THE KING'S SISTERS

THE KING'S SISTERS

BOOK THREE OF THE CROSS AND THE CROWN

BY

SARAH KENNEDY

www.penmorepress.com

The King's Sisters by Sarah Kennedy
Copyright © 2019 Sarah Kennedy

ISBN-13: 978-1-950586-13-4(Paperback)
ISBN   :-978-1-950586-14-1   (e-book)

BISAC Subject Headings:
FIC014000FICTION / Historical
REL053000RELIGION / Christianity / Protestant
FIC031020FICTION / Thrillers / Historical

Cover Illustration
The Book Cover Whisperer:
ProfessionalBookCoverDesign.com

Address all correspondence to:

Penmore Press LLC
920 N Javelina Pl
Tucson AZ 85748

DEDICATION

for Henry Adam Hill

subject matter is impressive, and *The Altarpiece* is a very promising beginning to Kennedy's *The Cross and Crown* series."—**Per Contra**

"If you love a great historical fiction series that is impeccably researched, this one is for you!"—**Celtic Lady's Reviews**

"A true page-turner."—**Historical Novels Review**

"Much of a historical novel's success lies in the author's ability to accurately cement the story in its time and place, and Kennedy excels in this aspect with detailed descriptions of the daily life of her characters, from clothing to architecture to medicine. . . . It is not necessary to read the first novel in the series to enjoy this book, but those finding this their first introduction to Catherine will surely search out the first novel to spend more time with this feisty woman in her richly detailed world."—**Foreword Reviews**

"Having chosen William Overton, Catherine Havens Overton, in Book Two of the Cross and the Crown series, now struggles to manage her wifely duties in his house, where her extraordinary gifts in physic and healing are feared as witchcraft as well as sought after by all, creating a difficult and dangerous situation. Filled with drama, suspense, vivid scenes and larger-than-life characters, *City of Ladies* fast becomes impossible to put down. . . . Kennedy is clearly as gifted as her main character, almost supernaturally at home in the 16th century as she combines the striking vocabulary of the time with her own poetic talents to create a rich and original tapestry of language. Such writing! Sarah Kennedy brings a lost world blazingly to life."—**Lee Smith**

". . . . In *City of Ladies* Kennedy takes her place with Daphne du Maurier, Anya Seton, Rosemary Sutcliff, and Hilary Mantel as writer of superb historical fiction."
—**Suzanne Keen, author of *Empathy and the Novel***

"I did not read the first book in this series, *The Altarpiece* – it's on my tablet – but I didn't feel any loss for not having done so. . . . by the time I was about a quarter of the way in I was hooked and had a hard time putting it down to go to sleep at night and one night I just didn't until I finished. Catherine is a fascinating character and I hope to find time to be able to read the first book in the series."—**Broken Teepee**

"It's not hard to see why *City of Ladies* is a contender for the INDIEFAB Book of the Year. Sarah Kennedy has quite a gift for storytelling and is sharing it with readers in her series *The Cross and the Crown*."—**Black Dog Speaks**

"This is a mystery, romance, political intrigue, story of women, exploration of the past, and a caution for the future. Sarah Kennedy brilliantly crafts her characters to drive a narrative that will have you guessing to the very end."—**San Francisco Book Review**

"In the spirit of Philippa Greggory (*The Other Boleyn Girl*), Kennedy delivers an intelligent and well-researched work of historical fiction that vividly re-creates the most tempestuous years of the English Reformation."—**The Sixteenth Century Journal**

"This book will thrill and delight lovers of historical fiction and mystery alike as well fans of C.W. Gortner and Philippa Gregory."—**History from a Woman's Perspective**

Chapter One

London, 13 February 1542

The Queen of England had been condemned to die. Another queen. Another charge of whoredom, and this time the evidence had been unmistakable. At Hampton Court Palace, where Henry VIII was hidden away, all the reveling, the feasts and dancing, the flirtations and love-making, had ended, once again, and the king had disappeared into his inner rooms after signing the death warrant. This time, it was Catherine Howard, once upon a time a carefree girl, then a queen, and now a wretch waiting upon an axe. A cousin, it was said, of Anne Boleyn. This one hadn't even made it to twenty years of age.

Watching from among the viewers who waited for the execution was another Catherine—Catherine Overton, once Catherine Havens. Once upon a time, a novice at Mount Grace convent in Yorkshire, then a married lady, with two children. Now a widow, this Catherine oversaw the kitchens at Richmond Palace and she had been ordered to witness the death and provide the details of the queen's demise to Lady Anne of Cleves, once also the wife of the king, now divorced and demoted to The King's Beloved Sister. Catherine could hardly believe, at first, that it could happen a second time, that Henry would kill another wife. But the laws were his, and Catherine had obeyed Lady Anne. Here she stood, doing her duty. But she was tired of death, and afraid.

And now Catherine Howard, the pretty royal girl, took her place in front of her former subjects on a bitter winter morning, staring up at her executioner like a child preparing to be corrected.

Why now, of all times, thought Catherine, to be forced to watch a queen die for being a whore? At the very time Catherine Overton suspected—no, she knew—that she, without a husband to her name, was carrying a child. Her stomach rebelled at the sight of the girl up there, preparing herself to die, and Catherine clutched her fur cloak tight, though her own belly was still as flat as any proper widow's. Like the queen, she'd allowed the court's frivolous mood to go to her head. *Now I will be found out for a whore, too,* Catherine thought, *and my family will be ruined.*

The queen placed her little feet precisely as she moved up the steps of the black-draped scaffold to the platform. She paused. Rumour had gone round that she'd passed the dark hours of her last days in the Tower practicing this moment with a chunk of wood, and the watchers were murmuring about it. The sun was pale and withdrawn, drooping in the sky. One scruffy woman in a tattered hood began to curse the king softly, and another whispered, "Stop your mouth. You'll be heard."

"She is just a spoilt child," Catherine muttered, "who made an error."

The swearing woman said, "Child or woman, queen or commoner, you'd keep your knees together if you knew what was good for you in this realm." Her companion elbowed her, hard, and she cowered into a leaden silence. Catherine shuddered. The nearby river's stench clogged the air, and she thought she would vomit.

The queen, above them all on the scaffold, removed her headdress and collar, and, handing them to one of the women in attendance, lifted her thick hair to bare a white neck. Catherine raised herself onto her toes to search the people. A few of the king's Council were here, their faces disinterested, as though they'd rounded up an unwanted hound. A man stared, and Catherine tried to shrink to the same height as the other women. Then the girl queen spoke to her audience, but the words wafted away. Catherine heard something about the King's Royal Majesty and huddled again into her wrap, waiting for the end. *Please let it come quickly.* The slight figure sank—she must have laid her head on the block—and Catherine saw the axe come up, catch a flash of early sunlight, and slice downward. One sullen thump and the viewers grunted. Someone wailed. It had taken only the one chop, thank God.

Next up was Lady Rochford, the queen's companion, her hair disordered and her dress half undone. She flung herself backward and side to side like a trapped animal, keening, and one of her women caught her by an arm. She stumbled up the steps as the queen's oozing remains, tumbled into a blanket, were sloshed into a coffin. Catherine's guts skittered, and she turned away as the axe flew up again. The thunk of metal against bone chimed back in echo from the stone walls. Catherine put her cold palm against her forehead until the whistling in her ears stopped and she could face forward again. Finally, the scaffold was empty.

"You must get yourself back home to Yorkshire right away, where you'll be safe." It was Ann Smith, Catherine's dearest friend, whispering into her ear. Catherine laid a hand on Ann's arm to steady herself and Ann went on. "There's no time to waste. You cannot be anywhere near London with a child in your belly. Not now."

People began to push forward, eager to be out of the foul air where they could sit by a fire with a mug of ale and retell the bloody events. The nobles were already gone, the blood mopped up and the bodies boxed.

"In the middle of winter? On the sudden? What reason will I give?" Catherine said. "The king will give me no permission to go. Nor will Lady Anne." She cloaked her face against the slashing wind.

Ann threw up her hood. "Give any excuse you can think of. You must go, or the law will come down like that axe. You could be stuck in the Clink for a whore. You could be hanged."

"I can be found easily enough in Yorkshire," said Catherine.

"Not as easily as you will be found in Lady Anne's household. No one will search so far. Have the baby away from all of these eyes."

"And who will I name as the father?"

"You know his name well enough. Just state the truth. He'll marry you, Catherine, if that's what you want."

"I know. But we need permission for that. Who will give it?"

"You might do it secretly," said Ann Smith. "In Yorkshire."

"Against the law?" Catherine felt her hands wringing themselves and shook them loose.

"Beg forgiveness later."

"Lady Anne will not let me go. Not now. But think, Ann. If the king marries again, that will lift his spirits. He must have another wife. And when he has one, all will be merry again. I think he might choose Lady Anne again. If I can just keep my secret until then, I will be saved. I can get my forgiveness without the marriage if I want and keep my position, too. Other women have done it."

Ann Smith scanned the retreating mob. The wind had come up again, and people were scurrying toward the gates. "There's no time to wait for Henry's good mood." She leaned close. "You have to go back to Yorkshire."

"And then what?" said Catherine. "My son will have to be told. And I cannot remove him from the prince. It would be too suspicious. And that means the prince will know. Then everyone will know. The king will know. And what if he is still in the killing vein? No. Here is what must happen. He must marry. He must take the Lady of Cleves back to wife. She will accept him. And she will speak on my behalf."

Ann said nothing to that. She pulled her cloak around her neck, and Catherine followed her friend's strong back. They did not speak again until they had shouldered their way beyond the Tower walls to the Thames and spotted a barge that would carry them back to Richmond Palace. A man, shouting at the river's edge, waved something gleaming. Metal. He pointed it toward the sky, and it exploded upward, shooting a cloud of smoke. A woman screamed, and Catherine grabbed Ann's elbow.

"What in the devil's name is that?"

Ann shaded her eyes with her hand. "It looks like one of those cannons for the hand. They say the wielder cannot hit the broad side of a horse with one of those. They make a large noise, though, and many men seek that these days."

"What machines of death will they dream up next?" Catherine paid their fare and slumped onto a board seat, toeing a slimy rag aside. The manservant who had accompanied them, Sebastian, had arrived before the women, and he sat without speaking across from Catherine, gazing into the dull sky.

Catherine could hold her tongue about the execution no longer. "She was Anne Boleyn's own cousin. She was too young to be a queen."

"Shh," said Ann, settling beside her. "Don't bring attention on yourself."

Catherine's head blazed again and she cooled her brow with her fingers. "I've been a fool, Ann. What will I do?"

"You will be silent and get ready to go home. We can manage there."

"It must be in the hands of Lady Anne. She trusts me. She enjoys my conversation. She will speak for me."

The boat lurched into motion, and Catherine's stomach heaved. She twisted and threw up her breakfast over the edge. Sebastian scooted further back, and Ann wiped her brow with a cloth. Catherine sat back and sucked in the damp air. "Thank God for the winter." She flopped the cloak over her lap.

"Wear roomy skirts. With plenty of pockets."

Sebastian leveled his eyes, grey and overcast as a dead mackerel's, ahead.

Catherine counted on her fingers. "Katherine. Anne. Jane. Anne. Catherine. Why are the ones who are divorced or killed the ones with our Christian names?"

Ann Smith pulled at the skin of her neck and tried out a smile. "I believe myself safe from his notice. I am getting the wattles of an old hen. And yet I hope he chooses a Frances next. Or a Cleopatra."

"Lady Anne is the one." Catherine snapped her fingers. "He must marry her again now. She will take him, and that will bring an end to all of our troubles."

"Are you going to play that note all the way back to Richmond?" said Ann Smith.

Catherine leaned into her friend and put her head back, watching the clouds form up together, then break into factions. "Once upon a time, I thought we might be two happy crones together, you and I. I hadn't thought to marry again."

"Who is a crone?" said Ann.

"Not us, to be sure. I suppose I am as much as married, in the sight of God." Catherine tried on a smile, but bit it off and swallowed her joy. "But I don't relish going to the church door like a sheep at market, about to drop a lamb."

"Marriage is only one way." Ann's hands were raw, and she rubbed them together, then blew warm breath into her palms. "But do you love him? Enough to give up your widowhood? A widow with money is a good thing to be."

"I know what you mean. Love and marriage do not always knit into a single cloth. He's a man. And men change. I don't know. I have refused him often enough. As I said, I hadn't thought to marry again." Catherine closed her eyes but could not remain among the images in her darkness and opened them again. She'd loved her first husband William wildly, and then he had become jealous. And then he was killed. But by that time she had not loved him anymore. "I never imagined there could exist so much death behind my lids. I still see the ghosts of William, of my mother, and all those murdered nuns, as though they had just departed life." A gull circled over their heads, and Catherine pulled her hood forward. "Some days, I am surrounded by specters, and they gnaw at my dreams."

"Then let your man press the demons out of you, if you want him. The living ones as well as the dead. Go to Yorkshire. You can marry him there and be done with it all. Or be done with him and live out your days as your own woman."

Catherine spat into the river and watched the oarsmen for a few moments. "Mark my words, the Lady of Cleves will expect Henry to return to her now. Her family will go to battle for it. She must force his hand. She will do it."

Ann raised an eyebrow. "She will be refused. By law, she is the king's sister. She agreed to it herself."

"But she will want the marriage renewed now that the Howard girl is gone. Oh, Ann. She must go to war and win him back."

"Our combats with Henry will not end until God ends him," said Ann with a weight in her voice. "He doesn't want Lady Anne. She's been shown that clear enough. She should make her peace."

"It is a shameful peace to her. She's a nun without the vows."

"Perhaps." Ann shrugged. "But she has land and jewels and more gowns than a woman can wear in one lifetime. She has servants and good wine. That's more than most of the nuns have."

Catherine shivered. "All true. Good jewels, too. Have you seen her ruby?"

"I have. Red as blood," said Ann.

Catherine said, "Lady Anne might come to him like the Trojan horse, all smooth, and overtake him before he knows what's happened."

"And if she succeeds, then we will all be happy and life will go forward. England will be all dancing and mirth."

"I can't speak of England. But I might be able to go forward without walking into a gaol cell."

The sky in the west was low-browed and dark now, threatening snow. The oily river slapped the sides of the barge.

"And why should she pursue him after this?" said Ann. "She doesn't want to lose her head, any more than you want to have that chap show his face to the world just now." She set her hand on Catherine's lap.

"But if he wanted her—" countered Catherine.

"He is not a king to want again what he's cast off once."

"It would be the easier course for him," said Catherine.

"And when has he taken the easier course in matters of love?"

"She is great friends with the king's elder daughter," said Catherine. "Perhaps Mary will speak for a reunion. She might even speak for me."

"Stay away from the Lady Mary," warned Ann. "She has the stink of Pope on her. At least you will spare yourself a scaffold on her account." Ann lowered her face against the filthy spray.

Catherine thought a while. "Henry will break up the Howard girl's household now. Her women will all have to go."

"Mmm. Another reason you must get to Yorkshire. Your sister-in-law is likely already headed that way. You can protect what's yours. And you can hide yourself until this time is past." Ann set her chin in her hand and stared ahead, into the fog. "It will pass, I assure you."

Catherine said, "I will ask Lady Anne if I may go," and then nothing more.

Richmond Palace emerged from the haze, and the two women stood, bracing themselves, as the bargeman steered toward the dock, drew them in, and tied up the vessel. Sebastian held out his arm, and Catherine took it. She offered hers, in turn, to Ann, and they joined the small group disembarking. The air smelt of rotten fish and cold mud and Catherine longed for the spicy scent of clean Yorkshire sheep and blooming gorse. She imagined she could smell the dirty lanes of London, wafting down the river from the east. The bile came up her throat again, and she vomited into the grimy water. The bargeman was asking the man with the hand cannon whether he'd seen the execution. "See it?" the man said. "The stuff spattered me all over." He dug a stained cap from his pocket to prove it. "That child had more blood in her than a fatted pig." He nudged the bargeman. "Hot, too. Felt it hit my face, I did." The man climbed onto the dock and disappeared, whistling, down the road.

"We are become an island of beasts," Catherine blurted, wiping her mouth. "I fear God has turned His face away from us all."

CHAPTER TWO

"All may be well without a removal to Yorkshire," said Catherine the next morning. She had come down to the kitchens from serving the morning meal, and she sat next to Ann at the table near the smaller fire. The big kitchen was a mess of hired cooks, brought in to prepare the great Valentine's Day meal. The king's younger daughter, Elizabeth, was coming, and the air was a cloud of flour.

In the lesser kitchen, a dirty-faced girl was pouring ale for Sebastian, who was back at his regular work, turning the spit. The highest iron pole held three skewered chickens, and he turned the impaled bodies with a doleful hand. Catherine said, "There is talk. The Lady of Cleves believes she will be queen again, as sure as my hand has nails. I told you it would happen. I will wait and see how the tide turns. If they marry again, the mood will shift. Tonight may show us something."

"She is deluded," said Ann softly, "and she should put a stop to her party. Someone should tell her. And then you must go from here. You think you can linger at this place, feeding her house and hoping on a dream, while someone is gobbling up your properties?"

"The queen was a child," said Catherine, lifting a bunch of carrots from a basket. "He has murdered a little girl this time." She yanked a wilted frond off. "But the Lady Anne is a woman and she likes to wager. She has the Cleves brother behind her." But Catherine bit her tongue. Henry's first queen, Katherine of Aragon, had had the whole of Rome behind her and still lost her battle for the king's bed. Catherine chose three turnips and an onion and shoved the basket aside. "These are almost pig food. What has become of the order for fresh vegetables?" She stood and shook the dust from her skirt. The maid at the fire struggled to help Sebastian. She pulled at one flopping, naked wing and let her skirt flutter near the flames, but when she shrieked and lifted it almost to her knee in escape, he simply stopped his work and stood, studying a spot near her chin until she grew bored and moved away.

"Girl," said Catherine. "See to some ale for the man, will you? Let him work."

Sebastian set himself to turning again, and Ann put a jug of ale within the maid's reach, but he did not touch the cup after she had filled it. The girl perched on the edge of the hearth, her chin on her fists, and watched. She seemed very small indeed. Catherine wondered what father and mother had sold her off to the palace. She said to Ann, "Elizabeth will be here any moment. Do you think the king will come to the masque?"

Agnes, Catherine's own woman, came in from the laundry on the last words. She was hunched from cold and headed for the fire. "Madam, they say the little queen ran through the palace to the king begging for her life and he shut his door in her face. They say she was screaming like a madwoman."

The little maid stared up, her mouth open. Sebastian set the spit into a notch on the frame and squeezed one chicken thigh. Blood squirted, and he took up the pole again. Catherine muttered, "Don't say that. Do not gossip." Then, louder, "Where are the fresh vegetables?" She dumped the old ones back into the basket.

"They're in the big room," said Agnes, her head lowered. "I've got the younger girls paring them."

"Very good. I cannot breathe in here." Catherine rose.

The pastry chef, painted in sugar and sticky white almond paste, presided over the baking room next door, and the two women ducked past him and his prissy band of helpers into the small side room, where Catherine kept her books and the better silver. She said, "Now, what else shall we have butchered? Lady Anne has ordered a pig and two swans. Those are readied." She checked off the items with a short quill. "Do we have the pheasants?"

"Being plucked behind the stables," said Agnes. "And what of those old turnips? Who will eat those?"

"Ann and I will eat them. For our health. You may join us if you like."

Agnes's mouth twitched. "It's a masque, Madam. There's going to be sweeties."

"Sweetmeats will give you the bellyache," said Catherine. "They will make you sleepy."

"I have the stomach for them," Agnes said. "I will see to the plucking." She got her cloak and headed out.

Through the half-door, Catherine watched the young woman go, dragging the spit girl along with her. She sneezed in the flour-haze. "It is perhaps too soon for the king to come courting? But he will maybe send one of his Council?"

Ann said, "To think that we will wear masks and dance and stuff ourselves like Romans. God should strike us down. Christ in the East, it makes me sick."

"We must obey when Lady Anne says we must and hope for the best of this."

They wandered back into the kitchen, and Ann perched on the edge of the table. "If God's going to strike, He needs to bestir Himself quickly."

"If you think of it, she's not so old and she's put up no fight against him. Maybe he is broken this time and will be happy to see her." Catherine lifted a couple of eggs from a bowl and turned them over at the window, then held one to her ear and shook it to listen for rot. It sloshed, and she set it aside. "He's done it before. He could show at the door, dressed as Robin Hood again or some such silliness. He could be Achilles. He has always loved costumes."

Ann said, "Shaking the pus out of that leg of his all over us. My God, it twists my guts. He wouldn't have her before, but if what she says is true, it didn't stop him from running his fat hands all over her. Can you imagine it? A man feeling a woman every night for half a year, then turning her out like a dog that won't hunt?"

Catherine leaned over and whispered. "It is sure she has a letter. The brother of Cleves claims that the king has had her in bed and must take her to wife again now. I heard her speak of it."

"Well, this king will deny it," said Ann. "He already has. He thinks her as ugly a woman as I am."

Ann had grown slender after they moved to Richmond, unused to the leisure hours of being in a former queen's service, even though her shoulders were still wide and her hands were calloused. Her brown hair looked thicker, even when she pulled it severely back for fear of getting a strand in the food. Here, she went by the title of lady-in-waiting, and her silk skirts shone with embroidery and fit her neatly at the waistline. Her skin was smooth and fair. She would have her choice of pastries and joints of meat at the masque dinner.

"Stop staring at me," Ann grumbled. "What is it? Is the sweat pasting my dress to my back?"

"You look as fine as any woman here," said Catherine.

"Hmph. Fine as any mower's wife, you mean." She fetched a basin of water and began rinsing the dirt from the eggs as Catherine shook and approved them, scrubbing the shells with a rough clout. Ann said, "How many boys do you think that girl had in her youth? The Howard queen, I mean?"

Catherine said, "Shh." But then she shook her head and added, "I keep recalling last Christmas. She was all jests and dresses. She danced with the Lady Anne. They didn't even notice when Henry went to his bed. That queen should have been playing at dolls, not at court." Catherine handed over two more eggs. "But we were all friends then. The sun shone on us all. Nothing seemed very sinful."

"The world does not seem to want women to keep friends," said Ann. "Is it true that the king has ordered women to be spied upon?" An egg splattered in her palm, and she wiped off the mess. She threw down the soiled clout and chose another.

"He's laid down orders about any queen of his. It's treason to conceal any misbehavior. Even from childhood," Catherine said. "I don't know how many boys the Howard girl had, but I hope she enjoyed them. They were probably the greatest pleasure she ever got." She could taste the words, bitter on her tongue. "I will hope Henry proves a better husband next time."

"You think he will reform his ways? Study the past, Catherine. He only changes when desire turns his sails. You couldn't have foreseen this. But here you are, and you must save yourself."

"Lady Anne would be a good wife to him. She loves him. I know she does." Catherine handed over the last pair of eggs and gazed out the window.

"How is that possible?" asked Ann. She took up the bowl and ferried it to the pastry chef. She returned with a couple of dead hens, their stiff claws hugging her thumbs, and tossed them onto the table. "You don't know what she thinks."

"Christ, Ann, I'm in knots." Catherine wrung her hands and, horrified at how much they looked like her mother's in the motion, stopped and tucked them into her pockets.

"Here," said Ann, shoving a chicken over. "Put yourself to work stuffing that."

Catherine ripped an old loaf into shreds and jammed them into the bird.

"You're putting dry bread into that," said Ann, taking Catherine's wrist. "Listen to me. You still have the house and the land. You are still young, Catherine, and still beautiful. If it is not Lady Anne, Henry's eye will light on someone else in time. Then the world may be different indeed. But time is something you do not have. We must go from here."

"Perhaps something will happen tonight." A woman's voice called from above stairs, and Catherine stripped off her linen apron. "It is Elizabeth. This killing will have her in a passion."

Ann said, "I think I hear a batch of unfolded napkins summoning me."

A small girl with blue eyes and unruly red hair showed her face around the door to the laundry, and Catherine said, "Veronica, go down with Auntie Ann, will you?"

"Yes, Mother."

Ann took the child's small hand in her rough one and swung her. The girl giggled and let herself be lifted onto Ann's hip.

One of the other kitchen maids came from the still room, rubbing her eyes, and Catherine snapped her fingers in the placid young face. "Wake up. It's almost the middle of the day. Ann Smith has laid a couple of old hens just there, and you will need to put onions and garlic in them. Be sure that all of the pin feathers have been stripped out." The girl blinked slowly, and Catherine clamped her lower lip between her teeth before she spoke. "There's a masque on tonight, child. Wake up and move your bones."

Richmond Palace was a cavern, and the voices upstairs carried all the way down to the kitchens. Many voices. Catherine set her feet gently on the stone steps as she ascended, preferring to make no sound at all than to set the hollows ringing with the clack of her heels. Her skirt whispered behind her, though, and she lifted it above her ankles. No one was at the landing, and Catherine wondered if her hearing had fooled her. "Hallo?"

Footsteps padded around a corner. It was weasel-faced Jane Dudley, another of the Lady Anne's women, looking less nervous than usual. She said, "Catherine. Let someone else manage the kitchen for once. The little one is here and we need you. She's in a fit of grief."

"Give me until you count one hundred." Catherine ran back downstairs, calling for Ann Smith. "Is there anything sweet? Any tart left from yesterday?"

Ann came in, carrying a pile of clean clouts. She sighed. "Let me see what's in the pantry," she said. The child Veronica dawdled behind her.

Catherine squeezed past the pastry chef's round buttocks and pulled plates and cups from a cupboard. She took a jug of ale from the floury table and poured a goblet, and when Ann reappeared with a plate of pear tart, she grabbed it and slapped it onto the side table. "I can make three servings of this." The chef sniffed and closed his eyes, unable to gaze upon an old tart, but Catherine sliced it, then slid the plate to Ann. "Will you arrange these and bring them up in a few minutes?"

"Is she frantic?"

"I haven't seen her yet," said Catherine. She poured half of the ale into one cup. She had good henbane on the high shelf in the still room, and she slipped down the empty hall and fetched a pinch for the drink without speaking. Ann was behind her when she turned.

"Keep this one separate," said Catherine. "On your life."

Ann shifted her eyes toward the cup and away again. "Elizabeth will want to see Veronica." She stepped aside to reveal the child.

Catherine bent to her daughter. "You will come up with Auntie Ann. You will curtsey to the Lady Elizabeth and do as she bids you. She will be taller but you are not to comment upon her appearance. You will not suck your thumb. Have you any small token of your sewing?"

Veronica trotted away, but returned in seconds holding a delicate handkerchief. A daisy with two leaves was embroidered in one corner. "I have done all of the petals."

"A perfect choice. You will fold this and present it to the Lady Elizabeth as a gift."

Veronica crushed the fabric against her chest.

"You can make you another," said Ann. "The Lady Elizabeth will have nothing from you at all if you keep it. Would you greet her empty-handed and make her sad, while you keep all to yourself?"

Veronica unfurled the handkerchief and regarded the work. "I will give it to her."

"Good girl," said Catherine, kissing the child on the top of her coif. "Come up with Aunt Ann."

Someone screamed upstairs, and Catherine ran.

At the center of the great front hall, The Lady Anne of Cleves was bent as though in prayer. Light from the high windows stabbed the dingy air, and Catherine stopped in the middle of one golden shaft to determine whether she should go on or retreat. Jane Dudley was posed with one hand against the wall and the other flat on her chest. Two other ladies, their backs to Catherine, were leaning, in hand-waving conference, toward each other. "Catherine," said Jane. "You must revive her."

Catherine pushed on through. Elizabeth Tudor lay on the floor. A cry slipped out of her and echoed from the ceiling far above them, and Lady Anne stroked the bloodless forehead, saying "Dear child, dear child. Come back to me."

Elizabeth Tudor was thin, even for an eight-year-old girl. Too thin. Her shins stuck out from the skirt like the legs of a marionette as she thrashed, and Catherine squatted beside her, pressing down on her chest. "Elizabeth? Elizabeth, I am Catherine Overton, speaking to you. What ails you? Tell me where you are hurt."

Elizabeth cast her eyes over the stars and sun painted overhead and let them come to rest on Catherine's face. She put her hand up. "I am sick to my death."

"Are you able to stand?" The two women tittered softly, and Catherine snapped, "This child is ill. Have you hauled her across England when she cannot even balance upon her feet?"

Jane Dudley came forward. "They are not responsible for her feet. I know these women and they have done all that becomes them to keep her from here tonight."

Elizabeth scrambled up. "But come I would. And I am here."

The women all dropped to their knees. The Lady Anne of Cleves said, "My child, you are recovered. A great joy." She smiled. She might have been beaming upon the girl, but even in her brightest moments of pleasure, the Lady Anne of Cleves, the King's Beloved Sister, had a face like a plastered wall. "You will dance with us this evening?"

"Stand," Elizabeth shrilled, and the women all unfurled. "It is here," she said, pointing to her narrow breast. No one spoke, and Elizabeth poked Catherine's chest. "Here, I say. Here is where I am injured." Her voice spiraled upward, like thin smoke. "I have been robbed of my peace of mind. I am stuck through the heart. They will try to marry me to some nobody. Some farmhand. Some lesser son with pustules on his face. I will not. I swear it, do you hear me? I will not!" She was panting raggedly. Her face was white. "They will kill me if I disobey. I will die first. But I will never marry. Never. And I will not dance like one of their trained bears."

Ann and Veronica turned the corner, and Catherine said, "You should take a draught to level your spirits, Your Grace."

Veronica came skipping when she saw her mother, then skidded to a stop and fell into a curtsey. Elizabeth pinched the smaller girl's chin and asked, "Is this my doll?"

Veronica smiled and offered the handkerchief, still rumpled but folded. "May I offer Your Grace a token? I have done the petals with my own hands." She glanced at her mother, and Catherine rewarded her with a shallow nod.

Elizabeth opened it and saw the daisy, then she put the handkerchief to her face and cried, "They will not force me! I will never marry, never!" She hugged Veronica and wept on her shoulder. "They will not chop my head off. Never! Do not let them."

Veronica, struggling to free herself, began to wail, and Catherine took the cup she had treated with the henbane from Ann Smith, who made a brief gesture at a curtsey and fled. "Here, Your Grace. Lady Elizabeth. Take this. Drink."

Veronica began to hiccup, and at that Elizabeth began to giggle. This started a skittery laugh in Veronica, and soon the two girls were on the floor, laughing in each other's arms.

"I have tart," Veronica managed to say, and Elizabeth took her by the hand and hauled them both to their feet.

"Where? Is it a doll tart?"

"No! It is pear!"

Elizabeth screeched, and Catherine steered the drink to her mouth. "Here, Lady Elizabeth."

The king's daughter drank the cup down and belched. She wiped her face and stood before the Lady Anne of Cleves. "When my brother is king, I will be his Beloved Sister, as you are to my father. I will do as he says and he will love me. Is that the way I must go to keep my head from being taken from my neck?"

"Ah, my little Elizabeth—" Lady Anne began, but Elizabeth held up a narrow hand.

"I will suffer his kindness and his direction and perhaps he will repay me with my life. I see how things stand. But if he seeks to marry me to some low-born idiot, I will cut my own throat before I submit. Do you hear? I will slash it myself! I will not have my head hacked off by a drunkard with an axe!"

The Lady Anne nodded. "Catherine, you will stay nearby?"

"Yes, Lady," sighed Catherine.

Lady Anne guided Elizabeth toward the great dining hall, and Catherine followed with the sweet and the ale, but Jane Dudley snagged her arm. "I would keep my daughter far from that one," she whispered. "Even those who love her say she's lost her wits. To have a masque, at a time like this, is bad enough. But to have Elizabeth here? It's lunacy. For God's sake, give that girl something to put her to sleep before the guests arrive or she will undo us all."

Chapter Three

"One can hardly be surprised that the girl's overwrought," said Catherine. Ann was folding big washing clouts in the clean still room to get away from the other laundry women, and Catherine watched her friend work while she waited for the maids who had gone out to the dairy to fetch yet more eggs for yet more custards. "She's seen two queens die on the scaffold, one her own mother." Catherine shook out one of the rags that had fallen to the bottom of the pile and handed it over. "Can you not get the laundress's girls to do this?"

"It eases my mind to put my hands to a task," said Ann. "Elizabeth didn't see her mother die. She wasn't at the Tower yesterday, either. Are you become the champion of the Boleyns and their kin now?"

Catherine's cheeks pulsed with heat. She'd spoken cursedly of them, it was true. "No. But she's seen it all well enough in her mind's eye. That can be worse."

"Yes. Imagination is a dangerous gift." Ann folded the last of her work and tossed the stack into a basket on the pavers. "If this Lady of Cleves wishes to keep her head, she will keep the mouth in it shut. She will lose this battle to be a wife." She hefted the basket, but Catherine snapped her fingers and a chambermaid came to take the burden from Ann, who wiped her hands on her apron and added, "If she angers him, Henry will take away this palace. All of the palaces. He will take the very clothes from her back. The king giveth and the king taketh away."

"As he could take Overton House from me," said Catherine quietly. "Surely Robbie's claim will be honored, even if his mother is called a whore? It is in the will. And he does well under the prince."

"Let's pray so," said Ann. "You must keep your head low."

Catherine added, "The prince favors him."

"It's a good position for the boy. There's none better."Ann. She looked around and found a cupboard to rearrange. "He can stay there until you sort your situation out. Then he can be told when it's all over. He will adjust to it."

"He may hate me for bringing him a new brother or sister." Catherine began to wring her hands, but again reminded herself of her dead mother and spread her fingers on her thighs. "He mustn't find out through rumour."

"Then clip rumour's wings. Go home. Make a story up and spread it abroad yourself."

A voice rang out a summons from the top of the steps, and Ann said, "That's my cue from above, Sister. I feel a sudden call to solitary prayer." She slipped down the hall that led back to the laundry.

"Don't forget to dress," called Catherine after her, but Ann didn't return. Catherine sighed and pushed herself to her feet.

"Elizabeth has laid her head upon the table," said Jane as Catherine came upstairs. "She snores like a fishwife and no one can move her." Jane's elbows shook, sending her long sleeves swaying as she marched off toward the big dining hall. "The girl does as she likes and no one corrects her. She will make a mockery of her position. She will amount to nothing. The tables must be decorated and she drools upon them."

"Are you yourself well?" asked Catherine. "Is your headache upon you?"

Jane turned. "My headache is sleeping on the table," she said, but she rubbed at the wrinkle between her eyebrows.

Anne of Cleves sat at the head. "Ladies," she said. "I have put my young visitor into a slumber. What do I do?"

Catherine and Jane bounced their curtseys. Elizabeth Tudor had indeed fallen into a stupor. Veronica had been allowed to sit next to her, and she had laid her own head down, facing Elizabeth's. She was mimicking the soft snoring. "Veronica!" said Catherine, pulling her daughter to her feet. "You do not ape the king's daughter. She has been long upon the road and her spirits are overcrowded."

Veronica pushed her face into Catherine's skirt. "I wanted to go to the place where the king's daughter went."

Catherine stroked the fine, bright hair. "I see."

"The little one meant no harm," said Lady Anne. "She sound like a small honeybee."

Catherine held her daughter against her legs. "Thank you, my Lady." She bent and whispered into Veronica's ear. "But remember that even the appearance of ridicule is to be avoided." She straightened. "What has happened here?"

Anne of Cleves pushed her plate away with a thumb. It held nothing but crumbs. Jane Dudley's portion had not been touched. The Lady Anne said, "She eat a bite. She say she feels sleepy. She sleep now like the angel. But table is no bed."

"Have her carried upstairs," said Catherine.

Jane beckoned two waiting women. "Do not let the men touch her." She turned back to Catherine. "What have you given her?"

"Tart and ale," said Catherine.

Jane's eyes slitted. "Is it enough?"

Catherine raised her hand toward the table. "You see how peaceful she is."

"She is the king's daughter," Jane said. "You must take care."

"I have taken all the care that I know. She drank the same ale that you and Lady Anne had."

"But she will sleep?"

"She will."

"Good. She is accustomed to the court physicians."

"Of course. And they take seem to have taken such very good care of her."

Jane smiled, a painful-looking exertion.

Catherine turned to Lady Anne. "I might perhaps remove to my home in Yorkshire, if I might have permission."

"No!" said Lady Anne. "I need my women about me. The king is broken-hearted."

Catherine nodded, seized her daughter's hand, and returned to the still room. The wind murmured at the windows and the frames rattled. The gulls screamed from the river.

Ann brought another load of her laundry to the table under Catherine's herb jars. "How does she?"

"Sleeping," said Catherine. "I would like to take the draught and go to oblivion myself. I asked permission to go and almost had my tongue bitten off." The panes rattled again, and she threw a clout at the wall. "That damned, pestiferous wind. What grudge does it have against us? I want quiet. I'm going to be sick." She stood suddenly and studied her stores. "Every one of my herbs smells like death to me." Catherine tossed the basket onto a shelf and flopped onto the stool again.

"That's normal enough." Ann stopped her folding and put her hand on Catherine's nape. "You wear yourself out with fear of the great ones. They're not your God. Let them fight their own battles. Go secretly. If you fear rumour, then there are women who want children and cannot bear them. Women in Yorkshire." She tightened the latches on the windows. "It's only a few months."

"Yes," said Catherine, scrubbing her eyes. But she was thinking of her stores of herbs. "Ah, God, an hour of dreamless sleep is much to be desired in this world."

They had almost a half a day's peace to finish preparing the food while Elizabeth Tudor rested. The Lady Anne and Jane Dudley were probably choosing their gowns and their masks. The palace was alive with preparation, the chambermaids about their business with the sweeping and the shaking of carpets before the evening gathering, the girls in the second kitchen beating eggs and folding sugar and cream while the pastry cook huffed and scolded. Catherine herself could grate the cinnamon and nutmegs while Veronica worked at her letters on a corner table down in the laundry. Agnes came in with an armful of old apples. "These will do well with that custard," she said. Agnes was a good sort, and Catherine felt a tug of regret that she had upbraided her.

The hours passed quietly, and the hens and pheasants were roasting to a golden crispness when doors opened upstairs. Men's voices deepened the palace's resonance, and soon enough Jane called from above. Catherine laid the spices aside. She did not hear Henry's big laughter. She said. "Will you finish this? Put plenty of honey in the sweets so that Elizabeth will eat if she wakes up." A grubby girl crouched in the corner. "Tell me your name."

"It's Marjory, Madam." The girl stood, scratching her leg through her thin skirt.

Catherine nodded. "Marjory, wash your hands and see to the salads. Ann!"

Ann Smith came up from the laundry again, already in her dressiest gown. It was brown silk with slashed sleeves and gold braiding at the bodice. "I look like a shaved rat," she said, yanking at the waistband. "I have no shape at all."

Veronica danced in behind her. "Auntie Ann! You are a princess! Where is your mask?"

"Child, you must need spectacles. I look no more like a princess than the man in the moon," said Ann. She held up a woolen cat's face. It had long whiskers of silk thread. "Here's my mask. I wish it were larger. I am monstrous."

"Rowr," said Catherine. She clawed at Ann. "Come, help me get dressed. Veronica, you want to do up Auntie's back?"

Ann turned and let the child tighten the bodice. "Ah," she said, patting her belly and adjusting her breasts upward. "Now at least they will know I'm a puss and not a tom."

The pastry chef blustered, "Madam, if you please." Veronica giggled, and they ran up the back stairs to their chambers, where Catherine's dress was laid out on the big featherbed. It was cream silk, with gold trim that matched Ann's, and Catherine peeled off her workaday clothing. The chambermaid had brought a ewer of rosewater, and Catherine washed quickly. Ann shook out the dress and helped her into it while Veronica twisted a ribbon around her own small coif.

"May I go to the masque, Mother?"

"You are too young," said Catherine, rolling on fresh hose. "You will stay above. Agnes will come and sit with you." Her mask, a tiger's face, lay on the sideboard.

Veronica's lower lip came out. "I will miss the dancing."

Ann took hold of the lip. "A rooster will poop on that," she said, and Veronica sucked it in again. "You don't want to dance with those old men anyway. Their feet stink."

Agnes knocked and peeked around the door. She had a platter of the vegetables and brown bread. "Look at you two," she said. "You will outshine the royal ones."

Catherine and Ann sat, but Ann just picked at the carrots. "These are old."

"They will keep you clean inside." Catherine pulled the bread apart and shoved a chunk into Ann's hand.

Ann ate one bite and stirred the turnips with the crust. "I have no appetite."

Catherine ate a plateful. "Vere, will you have Auntie Ann's portion?"

The child lifted a piece of turnip and put her tongue to it. "I will have the carrots."

Catherine handed her Ann's plate, and Agnes said, "Come, Vere. Let's sit by the window and see who trips as they step onto the dock." She put the girl on her lap and waved the other women off.

The tables downstairs had already been laid with the jugs of wine and bowls of bread and marzipan fruit—plums and strawberries, grapes and tiny oranges. The scent of the platters of roasted flesh and fowl reigned over the sweetness, though, and Catherine grabbed the banister. "I will vomit right here."

"Have a glass of the claret," whispered Ann.

"I cannot stay long," said Catherine. She surveyed the guests as they invaded the house. Eight so far. Not many more than the number of musicians. And no Henry. The women all held their masks before their faces or had fixed them to their headdresses.

John Dudley came in alone. He wore a close suit of black and carried a mask of raven feathers. He glared around and held his arms close to his sides. Then Jane, in midnight blue and a bright russet mask with blue feathers, came running from the dining gallery, and he raised a hand to her. His smile seemed to cramp his face, but he opened his arms for his wife, and she fitted herself to his stiff form.

Catherine said, "If any male and female were halves of a whole, Jane and John are. It's a marvel that they can be perfect together and so flighty apart. Two perfect night birds."

"They look like Satan's shadow to me," said Ann. "I cannot warm to them."

"When did Satan grow a second head?"

"Those two are his horns," said Ann, clapping her mask to her face.

Catherine put her mask up, too, to hide her laughter, but even through the narrow tiger-eyes, she saw him come in. Her child's father. The lust she always felt for him twirled in her guts, and she wondered for a moment if she could call it love. She knew that she should. Benjamin Davies was dressed as a green man, covered in silk leaves. His man, Reginald Goodall, was beside him in a huntsman's brown. Catherine nudged Ann. "Look there." Reg had been an Overton man before the death of Catherine's husband. Ann had said not a word when he went away to the Davies household.

Now Ann turned her cat's face in the men's direction. The color rose in her cheeks when she saw Reg, but she said, "They look like a couple of jesters. Go claim your half of them. Where is the wine?"

"This way." Catherine went on down, but not before Benjamin raised his eyes. She put her arm through Ann's and slipped into the gallery.

The long table had been set across the far wall, and Anne of Cleves presided, dressed as the Queen of Hearts. She wore a garland of pink flowers, and her hair, falling over her breast, was gilded by the candlelight. She smiled and waved. She was almost pretty, though sweat shone on her downy upper lip. Cups were handed around, and the serving men chased a couple of big floppy-eared dogs that someone had brought along. A quartet sat in a corner, tuning instruments. Beside Lady Anne hovered Karl Harst, her German steward, dressed as a satyr. He whispered into the Lady Anne's ear now and then and she nodded.

But the guests were too few for a party, and no one was laughing.

Catherine and Ann walked a circuit around the periphery. A lone lute player began to pluck a melody, but no one took up positions to dance. Anne of Cleves, bent over the table, was talking to one of her women, in pale blue. She might have been a storm cloud or Venus. Master Harst inched along behind the table on his plaster goat-feet to find a seat. A couple of strangers, a fat one and a tall lanky one, lurked in the corner, wearing dog masks. They spoke only to each other and the women made a wide margin around them.

Benjamin Davies was approaching. Everyone would see. He bowed, and one of his leaves dropped to the floor. "Lady Catherine," he said.

"Here in the dead of winter, you seem to have brought the fall with you," said Catherine.

Ann snorted behind her mask, and Benjamin picked up the leaf. Stuffing it away, he said, "Ann Smith, if my ears do not deceive me. I have brought a partner for you." He sidestepped, and Reg bowed to Ann.

"Oh, stand up, old man," said Ann. "You will get stuck down there."

"Your truth is ever my salvation," said Reg, bracing his back with one hand as he straightened. "When will we leave off this custom of torturing our spines to say hallo?"

Ann pulled at her waistband. "When women begin to breathe more easily in the world. Which is, to say it plainly, never."

"Perhaps you breathe better out of the open air," said Reginald. He lifted his mask and grinned. "We could retire to a closer spot."

"Not if you mean to close me in," Ann said. She gave him a slap on the arm, and he winced. "What sort of hunter are you, if you cannot withstand the touch of your prey?"

"You have always been a shrew to courting traditions, Ann Smith," said Benjamin. "And Reg is no warrior in the service of love."

Reg grinned. "A true, but a sharp, retort. Has he hit you, Ann?"

Ann looked down at her dress. "I seem to be unwounded yet."

Benjamin claimed Catherine's arm. "You and Reg will have to spar in private for a time, Ann." They fell to walking around the edge of the room. "The air at court is dirty with gossip," he murmured. "Keep moving." They passed the Dudleys and Benjamin nodded. Catherine glanced over her shoulder. Ann and Reginald were drifting toward the musicians. Their heads almost touched. Benjamin said, "Not many will come out to dance this night. No one is in a mood for S. Valentine. There is some wonder that quiet is not kept in Richmond Palace."

"Is the king in mourning?" asked Catherine.

"There's a general air of deep melancholy. He is fitful and angry."

"He will not come tonight?"

"Not tonight nor any night." Benjamin picked up a cup of wine and handed it to Catherine before he got one for himself. He bowed to a couple of the palace ladies and when the lute player finished, he stopped to applaud. Then they walked on. "The king goes on as though no queen ever lived and no queen was ever sought. He rages. They say he is much brought down but grieves alone. Some say his mind has let in the enemy and it is destroying him from the inside."

"He is gone lunatic?"

Benjamin leaned closer. "Do not say the word aloud. They say he burns with a fire that kills a man's reason."

"Is there any talk of taking the Lady Anne back as his wife?"

"This Anne? Of Cleves? No. Not even a breath of that in the air."

"She thinks he will. It would be useful if he did. She has a letter from the brother."

"Good God." The musicians had started, louder now, and Benjamin turned to see if couples were lining up, but the small crowd was standing in pairs here and there, not looking either to the music or to the Lady Anne. When the strings fell silent in ragged scrapings, ending with an odd squawk from the piper, the listeners clapped lightly and turned to themselves again."Catherine," Benjamin said, "you must come away as soon as we can manage it. Say you will. I have asked often enough for any man, and now the time presses us. No one will count a few weeks after the baby is born."

Catherine chewed her cheek. "Who will be the one to ask for the king's permission?"

"There's no asking of permissions. Not now. Not for anything, but especially not for our marriage. We must leave England. Go to the continent. I will sell the wool, and we can be gone before your shape is much changed."

"But my son—."

"He can stay where he is. He will surely not be punished on your account. Or I will fetch him and he can go with us."

Benjamin drank, but his eyes were flickering over the guests. "You know the queen's household has been broken up and the women are sent away."

Catherine's heart slid. "And have you heard aught of any of them?"

Benjamin laid his hand on Catherine's arm. "You mean your sister-in-law. I hear that she has gone, that she calls herself Lady Overton and talks of her great estate in the North. She is a straggler now and she may be desperate. She bears watching. But she has no claim. Your son will inherit the land. We can take your daughter with us."

Now Catherine drank. "My son will object to a new father who gives him a brother too quickly."

"I will win him in time. I swear it. You feel well? Inside?"

"My body is well enough. My mind is disordered." Catherine bit her lip and raised her cup toward the two strangers. "Who are they? The dogs over there."

Benjamin's lower eyelids tightened for a second. "King's men. They seem to have little to do but look for trouble. Everyone is counting losses now. Everyone has eyes on everyone else. Those two are shallows. Hangers-on. Steer around them. Everyone is looking to please Henry right now."

The musicians made another effort, and a half-hearted dance began with four couples, but before they had moved through three measures, a wail from above stairs broke the harmony. Ann Smith dropped her mask and stared at the ceiling. Everyone who belonged to the palace waited, unmoving, for Elizabeth Tudor to appear.

But the noise finally wound down to a thin whimper, then nothing. The silence held the hall for several seconds, then

John Dudley broke it with a cough. People began to circulate slowly again, but soon the guests were leaving, pleading the snow, the cold, the darkness. Most of the food sat untouched.

"I will take my leave, as well, Catherine," said Benjamin. "Prepare yourself for flight, and we can get our permissions and forgiveness later."

"Everyone insists that forgiveness will come," said Catherine. She shook her head. "Lady Anne will be in a state after this night."

"Let her howl if she wants. She is not your concern. Here is a plan. I will ride up to Mount Grace tomorrow. I will get your wools for the Dover market so that we will have ready money. I will sell whatever I can and return as soon as I am able. Stay on your guard. Confide in no one." He bent his head toward Reginald, who was pulling something from his pocket and pressing it into Ann Smith's wide hand. "They must come with us. It will put Reg into a consumption if he cannot cross swords with your woman now and then."

"She has never been my woman," said Catherine. "Godspeed, Benjamin."

He put his hand around hers quickly and broke away. Reg followed and they were gone. "What news?" asked Ann, coming up behind her.

"Men's news. Always men's news. And it is always expected that women will obey."

<h1 style="text-align:center">CHAPTER FOUR</h1>

"What token did he give you?" asked Catherine when they had retreated to their chambers. Ann was unpinning Catherine's head piece.

"Who?" Ann bent to work on the back of Catherine's gown.

"Oh, who. You know who. Reginald." Catherine shook out her hair, glad to be free of the heavy clothes.

Ann loosened her bodice and worked on her own coif. The strings knotted and she cursed under her breath.

"Well?" asked Catherine. She freed Ann's hair and leaned close to her ear. "Hmm?"

"Nothing. Foolish S. Valentine's Day foolishness."

Catherine said, "Let me see this foolish foolishness."

Ann held out her hand and a twisted gold chain, wrapped three times, slid into view. From it dangled a locket, and Catherine reached to open it. "Don't," said Ann. "It is nothing."

"If it is nothing, then I will not see a thing." Catherine had hold of the delicate pendant, and Ann sat back and let her pull the thing free. Catherine slid a fingernail into the slit and popped the locket open. On one side was a miniature of a Cupid. On the other Reginald himself. "He loves you!"

Ann snapped the locket closed. Her face was smoldering. "He is a fop to know no better than to waste his money on trinkets. I don't wear such things. He means to soften my mind. He is carried away."

"Benjamin thinks we should all be carried away," said Catherine, serious now. "He has gone to Mount Grace to get the wool for the markets. He wants me to leave England with him. I am to gather my things. You too."

Ann twirled the chain and it twinkled in the candlelight. The corner of her mouth crimped. "So he still wants to marry you? That is some good news. But I am not for leaving England. What would I do with myself?"

"Benjamin says that there are spies about. He seems sure that the Continent is the only way. He knows markets and buyers."

"Do you want to go?"

"No," Catherine admitted. "Robbie would stay with the prince. I don't know what I would do without my son."

The bell that summoned the household to Anne of Cleves's presence rang downstairs. Catherine had only heard it a few times, the last when the late queen had been arrested. Catherine and Ann tied up their shifts and threw robes and shawls over them. They slapped coifs hastily over their hair before they went out. Other women had already flocked into the hallway, clutching tapers and whispering, and John Dudley followed Jane from her chamber. They had obviously been abed.

"What? What's the trouble? Is there fire?" John was asking, but Catherine and Ann were already headed downstairs.

Anne of Cleves stood in the great front hall at the center of a clot of men. One of them was Master Harst, looking at the ceiling. His satyr hooves had been discarded on the floor and he stood bare-footed. Beside him was the fat dog-man. Out of his costume, he was moon-faced and looked like a ball of wax that had half-melted onto his own knees. His feet stuck out from chubby legs like dead fish. He clung to the thin fringes of his black beard with two fingers. His tiny eyes were dark, too, set so close in his face that they threatened to slide together. He'd settled into his own bulk, morosely staring into space. His companion was taller and lean, the color of dull flame all over. He wore spectacles, and when he glanced Catherine's way, the candlelight danced over their surfaces, making him look like a blind man.

As the household gathered in various stages of night dress, the Lady Anne stepped back to let Master Harst speak. Catherine wondered how much she understood when Harst flung up an arm in the direction of the fat man and said, "This gentleman is Martin David Martins. He is sent by the king to inspect this household. What is your title, sir? The accounts man? The revenue lost man? Ach, whatever you are." He scanned the small group. "Do you hear?" He turned to the women surrounding him. "This gentleman must be obeyed. He will be among us for the next few days." He indicated the glowering figure beside Martins. "This is Ciaran Barts, his man. You are all to accede to his wishes, as well."

"You go to your sleeps now," said the Lady Anne. She flicked her fingers toward the stairs and the women eased away. John Dudley muttered something about being called from his marriage bed for a penny-counter. Catherine pulled Ann Smith toward the steps down to the kitchen.

"A bottle of wine would help me," she said. "By my troth, I thought it might be the king."

The downstairs was a bustle of chambermaids and kitchen girls, washing up dishes and sorting dirty laundry. The pastry cook had probably taken the best of the leavings to his chamber, but the girls had set out a plate for themselves. The treats were already half eaten, and Marjory clapped a hand over her stuffed mouth when Catherine and Ann showed themselves at the door. "Don't mind us," said Catherine. In the corner cupboard she located a bottle of claret and a loaf of bread that hadn't been broken. Ann got a plate of butter and a pot of strawberry jam.

"I hope those girls keep an accounting of the sweets they put in their mouths," said Catherine. "If that Martin Martins is one of Henry's, he will take his balance from their flesh."

"He'd get more if he took it out of his own flesh," said Ann. "There is plenty of it." She shuddered. "That Barts fellow puts me in mind of a seething owl."

Upstairs, they sat by their fire, listening to the nighttime palace creak and groan. Catherine could hear men's voices from below. Or was that Lady Anne's heavy Dutch, complaining about something? They could surely leave all in peace until morning. She poured another cup and watched the flames in the hearth beat themselves against the darkness. More voices. Distant and angry. Was someone shouting in a far room? "The battle is coming," said Ann, and Catherine's skin tightened at the sudden sound of her voice.

"It may be that Henry is asking about Lady Anne's conduct. It could be a good sign."

"I expect it is a sign of something," said Ann.

Catherine said, "What will my son say to a new father? To a brother or sister?" She closed her eyes for a second and found them almost too heavy to open again when Ann spoke.

"He has seen other widows take men. He is only a little boy. He could accustom himself."

Catherine said, "The prince is only a little boy, as well, but they say he speaks his mind like a monarch." She brooded for a moment. "Even he has had a step-mother."

"And he's likely to have another. But in his world mothers come and go. Only fathers remain."

"And sisters," said Catherine.

"And they must bow to him." Ann touched the chain on her wrist. "I should return this."

"You should not! You have made him no promise."

"He has a right to think I have."

"Men and their rights." Catherine spat into the fire and the embers hissed. "They wrap a string of gold on us and believe themselves our owners."

"That sounds not like a woman bent on marriage."

Catherine laughed softly. "Oh, I am bent, but in what direction I will fall I cannot say." She ran her forefinger's nail along her bottom teeth. "Benjamin is not like other men."

"Nor is Reg." Ann lifted her hand and let the locket dangle. "He's just let his fancies get the better of him."

"And what of your fancies?"

Ann turned her hand, and the chain caught on the knot of her prominent wrist bone. She shook it loose. "I fancy quiet." She rubbed the locket. "He's a good man. If I wanted a man."

Catherine gulped down the last of her wine. "Let's sleep and let our dreams tell us what to do. Perhaps all will be well."

"I will get in with you tonight. I fear me it's going to be colder than the king's heart."

CHAPTER FIVE

Catherine dozed restlessly, with no dreams to lull her, and when she came down the next morning, Elizabeth Tudor was awake and sitting with the Lady Anne. The tragic remains of the masque had been swept from sight, and the floors, under the carpets, gleamed. A slice of untouched cheese in front of Elizabeth had grown a skin of dark oil, and Lady Anne was disassembling a poached trout. Catherine yawned as she curtsied, covering it with the back of her hand, and Elizabeth said, "Lady Catherine. Have you not slept?"

"The wind kept me awake, Your Grace." Catherine claimed a wide stool, and Ann Smith curtsied and excused herself. She was headed for the kitchen, Catherine knew it, where she could break her fast with a cup of good ale and the cold meat from last night without disturbance.

The fire was high, smoking a little from green wood, but its hot breath extended only a few feet from the hearth. The rest of the long room was still clammy and dawn-bitter, and Catherine pulled her shawl up to her neck. "And my nose alerted me to the morning," she said. "The winter begins to bite into my very flesh." She reached for the jug of ale and poured for herself. "I have never been a lover of February."

"Nor I," said Elizabeth. She wore a new cover of dark fur, and her skin looked white and dry as parchment.

"I could brew you a warm wash," said Catherine. "I have stores of rose petal and honey that will brighten your complexion."

The girl put a finger on her cheek, and Lady Anne said, "Will it improve one of my age? I will use this wash."

A thread of hope wound its way through Catherine's innards, though she knew it would not make the Lady of Cleves a beauty. "Yes, Lady Anne. It will work for any woman."

"I will have it," said Elizabeth. "I will take this water."

"How long do you stay with us? You will want to apply it more than once."

Elizabeth considered. "A fortnight. No, ten days."

The hope knotted into disappointment. "We will begin today." Catherine pushed back and stood, bowing. "I will prepare it now and have it sent to your chamber."

"No. You will come and apply it with your own hands."

"Very well." Catherine had no appetite, anyway. The smell of grease turned her stomach.

She was in her still room, heating the water, when she heard the men again. She waited, her hands in the pot, until they seemed to have gone by, then scooped in two handfuls of petals. She bent her head into the steam and closed her eyes. There was much to soothe the heart at the idea of marriage. The weight of a man to crush the mind's demons. A man. Her belly warmed, and she let her memory wander to the last time, at the New Year, that she had allowed Benjamin into her chamber. That must have been when she'd got the child. Everyone was in a holiday mood. She'd been on fire for him then, thinking of nothing else, and she'd let him pull her onto him as he leaned against the wall. It had been irresistible. It hadn't felt like a transgression. But it hadn't felt like love, either. He had asked her to marry him then, and she had said no. She breathed in the roses. They were heady, one of the few scents that did not revolt her.

"A small luxury for yourself?"

Catherine opened her eyes. Martin Martins hovered beside her. His mouth was damp beneath the string of a mustache. She said, "What do you do in the still room?"

"I must oversee every shelf and drawer of this palace. And what have you there?"

Catherine looked down. Her hands were deep in the water, and they were covered with softened petals. "Rose water. For the Lady Elizabeth." Their beauty was suddenly ruined for her.

Martins nodded and smiled. "The perfume is sweet indeed. It is no sin for a lady such as you to find a moment to enjoy it yourself."

"I prepare it for Elizabeth Tudor. As I said." The high window had fogged, and Catherine lifted the pot from the small iron grate. "If you will give way, please."

Martins slid one foot aside. Catherine called for Ann to bring the honey and a couple of eggs, and she poured the infusion into a large porcelain jug. Ann, with Veronica behind her, halted at the door. Her eyes passed over the man, then Catherine, and finally settled on the wall. Catherine asked, "Will you bring this in your pocket?" She handed her friend a cake of soap, and, lifting the container, skirted the horrible bulk of Martin Martins, who was scanning her with his rat's eyes. Veronica carried the washing clouts and an extra bowl behind the women.

When they were on the stairs, Ann whispered, "You have left him alone in your still room?"

Catherine nodded but said nothing until they had achieved the first floor. "I must not call it mine. He seemed to think I warranted watching." She knocked on the door with her elbow, and Ann opened it. Elizabeth stood at the window, and Catherine added warm water from the ewer by the fireplace to the wash. Ann took a stool in the corner and held the honey to the fire.

Veronica curtsied and said, "May I help you undress, Lady?"

Elizabeth patted her cheek and sat. Veronica's small hands worked the ties loose nimbly, and she laid the dress across the bed without letting it drag. Catherine held out one hand, and Ann poured warm honey into it.

"Who are those men?" asked Elizabeth as Veronica lifted her hair.

Catherine rubbed the honey into Elizabeth's wet palms, then took the clout from Ann and rubbed it down her back. She could count the girl's ribs. "They have some business with the Lady Anne. I'm sure it is nothing. Here now, splash your face."

Elizabeth did as she was bidden, and Catherine broke an egg, stirring it into a slurry with honey.

"We will smear this over your skin and let it dry."

Again Elizabeth obeyed. "Is there a question, that men come to oversee my step-mother?"

Catherine's heart leapt a beat. She had washed her hands and taken up a brush, and she gentled the bristles through the delicate, bright hair. "I haven't heard so. It is likely routine. An unpleasant routine but a necessary one."

"They are sent by my father, are they not? That is the routine you speak of."

"Don't talk while your face dries. He must keep watch over his people," said Catherine. She straightened the ends of Elizabeth's hair, holding it midway down like a horse's tail, and in the winter air it sparked and flew. She twisted it into a knot, then poked at the egg pack. "Just a few more minutes." She poured off some of the water into the bowl. "Soak your feet in the water now."

Elizabeth Tudor closed her eyes and they all relaxed. Catherine felt drowsy from the fire and the fragrance and curled up with Veronica on a large pillow. She was dreaming of her garden at home, of rows of apple trees in full blossom, shimmering with bees, when Elizabeth said, "Is it time?"

Catherine sat up, wiped her eyes, and shook Veronica awake. "We will see," she said, rising to meet the king's daughter at the window. Elizabeth's face was a smooth, expressionless mask, and Catherine tapped it. "Yes. Sit here." She washed Elizabeth's skin with a softer clout dipped in the clean rose water, then dried her all over. Veronica helped her back into her gown and sleeves.

A glass lay on the dressing table, and Elizabeth turned her face toward the light as Catherine fixed her headdress. "Am I beautiful?" she asked.

"As beautiful as any girl in the land," said Catherine. "As beautiful as a nymph."

"As a princess." Elizabeth traced her forehead with three fingers. "Soft. You are better to me than any sister."

"You smell like a garden."

Elizabeth kissed Veronica on the cheek and dismissed them. The maids would carry away the wash. They retreated to their chambers, and Ann said, "Our little Vere is ready to serve a queen."

Veronica rose onto one toe and pirouetted. "I am a queen's lady."

"Listen to the child," said Catherine. "But you were perfection, Vere. How did you learn to undress her that quickly?"

The small girl waggled her fingers in the air. "Each day I am set to write and write. My fingers have learned to do anything they are asked." She curtsied with a little flourish of her arm. "How may I serve you, Madam?"

Ann gasped. "God's Mother, Catherine, she is the image of you under that Overton hair. She could serve a queen indeed." She looked up, and Catherine knew they were both thinking the same thing. There was no good place for the girl away from England, either.

Chapter Six

For the next ten days, Catherine and Ann made plans for Yorkshire. They began packing their things, but only in bits and pieces, so that the chamber maids would notice nothing. Catherine directed the girls in the kitchen and prepared the wash water in her still room, listening for disturbances from above. Her daughter, called every day to serve the king's daughter, undressed and dressed Elizabeth Tudor without a misstep, which set Catherine up to hand-wringing again. Her daughter deserved a place in the world, too, after all. Martin Martins put his head into the chamber once, and Elizabeth shrieked. He withdrew. But still he watched, and still Catherine avoided him, slipping down the back stairs whenever she could. She had no word from Benjamin, and fell into her bed each night with a guilty relief at the silence.

Once, she took down the juniper and bit off a piece. Her stomach rebelled at the flavor, and she set it aside. Another day, she considered her stores of pennyroyal and tansy. Tansy would do it, but the herb was treacherous, killing as many women as it saved from unborn children. But if she could do it just right, she could save herself, without the assistance of anyone. Ann Smith came in and she pushed them to the corner of the table.

Ann lifted the pennyroyal. "What's this?"

"Nothing."

She set it down and chose the tansy. "This is not nothing, Catherine. You must think of your children if you don't want to think of Benjamin. You cannot put yourself in danger, and you cannot be sick with bleeding under the eyes of these king's men. The world has changed. You have changed. You could die."

"I am thinking of my children." But Ann's words were true. It was too soon for her to have felt life, so the soul had not entered yet. But the sickness would come. And the blood. And if someone at the palace knew anything about women's illnesses? There would be no concealment. And no forgiveness. She replaced the jars on their high shelf. For now. For now.

She washed the Lady Anne's face in the roses every afternoon, and held the glass for her afterward. "Do this make me fine?" asked the King's Sister.

"Very fine," said Catherine. In fact, it did smooth the skin. Lady Anne might be made to look as pleasant as her portrait. She said, as lightly as she could manage, "Have you a summons from the court?"

"No," said Lady Anne, "but weather is bad. Spring comes. That is the courting time. Marriages come after Easter."

"I think perhaps I should be in Yorkshire for the Easter season, Lady Anne. The new lambs will be coming."

Again there came the breathless "No!" Lady Anne gripped Catherine's wrist. "I must have full household of good women. You will be here with me if Henry should come."

"Yes, Lady," said Catherine. "And you will be as fresh as the flowers."

Lady Anne smiled at her reflection, and Catherine was dismissed.

Down in the still room, she said to Ann Smith, "Lady Anne is preparing herself for battle. She looks better. Younger. She still says that I must stay."

Ann scoffed. "Your imagination carries her away. Don't speak of it again. She's got her battle. Let her fight it. You and I will go."

"As soon as we can do it." But she hoped as hard for a message from the king, asking for the Lady Anne.

On the morning of the tenth day, Catherine and Ann woke to women's voices. Elizabeth was downstairs in the entry hall, scolding someone about the cut of her hood. "She is going," said Catherine, just as her name was shouted. "We will be freer now. The king will know we're alone." She dressed in minutes.

The Lady Anne was fussing over Elizabeth, pulling her furs up to her ears and pecking at her head. "You keep in the warm and you eat. Mind your music."

"Yes, yes," said Elizabeth, like any girl longing to be away. But when the men appointed to accompany her were stomping their feet outside, she grabbed Lady Anne and clung to her. She hid her face in the wide bosom for a few seconds, then looked up into the woman's face. "May I return?"

"Whenever you want, child," said Lady Anne. She held Elizabeth until one of the ladies coughed her impatience, then she broke her grip.

Elizabeth took two steps toward the door and slid to the pavers. "I cannot go! They'll put me in prison and force me to marry a nobody. A pig farmer or a lesser son. Let me stay,

Lady Anne. Let me remain with you. Do not send me to be married off."

"No, child. No one will do that," said Lady Anne. She laboured herself down to her knees and put her face near Elizabeth's. "You are just little girl. No, you would not marry no one you don't like."

"And you will not marry. Not ever. Vow it to me."

Anne of Cleves fingered the lacy edge of her bodice. "I marry no one. It is not permitted me. I am the King's Beloved Sister. I obey no one but the king."

Elizabeth rounded and saw Catherine. "You vow it, too. You will not marry."

"I am my own mistress, I thank God," said Catherine evenly.

The women stood in a circle, staring at their hands, until Elizabeth stood, smoothed her skirt, and snapped, "I am ready. What are you waiting for?" A manservant whisked the door open, and the king's daughter walked out without another word.

Lady Anne's face went flat and hard, and she retired, sending her women off with a wave of her hand. Ann Smith guided Veronica out of the room, probably down to the kitchen for a sweet, but Catherine stayed, watching from a side window until the procession had settled onto the wide barge. The lawn and gardens lay bleak and barren, and the river wound away, a strip of iron. She dropped the curtain. Someone's raised voice echoed through the palace. A door slammed, and Catherine turned.

Jane Dudley stood before her, her hands folded over her belly like an angry mother. "Can you provide a distraction, please?" Catherine had lost count of how many children Lady Dudley had. It was no wonder she suffered the headache.

"Who wants distracting?"

"That man, that what-do-ye-call-him, that money-man," said Jane. "Martin Damn-him Martins. He's taken over the entire house, Master Harst and all of the manservants, too. Another one has just arrived in back. He must have come up the road. Chandler Ellers. Ellers Chandler. Whoever he is. Martins claims to like your face and he'll leave Lady Anne alone if you show yourself to him. You might pull that bodice a bit lower, as well. Give him a figure to gape at that is not in a book. Master Harst's gone to get Lady Anne for another interrogation. My God, they're dreadful things, these men with names that tangle my brain."

"How do you feel this day, Jane?" asked Catherine.

Jane Dudley waved her hand at nothing. "I am well, well. I am well, I tell you." She breathed through her nose like a stalled mare. "These Germans do us no good. They set the country on edge. I don't know why we keep them."

"Martins is English," said Catherine, but she got no reply and followed Jane into the front hall. Martins, looking even shorter under the high ceiling, had adopted a court posture, with one toe twisted outward. He seemed to have risen from a puddle of himself. His right hand clutched one of the hand-cannons. The king had taken lately to wearing enormous padded shoulders and wide sleeves to conceal his expanding girth, and all his men were required to follow suit. On a short, fat man, the effect was that of an overstuffed puppet with a tiny head and hands. On the inflamed Barts, standing next to him, the impression was devilish. The excess of fabric was making courtly gestures a hazard for them both, as they flailed themselves into bows. The newcomer was maneuvering his arms out of his cape as Jane and Catherine approached. He was squat, with long narrow eyes, and when he trained his gaze on Catherine, she thought of a glaring toad.

"What is that thing on your hip?" asked Jane. "I wonder it doesn't tip you sideways."

"A curiosity to amuse the King's Beloved Sister of Cleves," said the man, drawing the weapon from its leather hanger, "and a new fashion that every gentleman requires. It is a wheel-lock." The weapon wobbled in his hand and he struggled to show it off. "Don't be frightened. I've not packed it with shot."

"Do let me see," said Catherine. She leaned toward Martins slightly.

"Ah. Catherine Overton. The widow. The lady who prefers to stay below. The nun who triumphs over the king's will. Such a novelty. With your face, you might do better for yourself." The man tried to both bow and brandish simultaneously, and the weapon almost hit the tiled floor. "What have your girls conjured up for dinner today?"

"Come down and I will show you," said Catherine. She twisted her mouth into what might pass for a smile.

"The moment I am done here, I am yours," he said. He slid her way, like a cross-eyed slug. His companions glided along behind him.

"You are done," said Anne of Cleves. She reappeared at the top of the stairs in yet another new dress, this one the green of deep forests, embroidered with blue and silver thread. She did not smile, nor did she offer her hand. Her advisor Harst and his manservant bristled behind her, unspeaking, like two brown pillars.

"Not just yet," said Martin Martins, working the firearm back into its leather loop. "I must bring back a balance. And if you are not disposed elsewhere, we will work."

"Can you not breathe a while?" asked Jane.

"I cannot. The air in this palace is corrupted. I have been informed of some suspicion of thefts. I believe I have found some jewels missing. A ring, for one. A ruby ring that the king claims to have given as a gift. Has it been seen by anyone? It is rather large."

"You have not seen the ring, Catherine?" asked Lady Anne, descending heavily. She was breathing through her mouth. "It has the pearls around, and I cannot put my hands on it."

Catherine held out her bare fingers. "I do not wear rings. My work prevents it." Henry had given her a ring one time, years back, a fine garnet. But she had never even slid it on. She wondered for a moment where it was.

Jane said, "The king has been most generous to his loving Sister. She is not so constrained that she must count every stone in her possession, is she?"

"You have not heard the news?" Martins' mouth tightened at one corner, as though he'd bitten a gooseberry. "The queen is dead. She has paid her debt to the realm. But her excesses have put the king in mind of accounts. Master Harst will confirm this, won't you, sir?"

The dark-haired Harst shifted to one foot and said nothing.

"Ah. The Dutchmen cannot fit their tongues to our English. What a misfortune."

"Where is she to be laid?" Catherine asked.

"Who?" Martins asked.

"The queen."

"She was a whore. What difference does it make?" Martins said.

"Any Christian ought to be laid to rest like a Christian, even one who has been found guilty of crime."

"Oh, my dear lady," said Martins. "We can all be found guilty of crime, every mother's child of us. Treason is a more serious matter. It makes a war within a realm, within a man's very breast. Or a woman's."

Anne of Cleves asked, "And now he seek me back? That is your business in this house? To see that I am worthy?"

"Yes," said Martins smoothly. "That is all. Why do you resist so?"

Anne of Cleves said, "You may look. All here is in order." The planes of her face were taut, and in the slant sunlight, her eyes looked hooded. Those heavy eyes seldom opened in surprise anymore. She folded her fingers and laid her hands against her skirt. "I send gift. Henry send gift to me. You examine house as pleases you. I have the ledger book." She trudged toward her writing room, her gait not quite elegant enough for the fabric. The men all went after her.

"Do you think it wise to ask to return to Yorkshire in these times?" asked Lady Dudley when they were alone.

"If the king's wife can return to being a daughter of Cleves after six months of marriage, I can return to my own lands in my widowhood now and then."

Lady Dudley cast her a level look. "The queen's household has been dismembered. Her women were sent off with only the clothes on their backs."

"I have heard as much."

"You had a sister-in-law among them, did you not? A former nun?"

"My husband's sister. And, yes, once a sister of my convent. Now one of the king's sisters. Margaret. She will surely go to Yorkshire. She is likely already there. In my house."

"There are two letters arrived for you."

"I trust the seals are still intact," said Catherine.

"Intact as my daughters." Jane stared at the closed door of Lady Anne's study. "She thinks this interest in her will lead her back into the royal bed. But you know as well as I that when this king truly means to make love, he does not call for a reckoning beforehand." She turned away. "That always comes after."

CHAPTER SEVEN

"Jane has remembered that I asked to leave," said Catherine. She and Ann were alone in their chamber, and Catherine turned the key in the lock before she laid a letter on the table. "That woman lodges everything in her brain and keeps it under lock and key. She is probably spying on me for Lady Anne."

"I expect you will smell the smoke if she gets too close." Ann took up the letter. The seal of Overton Hall had been mashed into the wax disc, and she ran her rough thumb over it before she opened the paper. "I thought you would have a letter from Robbie."

"And I have one. This one is fuller of news. It's from Yorkshire."

"From Eleanor?" Ann squinted at the script and laid the missive down again. "The girl writes better after a few years' study than I will ever. But I don't suppose anyone cares to see a pen in this old hand."

"Your hands are strong, as they need to be. And not old." Catherine flattened the letter between them. "It's Eleanor's writing, but she speaks for her husband as well." She pointed to the signatures of the two stewards and Ann nodded. Catherine said, "She reports that Margaret has returned, convinced that all the ladies of the queen's chamber will be taken to the Tower for traitors. Benjamin has been and gone. Eleanor asks for my return. It gives me my reason to go."

"Margaret should have been arrested before now," said Ann. "She is more murderess than traitor, and the bodies lie almost under her very feet."

"She will swear that she was innocent as a snowdrop in all that. The whole village heard my husband take the guilt for those women's deaths onto himself." Catherine crumpled the paper, then smoothed it again. "She let him die with her crimes on his name. She never did anyone any good, not in her whole life. And we are constrained to forgive. It makes me burn. But listen."

The latch rattled, and a soft knock followed. Catherine folded the letter while Ann unlocked and opened the door. Agnes stood there with Veronica, who balanced an old apple in one hand. "The child will have her Auntie Ann to help with her letters," the maid said. She guided Veronica into the room and curtsied her way back out.

Seeing the paper, Veronica ran to the table. "What news?"

Her red curls escaped from her stiff coif, and Catherine folded the stray hair into the cap. "Come up here, Daughter. We have a message from home."

"This is our home now, Mother, isn't it? Aren't our goods here? And our Lady? I am in training to be a lady-in-waiting." She bit into the fruit and spat a brown slush into her palm. "The apples have gone rotten."

Ann said, "Come with me, girl. I'll find you a solid one. Bring that for the pig bucket." The child leapt from her mother's lap and carried the shriveled fruit delicately by the stem. When they had gone, Catherine reopened the letter.

Greetings from Yorkshire Lady Overton,
We suffer a cold late winter and the grasses are froward,
but the sheep are fat with hay and theyr wools are
soft. Your father has brung some last years fleeces
from the Mt Grace fields and we have much to sell.
Master Benjamin has visited and taken it all away.
You know your husbands sister Margaret has showed
up from the court. She tells sad news of the queen who
is no more. Benjamin and her spent many hours
locked in closed conferrences, but have parted friends,
Benjamin with some pieces of the furniture that he
says will sell high in London. Joseph and me have
secured all account books and receipt books in the
small room of the loft under lock. Margaret watches
from windows but I tell her she is safe at home but
who knows what soldiers do now these days. We
would be glad for your appearance here among us to
keep order. I am quick with another child and feel life
from last week. Kiss small Vere for me. Do you hear
aught from Robbie?
Your loyal and humble stewards,
Eleanor (and Joseph) Adwolfe

Catherine wondered how tall Margaret's maid Constance
had grown since she'd left Yorkshire. She would show that
red hair, that Overton hair, in the village, and it would cause
talk. Catherine chewed her lip. Her children were the true
Overton heirs. A husband would help her keep it that way.
But a husband gotten without permission? The land might go
just the same. Catherine rose and, folding the letter again,

opened the door. She had turned toward the back steps to the kitchen when she heard the shouting below. Creeping to the main stairs, she leaned against the wall to listen.

Lady Anne was saying, "Prepare! I go now!" and Jane Dudley was shrilling to the maids.

Catherine stepped into view and Lady Anne said, "Catherine. The king calls for me. You will wash my face."

"Yes, Lady Anne." Catherine bounded down to the kitchen and fumbled through her stores for roses, calling for the maids to bring hot water.

Ann came in from the laundry. "What is it?"

"Henry has called. She's going to him." Catherine's hands would not do her bidding, and she dropped an entire stem into the water when the girl brought the bowl. "Ah, God's foot, we are saved. I'm saved. Get some rosemary to go with this."

Ann retrieved the rosemary and shredded the needles into the wash water. "Let me do this."

Catherine shook her hands until they stopped trembling and lifted the bowl. "Pray that she looks like a princess," she said.

"You mean a miracle?" Ann said.

Lady Anne's women were already doing her hair, and she was ordering skirts to be shown. "That one," she said. It was blue, with silver threads. "I wear that one. Catherine, fix my face."

"Yes, Lady." Catherine elbowed past the other women and stroked the skin of Anne of Cleves. There was little to be done for her. "Have you powder, Lady?"

"Cosmetic? I wear no false face," said Lady Anne.

"Not a mask," said Catherine. "It is almost a physic for the complexion." She trotted down to her own chamber and found a box. Returning, she showed it in the window light. "You see? It is almost invisible. Almost not there." She dabbed Lady Anne's cheeks and chin and nose. The Lady blew through her nostrils and said, "Am I finer?"

"You are," said Catherine. "May God shine on you." She picked up the bowl and fled before she had to tell an outright falsehood.

The Lady Anne would not return that night, and Catherine meant to stay in her still room with Ann Smith, sorting and arranging, packing up what she would want to take with her. But Martins was upstairs and she could not hear what he did. The third time she went to the stairs to listen, Ann said, "Sit. When the word comes, if the word comes, it will come in thunder. You will not miss it."

Catherine returned, and Veronica was brought by Agnes to help. She said, "Mother, you have opened and closed that crock four times. I have counted." She held up four fingers.

Catherine looked at Ann. Ann looked at the child and said, "Your mother is making sure of herself."

"I will make sure," said Veronica, re-opening a jar of sage and sniffing. "It is sage."

"And it was sage the last time you smelt of it," said Ann. "Sure as this world."

The palace went to a quiet sleep, and Catherine finally retreated to her chamber, but she lay awake, watching. If Anne had been summoned of an afternoon, perhaps it had been planned for her to go to the king's bed. Perhaps she was there now, making England well. But the image gave her a chill, and she pulled the covers up and curled into a ball.

64

Chapter Eight

Lady Anne did not return in the morning. Nor at noon. The sun was already tangled in the western trees when the barge came, and Catherine forced herself into patience by showing the kitchen maids how to roll out a coffin without tearing the pastry. She ripped a piece off and showed them how to mend an error. The voices rang upstairs, and still Catherine pushed at the roller, saying "You see? Any mistake may be corrected." She almost believed it.

She handed over the job and wiped her hands. Listened. Ann Smith came in with Veronica on one hip. "She's returned."

"Can you hear what they say?"

"No. And I will not eavesdrop, neither. Not with this one in tow." She bounced the child.

"I cannot wait," said Catherine, but as she crept to the stairs, she heard nothing like celebration. It was the Lady Anne. But she was shouting.

"I sequester no thing. You cannot say I do such action. I am Henry's loyal subject and his sister. I have been his wife. We give the gifts, one to the other. He give me the cramp rings as a token of love."

The accent made Anne's words thick, and Catherine's ears strained. But the man's accusation was easy enough to hear.

"There are discrepancies, Lady, and someone must be held liable for them." A long pause soaked the air. "It is not as though the king has denied you anything. Do you offer gifts in hopes of something to which you are not entitled? Would you shame the king? You will not do it, I assure you, nor will you have your brother's butter-boys grease your way into his bed or out of his realm. He has treated you right well, like a sister, but I see the sort of house you keep here."

Catherine laid her head against the wall. Lady Anne did not respond. Soon, a door boomed shut, and Catherine backed on her toes down the hall, then turned and ran to the kitchen. She did not want to hear the woman weeping. Martins would answer for it. Let him. "Ann," she said. "That man has attacked her character, and her barely in the door. Come, we can hear better upstairs."

They took the back way, but no one was talking. They loitered for a while, then retired to their chamber. Catherine turned the key and sat on her bed for a few minutes, waiting for any call from below. But nothing came. "I believe she has gifts from the king. That's something. I heard her speak of cramp rings."

"Those are toys between friends," said Ann. "He might give those to anyone. He gave you a ring, remember?"

"I do." Catherine still carried the letter from Eleanor in her pocket, where she'd put it after reading it to Ann the night before, and she removed it. "But these rings are a new gift, and Martins has made an accusation upon them. It could be his undoing." She folded the paper twice more, making a packet of it small enough to slide into the cubbyhole of her desk.

Ann shook her head, "Or our undoing. Hide that in one of the trunks so it goes with us.

And Catherine pulled the letter out again. She said, "Take Vere down, the front way, and listen as you go. I cannot be seen to have my nose in their conversations."

"Catherine—" said Ann. But she went.

Catherine opened her clothing chest. She secured the letter under a strap in the lid and slid a pair of gloves in to conceal it. Then she sifted through the old unfashionable sleeves and skirts. Something could be made of these suitable to the Lady of Overton House. Not too fine but rich enough to show her station. She would need looser garments. As she mused, Catherine's fingers touched an unfamiliar pillow of velvet. She pulled the item out, into the light. It was a soft black bag, one she had never seen before, gathered and tied with a gold cord that ended in two large tassels. Catherine could feel what was in it before she loosened the knot and emptied it into her hand. The bag was full of gold, angels and crowns. And they certainly were not hers.

CHAPTER NINE

The Lady Anne's voice could not be ignored, even coming from as far away as her game room. "I write letter to the king," she was shouting as Catherine came down the front stairs and peeked in. Jane Dudley sat at the table, dealing cards, and the King's Sister sat across from her, pounding the arm of her chair as she spoke. "He see his error. I will be his wife. I am his wife. This man will be hung like the villain he be."

"Yes, my Lady" said Jane Dudley. She glanced up when Catherine entered. Her chin lifted, and Catherine backed up a step, waiting for instructions.

Anne of Cleves's eyes were on the fire that twisted and popped in the hearth. "That girl betray him and now he will see. I will be his wife. I will have the baby now. I not very old. You have many baby."

"Many," said Jane. She laid down a card. "You have a comfortable situation here. Not many would choose to change it. You might be content with this palace."

"I am queen. I should have baby." She raised her hand at Catherine. "You have baby. Two. And you have been in the convent."

Catherine curtsied and kept her eyes on the floor. "Yes, my Lady."

"How do you be a widow and the sisters cannot marry?"

"The king granted me leave," said Catherine. "My case was exceptional. I was only a novice, and I was carrying a child. My husband paid well for the king's ear." Jane cut her a glance, and Catherine felt the blood take over her face. She added, "He spoke well into the king's ear, I mean to say. Most of the sisters cannot marry under the king's law."

"Ha." The Lady Anne plucked a card loose, examined it, and threw it down onto the table. "And now you are widow. So you are one of the king's sisters now. Like me."

Catherine said, "You have hit the target, my Lady. And would that we were all Beloved as well."

The Lady Anne put her head back and laughed with her mouth open. The sound was like a blade through the air. "You are the wit, my Catherine. Is she not, Jane?"

"Yes, my Lady, a very ready mind." Jane lifted a card from the spread in her right hand and slipped it back in, nearer to the left.

"You must never leave my side, witty Catherine," said the Lady Anne.

"I have a letter from my stewards in Yorkshire," ventured Catherine. "They ask for me to return and help them keep order there. My sister-in-law is apparently upending the household."

"But you have the stewards, do you not?" said the Lady Anne. "They will keep the orders for you. No, Catherine. Your place is here. With me."

Catherine backed silently, then turned and ran on down to the kitchen, where the maid Marjory was stirring a pot of water with a large pewter spoon. The pot was otherwise empty. "Have you not got those hens on to cook yet?"

"The water won't boil," the girl complained. She dipped her finger in and tasted it.

"It's just water. Let it be. You stir all the fire out of it," said Catherine, taking the spoon. "Go get their heads off, and this will be hot enough when you return."

"Which ones?"

"The oldest ones. You cannot tell?" Catherine bit the tip of her tongue and counted ten. "One has black feathers in the wings and the other's comb has been frozen off."

Marjory stared at the wall, seeming to lodge this information somewhere, then pulled on a cloak and, leaving the door unlatched behind her, wandered toward the poultry yard.

Ann Smith came in with a clutch of vegetables from the cellar and fastened the door. "Whew. I feel a cold wind blowing."

Catherine slung a handful of sticks on the fire and the embers hissed. "The maids in waiting have been taught only to dip and say 'my Lady' and carry their skirts just so and the kitchen girls don't know how to heat a pan of water. Are we making all of our English girls stupid? It's no wonder that the queen got caught with her skirts up." She slapped the recalcitrant pot. "But listen to me. The Lady Anne is on fire for marriage. I think she will win the day."

Ann flicked a knife blade against her thumb and began trimming the tops of some carrots. "You still want the maids all to be Margaret Mores."

"I want them not to be idiots who cannot learn to kill a chicken before they find their own heads coming off. I want them to pass under the eyes of the king's men unnoticed."

Ann laid the carrots upon a block in a row and removed their heads at a stroke. "She has been speaking of marriage, has she?"

"She knows the nuns of England must still be nuns, with or without their church. But she laughs at it. She has the heart to fight for him. Will that not go well with him?" said Catherine to the pot. She took the wooden spoon and stirred the water, then threw the spoon down in disgust at herself. "Will it?" She whirled around. "Do you hear?"

"I cry you mercy, I thought you were asking the pot," said Ann. She scrubbed the carrot skins with a rough clout. "He will set her straight fast enough, I warrant."

"I heard her say it myself." Catherine joined Ann at the table. "She wants children. She told it to Jane Dudley. If he had rejected her, she would show it. She would tell it outright."

"And what did Jane say?" Ann examined the vegetables, stopping to gouge out a black spot.

"She said nothing. Lady Dudley will not be said to have an opinion at all about royal matters."

Ann leaned forward and whispered, "Lady Anne should get her another new dress and give her thanks to God that she has a head on her shoulders for wearing the hood to it. Her man Harst should tell her if her women will not."

"Harst was her brother's man before he was hers and the brother wants the marriage. It may be that she has bought a dress or two too many." Catherine paused. She could hear her heart thumping in her ears. "I heard that Martins say that the books do not come to a correct accounting."

"You see?" Ann threw down the carrots and took up a turnip. "The king doesn't care how much money she spends as long as she bows and licks his toe and says 'your Grace is the godliest monarch on the earth.'"

"I pray that you say right."

"I did not say it would win her back into his bed."

Catherine pulled the velvet bag from her pocket and, listening for steps, laid it on the table. "And what think you of this?"

"Very pretty. It looks like it belongs with mourning weeds, though. Lady Anne will not be wearing black any time soon, I suppose?"

"I found it in my storage chest."

Ann looked at it more closely. "When did you carry it last? I have no memory of it."

"I have never seen it before."

Ann laid the paring knife aside and lifted the bag. Squeezed it. Her brown eyes came up to Catherine's. She pulled the strings and the coins fell onto the table. "Angels."

"And crowns."

Ann stirred the coins. "There must always be crowns contending with the angels these days. Put it away."

"Should I leave it where it was?"

"Among your things? No. Whoever put it there knows where it was. There are no locks in Richmond that are not subject to the hammer." Ann palmed the money back inside and knotted the strings. "You must give it over. Put it into the Lady Anne's hands and say you found it. If someone asks you more about it, you can blink your green eyes and look as astonished as the next woman. Innocent as the day you were born." Ann hefted the bag again in her right hand.

"I was not born an innocent. I was born with the stain of sin on me. And I am going to bring into the world another with the same stain."

Ann's eyes were dark. She set the bag into Catherine's palm. "Stop thinking so much. Get rid of it."

"All right." Catherine stood, sliding the bag away. "But who put it among my things? And when?"

"I can't imagine."

"Could someone have dropped it?"

"Someone who happened to be leaning over your open clothing chest?" Ann shook her head and reached for some onions. "Someone has been in your chest, and the same someone may have seen that your things are packed."

"If Lady Anne is retaken, it will not matter so much. Benjamin can see to Margaret for me."

Ann chopped a large onion open and its walls fell apart. She gathered up the broken skins and threw them into a bowl. "I expect that Margaret would enjoy having your Benjamin to see to her. Keep your chest locked, Catherine. And check it often. If the king comes to believe that his Beloved Sister is deceiving him, no one in the household will be outside suspicion. We need to go before that falls upon you."

Chapter Ten

Jane Dudley was calling, "Catherine!" and before they could move, her heavy heels came smacking down the stairs.

"Take this," said Catherine, stuffing the bag into Ann's pocket. "Hide it in my still room."

Ann pulled herself back into shape and bent over the remaining onions as Jane progressed into the kitchen. "You're needed. They've done with the accounts of the wardrobe, and the Lady Anne will have them entertained before we feed them. Put them into a better frame of mind. Can you manage it? Ann Smith, you come too."

Ann lifted a carrot and waved it. "These must be cooked."

"Oh, leave them for the maids," said Jane Dudley. She snatched the carrot and flung it onto the table. "They're soft as a priest's peter anyway." One of the maids wandered in with a handful of clouts from the laundry, and Jane gave her a soft slap on the back of the head. "Get those roots into a pot, will you, girl?"

The girl offered a stiff curtsey but her upper lip went white. "Yes, Madam."

Ann said, "I will just change my apron."

She disappeared up the back stairs, and Jane Dudley called "be quick about it" to her retreating footsteps.

"Where are they?" asked Catherine. "Those villains, I mean. Martins and his little court."

"They're in back garden," said Jane, "waiting for someone to worship their codpieces."

When Ann rejoined them, Jane handed out cloaks and led them out and around the palace. The long back lawn apparently made a fine shooting range, and Martins, when he spied the women, took a wide-legged stance to prepare himself for a stunning performance. Beyond them, a large apple awaited its execution upon a wooden plinth. Catherine hunkered against the wind, and Ann Smith threw her own cloak over her. Jane Dudley hunched under a cape of furs on a stool nearby, the red-faced Barts and narrow-eyed Chandler, mimicking Martins' stance, beside her.

"I can barely see your target from this distance," said Catherine. "You haven't a prayer of hitting it."

"You shall see, Lady," said Martins. "You observe how I rotate the dog thusly." He moved something at the rear of the weapon and a metal pan opened. He made a great show of packing and pushing, then produced a ball which he displayed between forefinger and thumb. "This will replace the point of any arrow in existence." He forced the pellet into the weapon and took elaborate aim, rocking from one dainty foot to the other. Chandler also posed as if to aim. Finally, Martins' thumb moved and an explosion enveloped his hand in smoke.

Catherine's heart jumped into her throat, and she grabbed Ann's hand. "Christ's wounds, it's got a demon in it."

"It is the new learning, Lady, no demon," said Martins. He waved the smoke away and peered into the distance. The apple sat unmolested, but a branch from the small oak nearby lay splintered on the brown grass. "Ah, a miss this time. But a hit next shot. Does it not give a frightful appearance, Lady?"

"A frightful appearance," assured Chandler.

"It appears that we will have fruit tart for supper after all," said Catherine. "You will not fire upon me if I rescue the poor victim, I trust?"

Lady Jane pulled her furs close and stood. "I must attend to Lady Anne," she said, ducking indoors. "I cannot endure such noise."

Barts sat where Jane had been. "The mechanism perhaps needs, hm, some regulation. Give it to me." He held out his hand and Martins laid the wheel-lock into it.

"You know how to make the changes?" Martins watched as the other man turned the weapon over. Bart's cheeks were wind-burned, and with his sandy hair and spectacles catching the sunlight, he looked scorched all over. Chandler hung over the other two, silently watching.

Catherine walked with Ann Smith down the garden and tossed the apple to her friend.

Ann caught it with one hand. "The men will perfect their firearms and make the world safer?"

"Safer for Englishmen and their God, no doubt," said Catherine, as they walked back. The men were still attending to the wheel-lock. "They will fire us all straight into heaven if they have their way." She slowed her pace. "They seem more intent on their own pleasure than on driving Lady Anne into submission just now. Can that mean a wedding to follow?"

"Henry has never revoked his will in matters of his desire. Only in matters of faith."

"But now that he's been proven a cuckold," said Catherine, "maybe the wind's gone out of his sails and he'll want to board a more sober woman."

"If there is still any wood in the mast." Ann sniggered.

Catherine lowered her voice. "He is older now, and fatter. Perhaps he no longer wants a woman that way. I am sick, Ann. I must get inside."

Martins raised the weapon as the women came up and the engraved leaves and vines upon the hilt glittered, even in the dull sun. "We have it! Shall we shoot again?"

"Not this day," said Catherine. "We're going to sacrifice this apple to a coffin of pastry in celebration of your new-found power."

"We have given you a gift, then. A boundless happiness to me. I would that you had every yearning of your heart. It is not too much to ask, is it?" He waved the weapon around. "A woman seeks her yearnings, I have heard."

"My deepest craving this moment is to get out of the cold," said Catherine.

"A simple woman with plain needs. A rarity these days. Do let me know if you have any troubles from which I can free you." The man laid the barrel into his palm. "Very well, ladies. You return to your pots and pans. You have us to protect you."

"A great reassurance," said Catherine as he claimed her fingers for a damp kiss. Her stomach revolted at it, and she ran.

The fire was ablaze in the kitchen, and Sebastian hooked the spit into the notch and sat for a drink. Catherine, dropping her cloak, turned her back to the flames. Heat touched her hose and the muscles in her thighs stopped shivering. "Thank God for warmth." She knelt and emptied her stomach into a bucket.

Ann laid her hand along the thick curtain. "That third one's got the weapon now. What's his name? Chandler Ellers?"

"Ellers Chandler. I believe he is a lawyer, so he may have a name that runs both ways."

"Whatever he is," said Ann, "some conference is putting their heads together. Changing the course of the world. God on the cross, they can hardly tell their scabbards from their codpieces."

One of the chambermaids came down, holding Veronica by the hand. The child clutched a feather duster and swiped at the walls and floors.

"Are you making a cleaning girl of my daughter?" asked Catherine. "Give me that, Vere."

"It's mine!" the child protested, but Catherine hooked it out of her reach.

"She likes to see the dust fly," said the maid, looking at her feet. "I didn't mean no harm by it, Madam."

Ann laughed out loud. "She is practicing to be a member of the king's court, Catherine. Plenty of dirt flying there."

Veronica put her thumb in her mouth, sulking, and Catherine removed it. "Oh, no, small lady. No sucking. You are just like your brother, and I almost resorted to sewing a glove to his sleeve to save his teeth."

The girl tucked her thumb under her four fingers. "I will be good, Mother."

"Yes, you will," said Catherine. "And then perhaps you will be called to serve the royal children, too."

The maid had backed silently from the room and Sebastian retook his post. "Have you a letter from my brother?" asked Veronica.

"I do," said Catherine. "He writes a good hand, and he asks after your health, as a good brother should."

Veronica leapt onto the bench. "He is the prince's best companion, is he not?" She clapped her hands before her face. "And the prince will be king, and my brother will be the king's counselor. And I am his sister and he will reward me."

Ann laughed again. "Your fancy runs off with you, girl."

Catherine said, "He is not always in the company of the prince, but he can ride with the best of them. He will move up with the court and perhaps one day he will be at the prince's right hand. And, yes, my girl, you are his sister."

"Read the letter to me, Mother, if you please."

"I have it upon me." Catherine pulled the paper from her pocket. "He begins 'Dearest Mother.' Isn't that a good boy?"

"All brothers say that," said Veronica. "That is nothing."

Catherine flapped the letter on her head. "All right, you monkey. He says 'I am much upon my new gelding, and he flies as fast as the horses of the prince's stable. I thank you for him. I pray for you every night, and for my little sister. His Grace has favored me with larger chambers. I do well and serve my father's name proudly.'" Catherine stopped a moment, skimming the paper. "'I send you my love and duty. Your son, Robert Overton.'" She folded it and stuck it back into her pocket. "Does he not sound like a young man?"

Ann said, "I know few boys of six years who write such messages."

Catherine glanced at her friend. "He was always good with his letters," she said. "Now, Mistress Veronica, where are your lessons? You were to show me how well you can spell your name."

Veronica traced a circle in the wood of the table. "I will do it just now."

"You have not even begun?" asked Catherine. "Vere!"

Ann took her by the hand. "You will do it now, indeed, my small madam. And I will watch you as I fold the linens. And I will secure that other bit of stuff as well." She dragged Veronica off just as Jane Dudley came into the kitchen.

"You are wanted upstairs, Catherine. I believe that Martin Martins cannot contain himself if he does not aim his weapon for your admiration one more time."

Chapter Eleven

Martin David Martins was saying his elaborate, oily farewell, and he pivoted, leg extended and codpiece displayed, when Catherine came up. He grabbed her hand and laid his lips upon it. Then he rose and drew her close, whispering into her ear, "So many temptations, Lady, and you so deserving. Do let me know if you lay eyes upon that ring. Or anything else of value. I have heard that you like to have a man in attendance. Let me be of service to you."

So he meant to come again. Catherine retrieved her hand and wiped it on her skirt as soon as the man's back was turned. Jane Dudley stood in the doorway, her eyes following Martins until he was riding away. Catherine's breast unwound, but midway to shutting the door upon the horrible squat man, Jane opened it again.

"Who is that?" she said. "Catherine, don't leave just yet. That is another of your suitors, is it not?"

Catherine stepped forward, pulled the door wider, and stood beside Jane. The man had stopped to greet Martins and was now riding toward them. His mouth was tightened into a measured smirk. "It is Benjamin Davies and his man Reginald," said Catherine. She almost stepped outside but recovered herself. "He comes with news for me. Tell him I am in the kitchen."

"The Lady Anne must see him. Don't hang on him and be sure you produce him quickly." She closed the door. The men would take their horses around back first. "What's the matter? What's this news he brings? You seem to know it already."

Catherine's heart was galloping. "Benjamin has invested monies with me. And with my father. I expect he brings me reports of our yields. Nothing more." She rubbed a patch of pain in her forehead. "I owe him a great deal."

Jane's eyes drilled into her. "Does he mean to marry you? There will be no permissions given now, you mark me. And then there is Lent. And Lady Anne in such a state—"

"I know nothing of any permissions, asked or received. Benjamin was a great friend to my husband. I mean, to my husband's older brother. He knows all the wool markets. He has profitable friends in Dover and Calais. But the king's orders? I have nothing to say to them." Her heart was giddy and would not stay down in her chest.

"When has that ever stopped love from rushing to its final destination?" Jane was now smiling, but only with one side of her mouth. The other side seemed to frown. "Come, Catherine, don't look glum. I've never heard your words tie themselves into such knots. He seems well enough. At least he doesn't affect those great shoulders the other men wear. God's wounds, they look like stuffed dolls."

"No," said Catherine. Her guts were as tangled as her tongue. "Benjamin Davies is quite immune to the contagion of fashion."

Jane pinched Catherine's cheeks. "Look how rosy a young widow you are. And what a bad little sister." Then she sobered. "But take care for yourself. And for all of us here."

"I will only be a few minutes with him." Catherine ran downstairs, pulled on a cloak, and went out. The air was frozen and bright and breathing was like drinking from a cold stream. The first lettuces would be showing their green crowns already. Catherine was shooing the gulls as the group of men rode around the house and pulled up short. The two in the rear bore a deer on a pole between them.

Benjamin Davies, in the lead, leapt from his Caesar and hailed Catherine. "What are you doing, tromping through the mud like a serving woman?" He swept off his hat and bowed, but his eyes were laughing at her. He was still broad in the shoulders, without benefit of padding, and still wore his dark beard long, too shaggy for court style. His coat was plain and his breeches were simple woolen. No codpiece. His black hair had grown even longer and curlier, hanging over his shoulders, and the window lit up the white strands in it. He bowed and said, "I bring you a token, Lady, if you will have it. I felled this beast with my own hands."

Reg Goodall was dismounting behind Benjamin, waving for the other men to ride on up to the stables. Their horses sauntered forward, and the ones carrying the deer high-stepped and snorted as their riders turned them to display the dead animal. It was a young buck but a fat one.

"Reg. It's good to see you well." Catherine laid her hand on the animal's flank and removed it, not liking to feel the hard, cold muscle under the soft hair. She said to the men, "Take it to the shambles in the back and ask for Hubert. He will oversee the dressing of it."

The men dipped their caps and rode on, the dead ears and tail swinging as they went. Reg was looking at the kitchen door, and Catherine said, "Go on in, won't you? She's hiding in the laundry." He dipped his head and hurried toward the house.

"And how do you, Catherine?" Benjamin resituated his hat. "I don't suppose you will let me kiss your hand?"

"You needn't play the courtier until we're inside," said Catherine. "You wear the mask so tightly that it will grow to your face."

"Oh. A hit." Benjamin touched his breast. "You will injure me to my grave."

"Go to, Benjamin, you mock me," said Catherine. Her cheeks flamed and she wanted to cover them. "Do you bring news?"

"Your sheep are fat and woolly. The village is full of gossip about your son. They say that Robbie is the center of his circle, shining among the other pages as a gem set in dull metal. They are sure that he will be as handsome as his mother is beautiful and will ride in with you and restore them to their glory."

"How long have you been returned?" Catherine walked on toward the garden and Benjamin was forced to follow.

"I have been at my country house for a day, just long enough see my daughter and to shoot you some meat. I have gathered some things from both of our houses to sell. Your leftover wool has been bundled for sale, and there will be more coming with the warm weather. Much more. Your father and Joseph Adwolfe have managed the works like old sheepmen. They are born to business. My daughter has made herself mistress of my own house and I have no worries in that corner."

"I had a letter from Eleanor. She says that you and Margaret were much together."

"I would not say 'much.' I told her that I would take some sticks of furniture to sell and that you were still the rightful owner of Overton House. She disagreed. I told her that it became a spinster sister to look over her family's property in their absence. I may have mentioned a court of law. Then she came to agree with me. Or at least she said she did. She did not object when I carried out the furniture."

They had reached the protected edge of the vegetable patch, and Catherine knelt to examine the tiny leaves pushing through the cold soil. They were larger where the sun shone all day, and she nipped one and tasted it. Sweet and tender. She stood, brushing her hands together. "And?"

"And what? You will have a pot of money, as soon as I can go to the market. The wools are ready, and they are very fine. I will not leave this island as a beggar."

"And so you are decided for the both of us?"

"It is the only sensible decision. You cannot stay here."

Catherine rocked back onto her haunches and shaded her eyes to look up at him. "I have news for you. The king has had the Lady Anne to him."

"What? For a wife?"

"Well, not fast. Not yet. She has been called to him, though." The sun was behind Benjamin, and she couldn't make out his face.

"It may mean something. I cannot tell."

"Will Margaret make trouble when she hears the news of me?"

"Perhaps. But the law will be on your side. That Connie is with her. I wonder that the mud didn't sink her along the road. The ways are almost impassable. She broke two wagons and was carrying nothing but her clothes and some old bushes." Benjamin squatted to Catherine's level. "The maid has grown to look almost the image of Robert Overton."

Catherine stood and wiped her hand on her apron. Benjamin stood beside her and offered his arm, but she didn't take it. "Constance is as much an Overton as my own children are."

"Oh, no. She is not and you must not say so aloud. Your children are William's by law and that one is Robert's bastard."

"Robert and William are both dead anyway. Lower your voice." Catherine stepped aside to let Marjory walk past. The maid had a pile of the soft carrots in a clout and she was headed toward the pig pens. Catherine said, "You might cut out what can be saved from those before they go into the slops."

"Yes, Madam," said Marjory wearily. Her eyes were on Benjamin.

Catherine chose a handful of skinny green onions and toed the dirt back over the tiny holes in the soil. They walked back without talking, where Catherine closed the door behind them and pulled Benjamin into the side kitchen. "Come away from the window. You'll create a spectacle."

"Are you worried that the maids will see us?" He sidled closer, hip to hip with Catherine.

"Gossip can get a woman's head cut off." His hand was on her waist and she tried to ignore it. "Tell me what else you know of Margaret."

Benjamin put his lips in the hollow under her jaw and murmured, "All I know is what I have told you. She returned to Yorkshire after the little queen went to the block. She brought a queen's ransom in clothing. She is holed up in her chamber like a fox in its lair."

"As Eleanor said in her letter."

"Mm-hm. And Eleanor is a gem, playing the saint when Margaret is in attendance, 'yes, Madam'ing and 'no, Madam'ing' as though her tongue were made of snow. I can see the fire in her eyes, though. If she knew a way to cast the devil out, she would say the spell."

A laugh twisted in Catherine's throat and she choked on the mean knot of it.

Benjamin patted her back and let his hand wander to Catherine's nape. "Don't throttle yourself with joy."

Marjory came in and passed through to the laundry with the dirty clout, empty of carrots, dangling from her fingers.

Catherine watched until she had gone. "How do my servants get along?"

"I spoke but little to them. They go about their tasks as though they know how to do them. The house is clean and the fields are neat. I spent my evenings alone with the best wine from your cellar." Benjamin grinned and Catherine feinted a slap.

The big skewer squeaked in the next room, and Catherine said, "Come this way," leading Benjamin to her still room. "Benjamin, I think the world turns our way. But I worry for my son. Robbie will not approve of my marrying again." The man sat forward and Catherine let her tongue go. "He has no father and he feels the loss."

Benjamin said, "Shall I fetch him then?"

"What will you tell the prince? That his company was not good enough for my son?" Catherine guided Benjamin's fingers to her skirt, but there was no swelling yet. She spoke without looking up. "I want him to stay with the prince."

"Then stay he will." He patted her belly. "You may write to him and tell him how things are."

Catherine sighed. "Christ's foot, I am a fool." She could not tell him that she did not want to leave England.

"You are no fool, and our plans are sounds. Robbie's too young to manage your house, and he requires finishing. Your properties are in good hands for now. Joseph has invested your profits in the Mount Grace buildings and more sheep for the House lands. He's turned joiner, too, and has set up a dozen woodworkers in the village. Leave Robbie where he is, and we will tell him when we are married. He will find me a good father, and all will be well."

Catherine's stomach tripped. She got a bowl down, filled it from her pitcher, and, pulling the onions from her pocket, swished them until she slopped the water over the edge. Benjamin handed her a clout, and she snatched it away without looking at him. "I could not bear to injure my son. He was injured enough by his father. He knew William never loved him."

"Give him time. He wants to prove himself and he lacks a man to show him who he is. He wants to wear the sword before he's mastered the dagger." He swiped an onion and bit off the nub of pearly bulb. "Let him accustom himself to the notion of me. He will, in time."

"You sound like Ann Smith." Catherine snapped the greens and sprayed water all over the table yet again. "Hellfire," she said, pushing the rag around. She glanced up at Benjamin. "You have never had a son." She tossed the ravaged, undergrown onions onto a plate. They looked pathetic, like something born too soon.

"No, but I have been one. You say he wants a father. Let me try out the part."

Catherine swished and shook the dirt from the bulbs. She was smiling and it felt good.

"You're pleased to hear it?" asked Benjamin.

"Yes. It eases my heart."

"And I will keep our secret quiet until we can act." He shoved the bowl aside. "It will be soon enough. I have to get that wool sold, though. May I come visit you openly?"

"You may not. That man of the king's still dogs our heels. He hangs on Lady Anne like a plague. His eyes go everywhere and we must be perfect."

"He is not here. I met him going out as I came in. But you know that." When he stood and offered her his elbow, she let her hand slide through it this time, and she liked the close fit of their arms.

"You will behave? We cannot have talk, even among the women. Everyone is wound to the breaking point. You should have seen Elizabeth. I thought she would tear out her own hair."

Benjamin let her go and sighed. "I will behave myself, at least until dark." He reached for the bag at his hip. "I have brought you a purse of ready money for to use as you see fit." He offered a red silk pouch with a gold drawstring.

"I cannot take your money," said Catherine. "I will not."

"It is yours," Benjamin replied, pushing it into her hand. "I will get twice this if the wools go to the Calais buyers in this dead time. Oh, and I have a present for Vere, from Havenston." He pulled out a poppet, with dyed wool for hair and a plaid shawl over her dress. Someone had embroidered a smiling face on its stuffed linen head. "Mistress MacIntosh fashions them for the children in Havenston."

Catherine took the doll and straightened the tiny coif. "It has a sweet expression." She let him take her by both shoulders and kiss her full on the lips. Her eyes closed, but he pulled away and she opened them again.

"Don't look like that or I will take you upstairs right now." He set her away from him.

A wind rushed through Catherine's head and she thought she would faint, but Benjamin caught her and put his hand over her mouth. "Quiet. The whole household will hear you."

Catherine could feel her blood beating against his palm and pulled his fingers away. "I said nothing."

Agnes came from the laundry, wiping her hands on a clout. "Madam? How do you?" Marjory was behind the older girl.

"I do very well." Catherine fingered a lock of hair back under the edge of her hood. "Very well indeed. What? Why do you ask?"

Marjory shook her head and glanced over Benjamin. "I thought I heard you call out."

Someone laughed, then Reg Goodall and Ann Smith, smelling of soap and water, entered the room. Ann's hands were red, and she shook them dry, saying, "Lady Catherine was just praying, weren't you?" She winked and Catherine's face raged with heat. Marjory threw panicked looks around, curtsied awkwardly on one knee, and stumbled out. Ann said, "Benjamin Davies. Hello to you. I thought I might find you here with Sister Catherine. The entire house will know of your arrival."

Catherine rushed out, toward the kitchen, and almost ran full into Sebastian. "Pardon me, Madam," he said, backing up. "I've been left to fill my own jug." His hands were empty, but Catherine called Marjory, who came running again from the direction of the cellar.

"You've forgotten to keep Sebastian in ale," said Catherine.

"But I've just filled it," said Marjory. "Just now."

"My error," said Sebastian. "I failed to see it." He bowed and retreated to the kitchen.

Catherine followed. A cold pitcher of ale sat on the side table in the big kitchen, and Sebastian poured himself a large draught while Catherine got wine and four cups. She could hear Benjamin talking as she came down the hall and through the still room door.

Ann was holding the doll. "Where did you get the little Scotchwoman?"

"Mistress MacIntosh," said Reg. "She makes them."

Ann looked at Benjamin. "Is Margaret in Yorkshire?"

Benjamin said, "Secreted in her chambers from the eyes of the king, or so she hopes."Ann poured for Reg, then slid onto the bench, propped the doll against the window, and picked up the last cup. "Mustn't let this go to vinegar." She drank. "The queen is all bones by now anyway."

They drank in silence, watched by the startled eyes of the poppet.

Ann announced, "Happier talk. When will the king marry again?"

"There's no time before Lent," offered Reg. "And he has to find a woman."

"There's a lady here ready to do the duty" said Ann. She set her gaze on the doll. "Perhaps she will talk her way back into the king's bed and then we will have two chaps on the way. They can wait until after Easter to marry. The weather's yet cold enough for thick skirts." Her hand traced the scar on her throat. "You know what they say. A first child of marriage can come any time. It's only the second that takes nine months."

"Henry will not marry the Lady Anne again," said Benjamin.

Ann took one of Catherine's hands. "Ah, well. He might marry someone else. He might be trying them out as we speak."

Catherine laid the onions into a wooden bowl, then sprinkled them with oil and vinegar. "The Cleves brother will push forward, now that the breach has been made," she said, "even with the king's men sniffing about. They may hang themselves with their inquisitions."

Ann said, "Let them do it then." Her voice was softer. "She doesn't even know how many rings she owns."

"I hope he takes her again. It would make everything easy. I pray for it." Catherine dragged her hand through the vinegar and lifted the onions. "Have you got a clean clout?"

Ann pulled one from her apron pocket and laid it flat on the table.

"Is this why you set yourself to work like a Trojan?" asked Benjamin. "You think God will send you an answer to your prayers? I tell you, you will not find your salvation in a bowl of salad."

Catherine laid her hand on the clout and watched the moisture disappear from her nails. She covered her nose and let the scent of the vinegar open her head. "We have never been free since the convent was closed. Forgive me for talking of the old times, but we must take what we can. Your king has never been the friend to the sisters that the convent was."

"You think the Pope takes better care of women?" Benjamin leaned back and linked his hands behind his head.

"I have never laid eyes on a Pope," she said. "I expect he's like other men when they get crowns on their heads. It weighs down their brains and they turn tyrant." She looked up and saw the wounded darkness in Benjamin's eyes. "Forgive me. I didn't mean that I prefer the past to the future. I was not speaking of you or Reg, but of freedom as a principle." She faltered and her heart shriveled with misery and guilt. "Don't listen to me." Catherine went to the door and, when Reg opened it, peered out. No one was listening there, and she said, "Let me refresh us," but at the kitchen, she heard the scuttle of shoes and went to the wine room instead. She got a bottle of the good claret and returned. "Now pitchers not only have ears; they have ears against closed doors."

"And they call this reform," said Ann. "The king trades in one wife for another, and all his people trade each other for a few coins. We hear the Latin, then we hear the English, then it's Latin again. I am not as sure of this marriage for Lady Anne as you are, Catherine. We have become so reformed and reformed backward that we are not to be recognized at all. We are neither fish nor flesh."

Catherine smiled. "That leaves only fowl."

"I see nothing foul in you," said Reg, and Ann's face flushed.

Benjamin grinned. "I wondered when you would find your tongue, man. I suppose your eyes work better than most. And Ann Smith, you do look as though the river air has done you some good. I wonder that you are able to keep your mind upon your work."

Ann pushed herself to her feet. "It matters not to me whether men's tongues or eyes work. And I have duties of my own. You all may work out the problems of the land, will you? It makes no difference to me." She drank off the remains of her cup. "This is for Vere?" she asked, picking up the doll.

"Yes," said Benjamin.

"Good." She shoved past Reg. "I will take it to her."

Catherine watched her go. "You might go after her if you would, Reg."

He shook his head. "Her spirits are raised and she will need to be alone to settle them. I will see her when she wants to be seen. She is afraid for you. She wants to see you safe."

Catherine regarded the man. "You know her right well."

"As I said. I know her," said Reg. "Her mind is armed against me."

"She had a bad man once, a long time ago," said Catherine. "It's left its battle scar in her."

"I know of it. He gambled away her money, then went off and died. It doesn't change her worth, not in my eyes."

They sat silent for a moment, then Benjamin leaned forward. "She speaks true about this king, though. He is in a black mood. He tosses one way and then the other. He looks to lay the blame somewhere. A woman would be a most convenient target. And he doesn't want Lady Anne."

"What would he blame Lady Anne for? That he cannot keep a wife? That he keeps chopping their heads off?" Catherine squeezed her cup.

"We'll speak more of this later. Now, I must go perform my obligation to the ladies upstairs." Benjamin stood and took Catherine's hand. "But be sure I would rather be here with you."

Catherine remained at the table, with her door ajar, until she heard the voices raised in greeting and announcement above. Anne of Cleves always saved her receiving room for unwelcome guests, and they had met in the front hall. Lady Anne's deep accent followed Jane Dudley's clipped soprano notes. A few bass sounds that must have been Harst. Catherine closed her eyes and listened to the easy harmony of their playacting. Someone, it must have been Lady Anne, said "the king," and Harst said "good sir" twice. Jane Dudley's bird-voice always had a tremor of alarm rippling over the top of it, and when she said "my Lord" Catherine could tell she meant her husband. Jane never mentioned him without a slight gasp at the center of "Northumberland." As though it was the name of a wilderness instead of the man's title. And yet, they always seemed devoted to each other. Catherine wondered what so consumed them.

"Catherine. Catherine! Come up." It was Jane, of course, trilling from the top of the stairs.

"Coming." Catherine opened the door to the smaller kitchen and almost fell over Temperance and Marjory. "Tell Sebastian to start the meat from that deer."

"I hear you, Madam," said Sebastian from the larger room.

Catherine met Jane at the top of the steps. "Master Davies and I have already said our greetings," she said. Benjamin approached in his courtier pose, ready to kiss hands. "I am afraid I collared him at the back and forced him to maid it for me in the garden."

The man bowed anyway. "Lady Overton," he said.

Jane smirked past him at Catherine. "Didn't I see you together at the masque?"

"Mm," said Benjamin. "You may have done. I like a dance with a beautiful lady as much as the next man."

Jane Dudley laughed. "A dance, is it? Be careful you don't slip on your tongue, sir. Now come. Lady Anne should not be standing at the door like a serving maid." She gathered her skirt in her fist and swept away.

Benjamin raised his eyebrows. "Have you spoken to Jane?"

Catherine said, "Not a word. But she has the eyes of a falcon and the faculties of a fox. Come."

Jane was laughing as they entered the game room. "She's keen to make you her waiting gentlewoman, Benjamin Davies. Perhaps you will hold the Lady Anne's train when she sits to wager."

"Whatever the lady requires," said Benjamin. He smiled at Jane but his eyes were sullen.

Anne of Cleves settled herself into her cushioned chair at the table, Harst at her side, and she stared up at Benjamin. "You were the man of greens."

"You have spied me out," said Benjamin, repeating his bow. "And now I am a man of mere dirt and have come to serve you."

Lady Anne said, "I require company."

"You see me before you," said Benjamin.

"Cards," said Lady Anne. She lifted one haunch and dusted her own backside. "They will amuse us."

"I will sit the fourth," said Benjamin, "if you will partner one of the ladies, Harst."

"I will have you," said Lady Anne. She pointed to the spot across from her. "Harst, you have Jane."

"What of Catherine?" asked Benjamin.

Anne turned. "Catherine no likes cards. Do I say right?"

"Forgive me," said Catherine. "I have no head for it."

"You have no head for no games." Lady Anne tapped her temple. "All serious. Like a lady scholar."

"It is my weakness, Lady Anne."

"But we eat the better for it, and you are your own woman." Anne of Cleves stopped and looked over the small group. "Our Catherine has her works laid out for her and will take no time for the leisure. The leisure is the way of the English, and yet she labour like the horse in the field. I cannot do without her."

"Yes, Lady Anne," said Catherine. She waited until the cards were being shuffled and headed back downstairs. She was alone in her small book room, looking over her own expense lists, when Benjamin returned.

"Still in the dungeon?" Benjamin leaned on the doorframe. "When will you begin to value yourself more highly and live upstairs?"

"I value myself at my worth. This is all my realm," said Catherine. They removed to the less private kitchen, where she shooed the two maids from the big oak table and dismissed Sebastian while Benjamin sat. She fetched a bottle and two cups, poured, and sat across from the man. "I haven't asked after Diana. How fares she?"

"Happy as any daughter. She has my purse strings and the running of the house. She is on the lookout for a rich young man but no one has passed her tests yet. Sometimes she says she will live an old maid, since my brother has sons enough. She misses your company."

"She needs higher companions."

"She has no taste for court life. She does not relish a hermit's life, either, though."

Catherine glanced over her shoulder then leaned across the table. "Did Lady Anne say anything about the king?"

Benjamin leaned forward in turn. "No. Not a word." His fingers touched Catherine's. "All her talk is of that accounts man."

Her skin sparked a little, and she let their hands lie together. "My books will show nothing to alarm him." Catherine let herself take gentle hold of Benjamin's middle finger. She stroked the nail, then sat back. "We mustn't."

"Why?" He did not reach for her. "We have managed it before. And there can be no more peril than we are already in."

"Jane suspects us. There can be no breath of scandal to blow about this house. Not now."

"No. Nor will I bring it on you." He drew a paper from his pocket. "But I have brought you this and I want you to study it."

Catherine read. It was a list of names, with cities and second names beside them. None of them English. "What is this?"

"Hospitable destinations. People on the Continent who would shelter you should things go badly in the next few weeks with this king and his moods. Their places of residence and English ambassadors who will direct you to them. I would find you."

"What are you telling me?"

"Nothing new. This is for you to keep in case we need to go from England in separate ships. The king will cast his eyes about for a new wife. He must. If it is this Anne of Cleves, I will eat my big toe. But if he cannot mend his heart, and the weather should turn stormy, you can choose your path from among these and I will discover which way you have gone."

"This is not safe, Benjamin. I fear it is not wise."

"This is only if matters come to such a head that you must go quickly. If need be. That's all. Put it away and have it if you need it."

"Travel alone? A woman with a child alone?"

"You will have Ann Smith. I only say if worse comes to worst."

Catherine folded the paper and put it into her pocket, next to the letter from her son. "Now I have something more to show you." She ran to her still room to fetch the velvet pouch from an empty herb jar and laid it between them. "I found it among my things while you were gone. What do you make of it?"

Benjamin shook his head. "What is it, an old relic? You must dispose of it." He felt of the fabric, then pulled the drawstrings open. He whistled, low, as though he were calling a falcon, and laid it down again. "Why have you not turned it over to your Lady?"

"I haven't found the opportunity. And with that man about the place—I was afraid."

"Get rid of it. Give it up. Say you found it today."

"The same advice that Ann has given me. Speak of the devil—

Ann Smith stuck her head in from the hall. "I thought I heard whispering. Hello to you, Benjamin Davies. Are you finished upstairs?"

"I have lost a hand at cards most nobly."

"And you are alone?"

"He is in the stable, Ann, looking after the horses."

"I simply asked a question of you," said Ann. But she was gone.

"Come," said Catherine. "I want you beside me when I do it." They stood and for a moment they were face to face. He stepped forward, and Catherine let herself walk into his arms. She turned up her face and let him kiss her, his hands on her back, then her breasts, then between her legs. It felt natural and fine, unlike any sin she had committed.

"God's blood, Catherine. Let's run up to your chamber first. They won't miss me."

"No." She pushed him off. "Enough. Not in broad day."

"We've done it under the sun often enough."

Her ears thudded with wild blood, and she held her breath until her heart calmed itself. "Come with me." She spun and trotted up the steps, Benjamin close behind her.

They stopped in the front hall and listened. No one was about. His body was against her back, and she could feel him, even through the thick skirt. "Back away now." But she was biting a smile from her lips.

Jane Dudley came through with Lady Anne. "Where is the food?" she said.

"Oh, I have clean forgot it," said Benjamin. "And my man has deserted me."

"We cannot play the cards on empty stomachs," said Lady Anne.

Benjamin said, "Lady Catherine has something to give you."

"Yes, I have found something." Catherine laid the velvet pouch in Lady Anne's hand. "I discovered this among my private goods. I have not seen it before and was troubled that someone might have dropped it without knowing."

Lady Anne spilled the money into her palm. She lifted one of the coins into the light. Then she raised the pouch itself, weighing it. "It is a large thing to be lost."

"The more reason to find its owner," said Catherine. "I am sure whoever has dropped this is frantic."

Jane Dudley took a few of the coins. "It's very kind of you, Catherine. I am sure the Lady Anne will seek out the owner." She returned them to the pile. "And I will be sure that Martin Martins includes these in his reports. Meanwhile, we will use them in jest for our games. Madam, will we play again?"

Anne smiled. "Yes. Will you play now, Catherine?"

Catherine curtsied. "Forgive me, Lady Anne. But no."

"Ach," said Anne. "It will be just Jane and me." She waved one hand in the air. "You are forgiven. Benjamin, you will be Catherine's accompaniment?"

"If you will give me leave," said Benjamin, bowing. "I think I have shown myself a poor partner to you."

"Yes, yes. Harst is bad player too. Go on and make the love between you," said Anne. Jane cut a quick look over her shoulder as they turned to go.

"You must make a thorough search of your things on a regular schedule," said Benjamin when the others were out of hearing. "And put that paper where no one can find it. I cannot say whether the country will turn right or left now. But move it will." He checked the stairs for onlookers and, turning, took her by the shoulders. "Catherine, do you hear me?"

She smelt the fresh ale and bread on his breath. It was like the outdoor air. "I hear you," she said. She touched his face with the fingers of her left hand.

"I will ride to Dover and trade your shearing. It might be slow travel. The ways are all muck and winterish. But I will return, and then we will go together, let anyone say what they will. Until then, be like the watchman in the tower, looking out for the enemy."

"And if no enemy appears, I must be silent. My mouth cannot endure it."

"Then let me give you mine." He put his lips on hers.

"I've told you. No whiff of scandal here." But a muscle in his temple squirmed, and she pulled him to her. Her body warmed against his, even through the thick wool.

"Your own lady has given permission for us to 'make the love.'"

Catherine grinned, despite herself. Such a relief, to feel happy, even for a moment. "Indeed she has. Upstairs," she whispered.

He turned and took the stairs two at a time. Catherine closed her eyes and counted until she could no longer hear his boot soles. She counted another ten, said a prayer for her soul, then took her quiet way up to her room.

Chapter Twelve

The next morning, Benjamin was gone and Catherine found herself sitting at the long table, alone with the king's man, who stood at her right. "There are funds missing," said Martin David Martins. His forefinger tapped an open accounting book, and the sun gilded the bloody, chewed rim of his nail. "And the jewels have not been found. I hear you have had a suitor in the house."

The man ought to wear gloves, thought Catherine. It might stop his bad habit. Or at least conceal its effects. "I am a widow. And what have I to do with the household monies?" She leaned backward to stay clear of the codpiece. It had been embroidered with small gems and two gold tassels that bounced as Martins swayed on his little feet. He did not reply, and she said, "I have control of the kitchen expenses, and you may see into the comings and goings of all the meat and bread that you please." She was still lost in memory of the afternoon before, the man's body over hers in daylight, a sin by any reckoning, and the sweetness of his scent. The musk caught in his long hair. The hardness of him, opening her body and filling her with warmth. She had shown him the dark new baby-line that ran from her mound to her navel, and he had traced it with his tongue. Her belly muscles twisted a little at the thought, and she felt a murmur pass her lips before she could clamp her mouth shut. He would return before the strawberries were ripe. She said, "I have business in the North. I will be leaving soon."

"You have business here and you must stay." Martins raised the edge of the book and let it fall closed with a thump. A puff of dust made Catherine sneeze. A napkin appeared before her eyes. "Let me offer you my assistance. Now that you are without your man."

"I have been without a man for these three years." Catherine pinched her nose. "I can take care of my own face. I have tasks and you impede me."

Martins strolled to the window and crossed his arms. The sun glared down from its high seat and gave him a ghostly cast. He seemed a man of wax, softening in the warmth. "You might have a more prominent position here at Richmond. Or somewhere closer to the king's service." He turned. "You have youth yet. A smooth skin. A man might call you beautiful."

"I am overcome with joy. Let me run and buy myself a glass." Catherine rose and moved toward the door.

"I do not mean for you to flee," he said. He moved toward her faster than she thought such bulk could travel, and halted, quivering in the flanks, in front of her. "I could do you favors, Lady."

A line of beard and mustache still embroidered his lips and chin, and the poor thin hairs clung to drops of sweat. Or water. Or spittle. The man's forehead was a shining dome, and Catherine felt her bile begin to boil up. "I need no favors, but I thank you for the kindness." She backed away a few steps to get some untainted air. "My business lies in the North, as I say."

Martins stroked his face and the beard flattened. It looked drawn on. "You have a devil in you. Hmph. They say the old sisters cannot reform themselves in the ways of the new world. Is that how you came to be a widow? Did the demon in you do away with your man? A man you ought never to have been allowed?"

A cold fear bit through Catherine's chest. Her hand stopped on the door latch. "My husband died in a contest of honor. He killed the man who spoke slanders of me."

"It's said that he died after a long illness. And you in the house there with him. You know that some say the king was bewitched when the Lady Anne came to his bed."

"I have nothing to say about the king's bed. And you should stop your ears against such talk."

"And your husband's sister, spirited away. So they say."

"If any spirit took my sister-in-law, it was the one under her own heart. It took her directly into the queen's own chambers, and then out again. Even now she treads the earth as other women do."

Martins nipped the edge of his thumb and dragged off a sliver of skin. He chewed thoughtfully, then spat. The thumb brightened with a bubble of blood and he tongued it. "Margaret Overton, is that right?"

The fear squirreled down Catherine's sides now and she crossed her arms to keep from scratching him. "Yes. As you seem to know right well."

Shrugging, the man returned to the accounting book and riffled the pages. "She is said to be in the North. Is this the business you speak of? Such a wild place." He looked up, squinting. "Have you had word of her?"

"You're telling tales. You've heard nothing of Margaret Overton."

He pushed his lips together. "She was in the disgraced queen's service. That is all I need to know. You have a son, do you not?"

"Robert Overton. He is in the prince's household, and he will have the house in the North when he comes of age."

"I see. Very well placed. So. You and the Lady Anne of Cleves have much in common. A history of witchcraft. Houses to call your own. Good placements. Much in common, a man might say."

Catherine gripped the latch again and reined her voice to a steady pace. "We each have two feet and two eyes and hair upon our heads as well."

Martins slid closer, his wide hips and legs driving the top of him forward. It was like watching a chess piece being moved by an invisible hand. But now he was upon her, the close-set eyes driven almost together by the intensity of his stare. "Such a head of hair, too. A man would like to see it uncovered." He reached for her hood.

Catherine flinched, grabbing at the headpiece. "Do not touch me. It is not seemly."

"I will have you uncovered, and who is to stop me?" He yanked the hood sideways, and Catherine's hair came down. "You have had a man on you already. It will not harm you to be touched."

Catherine still wore the coif underneath, and she clapped her hand over it, but the dark curls fell down her back. "Is this enough? Will you have me stripped for your entertainment?"

Martins held the hood at arm's length with one hand and fingered the ends of Catherine's hair. She closed her eyes against him, but the darkness brought his stench more sharply to her mind. Cooked meat and old fish. He breathed like a man newly come from a joust. She tried to imagine Benjamin, but the image would not hold. She clamped the inside of her cheek with her teeth, trying not to retch.

"I have not hurt you, have I?"

Catherine felt the hood being thrust into her hand, and she opened her eyes. Martins said, "I can be your friend, Lady Catherine. You want a friend. A true friend. You will stay here, safe as a nestling under its mother."

"Yes," said Catherine. Her teeth threatened to chatter. "You have been the soul of courtesy to me."

He smiled at this. "Does someone in the Lady Anne's circle keep a few coins aside for herself? Is there someone who has expenses that can't be recorded? She would confide in you, wouldn't she? Any lady could trust you, a woman so much like herself. One who maintains a . . . a humble position in the palace. Has someone promised you something? You needn't fear for yourself." He twisted a curl of her hair in his fingers again. "The Lady Anne's good name is my only object, an assurance of the purity of her companions and her books."

"My books are kept by my stewards in the North, and the Lady Anne's are not my province. I am no more like her well-bred ladies than is my pony to Pegasus. I serve her in the way that best suits me. I was not raised to fineness as the others were." Catherine forced the hood back over her hair. "I must see to the dinner for you and the others. And I must rearrange myself."

"You ladies, always arranging yourselves. Yes, I see how you manage it, with your pins and your powders. Some have had their arrangements done for them." He leaned past her and opened the door. "Or undone."

Catherine fled through the high hall and down the stairs to the kitchen, where Ann Smith was showing three young maids how to cut a half of venison. The four women turned from their task, raising their red hands into the air to keep the blood from their aprons. Ann held a large cleaver, and Catherine recoiled at the blade. "Sweet wounds of Jesus, put that thing out of my face." She splashed herself in the basin and, collapsing next to the hearth, asked, "Where is my daughter?"

"She's in the laundry with Agnes, practicing her embroidery," said Ann, "as you instructed her to do." She handed the instrument to the first maid and said, "Cut there. Through the center of the joint where the bones come together. The leg should come free in one piece." Ann rinsed her hands, then tossed the used water into the sluice that ran to the river. She squatted and put her hand on Catherine's shoulder. The maid wrestled with the corpse until the joint sprang open, sending thick blood spooling to the floor.

Catherine said, "I'm—I don't know what I am." She put her hands over her eyes and shouted, "Will you take that dead thing into another room?"

The maids froze, terrified, the table strewn with pieces of flesh. Ann said, "Take it out."

Sebastian moved to help, and Catherine said, "Leave it. It's nothing. I don't know what I say. I'm going to be sick." She ran to the slop bucket and vomited.

Ann opened the back door and shooed, and the girls, holding up their hands, scuttled out. "Rinse at the trough!" she called before turning back to Catherine. "Who has put you in this frame of mind?"

"It's that man. That money-man. Martin Martins. Martin David Martins. He as much as asked me to trade my body for my freedom. He means to lay something treasonous at the Lady Anne's charge. Or at someone else's. He means to find something to show the king. He means to raise himself. And I must sit like Penelope and wait for a man. I cannot do it."

"You're no Penelope. She knew her way around a needle," said Ann, but Catherine did not smile. "I have always thought her as boring as a caged partridge anyway. You need not wait at all, you know."

Catherine pulled the letter from her pocket. "Let me read something to you."

Ann fetched a towel and cleaned Catherine's face. "Isn't that the letter from Robbie?"

Catherine shook it out. "The very one."

"But I have heard it already."

"Not this part. I passed over it for Vere's sake. After he speaks of his father, he says, 'My lady mother, I hope not to see you fit another man to my father's place. The prince maintains that a widow keeps her soul intact by keeping her body faithful to one husband. Keep to the good, Mother, and submit yourself to my father's memory.'"

"No boy has writ this," said Ann. "He has been listening to someone read out of a book of morals. Something by one of those Protestant men. They want their wives to be children."

Catherine folded it again. "It's his hand. He doesn't even acknowledge that the gelding was a gift from Benjamin."

"Did you show this to him? Benjamin?"

"No. I as much as told him of its meaning."

"How can a little boy mean anything at all in speaking of his mother's marriage? This has been writ by one of the prince's men."

"I will not be dictated to, not by my own son. Does he threaten me?" She gnawed her lip. "My own Robbie?"

Ann said, "Boys parrot what they hear. That's all. Your worries should be coming to an end, Catherine. You may not be Penelope, but at least do not be Joan of Arc and run headlong into trouble. It may come to meet you if you seek it out."

Sebastian lifted the heavy spit, fat with impaled hens, and it clunked into place like a lock.

III

Chapter Thirteen

The weather grew warmer over the next week, and the air of the palace became fetid with bodies sweating under unwashed wool. Ann Smith crept into the upstairs rooms in the afternoons, while the ladies were occupied at cards, to gather the stale clouts and napkins and shifts from the corners and under the beds. Catherine came and went, ordering the maids and counting the barrels of wine, all the while listening for the sound of Benjamin's horse in the lane. Her front was still flat enough, but her hand crept over her skirt, smoothing the fabric again and again.

The king called the Lady Anne to him again, and though she was only absent the day, she returned to Richmond full of laughter, giving out ribbons to the younger girls and cheap rings to the ladies. She dropped her cloak in the front hall and did not look back to see if it had been taken up.

Ann Smith met Catherine on the back stairs the next morning. Ann was carrying a pile of stained hose, and Catherine followed her back down to the laundry and watched her friend dump the lot into hot water. "The whole place stinks of piss and dirty women." Holding her nose, Ann stirred the mess of cloth with a wooden paddle. "Lady Anne is in a distraction, and her women are left with nothing to do."

Catherine sat at the table. She'd left a bowl of apples here earlier, thinking she heard men in the back, and now she set to dividing them, the firm from the rotten, and laying the useable ones on her left. She said, "The maids copy the ladies. All they want to do is gossip and bicker and flirt with the boys who bring the wood. It will put them into trouble."

"Perhaps Lady Anne might set aside the gambling and dreaming and have a care for her household," said Ann. She lifted a handful of cloth, sniffed it, and slapped it into the water again.

"The ladies pretend not to understand what she says," said Catherine. "I pity her, by my troth, Ann. The king needs to tell her aye or nay. To keep her in this waiting is a tyrant's trick."

"If I were Lady Anne, I would get my marriage or I would get it out of my mind." Ann scrubbed the filthy clothes together and transferred them, dripping, to a steaming rinse pot.

Heavy-soled shoes came clopping down the stone stairs, and Catherine put her finger on her lips. Jane Dudley called from the front kitchen door and for a second time the apples were left where they lay.

"What is it?" Catherine asked, wiping her hands on her apron as she entered the kitchen. The hearth had burned down, and the pot upon it was cooling. The supper joint had been left to blacken on the underside, while the top was bloody and raw. "Where is Sebastian?" Catherine flipped the skewer and secured it, then opened the back door and scanned the grounds. Sebastian was nowhere in sight.

Jane Dudley watched Catherine from the doorway. "This is no task for a lady. Come upstairs. You'll stink of grease if you stay down here."

"And who will feed the people up there? Our spit-turner seems to have taken himself off." She wiped her brow with her forearm. "What is wrong with the young ones these days?"

Jane shrugged. "The same as always. They are not beaten and so they run wild."

"I will not beat them." Catherine removed the pot and held it to the window. It contained nothing but a dry scum at the bottom and she slammed it onto the grate over the small oven. "I will not beat anyone."

"Get one of the older maids to take a stick to the girls. That'll bring them around," said Jane.

"No, that's not the way." Catherine searched for the salt tub and found it behind the kindling. "Look at this." She picked wood slivers out until she could get enough of a pinch to season the meat. Then she heaved the skewer over again and sprinkled a second coating over the whole thing. She flung open the back door and almost ran into Sebastian, who pushed past her with a brief apology and took up the spit. Still Jane stood in the doorway, and Catherine finally asked, "What is it, Jane? Is someone in need of another hand at cards? Is there a codpiece that requires veneration?" She caught her lip in her teeth. "Forgive me." She stepped into the hallway with the other woman.

"The Lady Anne has need of a physician's touch. She asks for you."

Catherine stepped backward. "If she needs doctoring, you should call her physician. I manage her kitchen. That is all."

Jane twisted her mouth into a knot. "You are aware that the king has called Lady Anne to him twice?"

"Yes. And I am aware that she has come back again, alone." But now Catherine came forward. "What is it? Is there news?"

"Has she caught the fatness from him?" Ann Smith said. She glanced back into the kitchen. Sebastian had turned the meat once and was picking at the black crust. It dripped blood from the raw side. "If that's the sort of cooking that gets done, she'll thin down quickly enough."

"Ann Smith!" gasped Jane. But then she chuckled. Then she coughed and straightened her face. They all watched as Sebastian, grunting, locked the skewer into place, palmed the sweat from his neck, and sat for a drink. Jane said, "No, it's not her diet. There is a rumour abroad that the Lady Anne carries the king's child."

Catherine grabbed Jane's sleeve. "The Lady Anne has been in the king's bed? So he's taken her back as his wife in troth?" The arm stiffened, and Catherine let her go.

"As far as I can determine, she is still a maid. You must examine her. You must speak to her of women's things."

"Has she missed her flowers?"

"I cannot ascertain that. Sometimes she seems to say yes and other times no."

"And I am to be the one to explain to her how she might or might not have gotten a baby inside of her, is that it? Is that all?"

Again, the shrug. "Someone must do it."

"Good Christ above us. She is the same age that I am. Surely someone has shown her the bare elements of the procedure. Has she not seen a mare in season? One of her bitches?"

Another shrug.

Catherine rubbed her forehead. A finger of pain stabbed at her right eye, but she said, "Very well. Lead on." She caught of glimpse of Ann Smith, arms crossed, in the doorway to the laundry as she followed Jane Dudley from the kitchen and up the two staircases to the Beloved Sister's chambers.

Anne of Cleves perched upon the edge of her great bed. Still in her prim nightclothes though the sun gleamed from its zenith, she folded her hands and nodded as Catherine came into the room behind Jane Dudley. The two women curtsied and the King's Beloved Sister nodded. Jane withdrew backward, leaving Catherine alone with Anne of Cleves.

"My Lady, how do you?" asked Catherine. She was still balanced in a curtsey.

"You judge me. The belly," said Anne. She laid her hand on Catherine's shoulder and pulled at the edge of her sleeve.

Catherine rose. "My Lady. May I lay hands on you?" She put out her left hand, palm up, then pulled it back and offered the right instead. "I must touch you."

Lady Anne slid backward on her haunches until her feet stuck out like a child's. She seemed a complete innocent as she watched Catherine scrub her hands together to warm them.

"My Lady, I believe that you and I are almost of an age," said Catherine. She approached the other woman and laid her fingers on Lady Anne's throat. The life was pounding hard under the skin. The woman was frightened, and

Catherine put her palm softly against the insistent pulsing. "I will not hurt you. I will look at your eyes now?"

Lady Anne poked her head forward as a hungry pup might, and Catherine laid her thumbs along the lower eyelids. The skin was clear and firm, the eyes bright. She felt the forehead. It was cool, slick with a light skim of sweat. The breath smelt of ale and the musky, sick sweetness of new rot. She should have her teeth examined, Catherine thought.

"We are one age?" asked Anne of Cleves.

"Almost." Catherine lifted each of Anne's broad hands and flattened her fingers. The nails were smooth and pink, the knuckles softly dimpled. "Will you lie down, please?"

Lady Anne put her head on the pillow and swung her feet onto the bed. Catherine removed the blue silk slippers and squeezed the ankles. The woman had dropped some weight in the last months, but her legs were strong. Catherine could feel the seams between the muscles. The blood channels stood out behind her knees, and Catherine, laying her palms there, felt the warm thudding. The kneecaps were solid and prominent. Her skin was hairy.

"And Lady Mary? The king's daughter. She is our one age," said Anne.

Catherine's hands stopped. "You might say so. Within the year."

"She is good girl. She will visit us soon."

"She would be a great companion to you." Catherine moved to the Lady Anne's side. "Now I will put my hands upon your belly, if I may have your leave."

Lady Anne nodded. Her skin felt as any well-fed maiden's might, with a comfortable roll of velvety fat. She smelt faintly of soap. The only remarkable feature was the wide spread of dark curls, visible through the linen, that sprouted not far below her navel. She was hairy all the way from her ankles. "When did you have your flowers?"

"Flowers?"

"Your woman's bleeding. Your monthly?"

Anne scowled at the canopy. "The days of rain. Yes. During the rain."

It had rained half the days of the last month. "Tell me of your visit with the king."

"He send for me." Lady Anne hoisted herself onto her elbows and watched. "He have me to eat the meal with him. Like his wife."

"You sat at table with the king?"

"Yes."

This was good. "And were you abed after or before?"

Lady Anne lay back again. "I have the pain."

"Where is it?"

Anne placed her hands over Catherine's, adjusting Catherine's fingers to her lower belly. "This place. This is the place for the babies. I pray for it. I have been told that prayer will do much. That the king may bring me to life."

Catherine nodded, but her hope was twisting away like a specter at dawn. Lady Anne was perhaps fuller than she ought to be. "Let me touch you on the ankles again?" She felt her way down the thighs to the knees, then to the ankles. She had been right the first time. The legs were unswollen. She lifted each of the hands in turn again, this time kneading the wrists. She laid them down carefully on the yellow silk cover. "Was your visit with the king satisfactory?"

Anne of Cleves lay unmoving. Then she said, "The king sit beside me. We eat the white fish and drink the sweet wine."

"That is all?"

"He give me the gift of handkerchiefs. They have bluebells. Very pretty."

"And you left him then?"

"He kiss me." Anne sat up and touched her right cheek. "Here. And he whisper into my ear that I am his Beloved. His lips touch me here." She tapped her right ear.

"Have you had any sickness of the stomach? Any puking?"

"I drink the sweet wine. It sits in me very happy."

"May I look upon your belly? Under your shift?"

Lady Anne clutched the fabric, then let go. Catherine pulled it high enough to gaze upon the skin. Smooth and pink. No dark line. No swelling. She adjusted the shift further upward. The breasts were small and pink. Catherine covered the Beloved Sister again and stepped backward to allow Lady Anne to slide forward enough to put her feet upon the carpet. "Lady Anne, you do know how a child gets into a woman, do you not? The only woman I know of who got a child through her ear was our Lady Mary."

"The Lady Mary?"

"The mother of our Lord," said Catherine evenly. "You know that a woman must take a man inside of her to get a child. The man's part into her female part. Between her legs."

Anne's upper lip tightened and her left hand cupped her mound. "It is what that girl queen did. It is very dirty. They say treason. They cut her head off." Anne made a chopping motion against her palm with the side of her right hand. She did not look altogether displeased.

"You did not do this act with the king? This act of putting the male part into the female part?"

"I have been told that I must pray. He is the king. His breath is royal."

"But it is not divine." Catherine placed Lady Anne's hands onto her lap, then helped the feet back into the slippers. "I will fix you a tea, Lady, and it will tell us your condition."

Anne's eyelids lifted and she pointed to her chest. The blue. I will have the blue gown with the gold threads."

Jane Dudley flew into the room. "I will do the dressing if you will bring the tea." Lady Anne was absorbed with the unfolding of the skirt, and Jane added under her breath, "It had better settle this matter for good."

CHAPTER FOURTEEN

"Will you fetch me some lettuces?" asked Catherine, entering the kitchen. She expected to find Ann Smith.

Instead, two maids leapt at her words. One of them was the grubby Marjory. They had been sharing a pot of ale, and one of the cups slopped over onto the floor. "What does it look like, Madam?" asked the smaller of the girls while Marjory ran a dirty clout over the spill, smearing it into the grease.

"Do you not know lettuce in the garden?" Catherine snapped. "It is the most common of leaves. We eat it as salad." Catherine took the clout from Marjory, who'd remained on her knees. "Now go on outside."

The maid pushed herself to her feet, and a coin dropped from the pocket of her apron. She grabbed at it and shoved it away from sight, but Catherine held out her hand. "What is that?"

The girl's jaw muscles clenched, in and out, and she cast a rabbity look at her partner, who'd plopped back down. "'Tis nothin'. Found it in the gravel out back and didn't hurt no soul to pick it up. Temp'rence'll say it's so, won't you?"

Temperance was a riot of disorder, hair falling from under her coif, hose a lattice-work of holes, showing all the way up the leg she'd hoisted onto the bench. She gnawed diligently at the corner of her little fingernail. "Aye. Found it in them rocks. It's not nothin' to nobody. Nobody says it's gone missin' neither."

"And you didn't think to make your discovery known?" asked Catherine.

The two girls kept their eyes on each other. Temperance's mouth had scrunched into a resentful smirk. "Not given our wages to do no thinkin', Madam."

Catherine's palm itched to slap the grin off the dirty face. She sank her fingernails into her palms and counted ten. There was no baby. There was no baby in Lady Anne. To claim a false one would ruin all. Ann Smith came through from the laundry, with Veronica on her hip, and stopped, surveying the kitchen scene. The child squirmed to be set down, and, when Ann had freed her, ran to her mother with a tablet of letters.

"You will see, Mother, that I have finished making my name in full." The little girl held up the work, and Catherine relaxed her fists.

"Very handsome, Vere," she said. The letters were perfectly formed, and the child had decorated the capitals. "I'm pleased."

The two maids slid toward the door, and Catherine said, "Not just yet. Give me the coin." She suddenly couldn't recall their names. "You."

Ann Smith said, "Marjory. What have you got?" The girl jammed her hands into her pockets and Ann shook her by one arm. "Give it over." Ann reached into the pocket and retrieved the silver. "Is this what you require, Catherine?"

"It is." Catherine held out her palm and Ann dropped the coin into it.

"I found it," insisted Marjory.

"Aren't you the girl with the lucky stars shining upon you?" said Ann. "She found a couple of silk ribbons last week. And Temperance found a lace cap the day before that."

"They's stuffs layin' about like nobody wants 'em," said Marjory. She stuck out her lower lip. "It's everwhere a body looks. Just throwed down like trash," added Temperance.

Catherine said, "It is not your concern what is thrown down or what is left. You do your tasks in the kitchen and you leave things where you find them. Do you hear me? Now, go find me that lettuce. See if there are prunes in the cellar."

Marjory and Temperance made a show of studying Catherine's closed hand, then sidled out without another word or shadow of a curtsey.

"God's blood, the young ones these days are full of demons," said Catherine. "They will have us all in the Clink."

Ann fetched a crock of prunes from the pantry and set them on the table. "Here is your fruit. It's true, they are full of the devil. But it is also true that the household things are strewn about like floor coverings. It is almost as though someone means to tempt them to steer off course." She cut her eyes at Sebastian, who set the skewer in its notch, bowed, and walked out the back door.

Catherine set a pot of water over the fire. "She is careless. And she teaches the women around her to be the same. But a lady ought to be able to trust her women." Catherine stared out the back window at Sebastian, who was headed for the bushes. "That woman is no more with child than Sebastian is."

"The Lady Anne?"

"Yes. She has not even been in the king's bed. Someone has put it into her head that the king can breathe a baby into her. Can anyone be that innocent? At her age?"

Ann sat and let Veronica crawl onto her lap. "Is she honest?"

"What has she to gain by being otherwise? Do you think she means to trap the king with a pretended baby?"

Ann's eyebrows went up. "It might work long enough to get her back into his bed in truth. At least long enough to get her head chopped off."

"How vain would he have to be to believe that his presence has got her with child?"

Ann twirled a loose strand of Veronica's hair and said nothing.

"Yes," Catherine said. "Perhaps that's it. It's a fool's plan. And I haven't time to play the fool with her. And she is hairy all over. Legs, belly. I think our Harry would not bed a hairy woman."

Ann grinned. "You could cure her of that."

"I would have had done it with a carving knife if I had known. There's not enough arsenic in England, nor cat's dung neither, to burn it all off. It's not been taken off for months, if I am any judge. Not since before she was with the king."

"Is that why you give her lettuce?" Ann asked.

"She is constipated. There's only one thing she's carrying."

Ann snorted. The girls were returning, chattering and pulling wounded faces at one another. Sebastian returned as Temperance scuffed across the threshold as though she meant to break it free. She slapped the leaves down and curtseying with a simper, retreated back outdoors. Marjory went behind her without so much as a nod of her head.

Catherine sifted the offering. The lettuce was small, torn and dirty. "There is better than this right at the path's verge. Large leaves. Those two are so full of piss and vinegar they may never be worth anything."

Veronica hopped down and tugged on Catherine's skirt. "Mother, I am full of piss as well."

"Child!" said Catherine. "That is no way for a young girl to talk." Veronica plugged her mouth with her thumb and Catherine pulled it loose again. "Forgive me, Daughter. It was I who said it first."

Ann said, "Come, I'll take you, Vere."

Catherine stoked up the fire in the second kitchen and watched the pot refuse to boil until Marjory finally tiptoed back in and laid more lettuce, big, fresh leaves, on the table.

"Will that do for you, Madam?" Marjory's face was pale and puffy.

Catherine lifted the new stems, smelt them, and nodded. "You understand that you could find yourself swinging from a noose if you are taken as a thief, young as you are, don't you?"

The maid sniffled, and Catherine peeled a few of the leaves free. She held one up. "It looks almost like a green sail."

"Madam?"

Catherine went to her still room and returned with some rue. "Look at the difference in the shapes. Even dry, you can see how this one curves and folds upon itself, like the petals of a flower. It's a potent medicine, not one to be taken in quantity. It is as though the leaf warns us that the physic within it will bloom when ingested. In large amounts, it can kill. In small amounts, it heals. The lettuce lights itself from within. It wants to be consumed."

Marjory plucked the dry leaf from Catherine's hand and held it toward the window. "Does it speak to you, Madam?"

"In its manner," said Catherine. "The whole garden speaks with God's voice, if you listen. It is the breath of God that pushes forth both leaf and flower." The kitchen maid put her

tongue against the rue, and Catherine laid her hand on the thin shoulder. "No. It contains poison. I do not jest."

The girl threw the leaf on the table, and Catherine set it far aside. She ripped the lettuces in half, then in half again, put them into a bowl, and ladled hot water over their tops. "That will be enough." Catherine tied the rue into bundles, and held the bunch upside down. "When they are fresh, you hang them. Like so." She took them away from the table and by the time she returned, the lettuce drink was ready. "Stir a spoonful of honey in, will you?"

Marjory did as she was bidden, clacking the spoon against the edge to knock off the stray drips just as Jane Dudley came downstairs. "Have you the physic for Lady Anne?" she asked.

"Just here," said Catherine, pouring a cup of the tea. She spooned out some prunes and laid them on a plate with a chunk of bread.

Jane sniffed and wrinkled her nose. "Would this cure me?"

"No. I'll fix something suited to you." Catherine waited until Jane's footsteps reached the top of the steps. "Where is Temperance?"

"Out in the yard." Marjory dusted the floor with her toe.

"You must instruct her that picking up things will put her into water as hot as that tea," said Catherine. "And the taste will be just as bitter as the rue."

"What will you do with my coin?"

"It is not yours. Learn that. Learn it now. I will return it to the Lady Anne or her steward. I will tell her that it was lost and now is found. I will not say your name nor Temperance's. But you must take your lesson from this. You must."

Marjory touched her throat. "I am too young to be hanged, Madam."

"You are older than our late queen was by more than a year. And her youth did not keep her head from rolling into the straw when the axe fell."

CHAPTER FIFTEEN

Just after the midday meal the next day, Lady Anne's wailing began. The waves of agony reached all the way down to the still room, and Ann Smith, who was sewing while Catherine fanned some old herbs, smelling for mildew, put her hands over her ears. "Is she crying because she is not with child?"

"She is probably in pain with her purging," said Catherine. "And she has another letter from her brother." She rehung the stems and began mashing wort for an infusion. Veronica hopped onto her lap. "Jane says he insists that the king marry her again to save the Cleves honour. Why will he not decide? This waiting will be the death of me."

"Yes, what an honour she would have if he takes her." Ann stuffed the pillow she was making with dried lavender blossoms and began to stitch the last corner closed.

"A weighty gift to be sure." Catherine inhaled. "That scent is heaven. You sew like the angels."

Ann handed Veronica a single heavy-headed stem. "That's for you. Don't shake it or the beauty will shatter off."

Veronica held the lavender to her nose. "This pillow is for Mistress Dudley? So that she will not scream and shake so? Is that right, Mother?"

"Shh." Catherine put a finger on her daughter's mouth. "Lady Dudley has her spells. But a small girl does not see such things, nor does she speak of them. A small girl looks at her toes and says nothing, as though the greatest truth were written in the cracks between the pavers."

"It is tiresome to be a small girl." Veronica laid her head against her mother's breast and waved the dead flower back and forth. "When will I be old enough to see her spells?"

"Oh, Vere, it's difficult to know. Our eyes are not our own. You may note well enough but your eyes must not be seen to understand. It's hard to explain."

"Jane has high aims for her children," said Ann. She bit off the thread and squeezed the pillow. "This should please her, don't you think?"

"If anything can," said Catherine. She set Veronica onto the floor and scraped the wort into a cup of wine. "I suppose she has so many that she can sacrifice a few to her aspirations. Children, I mean. I hear that the boys are raised to overreach themselves. Even if I had as many sons as she has, I would prefer them not to stretch their necks so far out." She looked into the cup. Ann said nothing.

"When the young roosters stretch out their necks, Auntie Ann or Agnes chops their heads clean off with a hatchet," said Veronica. She slapped the board with the side of her hand. "Like that."

Catherine clapped her hand over her daughter's. "That's right, Vere. Just like that. Remember it and keep your head tucked in. Now you two stay here in the quiet while I deliver these."

Holding the pillow under one arm, Catherine carried the treated wine upstairs. The sobbing had ceased, and the palace throbbed with silence. Jane Dudley's door stood ajar, and Catherine found her in bed, one arm flung over her forehead. A chambermaid sat on a stool nearby, squinting at the embroidery in her lap.

"Jane?" Catherine said softly. "Are you awake?"

Jane gripped the bed curtain and tried to sit up. "I'm cold, Catherine, and yet I sweat so. My heart. It twists like a snake in my breast. Here. You feel."

Catherine set the cup on the table and slid the pillow behind Jane's head. "Lie back and let me feel it." She pushed the other woman down. "Put your head there and breathe. Not so fast, Jane. Your air will run off with your body like a wild mare. Quiet. Slow and steady."

Jane turned her damp, pale head so that her nose was mashed against the lavender-stuffed linen, and Catherine laid her hand on the woman's narrow breast. The heart went raggedly, to be sure, but less like a viper than the fluttering of a small bird trapped within the bones of Jane's thin chest. She smelt of stale urine and woman's blood, like a stagnant bog.

"Breathe more slowly. Slow. Hold your air if you must."

"What is to become of us if this brother will not cease?" Jane muttered. "He is insisting upon the marriage. What will we do if he gathers an army against us?"

"What is ailing you?" asked Catherine. She glanced over her shoulder at the maid. "Leave us. And latch the door behind you."

The girl tossed the needlework into a basket and sauntered out. The door swung closed slowly behind her. After a few seconds, it clunked shut.

Catherine said, "Would she not be happier if he married her? Would we all not breathe easier?"

Jane twisted her neck and her head flopped back and forth until Catherine lifted her to sitting. "He will hate her for it. She will steer us backward."

"Drink this." She put the wine to Lady Dudley's lips. "It is physic. It will calm you."

Jane gulped the draught, letting it run from the edge of her lip and drip from her chin. Catherine wiped her face with a handkerchief. When the cup was empty, Jane fell back again, and Catherine smoothed the soaked hair. "Tell me. What is it?"

"If she is queen again, this island will be at war."

Catherine started back. "Jane, you let your fancies ride you for this? Lady Anne has had pleasant visits with the king. That is all. You infect the very air with your worries."

"Why did he make a foreign marriage at all? It puts the whole world against us. My children."

"We all have our children to place in the world, Jane. Yours have greater advantage than most. They will go as far as you push them. But a mother can aim too high. It is not wise. Nor is it safe. Now sleep and let these fears fade. Let your mind take them for clouds and a summer wind will come to carry them into the sun. You're letting the devil into your intellect. Come, we live in England, not the duchy of Cleves. If he takes her again to wife, it is not for us to nay-say him." Catherine beat down the urgency in her voice.

Jane turned onto her side and seemed to sink toward dreaming. She shoved her nose into the pillow again. "She will turn him again to the old ways. And the Catholics will devour us as tidbits. My children."

Catherine stroked Lady Jane's hair until the woman was snoring, then she took up the cup and tiptoed out. The maid crouched across the hall. "Shall I go in, Madam?" she asked.

"She sleeps," said Catherine. "Will you wait here? The lady needs rest and silence, but if she wakes, I want someone close by to hear her."

The girl nodded, and Catherine went on her toes all the way back downstairs. The two kitchen maids were preparing the late meal, pulling cabbages apart while Sebastian turned a joint of pork over the hearth.

Ann Smith entered from the laundry, carrying an armload of kitchen towels, and surveyed the room. "How much have you finished?" she asked.

Marjory said, "Almost the basketful, Madam."

"See that you do them all." Ann's eyes met Catherine's. "How does Jane?"

"She is excited beyond her spirit's capacity. Such a condition makes a woman feel as though she is splitting her skin. She's afraid that the talk of marriage will put her children at a disadvantage. She talks of a return to the Church."

"All mothers worry about their children. Don't they?" said Ann.

Marjory laid down the blade and swiveled on the bench. "That fat shadow Master Martins has been back here and I heard Master Harst speaking to him."

"What of that?" asked Catherine. "He is here half the days of the week. Has he found something more?"

Marjory's eyebrows went up. "I heard Master Harst say that the ledger books should be returned to Lady Anne and asked what Master Martins thought of it. And Master

Martins said nothing to it. My father used to say that if a man's heart is clean, his thoughts are always ready to be known. Is that fat man honest, Madam?"

"Back to work, Marjory," said Catherine. "Let the ones who are paid to keep the books keep them. The thoughts of the king's man are his own. We have nothing here for him to find."

"Yes, Madam," said the girl, picking up her knife.

"Are you so sure that nothing will be found?" asked Ann.

"I am sure of nothing these days but what I stir with my own hands," said Catherine.

Sebastian drank a long draught of ale and turned the scorching spit.

CHAPTER SIXTEEN

The whispering had been going on in the writing room of the King's Beloved Sister since the latest letter's arrival. The women of the household served the noon meal, but the Lady Anne did not come. They put out cold meats for supper, but still the Lady Anne did not appear. Jane Dudley sat with Catherine and ate nothing. The other women filled their plates at the lower end of the table and stuffed themselves in silence. Ann Smith had elected to remain in the kitchen. Catherine spun her slice of leftover roast pig with a chunk of white bread and lifted a slice of the soft apple from the sauce to her mouth. She had ordered it to be flavored with sage and she savored it upon her tongue before she swallowed. But the chunk lodged in her throat and she had to swallow a mouthful of ale to get it down. One by one, the women drifted from the table, leaving Catherine and Jane Dudley alone.

"What do they speak of for so long?" asked Jane. Her fingers clung, white-knuckled, to a silver spoon. "They are just numbers. They reach a certain sum or they don't."

"The letter, maybe?" asked Catherine. "From Cleves?"

"Yes. That brother. What does he think? That the king has gone blind in the last two years? I have a note from my

John. He says there will be no remarriage for our Lady Anne. Let's pray for it."

Catherine choked on another bite and spat it onto her spoon. "And how does your husband?"

Jane Dudley smiled. "He complains of his stomach, but he has always carried his worries in his belly. I would send you to him if he would allow it. You could give him the cure."

Catherine shook her head. "I prefer not to serve men. I tend women's ailments."

"So you say. Why is that, Catherine? They say you once tended men. Your own husband. You might be at court if you sought a place."

"So might you. And yet here we are."

"My children are at court. And I am here because I pity the Lady Anne and the situation pleases me. I do not mean to stay until I die."

"Nor do I." Catherine made a demonstration of looking about the great dining hall. It was dark, and the timbers of the high ceiling seemed to hide faces in their grains. "I would that I had my own books and garden about me."

"The holy sister still lives, cloistered somewhere inside you?"

"No." The word came out fast. She sat silent for a moment. "The work of my hands brings me closer to God." She looked into Jane's eyes. "Without priest or priory. I will not be here forever, either, I tell you. I may go sooner than you think."

Jane threw her spoon into the air. Retrieved and spun it, then tossed it again. "And what do you hear from Yorkshire?"

Catherine considered the question. "My stewards and my father have improved the flocks by three dozen. We have more wool than our women can work through in the year."

"So your church is a drapery now." She pushed back the chair. "I see why the priory and priests are of so little concern to you. The buildings make a better profit as they are. What about Benjamin?"

"He helps. He knows the markets and gets the best prices."

"Benjamin is a good husbandman then?"

"The profits are the result of labour and diligence. I have good stewards, and my father finds that the business eases his old heart. I like the planning of it. Do you see a fault in that?"

"And you have made Benjamin Davies your knee-scraping servant?"

"Benjamin Davies has invested good monies in the Mount Grace wool. He was a friend to my husband and did much to try and bring him to a fair reckoning with his troubles. Would you have me withhold his earnings?"

Jane arched one eyebrow. "It is far from me to say what you might or might not withhold from him. That is surely the king's prerogative."

Catherine studied Jane's face but saw no flicker of irony there. Or condemnation. But she stood and said, "I have been a loyal subject of my ruler. There is work to be done below." She ran to the kitchen, calling "Ann, are you here?" Veronica sat at the table, head bent over a scrap of paper. A prayer book lay open before her and Catherine could see that she was toiling at the first words of Psalm Twenty-Three. "You do well, Vere," she said. "Have you eaten?"

The little girl laid her head back so that Catherine could pat her smooth face and said, "Marjory has given me a pie with pig and carrots. She promises that I might have a rhubarb tart if I finish my letters."

"Good girl."

Ann came in. "Is the conference still underway?"

"Jane says that he will not marry her. How long can this struggle go on, Ann? Does John Dudley know who the king might marry?"

"Mm. The royal fish might feed multitudes, but only if it were fresher."

A door slammed upstairs and they both stopped to listen. Shouting shattered the air, and Veronica pressed her new quill into the parchment. No one moved, and another door boomed overhead. Catherine placed her hand on her daughter's shoulder. A woman's footsteps hurried past the top of the stairs. The heavy accent of the Lady Anne's voice came to them, but not the words. The lighter tremor of Jane Dudley's voice followed hard upon. One of the younger maids peeped in and withdrew again without fully showing herself.

"Catherine!" Jane called.

Catherine lifted Veronica into Ann's arms and shooed them toward the laundry. She swept the girl's writing onto a high shelf and turned her attention to the hearth. Sebastian stepped back.

"Catherine!" Jane Dudley stepped into the kitchen. "Did you not hear me?"

"Forgive me. The fire was taking my attention." Catherine feinted a poke at the burning kindling. "It keeps wanting to go out."

"The Lady Anne needs nourishment. She is in a state." Jane was clutching her skirt in her hands, crushing the velvet.

"There is food on the table. Jane, will you take a drink?" Catherine went to the pantry, almost tripping over a little maid who scurried out of her way. She poured two cups, walked to her still room to stir a helping of the wort into one, and returned. "Here. You have had a trying morning."

Jane drank. Catherine sipped.

Jane stepped closer, almost whispering into Catherine's ear. "She will be humiliated if she begs for the king to take her again. She will be humiliated by her brother if she does not."

Now Catherine drank deep. "What will she do?"

"What indeed." Jane peered at the dregs of her cup. "What woman wants to brag of how disgusting she is to all of the men around her?" She waved at Sebastian. "Go outside, you." He went.

"Yes," said Catherine. "I heard how proud the queen sounded when she was on the scaffold for being a beauty. And what occurred this morning in the writing room? Has the king said no to her at last?"

"Martins claims that she is spending more than she says. He intimates that she is concealing her spending. It sounds not like news of a nuptial sort." She smiled.

"Henry wants her gone," Catherine concluded.

"Her absence might make the king's path easier."

"Ah," said Catherine. "Yes. The king's path has been so very difficult before now."

Jane's right eyelid flickered. She regarded Catherine carefully for a few seconds. "Yes."

Catherine could not hold her tongue. "And so very crowded."

"What do you mean?" Jane's eyes sparked.

"Nothing," said Catherine, turning back to the fire. "I meant nothing at all. A king's way must be peopled. That is all."

"I expect that Martins will receive a nice advantage from a discovery of thieving. A windfall for him, no doubt." Jane left without speaking further.

"Are you trying to get yourself arrested?" Ann said, coming into the room. Veronica was not with her. "You don't know who Jane talks to."

"I almost said 'crowded with bodies.' But I stopped my tongue in time." Catherine carved a piece of undercooked meat, slapped it onto a platter, and spooned the sauce from the pot over it. It had thickened to a gelatinous mass, and she stirred a spoonful of wine into the mess. "This will settle her enough to send her to her gaming table."

"Let's hope she is keeping track of her gambling debts," said Ann, "or she and all of her women will find themselves in the Tower."

"We're her women," said Catherine.

"I know," said Ann. She looked at the bloody meat. "I will fetch Sebastian."

Catherine found Lady Anne in the dining hall with Jane Dudley, and she set the plate down with a slight curtsey. The maids had replaced the dirty dishes with clean ones, and Catherine gave silent thanks. "Forgive me for tardiness. I hope this will nourish you."

"More pig?" asked Lady Anne.

"Yes. It is plentiful just now. Pig with apple."

"Mm. Good. What is the flavor?" The Lady Anne seemed to study the rafters as she chewed.

Catherine choked down a gag. "A large pinch of cinnamon."

Anne of Cleves swallowed, the lump of her effort as visible as a small animal writhing in her neck. "You will cook this dish for our guest."

"Guest? Who will be visiting us?"

"The Lady Mary."

"When? Today?" Catherine's gaze skidded toward Jane Dudley, whose mouth had fallen slightly open.

"Soon. You have made the acquaintance of her," said Anne. "She say you know her." Anne helped herself to another mouthful of meat. "She say she hope to see you. She know you of old, she say. Did you serve in the household of Lady Mary, Catherine?" Anne burped luxuriously and patted the small bulge of her stomach.

"I was in the household of the Lady Elizabeth once," said Catherine. "The Lady Mary was sometimes there."

"And you were removed, were you not?" asked Jane. Her eyes glittered. She looked a little wild. "You were sent home."

Catherine rose to her full height. "My husband was ill. I removed myself, to my own home. Do you blame me for that?"

"I judge no one," said Jane. "But we all know your past, Catherine, and Mary's stubborn nature is the block you might stumble upon." She turned to Lady Anne. "I beseech you, postpone this visit. Richmond Palace needs no more scrutiny than it presently suffers." She flicked a look at Catherine.

Lady Anne now rose and stared down at Jane. "Mary is of the close age with me." She lifted her hand. "Catherine is of age also. We will be three together. Jane, you may go if you are not happy with me."

"The king will hear of it," said Jane. "He must. Don't bring her here. Not now."

"What will the king hear of?" said Martin David Martins. He waddled into the room like a plucked duck and fastened his fleshy hand onto an entire loaf of bread. Ciaran Barts leaned against the doorframe, cleaning his spectacles with his handkerchief, and the squat Chandler settled beside him, narrow-eying the room. Out in the hall, Karl Harst huddled over the knot of his own hands.

Jane said, "He will hear only things good and proper of this house. Reformed things."

Martins ripped a bite from the heel and ruminated. Then he swallowed hard and said, "You must confide in me. It is upon my word that the king judges you. I am his eyes and ears."

Anne of Cleves threw down her napkin. "I hide nothing from the king." She yanked her skirt free of the table legs and trudged from the room, calling, "I will have the Lady Mary here. I will have anyone here that I want." Martins' gaze followed her as she went.

CHAPTER SEVENTEEN

March had come in cold and wet, but as the day for the visit approached, the breeze blew in a few green-smelling days, winter breaking apart for spring, despite the calendar's insistence upon Lent. Catherine was stuck within doors, preparing the kitchen and overseeing the deliveries of bread and wine. So much wine. Benjamin should have returned with her money by this time. The cellar was crowded, the barrels stacked almost to the tops of the walls. Like bloated coffins in a tomb, thought Catherine. He would come, and then she would go to Yorkshire.

On the day before the royal arrival, the men brought in a large catch of fish and the maids brought up all of the remaining carrots and parsnips from the root cellar. They were strewn across the big kitchen table, and Catherine sent them back for cabbages and onions and apples. Ann Smith disappeared into the laundry, pleading the need for a great washing. She took Veronica with her.

The time passed in a rush of food, killing a few old geese and hauling in more fish. Catherine set the maids to sorting a fresh delivery of new fruits, some for sauces and some for tarts. Catherine herself inspected the stocks of French wine, holding the bottles to the light and discarding any that looked cloudy. Veronica whined at being sent to the laundry to make her letters, but Ann Smith promised a special sweet made of the tender new strawberries and cinnamon, and the girl finally followed, sulking, to the table beside the washtubs. The kitchen was a shambles by the time Catherine fell into her bed at midnight.

The next morning was bright, and Catherine escaped the havoc by disappearing into the west garden. Trimming stems from the rosemary bushes, she worked alone, practicing what she might and might not say to Mary Tudor. Catherine was holding the needles of a woody branch, and she nipped the end of her right forefinger when she snipped. She cried out, and a berry of blood swelled out and fell upon the green herb. She put the cut to her mouth, inhaling the tangy scent of metal and leaf. "I will crack like a stick," Catherine muttered, ripping a branch loose. She shoved it into her pocket.

"Is that what you have waited for? To break at the last moment? It's not like you. Will you go back to hiding him in the bushes and the cupboards?"

Catherine whirled to find Ann Smith, a basket of eggs on her hip. Catherine's face went hot, and she put her uninjured palm on her cheek. "We never did. Not in the bushes."

"You've been out here for hours. What have you done to yourself?"

Catherine sucked the wound. "My finger bleeds, that's all. I am just confessing my sins to God. Don't listen to me."

"You'd better stand up and listen for yourself," said Ann. "There's horses coming down the north lane and you don't want them to find you talking to the bushes."

Just as she finished speaking, the Richmond Palace dogs came storming from the barns, snapping at the air, and all of the women, Catherine and Ann among them, fled back to the house, where they could watch from the safety of the kitchen windows. The riders blew in, raising small armies of dust and kicking at the dogs' snouts, sending them howling. The lead man swung himself to the ground and motioned for the others to go around to the front of the house, and when they had turned he led his mount into the stable, calling out a loud hallo. Catherine went in search of the kitchen maids. They were huddled together in the laundry, on their toes at the window, whispering and squealing. "Is she come?" asked Marjory when Catherine burst through the door. "Is the king's daughter here?"

"I expect she is," said Catherine, "or close behind them. She may come by water. Have the butcher dress the biggest of the catch for supper. Set the herbs that are on the table into the meat and keep one stem back to drop into a bottle of claret. Carrots. Did we get carrots with the apples? See if there are young peas in the glass house yet. Fry up the onions. And put together some custards. Ann has the eggs, and there are nutmegs on the top shelf in the pantry." She was pulling off her apron with one hand and fixing her hood with the other. She discovered a patch of dirt on her skirt and cursed. "Where has Ann gone? Where is Sebastian? Hand me that brush, Agnes." She beat at the soiled spot but it would not come out. Her finger split open with dark blood again. "Sweet mother of God, I look like a—"

"A what, Madam?" asked Agnes. She knelt in front of Catherine and, taking the brush, worked at the stain. "See? It comes right off if you knock it downward. Ann is just there, folding napkins for the table." She pointed. Ann had gotten to work right behind her.

Catherine felt the blood pounding her cheeks again. Her finger throbbed, hot and swollen. She put her left hand upon Agnes's head. "You're a good girl," she said.

Then came the call from upstairs.

Catherine wrapped her wound, put her hands together, took a breath, and went. She took the cold steps slowly, counting as she rose. It would be nothing, she told herself. Mary Tudor was simply another visitor. Another woman cast off by Henry. It would change nothing. It was not a crime. It should not be a crime. She set her hand on her belly. It felt like a pouch and she sucked in. She could look hollow for now. Benjamin would come soon. He would. "Never in a cupboard," she muttered to the stone walls.

Jane Dudley had already turned back to the visitors when Catherine rounded the corner into the room, and they walked, one behind the other like lady and maid, toward the two royals. Jane Dudley squatted a tight curtsey, bent her head, and retreated. Catherine was left with the king's Beloved Sister and the king's elder daughter.

"Lady Mary," she said, dropping to her knee.

"Catherine Overton," said Mary. "Stand up and let me look upon you."

Mary Tudor was narrow-boned as a young bird, and her gaze had grown flinty. Catherine stood and said, "My Lady, I am glad to see you well. My thoughts have been ever with you."

"As you yourself have not been. Do you recall our conversations at Hatfield House?"

"I do. Those days are dear to my heart."

"You might be lady of your own properties. And yet you stay here, doing your battles with a dirty kitchen. Is this your choice? What has happened to your hand?"

Catherine glanced at Lady Anne, who pondered the wall, arms crossed on her belly. Catherine considered a moment. "It was the king's wish for me to serve his Beloved Sister. The Lady Anne has an excellent kitchen, and I find a great joy in teaching the younger girls." She lifted her right hand. The linen was soaked on one side. "I injured myself in the garden just now."

"And you find Catherine a satisfactory companion?" Mary asked Lady Anne.

"She is good cook and good manager," said Anne of Cleves, patting her stomach. "She keep us all in good flesh, even in the Lenten time." She put her arms on Catherine's and Mary's shoulders. "And so we three, we will all be sisters, will we not?" Her eyes had found Mary's and the hoods of her eyes lifted.

"Sisters?" asked Mary. Her eyes softened. "Yes. We might be. How might we show our love to one another?"

Anne let her head rock from side to side. "We will play the cards together." She pulled Catherine closer. "You will let the below girls do the cooking for now."

"But I—" Catherine began.

"You will play," said Mary Tudor. "We must rein Lady Dudley to play the fourth."

Catherine nodded. Anne of Cleves waved her hand. "You. You leave us." The other ladies and maids curtsied and ran off.

Lady Anne led Mary Tudor into her gaming room, and Catherine stepped to the stairs that led down to the kitchen and called for Agnes. "Bring food. Wine and cheeses and bread. Where Lady Anne plays at cards. Choose another of the girls to help you serve. Three cups." Agnes scuttled off, and Catherine hurried to follow Anne of Cleves and Mary Tudor.

The two women had settled at the small table, and Anne was already shuffling the deck. These were brightly painted with Greek gods and goddesses, Poseidon threatening the sky with a trident, grey-eyed Hera scowling from the heavens. Athena, armed against all comers.

Mary Tudor was twisting a ring on her thumb when Catherine entered, and she rose to pace the room. Catherine went to her knees until Mary snapped her fingers to raise her. "He must not have another," said the king's daughter. She strode back and forth, stopping finally at the window to jerk back the drape. But she then dropped it as though it had scorched her. "You must tell your brother to stop writing. My father should not marry again with anyone."

"He give me much," said Anne quietly. She had laid the cards down and began lifting them one by one, setting them face up in a second pile. "But this sisterhood shame me. My brother say this."

"Shame," said Mary. She went a circuit around the floor again. Twigs from her travels had gathered in the hem of her skirt, and Catherine itched to pull the nest free, but Mary kept walking. She was talking low, almost to herself. "I have had a lifetime of shame. And my mother. She died of it. You must stay as you are. You are safe. You live in comfort. What shame is in that? And your brother. He is in Cleves. Let him stay there, where he cannot lay his hand upon you. Brothers. They are born to torment their sisters."

"I am not queen," murmured Anne.

"Nor am I," said Mary. She halted and clutched her skirt in her fists. "Nor am I ever like to be if he has another son. As things are, I will also be the king's sister if that boy grows to manhood. He already struts like a monarch and makes his little speeches and I can hardly bear it." She dropped into a chair and put out her hand. "Catherine, I am glad to see you sit with us. You are with us, are you not? Three sisters, happy without men."

Catherine nodded. "I am with you, Lady." She sat.

Anne tossed out the cards listlessly. "Where is Jane?" she said, and Mary picked up hers without looking at them. Catherine was not dealt in, and she didn't ask for a hand. Better for the Beloved Sister and the outcast daughter to wager with each other.

"What will I do here?" asked Lady Anne. "My brother say I am locked away like a nun."

Catherine's finger wept blood through its windings, and she made a fist to contain it, but the wound complained, and she opened her grip to find a stigma upon her palm.

"Your brother is a tyrant and a villain," said Mary. "Brothers believe they may rule their sisters' fortunes as well as their hearts. You must not demand what your brother demands. Brothers may be defied. Even if they are—" She stopped there and squinted at a king of hearts before her. She laid it down, revealing Zeus wielding a thunderbolt.

Lady Anne's shoulders sagged and she fanned her cards. She picked one out and tucked it back in. "But I will not even ask for audience no more?"

"He will scorn you again. And that would be shame indeed." Mary skidded the king of the gods away and tapped the table with the edge of a pink Eros. "Ignore your brother. Brothers grow old. Sometimes, they die."

Someone knocked at the door, and the Lady Anne called, "Enter." It was Agnes, with a large platter. She set it on the sideboard. She opened her mouth, closed it again, curtsied, wobbled, fell, and caught herself with one hand on the floor.

"Rise up, girl, and see to your kitchen," said Mary, without looking away from her cards.

Agnes scrambled to her feet and backed to the door. She banged her knee as she gathered her skirts to squeeze through.

"Is that one of your new prodigies?" asked Mary.

Catherine said, "She's a good girl. Just green and afraid of great faces."

"Hmph," said Mary. "I wish this face would terrify as well as some others. It might do me some good then."

Catherine served the wine and brought the plate of cheese and bread for the card table. "I treated this for you, Lady Mary. It is healthful for your stomach."

"Catherine. Always thinking of my body's health." Mary Tudor drank. "It pleases me."

"I am gladdened to hear it."

"But what of my soul, Catherine? Would you help me to keep that healthful as well?" Mary spread the cards in her hand and plucked at one.

"I would serve anyone's soul to keep it healthy," said Catherine.

Mary still scrutinized her cards, and Lady Anne let her hands flop into her lap. "We three sisters of one almost year. It means that we must be like the dairy maids at their work."

Mary smiled with one corner of her mouth. "The maids tell each other their secrets." Someone again knocked at the door, and Mary called, "Enter." The tallest of her men came into the room. He bowed, and she said, "Welcome, Peter."

He straightened and said, "Will we go to the, ah, chapel?"

"Wherefore to the chapel?" asked Catherine.

"He mean here," said Anne. She pushed open a door in the paneling that Catherine had never noticed before.

They crowded into a small room, unwindowed and dark. A wooden altar reigned against the far wall, with an elaborate, small gilded Virgin in a niche above it. The surface of the figure winked and sparkled as the man lit a pair of tapers. Mary knelt, crossed herself, and slid onto one of the wooden chairs. Anne of Cleves followed her lead, keeping her head down as she sat. The horseman settled himself behind the altar, removing his jacket and replacing it with vestments from a chest against the wall. He opened a square door, high in the paneling, and removed a chalice and censor, a crucifix and a cloth-covered plate. He was praying, and Catherine dropped to her knees, as she had done all of her girlhood, and prepared herself to hear the Mass.

The priest's prayers were smooth and efficient, and the three women took the body of Christ with a speed that Catherine had never before witnessed. The priest bent to Lady Anne and said, "Remember to pray for your desires." When they had concluded, Lady Anne kissed the crucifix that had appeared in her hand, then laid it in a hollow under the seat. Mary returned hers to her pocket. Catherine had none and so waited for a signal that she should rise. The priest was putting on his woolen riding jacket and becoming Peter the groomsman again. He pushed the square door back into place and nodded at Mary. The king's daughter tilted her head toward the next room, and the priest led them back out. The playing cards lay where they had been left, the Fates on top, fingering their woolen threads and watching the women reassemble themselves.

The light pierced Catherine's eyes, and she placed her forearm over her face until she could adjust to the human world again. The priest was bowing to his mistress and backing away. He twisted his hat onto his head, and withdrew from the room.

Mary and Anne sat at the table, as though they would resume the game they had never started, and Catherine fell, stunned, onto the seat between them. Her heart was storming around her chest, and she put her hand onto her breast to calm it.

"Are you ill, Catherine?" asked Mary.

"No. I am cast back in time and do not know my way toward the future. My breath does not know whether to come in or go out." She lifted one of the cards that had been rejected. It was the fool, in the guise of a Greek shepherd, and she threw it down again. "Who knows of this?"

"No one but we two. Now we three," said Mary.

"Does your father not suspect?"

"My father is the head of the church. The leader of our faith. Should he not know everything? Should he not have the power to see into the recesses of men's souls? Does he not have a halo under his crown?" Mary chuckled, a black sound.

"What of women's souls?" asked Catherine.

"Those he may not see so clearly," said Mary, "as hard as he might look." She looked at Lady Anne. "This is not the first time we have celebrated the true religion." Mary lifted her cup to Anne, and Anne touched her own to it. "My father is misled by evil counsellors. He ages and his senses run away with his wits. But we will have God on this island. Will we not, Lady Anne?"

"Whatever you wish," said Lady Anne.

"And you will not sue to him for your return. You will not sue to him for anything. You do not want it," said Mary. She gestured toward the great stone hearth, then to the ceiling, painted with the heavens and their constellations. "You see what you have. This. And the freedom of your conscience and the safety of your head. You do not want to be queen, to put your neck out for the axe."

"I do not," said Anne. Her hand rose to her throat and stroked it. "But no children."

"You want no children. This king sweeps them away as he does his wives. What if you should win him back? And reward him with a daughter? A daughter you loved and taught and who was your dearest love? And that daughter was wrenched from your arms and banished from your presence?" Mary's eyes showed spots of light, though no rays of sun fell onto her face. "And if you had a son, that would be a grievous occurrence to me."

"No children. No children," said Lady Anne. "I will have the freedom."

"We will worship together."

"Yes."

"And we will make our contentment together until we can search out a better path."

"Yes."

"We will not speak to the king of marriage," concluded Mary.

Anne of Cleves gathered the cards and stacked them into a neat pile. Mary smiled, and, sitting back, closed her eyes. She reached for Catherine's hand, laced their fingers together, and held on as though she would never let her go. Catherine could feel, through her wound, the erratic beat of life in the other woman's palm, like the pulse of a flame.

CHAPTER EIGHTEEN

"Are you awake?" Catherine spoke into the silver light of the bedchamber. Ann Smith lay next to her, but she hadn't moved or said a word since Catherine slid in beside her. The bed curtains stood open, and the round moon had nudged the darkness aside as it filled the window, etching the lead squares onto the covers.

"I am now," said Ann, rolling onto her back. She sat up and traced the shadows with her fingers.

Catherine lay listening, and Ann cocked her head, then fell back onto her pillow. Veronica slept in the small room beside theirs with Agnes, and Catherine finally threw back the covers and padded across the room to lay her ear against the door. "They can't hear, can they?" she whispered.

Ann's white nightcap moved back and forth in the moonlight. She patted the bed, and Catherine rejoined her. They curled, face to face, like girls. "You smell like Mary's perfume," said Ann. "Essence of incense."

"She would scarcely let me go. Or Lady Anne, either. It's as though she has to ensure herself over and over that we're real. And that we're still unmarried."

"Hmmph," said Ann. She rolled to her back again. "She wants a court of her own."

"She does indeed," Catherine softly said. "And she hears the Mass."

"Who?"

"Mary Tudor. Here. In this house. Lady Anne with her. Jane is right."

Ann stared upward. "Do you want to tell me how you know this?"

Catherine watched the moon tilt until its belly nudged the window frame. "I was with them. There was no saying nay. We were playing at cards, then we were hearing the Mass."

"Where did the priest come from?"

"He's the tall manservant. The horseman. The one who rides forward of the other men. His name is Peter."

Catherine's heart was trembling at the memory. Ann's breath went ragged and shallow, and Catherine turned to comfort her, but Ann was laughing. She covered her mouth with the blanket and turned her head into the pillow, but finally was forced to rise and dig out a handkerchief to blow her nose and wipe her eyes. "Peter? Peter? Did she name him herself? Sweet Jesus. That woman has the guts of a warrior." She climbed back into bed, still chuckling.

"A queen, more likely," said Catherine. "She is the image of her mother, every inch."

Ann scrubbed her eyes with the edge of the sheet. "You may be sure of that, and right through to the heart, too. Folks say she's lunatic, but that woman could lead an army into battle. She's more politician than her father could ever hope to be. If she's crazed with anything, it's grief and anger, and she aims to make someone answer for it. I think she will hit her target, one day."

"But Ann, don't laugh. She could be arrested for it. Tried for it. If the king discovers it, he will wink at his daughter if she shows remorse, but he will cut the head from Lady Anne's shoulders. I should have listened to Jane. But think of it. If a marriage did go forward, the king might relent. He's old and tired. The entire country might—"

"You are sure no one saw you?"

"I was with Mary, Lady Anne, and the priest. That's all. Mary made Lady Anne vow not to marry, but if the king wants her back, I don't know which way the fight will turn."

"That's hard," said Ann. "A promise to the little one may mean nothing, but Mary will hold Lady Anne to her word. Henry doesn't want her. Accustom yourself to it."

Catherine nodded. "But the king is still the king. Why must women betray women? Do we not have enough enemies without turning on each other?"

"I have no answer to that. We all have our battles to fight." Ann patted her hand. "All of us."

Catherine considered this as the moon rolled her bulky body on, casting long shadows behind her. "The moon is our sister," she said.

"How is that?" Ann said through a yawn.

"She is silent and alone and must remain so. She is a sister. Her eye is soft, because she is weary, and she seeks to conceal our imperfections rather than shine an angry light full upon them."

"Mm-hm. A sister."

"Ann, do you mark me?"

"Mm."

"If we women were more like the moon, we would gleam gently as she does, and not glare like the king. We would illumine one another. It is a priest who has filled Lady Anne's head with notions of a baby. This one or another of his kind. I am sure of it. And I once thought the priests held our salvation in their hands. They are as wayward as other men. And as deceitful."

Ann said nothing, but her even breath said she was asleep. Catherine turned onto her side, away from the retreating light.

The next Catherine knew, the room was bright and Veronica was crawling over her legs. She bounced there until Catherine opened her eyes, and then she said, "Auntie Ann. You wake up too." She had the poppet under one arm and she danced it across her mother's knees. Agnes came in behind the child, scratching her scalp. "How long does the Lady Mary bide here?" the maid asked.

"I haven't heard," said Catherine. She stretched and wriggled her legs to dislodge her daughter. "What do you call her? Your doll?"

"Just don't call her Ann or Catherine," said Ann, pulling off the covers. "We have enough of us already."

Veronica gazed into doll's embroidered face. "I have christened her Cleopatra."

Catherine let her laughter out. "She has been listening to you, Ann Smith." She lifted her daughter to the floor. "Down to the kitchen," she said. "We are on your heels."

Agnes and Veronica ran, almost bumping into the chambermaid bringing fresh water. Catherine splashed her face in the basin and pulled on a fresh shift. She twisted her hair up and jammed a clean coif over it. She had her skirt and bodice on before Ann had finished combing her own hair.

"Are you going on a journey that you dress with such dispatch?" Ann asked. "You can't go while Mary is under the roof."

"Don't taunt me. I am going to escape out to the garden before I'm called," Catherine said. "Could you take any longer to get yourself ready?"

"We don't all have the fire under us that you have," Ann said, but she set down the comb. "Give me three minutes." She threw on her clothes and was still adjusting her hood as they ran down the back stairs.

They stopped long enough to break their fast with a loaf, some cold meat, and a jug of small ale. The younger maids had their arms full of kindling baskets, and they paused for orders, but Catherine stuffed a chunk of bread into her mouth, pointed at the fading fire, and rushed out the back door.

The morning lay cold and damp before them, the sun chaste, veiled by shreds of cloud. The garden sparkled with fine nets of dew-covered web, strung between the young leaves. One spider had spun a dome among some old nettles, and the early light revealed thousands of tiny chambers. At the center, the dark queen hung, unmoving. Biding her time. It was too damp to work among the plants, but Catherine went anyway, the soft earth giving under her feet. "Look here," she said. "This spinner has built herself a palace."

"It is kept neater than some palaces I know. But this queen looks for someone to bite." Ann stayed upon the verge. "You will be mud to your knees. My shoes are already soaked through."

"Mud is clean," said Catherine, bending to extract a small thistle from among the new radishes. "Mud we have been and mud we will be again. There's no harm in it."

"Mud dirties the good and the wicked alike?" asked Ann, strolling along beside her.

Catherine tucked the straw further under the young berry vines, then turned over the baby leaves to check for vermin. "You do nothing but laugh at me." She pulled up her skirt. Her feet were slabs of fresh muck.

"I laugh with you, not at you."

"I am born to play comedy," said Catherine. She'd reached the far end of the plantings, and she laid a handful of weeds on the bare edge of the rows, then rested on a bench, sliding her feet along the long grass. A pair of gulls scolded each other and clopped their beaks on the air. The first stable hid the women from the palace. "How long should we wait?"

"Not much longer." Ann plumped down heavily beside her. "You are not ridiculous and you are no player. But your heart shows in your eyes for everyone to see." She regarded Catherine. "They are already green, though, so you can be jealous at your leisure and no one will know."

"What would make me jealous? I am more than I need to be. Would that he would come with the money. He said he would come." Catherine felt her cheeks smolder, and she bent to pull off her shoes and scrape the sides clean on the grass. "Let's make a new accounting of all the kitchen goods today. Pots and pans, utensils, linens. That Martins will not accuse me of keeping sloppy books."

Ann turned her face up to the fresh sun and breathed deeply. "You are better off spending your time packing up."

"It will not hurt us to be shown good huswives. Most of what is here we can leave, if we must. I will plead that we are preserving the reputation of the Lady Anne, getting the lists in order, and we will be in Lady Anne's good books."

"Are you sure that will do you good?" Ann gazed out toward the river. "Lady Anne has made her vow."

"So she has. It's Martins I'm thinking of." Catherine replaced her shoes. "It will busy us while Mary stays here. I must be busy."

"Very well, then, we had better begin." She stood and when Catherine was on her feet, she paused. "He should have been returned by now."

Catherine flushed a little. "I have heard it said that men are different, but husbands are all the same."

Ann said, "So that's your fear? That he will alter, like William?"

Catherine lifted a shoulder. "He's been gone a long time." Her ribs tightened under her skin. Her eyes were hot and she was afraid she would weep.

Ann put her arms around her. "Forgive me. My tongue flew before my thought. He will come. I know he will."

Catherine pulled away. "I hope so. He has all of the wool and some of the furniture. Is it not strange, that in the convent we claimed to own nothing and now I think of money so very often?"

"Money eases the way for many a woman," observed Ann.

Catherine looked up to gauge the passage of the sun. It was still early. "God must not recognize any of us in our conversions."

They were silent the rest of the way, and the house was too busy for the women to speak again. They worked at the accounts between mealtimes, and Mary called for Catherine in the evening, when the light was too low to write easily. Catherine went, leaving Ann Smith with the maids and the piles of dirty plates and goblets.

Mary Tudor was sitting alone in her chamber. No maid, no one to undress her. "Sit here at the mirror, Lady Mary," said Catherine, "while I unpin you." Catherine unfastened Mary's dress, then she took off the coif as well and sifted the dry hair with her fingers. "Let me wash this. A princess should have a head of silk. You have neglected your beauty."

Mary Tudor patted her own head. "Will I win a husband with fresher hair, do you think?"

"If you want one. Any man would be a fool to refuse you," said Catherine. But even in the sympathetic candlelight she saw that the jowls had already begun to puff and sag at Mary's jaw, and her hand traced her own smooth throat. "We are within a year of each other in age."

"And you have already worn out one husband. I expect you want another one."

Catherine stepped to the door and called for a chambermaid to bring a basin of warm water. "Thicken it with a pint of milk and put three sprigs of sage into it while it heats." She returned to help Mary out of her heavy silk sleeves. "I'm not married, Your Grace."

"Equivocation?" Mary's eyes were dark holes in the glass, and Catherine felt that the stars themselves might drop into them and disappear from the heavens. "They say that a certain gentleman is much in your company."

"I have my children to occupy me. My daughter is but little yet. My son is alight with opinions about my state."

"Children do not warm a woman's bed."

"Ann Smith sleeps with me when I am lonely." Catherine shook out the heavy, embroidered sleeves and laid them over a wooden stand to let them air. She hung the woolen dress on a high hook and pulled out the skirt for brushing. A couple of stems still hung on it. "You have traveled in the dust, Lady Mary. I will have this taken outdoors for cleaning."

"Everywhere I go feels dirty," said the king's daughter. She combed her hair with her fingers, and Catherine stepped up behind her.

"Here, let me do that." A brush lay upon the table, and Catherine parted Mary's hair and worked it smooth hank by hank. Snowy flakes floated from the strands, and Catherine put her nose to Mary's head. She smelt sour, like raw meat left too long in the sun. "How is your stomach lately?"

"Bitter."

Catherine nodded and kept brushing. A soft knock interrupted her, and she went to the door before it could be opened by the maid. "Thanks," she said, lifting the heavy bowl. The girl had a thick clout over her arm, and Catherine motioned for it to be thrown onto her own shoulder. "Now go."

When the girl had pulled the door closed, Catherine teetered to the small hearth and laid the bowl on the stones. "Will you have your hair washed?" she asked.

Mary Tudor came like a child and sat, her legs folded under her.

"No, Lady. Not on the floor. On this." Catherine dragged a cushioned chair backward to the fire and guided Mary Tudor into it. "Lay your head back, on this pillow." Mary obeyed, and Catherine wet a soft clout in the fragrant wash and rinsed it through the dry hair. Mary sighed, and Catherine squeezed the milk water through again and again, then worked the skin with her fingertips. "Let it rest now. Then we will flush it out."

Mary had closed her eyes, and Catherine tiptoed to the door, the basin balanced on her hip. The maid was crouched in the hallway, and Catherine whispered, "Bring clean water, heated." By the time the girl had returned, Mary was breathing through her mouth. Her skin was pocked and pasty, and her eyebrows showed bare patches, as though someone had pulled at them, hard. Narrow lines had begun to radiate from the lips. Catherine had remembered her as a stern woman, but a handsome one. A royal one, above the common sort of person. Now she was beginning to show a mortal's decay, the lines of the skull beneath the skin. If she were to get a husband, she would have to be quick about it.

Catherine sat on the pavers beside the sleeping Mary, watching the hearth flames contend with the air. She drove a stem she'd plucked from the royal daughter's skirt into the fire and, when the blossom end sparked, waved it like a banner until it burned itself out. She pitched the scorched stub among the logs and chose another. It had just bloomed with fire when the hesitant knock sounded again. Catherine tossed her little torch away and fetched the new basin from the girl at the door. She arranged the rinse water under the hanging hair and began gently to work the water through. Mary stirred, snorting softly as she came awake. She said, "And I will be young and beautiful again, will I?"

"You are still young," said Catherine, "and you will always be beautiful. You are the king's daughter. All the tales say that you must be the most lovely lady in the land."

"If I am to be so, then do not the stories say that I must hide my face to save the young men from themselves?"

Catherine got a polished wooden comb from the table and sat again to untangle Mary's wet hair as it dried. "I don't know that story. Tell me."

"Or is it that I must be veiled so that I can have a husband before my younger sister?" A drop of acid had fallen into the flow of words. "The younger sisters always destroy the elder ones, do they not? They will marry off that little brat before they find me a man."

"Who will have her?" asked Catherine, though a nub of pity clogged her throat. Elizabeth was red-haired and quick-witted, like her own Veronica. Strung tight, like a high-voiced lute. Daughters of shame. Catherine swallowed hard and kept combing.

Mary threw her head forward and plowed her hands through her hair. "It feels new," she said. She pressed it against her face. "Like a summer garden." She lifted it back and smiled. "You are still the lady physician, Catherine."

Catherine got to her feet behind Mary and lifted handfuls of hair toward the fire, letting them fall through her fingers as they dried. Mary sat quiet, letting her work. The hair was indeed softer. Finally, Catherine said, "I am glad for your joy. Will you sleep now?"

Catherine took the basin to the door and sent the maid in to fix the bed. She bade Mary goodnight and headed straight for the kitchen.

"Ann!"

"I'm here," came the familiar voice.

Veronica ran out of the laundry and wrapped herself around Catherine's leg, almost upsetting the water. "You monkey," said Catherine. "What game is this?"

"We have been in hiding, Mother, and no one has found us out but you." The child let go, danced a few steps, and withdrew the doll from her dress. "I am Cleopatra's rug. She conceals herself in my bodice."

Catherine laughed. "Who warrants such stealth, Daughter?" She stepped outside and emptied the basin under the nearest rosemary bushes.

Ann Smith closed the door as she came back in. "We're keeping out of the way of great ladies. They burn too brightly and we wish not to be charred in their wake."

"She speaks of wanting a husband, Ann." Catherine bent to look into her daughter's face. "Vere, the Lady Mary will wish to see you before she departs. She will ask after your brother and you must make ready a proper answer. You will not refuse to see the king's daughter, do you hear?"

"Not if she is the daughter of the king," said Veronica. The little girl put the edge of her finger against her neck. "The king will have my head chopped off if I do not do my duty."

Catherine gasped and she pulled her daughter close. "Who has been telling you such things?"

Veronica wriggled free. "The lady maids say that the king has the heads of little girls chopped off when they do not obey. Or if they laugh or if they smile at the little boys. I will obey, Mother, and I will do no smiling, not at any of the boys. Nor must you neither, Mother. That is what they say."

CHAPTER NINETEEN

Mary Tudor had decided by the next morning that she would progress to Hampton Court Palace and ordered that a barge be brought. Lady Anne stood at the bottom of the great stairs, flapping her hands in distress, when Catherine trotted up to oversee the laying of the morning meal. "But you are just arrived. We have not eaten the foods," Lady Anne was insisting to a trio of Mary's women. "We will have great party if you stay." The young women nodded obediently, but when Mary Tudor appeared from her bedchamber and ordered them to see to her clothes chests, they curtsied and fled up the steps, leaving Lady Anne to fly after their mistress to the dining gallery.

"Catherine, you tell her," said Lady Anne. "Make her stay. Her horses are here."

Catherine shook her head and slid into a seat low on the table. "With your leave, Lady Anne," she said, "I will trust the king's elder daughter to decide her own mind. The stable men can surely feed a few more horses."

"The Lady Mary knows what is best for her," said Jane Dudley, taking a seat at Lady Anne's left hand. "Her father has sent her a welcome, and she should tend to it in good time."

"And how do you this morning, Jane?" asked Catherine. Jane had been in her chamber since Mary's arrival, pleading the headache. "You have conquered the beast?"

Jane Dudley touched her temple, then pushed back her hood. "It besets me still."

Mary Tudor said, "Catherine will cure you, if you put your head in her hands. I feel myself to be a new woman." She trained a narrow look on the blanched face of Jane Dudley. "You could perhaps benefit from some renewal yourself. I hear that the weight of your husband's attentions wears you down."

"I will study upon it," said Jane. She snatched up a drink, but it was fuller than she realized, and yellow ale sloshed onto the table and ran onto her lap. She leapt to her feet and knocked over a salt dish with her hand. "God protect me," she gasped. The salt was instantly soaked by the ale and left no pinch to take up for tossing. Jane stared in horror at the evil mess before her, and no one spoke.

"Mother? May I break my fast with you?" It was Veronica, who came skipping into the room, swinging the poppet by one hand.

"What is that?" Jane Dudley screamed. "Is that an image? Who is that? Is that the king's sister?"

Veronica wailed. Jane Dudley threw a fingerful of the sodden grains over her shoulder and ran from the room. Anne of Cleves took the doll from Veronica's hand and said, "This do look not like me."

Ann Smith hurried in from the side door. "What has happened?" she asked, gathering Veronica into her arms. The child hid her head against Ann's shoulder. "What is the matter?"

Mary Tudor had laid her cheek on her hand, and Catherine retrieved the poppet. "It's a gift from Benjamin Davies. A Scottish woman in my town makes the dolls. It is a plaything for a child, nothing more."

"She thought it was my aunt. The Scottish queen," sighed Mary Tudor. She began to laugh, low in her throat. Then she stood. "That woman has a fire of ambition inside her, burning her alive. It's the way of our world now, is it not? For women to be afraid even of girls and their toys." She pushed the wet pile of salt with one finger. "They say that, when I was born, the people cheered in the streets. My mother told me that she wept, first for happiness, then for fear. But my father smiled upon me and the world seemed bright. Newly made. What think you of that? A handsome king, a beautiful queen. And their princess. And you had been born within that year." She put her hand over Lady Anne's. "And you," she said to Catherine. "It seemed a fairy tale, and I was to be the Queen of England. And then the sun turned its face and we were all in darkness. It is no wonder that we are ridden by fear of demons. We are all worn down."

Mary's maids came to the door and, flopping onto their faces, indicated that her chests were ready and being loaded to go. Veronica squirmed to be free, and when Ann Smith set her down, she squatted next to the row of maids.

Mary Tudor studied the girl, then she walked over and lifted Catherine's daughter by both hands to her feet. "You have raised her well," she said. "She is bold but she knows her position. And have you learnt your needlework, little Veronica?" She smiled. "Better than your mother has?"

Veronica's face twitched with alarm and she glanced at Catherine, then back at the king's daughter. "My Aunt Ann

Smith shows me how to do it. I have made this hem." She raised the corner of her dress and showed the plain shift beneath. It was stitched neatly across the bottom.

"I know your auntie of old. She has always been clever with her needle." Mary examined the work and smoothed the girl's clothing back into place. "Very good." She petted the girl's head. "This hair."

"There is ginger in the Overton line," Catherine put in quickly.

"In the Tudor, as well," Mary said.

Mary's groomsman, the changeable Peter, came through. "The barge is ready, Lady."

"Then I will say farewell."

Anne of Cleves rose. "Wait. You will wait this one minute." She bustled to her game room and reappeared, a box in her hands. "Mary. You will have this from me."

Mary took the gift and nodded. She handed it to her man, and the two women embraced. "Remember," said Mary.

"I remember," said Lady Anne. "Travel with God by your side, Lady Mary."

"And you." Mary took Catherine by the forearms and squeezed. Catherine tightened her stomach for the embrace, but it didn't come. "And you, Sister Catherine. Until I see you again."

Then she was gone. The tall groomsman led them out, like any servant. Veronica stood by the long dock, waving. The sun glared down and set her hair afire.

"Is she gone?" It was Jane Dudley, sweeping down the main stairs with one fist against her breastbone. "Quite gone?"

"Gone," said Lady Anne. Catherine called her daughter back inside and closed the door. The girl stood in the middle of the trio of women, looking up at one, then another. Lady Anne said, "Little Veronica, go fetch me some sweet."

"Yes, Madam," said Veronica. She curtsied and ran off, sliding around the corner to the back stairs on the soles of her slippers.

"She gives me worms in the belly," said Jane, "with those glowing eyes of hers. Like the fires of hell. They put me in mind of her dead mother, staring out of the grave."

"Her eyes are blue," said Catherine. But she had seen it herself, the dark light that always burned behind Mary's gaze.

Lady Anne said, "We women carry our mothers in us."

"Like ghosts," said Catherine. "You might expect her to show the complexion of melancholy. Sadness has been her meat and bread for too many years."

"We all suffer," sniffed Jane Dudley. "She has been treated right well since—. The king has taken her back into his grace as though she had never defied him. It shows great mercy in him."

"His mercy cannot be put into words," said Catherine. "I must see to my daughter." She started to go, but Jane caught her arm.

"I have the pain in my stomach again. Can you fix me a draught to it?"

The face of Anne of Cleves was a wall.

"I will bring it up shortly. Do not lie down if your heart burns. Walking is better. At the least sit upright. A straight-backed board chair. That will do for you perfectly."

"Ah. Very well," said Jane. "I will find me a hard chair."

Anne of Cleves smiled.

Downstairs, Veronica was helping Agnes slice a dried plum tart. "Like this, lamb," the maid said, tidying up the edges of the flaky coffin. "Now fetch me that cream." The girl brought it, and Agnes showed her how to make a flourish over the top of the fruit. "See? Guide it with your wrist."

Veronica laid a double-leaf of mint on top.

"Where are the younger girls?" asked Catherine.

"I haven't seen them," Agnes said. Her eyes flickered to the embers in the smaller hearth.

"I will see to that," said Catherine. She took up some sticks and tossed them onto the dying fire. "Will you walk with her up to Lady Anne? You'll likely find her in her game room by this time. Take another for Master Harst." She waited while they fixed a second plate, Veronica insisting upon pouring the cream. "Don't forget a pitcher of ale."

Catherine watched until Agnes had led Veronica to the top of the stairs, then started the draught for Jane Dudley. Chamomile and honey. Saffron to color it deeply. Then the wort and henbane. The strongest ale she had that would not take her over the brink to death.

Ann Smith came in from the back yard, lugging a shallow bucket of eggs. "What are you making now?"

"A sleeping draught for Jane. She complains of her heartburn again."

"What's burning in that woman is not in her heart."

"I know. But the heart can tell the rest of the body how to feel." Catherine set the honey and chamomile, thinned with a splash of the ale, over the fire.

"I meant she would have to have one for it to ail her. A heart."

Catherine laughed. "She has one, but it's eaten all through with her worries. Wherever the ailment is, I aim to put it to sleep. Have you seen Temperance and Marjory?"

"No, but I wasn't looking for them. Is Lady Mary departed?"

"Yes. Gone with a present in hand. A small box."

"What of that?"

"It was just the size to hold—well, I know not what. Ann, I have a great fear in staying in this place a minute longer. Let me take this up and put Jane down for a while. My God, how I wish Benjamin would return." Catherine stirred the drink and sniffed it. "Stay here." She tiptoed up to the front hall and leaned her ear against the door of the game room. Harst was speaking. It sounded as though his mouth was full. Good. She ran on up and found Jane Dudley in her chamber, crammed onto a stiff chair by the window. "I have brought your physic, Jane."

"Thank God. At last." Jane jerked to her feet. She snatched the cup and stuck her face to it.

"Take your time, Madam," said Catherine. "You will choke yourself."

Jane dropped the cup. It pivoted on itself and came to rest against her slipper. Jane leapt away from it. "It's getting me wet. Take it away."

The chambermaid, huddled in one corner, retrieved the cup. The edge was bent, and the girl tried to cover the damage with her finger. Jane turned away and braced her arms on the windowsill. She said, "This ache will not leave me. It eats my innards."

Catherine removed the cup from the girl's fist and shooed her out. "Jane," she said, shutting the door. "Is it your monthlies? Do you feel it swell with the moon?"

"No! Mayhap. I don't know." Jane fisted her hands and pushed them against her eyes. "It comes up in me like a fierce little animal and chews at my throat. It makes me mad. I am afraid." She began to beat at her face softly, then harder, and Catherine set the cup aside and dragged her from the window to the bed.

"Jane. Stop it. You must breathe." Catherine held the other woman's arms and helped her lie down. "Put your feet up now. Steady yourself. Come. Say a prayer." Jane shook as though a stormy wind tumbled through her, and Catherine leaned with her whole weight upon her. "Pray, Jane. Turn your mind to God. You will set the whole house alight with these fits." Catherine held her air. The woman smelt of old urine and she wondered how often she changed her undergarments.

Jane's eyes closed and her lips moved. Catherine tried to imagine her with a husband and children, in charge of a household, but the picture was an image of chaos. Then the praying ceased and her eyes opened, bright, as though someone had lit candles behind them. "I cannot breathe!" Jane hissed. "Those damned Catholics. Let me up!"

"Lie still," said Catherine. "Tell me of your children. Name them. Begin with the eldest. It is a boy, isn't it?"

The fiery eyes closed again. "Yes, first is Henry. My first Henry. He is a true reformed boy. An example to his brothers. The king will love him. Will love him."

"That's fine. Who are the rest?"

"Thomas. He died, you know. Then John and Ambrose. Then is . . . who is next? It is Robert. He is a lively boy. And great in pursuits. He will go far if I steer him right. Then comes Guildford. My dear Guildford. A boy beautiful as a cherub descended from heaven. Have you seen him? His name comes from my father, you know. He is my dearest. What God has in store for him—"

"Jane, have you had troubles since your last birth? With your water?"

"I leak. I drip like a broken basket." She clutched Catherine's hand. "They tear our bodies, then they tear our hearts." Jane mumbled a few more words, then closed her eyes. Drool slipped over her lower lip. She was asleep. Catherine listened, then examined the battered cup and slid from the room. As she came down, she met Marjory and Temperance. Veronica skipped behind them. "Where have you been?" asked Catherine. She took her daughter's hand to slow her down.

Temperance offered a sulky shrug, and Marjory said, "That Master Harst forgets all when food enters the room. I heard him up there." Veronica made snorting noises, and Catherine covered her mouth. Margery said, "Master Martins is coming again today, they say, with his troop of men. From the court."

"How very precise their timing is," said Catherine. They entered the kitchen, where Ann was waiting at the table. "Ann, will you walk into the garden with me?"

"I will walk with you," said Veronica, flourishing the doll. "Cleopatra must take her exercise."

"You will exercise your wits on your letters for now, young Madam," said Catherine. "Do you have a new word for each letter of your alphabet?"

Veronica hung her head. The poppet drooped in her hand. "Almost."

"What is 'almost'?" Catherine was headed to Veronica's writing table. She put her hand on the paper and her daughter came dancing over and jumped onto her chair.

"I have completed, um, almost four?"

"Four! Of your entire alphabet? How is that 'almost'?"

"It is almost that I am almost ready to begin my letters again," said Veronica, lifting her quill.

"A rhetorician," said Catherine, giving her daughter's head a scrub with her knuckles. "Get yourself to your work. Aunt Ann and I will return shortly."

Outside, the sky was clear and the sun high-handed as a monarch, shoving the clouds here and there and letting the wind worry the women's hair from under their hoods. Ann pulled her cloak tight and shivered. "Spring will never arrive this year."

"Better to freeze than to burn," said Catherine. "At least a body can don more clothes."

A trio of horses clattered through the far gatehouse, and Catherine said, "Is it Benjamin?" But she saw no Caesar, and said, "Those are the king's men. Come, run. I will not be seen."

They made it to the poultry houses and concealed themselves until the men had ridden to the stable and given over their reins to the Richmond men. Their voices came hearty and loud over the buildings, like men in triumph.

Then they faded and Catherine peeped around the edge of the shed. "Quick now."

They passed the edge of the garden, and Catherine made a show of plucking a few new weeds among the carrot fronds, just poking through the broken soil. She folded the offending plants into a green package and walked it to a wheelbarrow against the back wall, where she laid it to rest, then wiped her hands. Ann followed, unspeaking.

Catherine gazed over the cold green rows. New shoots showed bright, hopeful, in the sun. "She has given her a crucifix," she said softly, "or some other token for the Mass. I hope the king's men have not heard of it."

"Who? Mary?" Now Ann went to her knees, digging with a forefinger around an onion shoot that had got its head stuck under a clod. She sat back on her heels and patted the disturbed earth. "You mean Mary Tudor?"

"Yes. Lady Anne gave her something. She must not. It's an error that will be called treason."

"Or sin. Yet another heresy." Ann Smith heaved herself to her feet. A stick lay nearby, and she scraped the mud from her boot soles. "The king's men could not have heard of any such gift this soon."

"No. I suppose not."

"And do I want to know how you came by this new information?"

Catherine looked over her shoulder, though nothing stood there but the stone wall. "I saw it. The box, I mean. The room where the altar is lies behind the wall of her game room. If someone finds it, all her hopes are dashed. Someone must know the room is there."

Ann's lower eyelids hitched but her stare did not waver. "And what will you say about it when the king's men come with their swords to question you?" Now she turned and faced Catherine.

"What have they to question me about? They have nothing to say to me," said Catherine, but her words were cut short by a scream from the kitchen.

CHAPTER TWENTY

It was not Lady Anne who'd screamed. Nor Jane Dudley. The maid Marjory stood in the middle of the kitchen, either arm caught by Martin Martins and Ciaran Barts. Their accomplice, the flat-faced Ellers Chandler, stood behind them, his eyes slanted at the girl and his dagger at the ready. One hand worked the air, as though he wanted someone to hold, too.

"Madam," Marjory cried out when she saw Catherine. "You must tell them. I'm needed here. I can't be taken."

"What is this business?" asked Catherine. Temperance scuttled past the interior door, and Ann Smith went after her.

"What has she done?" Catherine asked.

Martin Martins opened his free hand. In his palm lay a gold crown. "She lifted this from the lady's side table. In her writing room. I saw her with my own eyes. Followed her down the stairs. She slipped it into her pocket, slick as a weasel. She is your girl, is she not?"

"She is a maid of this house. Marjory?" said Catherine. "What have you to say?"

The girl shook her head and stared at her feet.

"Let me speak with her," said Catherine. "Alone. You have my word that she will not escape."

The men's eyes communed over the girl's bowed head, and they let go at the same time. "I will return," said Martins. He waddled out with the inflamed Barts, Chandler skulking behind them.

Catherine set Marjory onto a stool. "Now, what has happened? You told me you would mend your ways."

Marjory's hands trembled and she laid them upon the smooth oak. "I never meant no harm, Madam. But they leave the stuffs just layin' about, like they want it taken. The ladies, they go about in their silks and their jewels, and the coins and the little things are flung down like they're nothin'. They're not nothin' to me. I cannot seem to stop myself. It's like the devil's in me, sayin' 'go on with you, Marjory, nobody minds you.' And I take. I would give it back, Madam. I wouldn't even lift a finger if it wasn't just there with nobody to care and everbody havin' so much and me almost nothin'."

"Oh, Marjory," said Catherine. "I pity you. By my soul, I mean that. I don't know what I can do."

Ann Smith entered the room. "There is nothing you can do. Temperance says that she was in the room when it happened, and that will not go easy with either one of them. Marjory admitted the theft when they took hold of her."

Marjory slid to her knees and clutched Catherine's calves through her skirts. "Madam, will you speak for me? I beg you, as a Christian, do not let them take me."

Catherine put her palm on the girl's head. Her thoughts swam in black water and she could not see her way through. "I will do what is in my power. It may not be much. Anyone might have trespassed in such a way." The spit squeaked, and they turned to look at Sebastian. He turned the iron handle and did not lift his eyes.

Martins and his men were thumping back down, and Catherine yanked the girl to her feet. "She is repentant," Catherine said, stepping in front of Marjory as the men entered. "She believed the coin to be discarded and she now sees the error of her decision. As Christians, we are bound to forgive. We are commanded to it. Everyone sins."

"I am sorry," said Marjory. Her legs gave way and she fell to the floor again. "I repent me of my ways. I will do anything to make it up to my Lady."

"It is not your Lady who will decide your fate," said Martins. He snapped his fingers and the two others marched into the room, Barts pulling a length of rope from somewhere under his cape. He hauled Marjory up and Chandler bound her hands before her. "Get the other one, too," said Martins. "She's the shadow of this one, sure as the sun shines." They nodded and scuttled out. Temperance screamed, and Barts dragged her in, also tied. "We'll be taking these ones with us, Lady Catherine. And you may spend your Christian words in prayer for their souls. Their bodies are mine. You should keep better watch over your charges."

"You will take these children to prison for a sliver of metal?" asked Ann Smith. "What sort of wolves are you?"

Martins smoothed his smear of mustache with a forefinger. "The sort that follows the law. We obey the king. You might want to do the same and keep your head out of a noose."

Catherine and Ann followed the men as they drove the girls upstairs, where Anne of Cleves waited. Jane Dudley stood beside her.

"They are little girls," said Lady Anne. "Leave them to be."

"I cannot report to the king that I have let thieves run loose in one of your palaces, Lady," said Martins. "Would you have me give such a message to the court? That you keep felons within your walls?"

"No. I want not that."

"Well, then." Martins bobbed his little upper half at Lady Anne and Jane Dudley. The fat bottom anchored him in place. "You will thank me when you see how much cleaner your household is."

"Thank you?" said Lady Anne.

"You are welcome," Martins said. He snapped his fleshy fingers, and Ellers Chandler and Ciaran Barts came to attention. They tightened their grip on the girls and filed out.

Catherine sat hard on a nearby chair. "We are none of us safe from that man's eyes. The law is a badger. Sneaking this way and that and snapping at anything in its path."

"He got what he want," said Anne of Cleves. "He goes now."

Catherine looked into the placid, wide face. "I wish that were so. I fear for us all. We have no one to protect us. You are the king's Beloved Sister, but we are his ordinary ones."

"Ordinaries?"

"His ordinary sisters. Ann and I."

"You share the father?"

"No." Catherine's jaw tightened. "Our father in heaven, Lady. We have been honored by our time with you, but this

—" She pointed at the door through which the girls had been taken. "This makes my heart tremble."

"What to do?" asked Ann of Cleves.

The lie came off Catherine's tongue like water. "I am sorely needed in Yorkshire. Ann and I crave the open fields and the village. Ann even longs for her own old washtub." In saying the words, Catherine felt her old home pull at her memory, as though she had spoken her longing into being. She could almost smell sheep and the wine-scent of drying grasses. "We were never destined for palaces and royal service. We were raised to serve God." Catherine looked into the eyes of Anne of Cleves. "I know you understand me. We must do what we can to protect ourselves. Other women have husbands to stand between them and the law. Jane has a husband."

"What of that?" asked Jane. "I am here as well as the rest of you."

"But at a word he would fetch you home."

Jane said, "So now you want men, is that it? After all that noise about keeping your chastities?"

Catherine felt the sting of her own argument coming from Jane's mouth. "If men will be tyrants to women for being women, then women need other men to keep them off us. If men were the Christians they claim, we would be safe enough without them or their laws. We used to enjoy some protection. But now?"

Now Lady Anne's long nose shone red at the tip. Catherine thought she might weep. "The man should protect his woman. I was queen." She peered at Catherine as though she had become short-sighted. "Am I not the queen?"

"Oh, Lady Anne," said Catherine. "I aim not to summon the spirits of the past. But I am afraid for us and I must leave your service."

"You go home? Away from me?" She grabbed Catherine's hands. "Tell me." The Beloved Sister had a grip like a soldier.

"I want to go," Catherine said, "with your leave, Lady."

The fingers hung on. "You will not spread the rumour of anything you have witnessed."

"No, Lady. I will not."

"Then we are safe. All safe. You will stay."

Catherine's palms ached from the piercing nails, but still Lady Anne had her. "Those men will not stop at two serving girls. He aims higher. We are not safe. Please let me go."

Lady Anne unwrapped her fingers from Catherine's. "I am alone."

Catherine retreated a step. "Lady—" she began, but the door opened behind them, and Master Harst came thumping in, bringing the smell of cold dog and straw. He was slapping his hands together.

"What is the huddling here?" he asked. "Women's secrets? We can have none of them, not now, not here. Leave the door open when you confer in private. They say we've got felons among us." He walked to the fire, put his back to it, and lifted his jacket to warm himself before he called, "News from Hampton Court Palace, Madam, which I will whisper in your ear alone." He leveled a look across the room.

"I must prepare our evening meal," Catherine said, backing out, "since I am short two maids." As she pulled the door after her, she could hear Harst saying "What have you told them?"

The kitchen was quiet, and Catherine worked herself into a sweat to keep herself from listening at the stairs. She would have to go, whether Benjamin came with the money or not. He would have to come now or travel again to Yorkshire. By the time the venison was roasted and the cabbages mixed with the leeks and carrots and Veronica had finished her lessons, she had decided. Within the week, she would be gone, and in the peace of her own house she could determine what was to be done about the pregnancy.

Jane Dudley called for all the women of the household to assemble. Ann took Veronica's hand. "That doesn't include me."

"Isn't Auntie Ann one of the household women?" asked Veronica, pulling her back.

"Your Aunt Ann is a woman of her own, not to be dragged into a fray," said Catherine.

"Ha!" said Ann. "I am my own because I hide. Would that a woman could be called her own by birth."

"Weren't you born?" asked Veronica.

"Born and born again," said Ann, "and I am still overlooked when they call. I thank my God and my coarse hands that I can duck my head and be counted among the pack animals."

"If you are a pack animal, then you must carry me!" squealed Veronica.

"Climb on, kitten," said Ann, dipping one shoulder. The girl scrambled up and Ann bounced her away, up the back steps to their chamber.

Catherine wished for a moment she could disappear with them, but Jane's voice had spiraled up a few notes, and though her mind still swirled in a dark pool of care, she submitted to her duty and went.

It was the old story. "The books still do not balance, and we will find out the culprit before the king's man charges us all with theft," Jane was saying. The ladies-in-waiting and their women slouched around in various attitudes of weariness and irritation. A couple of maids lounged on a bench under a window, and one was picking at a scab on her cheek. Jane thumped her narrow fist into her palm, and Catherine wondered if her bones would splinter. "You will all provide a list of your expenses, do you hear? You will leave nothing out. Two of the girls of this palace have been taken as thieves already, but this is more than a stray coin. Do you mark me?"

One of the ladies yawned expansively and said, "Jane, do you hold us from our meal for this? We are not the king's accountants, and if the council would like to inventory my hose, they are free to do so. We have heard this tale a dozen times and more."

The other women giggled, and Jane's hair seemed to swell under the folds of her hood. "I tell you, the books do not balance. There are monies missing. A valuable ring is missing."

"Perhaps they need your foot upon them if they do not balance. It feels heavy enough," said another of the ladies. She lifted one bored hand, the finger barely rising to point. "There stands Catherine Overton. That means our meal is cooked, and I do not favor cold meat. When you are given authority over my allowance, Lady Dudley, I am sure my husband will inform me." She gathered herself, beckoned to her maid, and swept into the dining gallery.

The others followed, and as they rustled by, Jane cried, "You listen. Listen to me. All of you. Catherine, you will hear me, won't you?"

"I hear you, Jane, but all of my wealth stands on its hooves in Yorkshire. I cannot bear this any longer. I must change my circumstances."

"But who will treat my heart? Who will prepare my sleeping draught?" She laid her hand upon her breast.

"Your husband may bring his physician to heal you."

"No. I cannot do without my treatments. You must stay." She was clinging to Catherine's sleeve.

"Everyone seems to know what I should be better than I myself. Now, let us eat. I will bring the wine."

She'd turned to go back downstairs when Anne of Cleves came running, her skirts in one hand. "Stop, Catherine. Stop!" she called. One of her manservants trotted along behind her, looking as though he was searching for a spot to get hold of the King's Beloved Sister. They both skidded to a halt before Catherine and Jane Dudley, who had plunged into abject curtsies. Anne of Cleves was panting, and she put her hands on her knees.

"My Lady," said Catherine, glancing up. "Are you ill? Where do you hurt?"

"No. No sick," said Anne of Cleves.

The manservant said, "Horses at the front. Lady asks for Catherine Overton. She's got a few men with her. A little maid by her side. She asks for you and will not remove from her horse until she sees you."

Lady Anne stood straight and laid her hand upon her breast. She looked like a great, thick bird. "She sit like a lady of means. You come."

"A lady of means? For Catherine?" said Jane Dudley, forgetting the curtsey and leaping to her feet. "Is it one of Lady Mary's women? Send her away."

Catherine glared at Jane. The woman looked like a skinny white crow, clapping her beak and stinking of rotten meat. The voices of the other women, running in at the sound of loud words, were a rush of squawks, and Catherine's chest felt stuffed with feathers. "I cannot bear any more," she said. "No more."

"The lady outside requires you," said the manservant.

"Where is Ann?" said Catherine.

"I am here," said Anne of Cleves.

"Ann Smith. Bring me Ann Smith," said Catherine. Jane went to the stairs and shrieked for Ann. Someone had Catherine's arm, and she leaned onto it. She looked up, into the white face of Sebastian. He stared impassively down at her. She said, "Bring me Ann."

Ann Smith came hurrying in, elbowing the man aside and taking hold of Catherine. "What is it? What has happened now?"

"She's here. I know it's her," said Catherine. "Out front. With that girl. Margaret's here."

Chapter Twenty-One

Margaret Overton had worked her way down from the mare she rode, and beside her stood her maid Constance, now a tall young woman who looked like her Overton father. Their serving men, strangers to Catherine, stared blankly from a short distance away. They held the horses' reins.

"Sister," said Margaret, stepping up to the door. She extended her hand. "And how have you been this many a day? I come from the Overton properties. We are doing well with the wool."

The wind blew Margaret's skirts toward Catherine, and Constance, gaping up at the palace front, bundled her fur collar up to her chin. Catherine recognized the cloak as one of her own.

"Catherine?" Margaret was saying. "Will you not greet your loving sister?" The hand was still out.

Catherine finally clasped it. "I greet you as a fellow creature of God," she said. "How have you traveled all this way alone, at this muddy time of the year?"

"I have hired me some men. I have business. They have brought us right along. Con, come in from the cold air," said Margaret, and the young woman trudged in behind her. Constance's figure still featured the extra wagon wheel at the middle, and her hood did not conceal the frizz of red hair. She scanned the broad room, one part sullen and one part envious. When she smiled, sharp foxy teeth appeared. Catherine could hardly imagine that Constance and Veronica were blood cousins.

"You recall Constance, I'm sure?" Margaret said, guiding her maid forward. "She has become almost a daughter to me."

The wind fingered its way through Catherine's dress, and she stepped backward, treading on the toes of Ann Smith. The other ladies had retreated, but Catherine seemed to hear their whispering as she went in, rippling along the tapestries upon the walls. Anne of Cleves had disappeared. Catherine asked, "And is that why she wears my clothes?"

Constance removed the cloak, and, not finding anyone to take it, draped it over her own arm.

"This rag?" asked Margaret, lifting one corner of the cloak. "It was moth holes top to bottom. Con only chose it so that her good wrap would not be destroyed along the filthy ways. Will you offer us drink? We have been upon the road all day and are dead on our feet."

"Would that you were," Ann Smith muttered.

"What's that you say? Ann Smith, you always did have a wicked tongue. Catherine, I wonder that you keep this woman. She doesn't have the manners to serve a royal lady's house." Margaret brushed past and gazed right and left. "Will you introduce us to the presence of the Lady Anne of Cleves?"

"She will ask for you," said Catherine. "Before you come in another step, though, you must tell me what you do here."

Margaret's head whipped back like a viper's. "I am a grown woman and the eldest daughter of Overton House. I have been released from my position at court. I go where it pleases me."

Catherine sucked the inside of her cheek between her teeth and bit down before she spoke. "And it best pleases you to come where I am?"

Margaret's upper lip lifted and a sound came past her tight lips. It might have been a piece of a laugh. "You," she said finally. "You think it is you I come to see? I have come to seek my husband and have been directed here. He is not at his home and I supposed you might tell me where he bides. He has monies, I think, that belong rightly to me."

"Your husband?" asked Catherine. "What are you talking of? You cannot marry. You were a nun." The whispers in her head blew into whistles, deriding her, and Catherine's heart threatened to knock its way through her ribs.

Constance laughed into her hand, and Margaret gave Catherine's arm a teaser's slap. "I know you have suspected. He will get permission from the king just as my brother was given permission to marry you."

"But I was yet a novice, barely a sister at all. And I was carrying a child. You had been under the veil for five years. You had taken your solemn vows. And the king is in no mood for weddings."

Margaret blinked. "We are all sisters now, are we not? All the same under the king's laws. Even the Lady Anne of Cleves. We are the king's sisters and we obey him. We may also petition him to favor us. Or we may have our men do it for us. In the name of Christian marriage, of course. And what if I were to carry a child? What if someone had made a conquest of me, with the promise of marriage? I might find myself to be just like you, Sister."

"You are with child? Whose child?" Catherine struggled to compose her face, but she could not force her muscles to obey. "Who is it that you think you will marry?"

Margaret finally sighed. "Sister. You goose. Don't play the simpleton with me. Benjamin Davies, of course. He is already as much as my husband."

Chapter Twenty-Two

A hand grazed Catherine's shoulder, and she whirled around, ready to strike. But it was only Jane Dudley, come to greet the visitor. Catherine huffed her breath through her mouth to keep herself from crying out. It made her feel like an animal.

"And this must be your sister, Margaret Overton," Jane was saying. "The Lady Anne will be surprised at this. Most surprised."

"The weather turned fair enough and the road looked smooth and so I came ahead without announcement," said Margaret. She dipped a little swoop of a curtsey. "I might settle myself into a chamber or take drink. We've not stopped for food today. Catherine, you see to the kitchens, do you not? Might you bring us some refreshment?"

"I will have food fetched up," said Ann Smith. She turned on her toe and ran away.

"Have you spoken to the king of this marriage?" asked Catherine. "Have you spoken to anyone? Have you come to ask Lady Anne to intercede for you?"

"Do we need her permission?" asked Margaret. "She is not the queen. Nor is she the head of our church. We will seek the good word of the king himself. He will not refuse a woman in my situation. He did not refuse you."

"What marriage?" asked Jane Dudley, looking from one to the other. "Who is married?"

"I am." Margaret bowed her head, as though she expected a blessing. Catherine wanted to crack her skull. "Well, as good as. We must go through the ceremony. But we are promised to each other, in word and in blood. It is a betrothal in faith and in custom."

"And where is the fortunate gentleman?" asked Jane. She searched past Margaret's shoulder, but Catherine heaved the door shut. The heavy wood groaned and eased itself into place with a sigh and a slight thud. Jane said, "The Lady Anne will expect to receive him as well." She added, "Your husband," as though the words might conjure him into existence.

"Benjamin," said Catherine. Her jaw ached, and she realized she'd been grinding her teeth. "She says she is married to Benjamin."

"Your Benjamin?" Jane said to Catherine, then trained her gaze on Margaret.

Catherine said, "I've not heard of banns being read. Nor do I see a ring upon your finger."

"Benjamin will not deny me," Margaret said. "He has been without a wife for many years now, and I have made him one." She held out her hands. "Look at the state of me. I have dirt beneath my very nails and I am made to stand here in the cloud of my own grime defending myself." She beckoned Constance forward with one finger. "You were witness, were you not?"

"I saw him in the house," said Constance. Her face had gone scarlet. "I heard Madam say that they had concluded their marriage." She covered her mouth like a shy girl. "It is not something to speak of among company."

"With no priest?" asked Jane. "When did you publish the banns? And why did Lady Catherine not hear of them? Who performed the rites?"

"Questions, questions, and still nothing to drink," said Margaret. She dusted one sleeve with her fingers. "We had no time for the old rituals. We will see to the church when the wools are sold and we have counted our monies. We have exchanged our vows and bedded. That is enough. The times are changed from what they once were, but every mother's son knows that vows and a bedding make a marriage."

Jane snorted. "That is no marriage, Margaret Overton, and it is not in me to say precisely what it is. I will ask you again. Have you published banns? In a church?"

"I have ordered them to be put up in Havenston. I did so just before we left."

"And just after Benjamin himself left Yorkshire. Is that right?" asked Catherine. "Who would put them up?"

"Do you doubt me? I have a witness!" Margaret shoved Constance forward, almost throwing her to the stone floor.

"She may have seen a man in the house. She may have seen three or four of them," said Catherine. "A man in your bed does not make a marriage. Who heard these vows of yours?"

"They were private vows, spoken between a man and a maid. They are binding. This is widely understood." She also covered her face briefly with her hand, the mirror of her maid. "He has conquered me. We are fast married."

Catherine said, "Bring the man here and have him witness it. Jane, have you a manservant who can ride?"

"Of course. But where is Benjamin? I thought he was traveling to Dover to meet a merchant."

"So he was. But that was weeks now. He might be returned to one of his houses by now. The London house is less than a day's hard ride. Another day or so will take a good rider to the country house."

"Save your man and his horse. Benjamin is not at either of his houses," said Margaret. "I left a letter telling him that I would be here. If he were that close, he would already be in the front lane to greet me."

Jane flattened her right eyebrow with two fingers. "This gives me the headache." She sent her maid, who was hovering in a corner, out to the stables to find a groomsman. "We will get to the truth of this matter one way or the other." She pointed at Margaret's nose. "Not a word of this to the King's Sister, do you hear me? I will snatch the hair right out of your head if you speak of marriage in her presence right now, especially a secret one. She is much distracted and you will not drive her to a frenzy."

Margaret leaned against Constance. "Lead the way."

"I thought you were well nigh dead for food and drink," said Jane. "Look there, I see the girls carrying something into the gallery. Go through and eat while I inform the Lady Anne that you are here."

"Come, Con," said Margaret. They walked off, Margaret using Constance's thick arm for a support. Margaret's hard high heels clicked as she went.

"What did you know of this?" Jane whispered fiercely to Catherine.

Ann Smith was approaching, and Catherine waited until her friend was in hearing. "I knew nothing of it. Not one word. The last I heard from Benjamin Davies was that he disliked Margaret's company and hastened himself out of it. I believed him."

Jane turned on Ann. "Did he say the same to you?"

Ann Smith held up two hands. "He said nothing to me on the subject. He spoke of wool and becoming rich. But I am not in his confessions."

Jane's maid returned, coming up the back stairs, a greasy manservant with dark hair in tow. The girl curtsied and retreated, leaving the man with his head bowed and his cap in hand. Jane said, "Look here. Have you got a horse that will travel some thirty miles before dark?"

The man scratched his hair. "Not afore dark, I think, Madam. He might get me there afore mornin', if he knows where he's headed."

"Very well. Get him saddled. Catherine, you see to it that this man knows the way. Find out where Benjamin Davies is. I will have to present that woman to the King's Sister." She breathed out an angry puff and looked hard at the man. "This has not made my day fly by any easier."

"Nor mine," said Catherine softly as Jane huffed away. She turned to the man. "What's your name?"

"Oliver, Madam. Is it true they've taken the little maids away?"

"I fear it is. Follow me to my work room, Oliver, and I will draw you a map. You must ride first into London, then north if no one is at the house there."

After the rider had gone, Catherine and Ann hid upstairs in their chamber, waiting to hear any noise from Margaret.

Some feet pattered by their door, and twice someone went running, but no voices sounded. Veronica had gone out with the poultry maids to gather the eggs, and Catherine watched out the window as the three came back, Veronica swinging between the arms of the two older girls. One of them had a basket in her other hand, and it threatened to topple.

"The Lady of Cleves will put Margaret straight," said Catherine to the window. "The King's Sister will put my sister down."

Ann Smith set aside the shift she was mending. "You will dig holes into your sleeves."

"What? What do you say?" Catherine looked at her crossed arms. She had scratched bald patches into the velvet. "Christ's Mother, I have ruined these. Help me get them off."

Ann untied the garments, and Catherine pulled herself free. "I can make something of them," said Ann. "Caps for Veronica. Or little gloves. You mustn't destroy yourself simply because you cannot get at Margaret. She tells lies and she will be found out."

"That woman." Catherine clenched her hands again. Her nails pierced her palms and she shivered, her arms goose-fleshed in the light cloth. "She means to be the death of me."

Ann sat again and began clipping the seam of a sleeve. "She means to claim a man. If that will be the death of you, then I agree."

"What do you mean to say?"

"Do you doubt him so easily?"

"No. Perhaps. No. Sometimes." Catherine knocked her forehead against the pane. The window was unlatched and it sprang open. A dark cloud swelled above them, and the wind smelt of green spring storm. "Where is he?"

"No man is worth pitching yourself to the earth for. But if you mean to leap, you will need to find a wider portal than that. I could barely squeeze a cat through it." Ann pulled a long silk thread loose and laid it aside.

Catherine turned and sat on the sill. "I accuse and scorn her for the same thing that I have done. With the same man. And I curse her for it." She scanned the sky over her shoulder. "It is coming up a tempest." A chuckle bubbled up her throat. "I am the worst of hypocrites. I look a fool, do I not?"

"You look like a woman in torment," said Ann. She shook out the fabric, smoothed it onto the table beside her, and took up the second sleeve. "You are more likely to get permission to have him than Margaret, if you still want him. She has only poisoned her own water by announcing this. But I have said it before. There are women who want children and cannot get them. You don't need him. You need only to get home. Now."

Thunder sounded and the big-bellied clouds pelted the side of the palace with rain. Catherine pulled the window closed and locked it. "I cannot trust him. And I will not give the baby away. I must get rid of it. That's the only solution."

Ann studied the stitches she was snipping. "It is dangerous. You know how dangerous it is. I have said this before, too. You could die. You promised me once that you would never turn to that again." Her eyebrows were scowling. She did not look away from her work.

"But that was years ago, and—" Catherine began, but the door flew inward and Jane Dudley came rushing in.

"She swore it," said Jane. She plopped onto a stool, holding her stomach with one hand. One of her maids waited in the hall, looking one way, then the other. "In front of the Lady Anne, in the middle of her receiving room, that Margaret of yours put her palms together and swore to heaven that she and Benjamin Davies are fast married."

"She is not mine. What did Lady Anne say to this?" asked Catherine.

Jane Dudley began to giggle like a girl, then she hiccupped until Catherine told her to hold her breath. Ann Smith glanced up, then shifted her eyes again to her work. Jane checked the door and shut it in the face of her maid. She leaned against the latch, as though someone might break in upon them. Finally she said, "Lady Anne ordered her out of her presence. Just like that." Jane snapped her fingers and began to laugh again. "Sent her out of the room and ordered her to leave Richmond Palace at once. She called her a wicked woman and a shame to her sex who would bring a shadow upon the entire household at a time when we seek most to please the king."

"The Daughter of Cleves said all of that?" asked Ann. She finished the second sleeve and laid it over the first one, flattening the nap with her fingers.

"Not in just those phrases," admitted Jane, "but her face was as red as a strawberry. I thought she would beat Margaret with her own fists." She dropped again to the stool. "I have never seen the like. Your sister cannot say I didn't warn her."

Catherine said, "So Margaret goes tonight? Have you seen the storm that's blowing in?"

"She asked to wait for Benjamin. She begged not be turned out on her ear. The Lady Anne covered her head with her hands and would not hear. And since Margaret seemed bound to remain in the room, she herself left. The Lady Anne left, with your sister standing like a wooden post. She left her there with that maid of hers." Jane Dudley stood and rubbed her stomach again. "I have a pain here in my middle, Catherine. Are you too disordered to fix me a tisane?"

"Go to your chamber and I will bring it to you."

Jane nodded and went, leaving the door open behind her. Catherine looked up and down the hall but the only movement was a lone chambermaid, dawdling at the window in the far wall to watch the lightning. Ann, from her sewing stool, said, "Go make the physic. No one will be travelling in this rain."

"Not even Benjamin."

Ann peered out the window, her hand hooding her eyes. "The clouds look like great grey hawks. Owls, perhaps. Do you take it to be an omen?"

Catherine came and stood beside her friend. Lightning split the sky and the thunder seemed to shake the foundations of the palace. "Like the finger of God," whispered Catherine, "pointing my way to destruction."

Chapter Twenty-Three

The rain droned all night, and Catherine lay next to Ann, listening for movement in the palace, but she heard nothing except the thunder, bellowing somewhere in the distant dark. She must have slept, because she woke with a jerk from a dream of Yorkshire and her first husband, William. He had been in the bed next to her, and when she turned to embrace him, she found herself touching the fat King of England. She said "Oh," but it was only Ann beside her, stretching.

"I dreamt that you were King Henry," said Catherine, throwing off the cover and feeling for her slippers in the dark.

Ann sat up and pinched her waist. "I will have to eat less supper, then."

Catherine squatted before the hearth and poked at the fire but the embers only glowed and smoked, and she finally crawled back into bed. She said, "Even the flame's spirits are low," but Ann was already asleep again, and Catherine lay on her back, trying to see Benjamin's face through the ghost of William's on the backs of her eyelids, until the pale dawn fingered its way through the shutters.

Agnes and Veronica were up with the sun, and they entered from the maid's chamber to wake Catherine, but she was already opening the narrow window. "The storm has moved on," she said. "Look, God is smiling all the way to Wales."

"Where?" Veronica climbed onto a chair to see the view. "I want to see the face of God."

"It's there, before you," said Catherine. "See how we're loved today?"

"God was angry at us last night," said Veronica. Catherine held her daughter's waist as the girl put her nose to the fresh air. "He was not happy to see Aunt Margaret."

Ann hauled herself out of bed and plodded over to the basin to wash her face. "The wisdom of God is without bounds."

Catherine said, "Here, child, you will fall," and pulled Veronica inside. "Did you hear anything in the halls during the night?"

"Not a cheep or a complaint," said Agnes. "I will run down and see what the gossip is in the kitchen."

Agnes lifted Veronica and was gone. Ann and Catherine dressed quickly and took the front steps down. No one was stirring except the chambermaids, listlessly dusting the furniture. No one had laid food to break their fasts, and the two women descended to the kitchens. One of the laundry maids was heating a couple of small tubs, and the dairy girls, newly assigned to the kitchen, were standing at the back door, staring out at limbs fallen over the gravel. Sebastian and another man busied themselves with axes and hand saws, clearing away the brush. Agnes was outside, holding Veronica by one hand. The poppet dangled from her daughter's fingers.

"Where is the food?" asked Catherine, and the maids startled.

"The rain, Madam," said one, dropping into a contrite curtsey. "It's got everyone out of sorts. There's boughs down all over the yard and the men have been out since before sunup. There's dead things in the river. I never seen anything so scaring to me."

"All right," said Catherine, "but the household will be clamoring for victuals. Get some cold meat and cheese and bread upstairs. Take plenty of ale."

"Yes, Madam," said a tall, black-haired girl.

Catherine and Ann went out back to watch the work. Agnes said, "The order is to get the lane cleared and the Overton horses saddled before the sun is over the trees."

"So she's going," muttered Catherine. "We will wait until she is far down the road, then we will go, too."

The wind was high, whipping the sawdust as the men worked. One window had been shattered by a loosened branch, and a young boy teetered high on a ladder, nailing boards over the offending hole. The women's hoods threatened to sail off. One of the younger maids came hurrying from the dairy with a bucket of fresh milk, its surface thrashed into tiny waves. She was holding her head low and almost bumped into Ann Smith. "Pardon me, Madam," she said without looking up. "The air is vicious this morning."

"Indeed," said Catherine. She watched a ribbon of cloud unwind high in the blue sky. "The whole world has come undone."

The stable boys led Margaret's horses out. They were already bridled and saddled, but their spirits were excited, and they stomped and pawed the gravel as they came. "Thank God," said Catherine. She turned to go back inside when another rider came galloping around the corner of the palace. He skidded to a stop when he saw the other horses in his way and, jumping to the ground, handed his reins to a groomsman before hurrying back to the front.

"That was our messenger," said Ann Smith, watching him go. "Oliver, isn't that his name?"

"Come from Benjamin," said Catherine. "He can ride, I will say that for him."

Ann said, "Should we walk through and hear the tale?"

Catherine shook her head. "We must not seem too anxious. We don't want Lady Anne's fury to fall on us."

Lady Anne had come downstairs and was sitting with Jane Dudley and her other women at the long table when Catherine forced herself upstairs, Ann just behind her. Their cups had been filled and they were being served bread and meat.

"Catherine," said Jane Dudley. "Have you been out to inspect the damage?"

Catherine nodded and slid into an empty seat. Margaret was nowhere to be seen. Ann took the spot below Catherine. A jug of ale sat before them, and Ann poured. Catherine's heart was banging, and she drank before she spoke. "The wind was most violent. I saw at least one broken pane and enough torn limbs to make a bonfire. It will be all day getting them cleaned away."

"Is that all?" asked Jane.

"It was enough," said Catherine. "The men seem to be bringing the horses from the stable. I wonder that the roof did not collapse upon them."

"Our rider has returned," said Jane, breaking a piece of bread and setting a piece of meat on it.

"Has he?" asked Catherine. "He is most expeditious. Has he brought Master Davies with him?"

Ann rose and curtsied to the table of women. "He will want refreshment. I will see to him." She backed out, but Catherine heard her running down the steps to the kitchen. She was going to see if he'd come in the back way.

"Your woman is most attentive," observed Lady Anne.

"Ann Smith is a gem among women," said Catherine. "I have always been blessed in having her for my sister."

Anne of Cleves buried her face in her big goblet of ale. She seemed to empty the cup, and a small belch escaped her as she set it down. "You seem both to be very blessed," she said.

Catherine put her palms flat on the table. "Was he home? Are they married?"

Lady Anne smiled. "Her man is not at his home."

"Oh. I see," said Catherine. "Her man." Her guts rolled over and her arms itched. She felt that her skin was being overrun with tiny feet, and she wanted to cry. "So there is no word."

"That is not what I say," said Lady Anne. "His man is home. The man who run the house. This old man. Jack he say he is."

"Jack Huff!" said Catherine. "I know him. Is he here?"

"No," said Lady Anne. "But he say his man no married. He swear it." She put her hand on her breast. "She must go now. I am sorry to know she is your relation."

A cry came up Catherine's throat and she let herself say, "Thank God for it."

"Yes," said Jane. She sipped from her goblet. "Thank God."

Catherine rose. "I must write a letter to my father and ask him about these banns."

Anne of Cleves sighed. "Very well, my Catherine Overton. Go write your letter."

Catherine ran from the room and flat into Ann Smith. They both almost fell backward and Catherine began to laugh. "Christ in the East, Ann, we will kill each other just as my heart's been eased a little."

"What?" Ann grabbed Catherine's arm. "Where is Benjamin?"

"I don't know," said Catherine. "But wherever he is, he is not married to Margaret. Come, I have no desire to kiss her hand as she departs. I must write to Father."

"If Margaret was able to ride here, then we are able to ride North. I say we go. Benjamin is not here. He is not there. We must take care of this matter ourselves."

"We are in agreement," said Catherine.

The letter was scratched at the big kitchen table within the hour, while Ann showed the kitchen duties to the maids and Veronica walked her poppet across the sill of the open window. Catherine re-read the message. It was innocent enough as far as the questions about Margaret were concerned. But she said that she would be returning and asked if Benjamin had perhaps brought her profits back to Yorkshire. It was a risk. She signed the bottom and scattered sand over the ink. Sebastian, back at his post, stepped aside to let her melt wax at the big hearth to seal the edge.

"And who will deliver it?" Ann asked.

Catherine waved the missive until the wax hardened, then tucked it into her pocket. "We might send Oliver today, if Jane will spare him. We know that he can ride and we can pay handsomely for his service. We will not be far behind him."

Ann nodded, but Catherine bent as she tried to rise and let her head fall between her knees. "I will be sick," she said.

Ann rubbed the back of her neck. "All will be well when we are gone from here."

Catherine felt the knots loosen in her back. She stood, slowly and moved to the back door for fresh air. Oliver was there, breaking up branches, and she stepped out to hail him, but just as the man looked up, a noise in the hall made Catherine turn. It was probably Jane Dudley. "Back inside," she said quickly, and Ann opened the door to find the kitchen empty, except for Martin Martins, waddling up to her.

"Madam. I will need to detain you."

"What? For what reason? What do you do here?" His swollen hand hovered near her elbow, and Catherine jerked away. "I am busy with a letter to my father."

"So I hear. Come with me." From the shadow of the hall, Ciaran Barts emerged into the light of the room. His red face shone, and his spectacles caught the untended flames.

Catherine and Ann pushed past the men and headed toward the stairs, but Martins said, "No. This way." He took Catherine in his damp grasp and steered her toward her own small room. She said, "Ann," over her shoulder, but he shoved her inside and closed the door behind them. The extra silver rattled in the baskets. She could hear Veronica wail.

Martins pushed Catherine onto the wooden seat, among her own books. His breath was rancid and she faced away. He said, "You will empty your pockets."

"I will not. I carry a letter. It is private."

"I will determine what is private and what is not. Laws are being flouted. Lies are being told. Women are making their plans, as though they think they are men. Let me see the letter." His fat hand was out, and before he could touch her, Catherine removed the paper and set it on his palm. He cracked the seal and read, tilting the paper into the one shaft of window light. "Mmhmm. Yes. Private indeed. I was told of this pretense about a marriage. I have heard of this man. He is not to be trusted. But I had not heard that you planned to leave your lady's service without permission. You are in serious trouble."

"I can go where I please. I am an Englishwoman. This is England."

"Oh, so now the women have become the law of the land. Is that it? No, lady. You go where the king tells you to go."

For a moment, Catherine thought to grab for the message and tear it, but Martins had already folded it again and secreted it in his jacket. "This with the other proofs will be most interesting. What have you to say for yourself? And after I have offered you such kind assistance?"

"I have nothing to say," said Catherine. "I am sick with your threats and suspicions. I have written to my father. There is no crime in that."

"Oh, there is crime, Lady." He went to the door and called. Catherine could hear a faint answer from somewhere. Then footsteps. Martins went out, and she could hear him conferring with Barts. Twice the fat man peeped back into the room to be sure she had not moved. The third time he returned and pulled the door closed behind him again. "Yes. There is crime." He opened his hand. Catherine's purse lay in it, and he threw it into the air, catching it as it fell. "What do yousuppose it in this purse? And where do you suppose it has been found?"

"It is my purse and you found it among my possessions. But what is inside belongs to me and was brought to me from my holdings in Yorkshire."

"And what of this?" He removed a paper from a pocket in his breeches and flapped it before her face.

At first glance, Catherine didn't recognize it. "What of what?" He thrust it into her face. Her head felt as though she had walked into a hot blizzard. Her blood began to rattle. "I am sick."

"I expect you are." Martins snapped the paper open. It was the list of merchants that Benjamin had given her. She had almost forgotten it. "I know the hand well enough. It's that Davies, isn't it? So you are an Englishwoman simply headed to her home? Or a traitor fleeing the king?"

"Where is Ann? I'm not well." Catherine squeezed her head between her hands, trying to steer her thoughts in a straight direction, but the snowy light flipped and danced before her eyes. "I must have drink."

"You must have what I allow you," said Martins. The wide shoulders of his jacket had begun to sag, and his codpiece was close enough to Catherine's face to make her gag. "You will admit it. You have concealed goods that do not belong to you. You have meant to make off with them, to leave the country without the king's warrant. You have like a whore enlisted your lady-in-waiting in this plan. You mean to abandon your young son, against the laws of the king and of God. You have committed thefts and borne false witness. You have rejected my most generous attentions to your welfare. Admit it."

"I am sick," said Catherine. "I have only tried to mend the breaks in this household, to help the Lady Anne to some happiness, and anything I have concealed has been in the service of peace."

"Peace. I will give you peace. And quiet. Yes, plenty of quiet. You will find the stones of your cell as silent as the grave. And one well-tied knot will give you all the peace you require."

The blizzard in Catherine's head whined and roared, and she put her head down again. "I am sick," she said again. "I must speak with Lady Anne."

"You may speak all you wish, but the Lady cannot help you. She will not."

"I must have the benefit of the law," said Catherine. "I must be allowed to speak."

"You may cry your heart dry, but the law of this land will be no benefit to you," said Martins, hitching the waistband of his breeches up. The codpiece bobbed, and the jewels embroidered on it sparkled. "Let the walls of your prison listen to your tale."

Chapter Twenty-Four

The King's Sister waited at the top of the stairs, with Jane Dudley scowling at her side. A couple of doughy men slouched behind them, hands idly resting on their daggers. Lady Anne squinted down at the group as they came up.

"You," said Jane Dudley. She pointed at Martins and he continued up the steps until his chest touched her finger. But she did not back away. "You Martins. You Martin what-do-ye-call-yourself David Martins." She swung the finger toward Barts. "And you, tall fellow, can you see my finger before your face?"

Barts sidestepped Jane and dragged Catherine toward the front door. Martins brandished his wheel-lock and Catherine heard him say, "You keep thieves in your very bosom, Lady Anne. Liars and whores and thieves." The other men sidled out from behind Anne of Cleves. One of them twirled his weapon as he walked.

Catherine yanked herself free. "I am no thief."

"Of course you are not," said Anne of Cleves. She drifted like a wall of silk toward the bell-shaped man.

"This one," said Martins, latching again onto Catherine. "I seize upon this one and her companion." He gestured with the hand holding the wheel-lock to his men. "You may search her chambers after we are gone."

"You may not," said Catherine, but Martins' men had already put on eager faces and taken the stairs. She called to Lady Anne, "You will not allow them to put their hands on my goods?"

But Anne of Cleves was staring at Martin David Martins. Ciaran Barts hovered beside Catherine, his spectacles twinkling as he looked from his master to the ladies. "You will make your searches and be gone?" Lady Anne asked.

"With your leave," said Martins. He tried out a courtly bow, his little head and chest bobbing over the great belly and legs. He looked into the dining gallery. "I see refreshments have been laid."

"You are surely too rushed to stop for a meal," said Jane Dudley. She curtsied to Lady Anne and bolted upstairs. Catherine had never seen her move with such dispatch. She left a scent of rotten urine on the air.

Anne of Cleves watched her go. "Where is the Margaret? The Margaret of Overton? She is the one who bring us such trouble." She beckoned to Catherine, and Barts brought her forward. "Your sister has done this."

"I don't know where Margaret is. I thought she was gone," said Catherine. She stared up the steps. "They are in my chambers. I can hear them from where I stand." She put her foot on the bottom stair. "You must release me to see what they're up to." But before she could move, Margaret appeared at the landing. She leaned onto the banister, Constance beside her, and one of Martins' men came up behind them. He had Sebastian with him.

Margaret said, "That is my sister, gentlemen. Catherine, what have you done?"

"I've done nothing. It's you, isn't it?" Catherine pointed at the spit-turner, staring down. "I should have known this tale came from you. What, have you been spying as you pretended to work?"

Sebastian was stretching a pair of Catherine's gloves, trying to get his sooty fingers into them, and Margaret slapped them out of his hand. "Do not take her things. Don't lower yourself."

Catherine said, "That purse. He told you of it, did he not? It belongs to me, I say. Those are my monies, the profits of my wools, and you know it. Margaret?"

"I know nothing of a purse. I thought the wools were not yet sold," said Margaret.

"He left me that," Catherine said. "He said he would take the amount out of the final price."

Margaret said, "Who said this?"

"Benjamin," said Catherine. "Benjamin is my—"

"Your what?" asked Martins. "Which lady has the husband? Are you in this with her?"

"I am a guest in this house," said Margaret.

Catherine said, "We must get the man here to answer for himself. And for me."

"And where is he?" asked Barts. "Why does he not come when he is called? Why does he not ride to your rescue? I think this man has won you both and has taken himself away."

Martin David Martins braceleted Catherine's wrist once more with his fat hand and squeezed. She would not turn to gaze on his form, darkening the door to the dining gallery.

He said, "It seems we may go." He pulled out the purse Benjamin had given Catherine and hefted it. "This needs counting and measuring. Have you been concealing the coins one at a time or did you take all at once? And this silk—it seems very fine for a lady of your modest duties."

"It was given me by Benjamin," Catherine said. "The purse, I mean to say."

"And he will not ever tell a lie on your behalf?" asked Martin Martins.

Margaret said, "He is *my* husband." But no one marked her words.

Catherine said, "Ask the Lady Anne of Cleves. Here she stands. Ask her if she has ever seen such a purse before or if I have ever touched her things without her leave."

"I never see such a purse," said Lady Anne. "She speak truth. She has money. It's none of mine."

Martins did not look at Lady Anne. He replaced the bag and worked his weapon back into its holder. "Such vanities may be bought with stolen money. And there is still the matter of the missing ring."

Catherine said, "Get out. All of you. And leave me be." She wanted to sling her arm from Martins' grip, but he was strong, and she clutched her skirt with her left hand instead.

Ann Smith suddenly jerked loose and said, "You will let us both be. We are no criminals and you are no men of the law."

"The law is what I say it is." Martin David Martins dropped Catherine's wrist and took Ann by the shoulder. She pulled away, and he held on, shaking her until her hood came loose. "No fighting, woman. You will come with me whether you want to or not. Your mistress, too." He flung her away.

Now Chandler and Barts moved forward, taking Ann's elbows. Margaret hooked her arm through Constance's and pulled her down the stairs. "He is mine," she said, and Catherine shouted at Chandler, "You will not take Ann! Not Ann. She has done nothing!" But Margaret and Constance blocked her way forward, and Martins held her back. Catherine could not elbow herself around them.

"Calm yourself, Lady," said Barts. Ann did not fight him, and he shook her again. Still she did not respond. He said, "We will want to ask this woman some questions." He and Chandler dragged Ann to the dining gallery, leaving Catherine with Martins and Margaret and Constance. Martins placed one hand on his weapon.

"Catherine," said Lady Anne. She was ashy-faced. "What do they find in your chambers? What is this purse they speak of? Are you married?"

"I am not. And it is nothing. Some ready coin brought to me by Benjamin, my own profits from my own wool," said Catherine. "How many times must I say it? Where is he?"

Lady Anne turned and beckoned to Oliver, who had come up the back stairs, cup in hand, observing the scene. "I was called," he said.

"Where is Benjamin Davies?" asked Lady Anne.

Oliver bowed and said, "Still in Dover, his gentlemen report."

"Cup belong to me," said Lady Anne, tapping the metal with her fingernail. The man blushed hard and handed it over.

"I don't mean to take nothing that's not mine," he said, cutting his eyes at Martins' wheel-lock.

"You had better not, boy," said Martins. He thrust his be-weaponed hip forward and stroked the golden butt. "We have eyes in every corner of Richmond Palace."

Oliver bowed and asked to be excused. He was backing away before Lady Anne gave him her consent.

The two men who'd taken Ann Smith returned, but they'd shut Ann in. Martin Martins called, "What does the woman say?"

"Nothing," said Barts, his face aflame with frustration. "She says the bag belongs to her lady and that the money was brought by Master Davies. She is firm."

"How much is in the bag?" asked Martins.

"Precisely the amount the books fall short," said Barts.

"That cannot be," said Catherine. "It's a lie."

"I say it is the same," said the man. "I will say it to anyone."

"Then it is proven," said Martins.

"Nothing is proven," said Catherine. "His word proves nothing at all. He can say that I have taken the very shoes from Lady Anne's feet and it does not make the words true."

But Martins had turned to Anne of Cleves. "We will take the Lady Catherine and her woman for more questions. They will stand trial for this theft, on my word and the word of the spit-turner. He has heard her speak of theft. He has heard her speak whorishly. She speaks treasons. She speaks foul words against the king."

Margaret said, "She cannot have monies from Benjamin."

"You must wait for Master Davies," cried Catherine. "My daughter! Who will care for my daughter?"

Jane Dudley now took hold of Catherine's sleeve. "The little one will stay here safe. We will watch over her."

Martins pulled Catherine loose. "The women must go with us." He dragged her toward the door. Chandler and Barts led Ann Smith out. Ann stared at her feet as she shuffled beside him. The palace was silent as the men bundled the women into the front courtyard. The sun was blurred by clouds, and the wind was whipping the high branches of the trees into submission. Sebastian followed them out, and when the air hit her face, Ann Smith wrenched herself loose and spat at him. "You are that lickspittle's toady and you disgust me. We are innocent and you know it. God will roast your soul."

"Must I bind you?" asked Martins. "I will tie you if you resist me. I will stop your mouth. Come on."

A small barge was tied up at the end of the dock, and Ann said, "Let me sit with Lady Catherine. The water makes her sick."

"That you will not," said Martins. You will sit between these men, and your mistress will fit nicely beside me." He freed the wheel-lock from his side and waved it around. A boy held out a hand to help them aboard. They must have ordered it before they came inside, thought Catherine. They had already known what they would claim to find.

"Go on," Martins was saying to Ann. "Get on."

"Get on," said Chandler.

Ann was surrounded, and she stepped into the barge. The water felt skittish beneath the boards as Catherine put her foot in, but Martins pushed her forward. They slowly moved into the river, Margaret's thin complaints pursuing until the winds blew them away.

Catherine closed her eyes and counted the slaps of the waves to keep herself from weeping. Agnes would be at Richmond and she would be kind to Veronica. Lady Anne would be kind. Jane Dudley knew the grief of a mother. And she would be redeemed as soon as Benjamin came. If he came. She opened her eyes. "Where will you take us?"

"To the prison, Lady," said Martin Martins. "As I have said."

"Wherefore?" gasped Catherine. "We have not had a trial."

Martins lifted one shoulder. "I have tried to warn you. I have tried to be your friend." He picked at a knot in his belt. "I might still be your friend, Lady Catherine."

Ciaran Barts teetered toward them until he could flop heavily on Catherine's other side. The sun on his spectacles gave him the look of a large, red grasshopper. "Your room will keep you until you know who to count as your friend."

"My room? I have no room. How have you known to make a room for me?"

Barts raised one shoulder and yawned. "We have known what we know."

They bore down on the city, and Catherine watched Ann ahead of her. Her friend rode slumped, and she winced when Chandler, on her left, drew her closer to him. Ann looked thin. She tried to glance once over her shoulder, but the man flipped a scarf into her face, and she startled back to her original position.

Catherine shouted, "Do not strike her! Don't dare to strike her! Ann, are you injured?"

Martins shook her, hard. "Keep your mouth shut, Lady. We will be heard. You do not want a crowd gathering to watch your shame, do you?"

A door had opened in a flat-faced, narrow house along the bank, and a woman stared from the threshold, clutching a crooked broom, as they skimmed by. Catherine's skin prickled and burned, as though a thousand tiny candles had been lit under her muscles. Her face flushed and she bent her head, pulling the hood tight. "Do they know?" she said softly. "Are there notices that we are accused as thieves?"

"They will know you're a criminal if you shout like one," said Martins. "They will think you a common whore."

Catherine's throat closed up. Shame heated her, God's face burning down on her. Thief. Thief. Thieves hung upon crosses with Jesus, she thought, and no one showed them mercy but Christ himself. No one mourned them. Their bodies might have hung on those evil trees until the birds pecked them to bones.

Soon, the pikes at the end of London Bridge shadowed them. Silhouetted against the sky, the skulls drying upon them. Traitors and murderers. Thieves.

"And so, ladies, we are arrived," said Martin Martins.

Catherine hung her head again and seemed to feel a hundred glowering eyes upon her.

Chapter Twenty-Five

The lanes running past Southwark Cathedral were dark as tunnels, the buildings leaning their heads so close together that Catherine ducked as they passed through. She seemed still to feel the roll of the river under her feet, and she trod the muddy street with unsteady steps. A woman opened shutters and flung a pail of slop out before them, and Catherine smelt old fish splash against her skirt. She would not weep. She clutched her own hands to create a distracting pain in her palms. Her heart skidded and flipped, and her arms were alight with something like small flames. Sunlight speared the cramped way here and there and made her eyelids ache. A great wall rose on their left, and she felt that a city existed somewhere beyond it, beyond the stink of the river's rot and filth. "Where are we?" she whispered.

"Madam, you will step inside here," said a man's voice.

Catherine strained to see into the gloom. She was wedged into a black corner, and her breath stuck in her throat. "Where? Where do I go? Where is this?"

"Here." The man offered his hand.

Catherine stepped forward without assistance and found her face against a cold wall. Ann fell against her. Catherine groped for her friend's hand.

"Come on," Ann said, pushing past and pulling Catherine after her. "We will go where we must." She stepped over the grimy threshold, and when Catherine stumbled over a flat stone, Ann caught her. "Be strong now."

Catherine crumbled to her knees. "I will be sick." She placed her forehead on the damp ground, but even the smell of moldy straw and rat dung would not bring up her food. She'd had no food. Her stomach heaved but would not disgorge. The mud itself seemed to hold the scent of blood. Someone was pounding metal upon metal. Clink clink clink.

Ann's hands slid firmly under her arms and Catherine was lifted to her feet. They were facing a guard, his eyes fixed over their heads. "This way," he said, turning.

Catherine's feet went forward, over the slick pavers and down a few steps to a short unlit hall. One high, grated window was smeared with sunlight, and the yellow square seemed to tilt toward them. They passed through a spiked door. It would surely fall shut and crush them. The place surely had a name. It surely had held innocents before, as the Tower had held its queens. Queens now dead and rotting in their tombs. Queens with no heads. While the king went on, searching for another woman to warm his bed. Too slow. Everything too slow for a woman carrying a child. And now Lady Anne would need another woman to mind her kitchens. If only she had left last week. Yesterday. This morning. Catherine's hand clamped itself against her throat. "What?" she said to no one in particular.

"This way," the guard repeated.

He entered a narrow, dark doorway, and Ann Smith stepped back. Catherine put her hands upon the stones on either side and hesitated. They were slimy and frigid. She pushed. Ann breathed fast behind her. "Samson would bring this down upon their heads," Catherine said. She pushed again and a muscle in her arm cramped. She gripped and her forefinger's nail slipped against the oily surface and cracked.

"This way," said the guard once again. Catherine dropped her hands and followed.

Their chamber was low-ceilinged and dank, barely three paces across. A granite bench squatted under one grubby window. The air smelt stale and frozen. Martin Martins appeared behind the guard at the open door. "Give them a taper and a flint. Give them something to eat. Today, at least." The guard nodded and, pulling the door shut after him, departed. A key snicked in a rusty lock. They were alone. The stingy light filtered in on them through one dirty, small pane, and Ann sneezed.

Catherine's chest was alive with beating things, and her breath felt ragged and shallow. "I will die," she gasped. Then the tears came, choking her. She could not get the air into her. "I am branded a thief. I cannot live under it." She collapsed onto the icy muck on the floor, her guts shredded and hot. "I am broken. I am turned the wrong side out. I will die."

Ann sat beside her, folding her skirt under her legs. "Quiet, now. We will endure whatever comes." Her hand found Catherine's shoulder blade. "Put your head down and sleep. It will heal you."

"Nothing will heal me," said Catherine. The sobbing caught in her throat again and she struggled to get her breath. "Veronica. What will they do with her?"

"She will be safe at Richmond," said Ann. "No one will let a hair of her head be pulled loose. Agnes will stand between that child and the devil if she must. Lady Anne will guard her. Even Jane will do it."

"What will she do without a mother?" The wail welled from Catherine's throat. The animal in her was loose and there was no caging it.

"Quiet, now," said Ann. "Catherine. You will unravel yourself."

"My daughter. She will be told that her mother is a thief."

"She will know nothing of the kind, whatever she is told. She will know her mother for herself as the good woman she is. Rest now."

Catherine laid her cheek on the dank stone and let herself cry until she had nothing left but dry coughing inside her. Ann's hand kneaded the bones of her back, and she felt herself slide into sleep.

Her dreams were filled with parties of strange animals, a bird she held by the wings that tried to snap at her nose. The specter had hands instead of feathers that grasped at Catherine's hair and when she threw it into the sky she saw that it held her children in its talons. Catherine cried out, leaping after the departing thing, but then she opened her eyes and found herself in the dark chamber. It was night, and Ann lay beside her, one arm over her shoulder. Her cheek was numb, and her hip ached. Ann slept without moving, breathing through her mouth, and Catherine eased herself from under her friend. She was hollow and shattered. She moved silently to the window and gazed out but saw only an enormous nothing. Another Catherine seemed to float above her, watching the woman she had once been prepare herself for humiliation and death.

"God help me," said Catherine to the window, but the darkness had not a word of comfort to say in response. The metal clanking started up again. Clink clink clink. At least they were not manacled. Not yet. Someone walked by outside with a torch in hand, and a dim circle of light moved with him. The grass, tufted in the stones opposite, scorched briefly in the dim flame, and the wall appeared like a dark mountain behind him. Catherine leaned forward, searching the blackness for candles or more people, but the night was faceless. "I have taken some love for myself. It is no more sin than any man would have committed if he'd wanted to. What more have I done?" she said to the blankness.

"Nothing that should have landed us here," said Ann behind her.

Catherine turned. "The very appearance of wrongdoing gets a woman's head chopped off. I should have kept us low and out of sight. I should have made Benjamin write me a receipt. I should have fled in the night. Taken you and Veronica and gone while their backs were to us. I should have known that Sebastian was all ears. All of that waiting and it's come to this."

"How could you have known?" said Ann. "Martins lied. He lied as though his soul was already safe in heaven. And Chandler and Barts lied right along with him. Sebastian is as light as a feather, and he simply followed the lead of his betters. They are the arrows that speared him on. Would that they had made him a martyr for some other saint than Henry." She put her hand on the glass and watched the steaming mark it left behind. "It matters not. Our heads are still upon our shoulders. I will keep mine as long as I'm able. You may have played holiday too loosely. It's no more than other women have done. They don't do it without men. It is no treason and I will never say that it is. And it is no thievery to place money that belongs to you among your things."

"I have brought you down, Ann. You should be with Reginald, in your own house. You should be married again. Have a child."

"No more of that," said Ann.

"And Benjamin? Where can he be? Has he played me false?"

Ann shook her head. "I pray not. He is perhaps our only hope now." She scuffed a stone loose with her toe, bent to retrieve it, and lobbed it out of a tiny hole in the corner of the window. They listened for its landing, the tiny click of its freedom upon the gravel below.

"Do you think he is married to Margaret in truth?"

"I believe nothing anymore without the proof of it before my eyes. I hope we may see the truth of him before we see our God."

Chapter Twenty-Six

Food was brought in the grey light of dawn, cold bread and a jug of ale. The gaoler dragged in a wobbling table, where he left the platter, along with a short stick of candle and a flint. Before he had stuck the key back into the lock, however, a man's voice told him to open up again.

A small sandy-looking man pranced into the chamber. He was shorter than the women by several inches, and his soft leather shoes were scuffed at the toes. He bowed and said, "I am Jason LaBranche and I am here to serve you."

"Serve us in what way?" asked Ann, backing off a step. "We have already been served, as you can see."

"I will serve as your lawyer." LaBranche smiled. "I will see to it that you are released. The charges leveled against you are not to be borne. Any woman might have a list of names upon her. A purse of coin. No court of law in England will convict a woman for having things about her."

"Our what?" asked Catherine. "Who sent you? What is this place?"

"Ah. The County Gaol. Thank God you are not in the Clink." He shuddered. "Or the Borough."

"I will be on my knees with gratitude this instant," said Ann.

The lawyer blinked at Ann. "You are in the liberty of the Bishop of Winchester. He oversees the laws here."

"A great blessing," said Ann. "He seems to have set us at a peculiar liberty."

Catherine said, "They say a ring is missing, and I have been charged with stealing it."

"How old are you?" asked Ann.

Jason LaBranche touched his cheek as though he hoped to discover a beard growing there. None seemed to be forthcoming. "I have twenty-seven years on me. My father was in the law and has taught me all that I know. My father's reputation goes before me and it will bring you along, too. You have nothing to fear. I see they have given you a portal. A great privilege."

Catherine snorted. "Who has sent you to mock us?"

Jason Labranche stepped back, pulling in his receding chin, so that it seemed to disappear into his skinny neck. "Your doubts may be well-founded, ladies. I hear that your movements have been under much scrutiny, that you have been unguarded in your words. But let me assure you, this charge will be found to be without merit."

"Who hired you?" asked Catherine again.

"Master Benjamin Davies." LaBranche bent from the waist again and flung his arm outward. "My father served his family and he retained me in case you should have need. Your man was at the Davies house and says that you are in need of assistance. And here I stand."

Catherine glanced at Ann, who was scowling at the beardless lawyer. "What man?" she asked.

"One Oliver. I don't have his other name. I was called upon by one Jack Huff."

So Oliver had gone on his own. And Benjamin had thought of their welfare, before he had disappeared. But there was no Benjamin. "What are we to do?" Catherine asked.

LaBranche brightened and skipped a step forward, skidding in the muck. "We will make your statements. We will write them together. I will speak with all of the witnesses against you and those for you. And I will see that your release is speedy and unrestrained. Put your minds to rest, ladies. Your situation is a common one. There are greater criminals than yourselves under the crown of England. Put this matter out of your minds and I will see to a dismissal." He snapped his fingers above his head. Catherine thought she saw a blossom of dust spill from them. "My father has taught me all."

Ann broke off a chunk of bread. "Thank God for the greater criminals. Though I cannot give half a damn what trespasses go unnoticed under the crown nowadays."

LaBranche regarded her with a look of horror. "You must not say so. I will be required by my conscience to make report of it if you say such things."

Ann narrowed her gaze through the fog of the cold room. "Who did you say is paying your wage?"

LaBranche fluttered a letter from his jacket pocket and flapped it in the air, but he did not let go of it. "Master Benjamin Davies. You may see his signature at the bottom. He agrees to pay all expenses associated with your defense if need should arise. But I am a man of law."

"Whose law?" Catherine reached for the order, but LaBranche popped it away. She asked, "How can I know that is a genuine request from Master Davies?"

"Do you doubt, woman?" LaBranche huffed. "Why else would I be here?" He gave the chamber a cool scan. It was damp, and a rat had made her nest in the broken stone of one corner. "It is not a place to which one hurries for one's pleasure."

"I would say not," said Ann. She tore a bite from the loaf. "We are very pleased that you have gone to such trouble for our sakes. I have no doubt that our minds will take as much rest from your words as they warrant."

LaBranche bowed yet again. "The trouble will be nothing when I have freed you. You will go on about whatever business women's lives are made of, and I will have my reputation. My reputation and my father's. Now you put your minds to preserving your complexions, and I will see to effecting your removal." He smirked at his own weak wit, replaced his cap upon his tawny hair, and knocked on the heavy door. The single eye of the guard appeared. Then he was let out. The key whined again in the lock.

"I feel the blessed redemption falling upon me like the spring rain," said Ann. She poured a cup of ale and gulped it all down. "Methinks it is rather cold."

Catherine stepped to the window, where she watched the young lawyer saunter past. He was whistling. Her breath clouded her sight, and her skin sparked again with fear. She started to speak, but something like a stone rose in her throat, and she could not get it up or down. "Ann," she choked out.

"What is it?" Ann came to her side.

Catherine rubbed her neck until her voice cleared. "Will he save us indeed? Is it as simple as that?"

Ann shrugged. "Benjamin has money. If anything can save us, wealth will be what does it. Money can do what intellects cannot."

"Wealth did not save my mother. Nor the Boleyn queen. Nor the Howard queen. Wealth is not saving the Lady of Cleves from her regrets and sorrow."

"It has saved Margaret thus far."

"Margaret has an evil star shining upon her. Its light looks much like a halo."

"And what do you think evil stars are made of? Gold, that's what, reflecting the sun. They have no light of their own. They just look as though they do."

Catherine nodded. "And looks are everything these days. The king is short-sighted as ever. He prefers not to see at all when heads roll in the straw."

Chapter Twenty-Seven

LaBranche did not return the next day, or the next. Agnes came with baskets of bread and cold meat and jugs of wine, but the lawyer did not. Two chambermaids from Richmond Palace came with blankets and clean clothing, but the lawyer did not. Catherine worried about Veronica, and Agnes, one evening as she was leaving, begged for permission to bring the child, but the gaoler refused.

"The lawyer could surely make him let your daughter visit," said Ann Smith when they were alone. She had fashioned a bed from the covers that the maids had brought and was shaking out the blankets, searching for fallen fleas.

Catherine sat beneath the window. "It's better this way. What a sight for a child, to see her mother locked in a dungeon."

"It is no dungeon," said Ann. "Call it our chambers. Our private closet. We seem to be the only ones with a solid door and a window." She wiped the table that they had pulled from a dark corner and laid out their food. "Eat. You will do no good sitting there fretting."

"It warms me," said Catherine, but when Ann poured the new wine, she joined her friend. "The clouds look angry. We will get rain tonight."

"Maybe a storm will wash LaBranche this way," said Ann.

Agnes had brought Catherine one of her receipt books, along with quills and ink, and she turned to a blank page and idly drew a setting for a broken finger. "I need more light," she said, and Ann came to look over her shoulder.

"You had better not show that to anyone," Ann said.

Catherine blew across the drawing. "I have repaired such an injury myself," she said. "I have not lost a single bone."

"I know," said Ann. "That is precisely why you must not show anyone."

The sky split and shuddered. "Here comes the rain," said Catherine.

It flew at their broken pane in silver sheets of water, but the window frame held. Catherine closed up her book, Ann brought fresh cups of wine, and the two women sat side by side at the table while the storm pelted the stones.

"The glass will be cleaner," said Ann finally.

"Clean enough to show us our future?" asked Catherine.

"Are you certain that you want to see it?"

Catherine laughed without mirth through her nose. A couple of sticks flew by, and the lightning flaunted itself again. Someone was moving in the hall outside their door, but no one spoke. It was likely only the guard. The sky glowered, darker and darker, and soon they were looking at blackness, shot through now and then with the brilliant streaks of the tempest. The room gathered gloom upon gloom, and they huddled together watching the heavens tear themselves open and shower down. "This feels like the view from the grave," Catherine whispered, and Ann said, "None of that."

The storm finally blew itself out, and a few stars poked through the shredding clouds. Catherine put her head on her arms.

"Can you sleep?" asked Ann.

"What else is there for us to do?" said Catherine.

"We can finish this wine," said Ann.

The drink was good and by the time they'd emptied the jug, the billows had dissolved. Catherine and Ann lay in the soft star light and slept until the sun flung a weak beam across the floor the next morning. Catherine rolled from under the blanket and leaned over to shake Ann.

"Let me be," said Ann, scooting under the covers. "There is nothing calling me to rise."

"Very well," said Catherine. She splashed her face in the small basin of used water and put her face to the window to dry. The rain had blown down large branches from somewhere and a few stones had tumbled from the wall into the lane. On the sill huddled a pair of young magpies, their wings hanging at their sides.

"Someone has lost the way," said Catherine.

"Who?" mumbled Ann from the floor.

"Two birds," said Catherine. "Just like us, they've been driven from their home and have landed in gaol."

Ann sat up. "What are you talking about?"

"There." Catherine pointed. "Look there. They're too small to be out of the nest."

Ann trudged over and peered out. "It's a pity," she said, scratching her scalp.

"One for sorrow, two for joy," said Catherine. The mother flew in and was circling the babies, bobbing around them, winging in a circle then returning. The two nestlings watched without comprehending. She dived at them from across the lane, but they hung onto their makeshift perch and flapped their beaks open. She jabbed a bite into one of them, then soared off, leaving them to cry after her.

"That's three. Three for a girl," said Catherine. "Someone might make pets of them."

They watched for over an hour, while the young birds cried and stretched their wings, but no one came and they did not lift into the air. "This breaks my heart in twain," said Catherine. "Do you think the gaoler might give them a morsel until the mother returns?"

"I will ask," said Ann, but as she stepped to the door to call, Catherine saw one of them fall. A huge dark mastiff bounded down the lane and grabbed it up in its maw.

"Ah God, no!" Catherine shouted, but the dog had the young magpie between its teeth and was shaking its head madly. The untried wings flopped uselessly and the dog eventually tossed the body aside and snapped for the other, which fell, as though bewitched.

The mother bird swooped in just as the jaws closed. The dog was fighting off the claws buried in its ears, but it wouldn't drop its kill. Catherine yelled from the window, but the flurry of feathers and fur was only broken up by a guard, who ran out brandishing a cudgel and pounded the trio until the older magpie flew off, the dog skulked away howling, and the second nestling landed unmoving beside the first.

Ann still had her hand on the latch, and Catherine said, "Don't bother. They're dead. One alone again. One for sorrow." She started to turn from the window when the guard returned, this time leading a trio of men carrying boards and saws. "What are they doing?"

"I thought you said they were dead."

"Men." Catherine's heart clenched and went cold. "There are men. Carpenters. Tell me I'm wrong."

Ann leaned over Catherine's shoulder. "Maybe there is damage to the buildings from the storm."

Catherine covered her eyes, but she had to look again. The men laid the stack of boards in the lane and one directed the other two back to wherever they had come from. They walked off, and the leader stooped to examine the wood. "They're fixing to build something," said Catherine. She could not say the word scaffold.

"We have not even been at trial," said Ann softly. She grabbed Catherine's elbow and Catherine could feel her nails through the sleeve. "They have to give us a trial."

"I believe so," said Catherine. She went to the inside door and called for the gaoler. When a grime-circled eye appeared at the opening, she asked, "What do they build this morning?"

The eye withdrew and she could see the whole face. The mouth opened to show a row of blackened teeth. "They's only one thing built by the men in these walls, Lady," the gaoler said. His eyes widened for a moment, and red-shot whites appeared. "They's a gallows on the roof here, don't you know? Musta got tore up in the rain. You won't see it, though, unless you're close enough that there's no mistakin' what it is." He chuckled and backed away.

"Wait. Wait!" said Catherine. "Where is our lawyer?" But the man did not return. She clutched the bars and pressed her face against them, but she could see nothing but the grey hallway. "Come back!" she called, but her voice echoed back to her from the long narrow passage.

"Don't waste your breath," said Ann, sitting by the window.

"What are they doing?" asked Catherine, returning to her side.

"Bringing more lumber," said Ann. "This can't be a hanging place. There's no room. They won't kill a woman right here on the gaol top." She turned. "Will they?"

CHAPTER TWENTY-EIGHT

Catherine and Ann spent the day in silence despite the new-kindled sunlight and feeble warmth through the open window. Hammering commenced, somewhere above, and they wandered over now and then to look out. But there was nothing to see except the high, dirty wall opposite their cell. A man trudged by, head down, and Catherine halloed, but he pulled his cap lower and picked up his pace. She pulled over a short stool and stood on it, pushing her face against the panes, watching. "If they mean to hang us, at least we might have the gift of fresh air in the meantime."

Ann paced the perimeter of the room. She stopped at the window and set her hands on Catherine's waist. "Come down. We are as innocent as anyone."

"Does innocence make a difference when a mask of guilt has been set upon one's face?"

"If our lawyer would spare a minute to visit us, I might ask him."

Catherine leapt down. "He must be working on our behalf. He must. My children. They must let me see my children."

Ann gave her a mournful look and took the stool that Catherine had vacated. She watched a while, then sat on it and put her face in her palms.

There was nothing to do. Catherine counted pits in the stones of the floor until her head ached, and Ann brushed their clothes and wiped their dishes, over and over. The gaoler looked in on them twice and passed on without speaking. The invisible hammering went on, making an evil harmony with the endless clinking of the manacle-maker. "I could plead my belly," Catherine said.

"And then you would be charged as a whore as well as a thief," said Ann.

The day passed, and then the next. The last wine bottle was opened and drunk, and the last chunk of bread grew stale. Catherine slumped over her book, unable to imagine anything to record. The wall opposite brightened and dimmed, flamed for a moment with a reflected sunset, and went dark.

The morning of the third day, Agnes appeared again, slipping past the scowling gaoler. She carried a large basket of bread and cheese and meat, and a young maidservant followed her with and empty bucket and a basket with bottles of wine. Under the wine were folded clean shifts for both women.

"Thank God you've come," said Ann, taking the basket. She held a loaf to her nose and inhaled deeply. "I was beginning to feel moldy inside."

"I have a bowl of butter, but it likely will not last in this air." Agnes motioned for the girl to come forward with the bucket she carried. "I will have her leave this one and take the used one." The girl threw a thick clout over the used bucket and set the clean one in the corner.

The three women sat, and the girl hovered by the door, rubbing her arms against the dankness of the chamber. Catherine and Ann ate, and Agnes poured them both drink. The bread was white and fine, and Catherine slathered hers with the fresh butter. "You are sent by God," she said. "I have never tasted anything better."

"I would have come yesterday," said Agnes, "but there was much commotion at the palace."

Catherine's teeth stopped halfway through a chunk of cold chicken. She swallowed hard. "What is the matter?"

Agnes glanced at the girl, who knocked to be let out. Agnes waited until all was silent beyond the door, and then she leaned over the table and whispered, "It is your sister. That Margaret."

Catherine sat back. "Is she still there?"

"No. Oh, no. The ladies have sent her off, but she has returned, demanding to know where they have put Master Davies."

"Has he still not come home?" Her heart twisted a little.

"No, Madam. No word of him. But your sister, she is not to be diverted. She cried down the house, even brought the Lady Anne to the door, wondering what the disturbance was about." The young woman smirked, then bit her lower lip. "Lady Jane was white with it. You should have seen her face. I thought she'd lost every drop of blood in her. I thought she might go after your sister with her very claws."

Catherine looked at Ann. "It is nothing to ridicule," she said, trying to sound a prim note, but Ann guffawed, and Catherine could not contain herself. She snorted and had to clean her nose on the edge of a dirty shift. "We shouldn't laugh."

"Why not?" asked Ann. "Why should we sit here in the dark and the damp and the smell of our own shite and be miserable while we wait to die?" She squeezed Agnes's arm. "Now, what of Margaret? Where did she think Jane was hiding Benjamin? Under her skirts?"

Agnes waited until the other two women had regained their poise. "I don't know. It never came out where he is."

Now Catherine shook her other arm. "Then what is the matter?"

"Your sister. Lady Margaret. She says that she is with child and that the father must be found."

Catherine stood and, in doing so, shoved her stool backward so hard that it fell on its side. "What proofs has she?"

Agnes's eyes widened. "I don't know, Madam. She didn't say. I thought Margaret would know. How does a woman know? Are there not signs?"

"Her courses would cease. She might puke of a morning. The smell of fat meat might repulse her."

Agnes's head turned from Catherine to Ann and back again. "I don't know."

Ann said, "Margaret would scarcely allow herself to be examined, Catherine."

Catherine's cheeks prickled with shame and she retrieved her stool. She mumbled, "Forgive me, Agnes. You surprised me."

"Oh, Madam, I have brought you hard news. But Master Davies is nowhere to be discovered and no one knows what's to be done. That Constance follows your sister about like the cat in the dovecote, holding her skirt and mopping her face and 'Lady'ing this and 'Lady'ing that. Your sister acts like a woman made of glass."

"And has she insinuated herself back into the household?" asked Ann.

"Lady Jane called her a slut and drove her from the door," said Agnes. "Lady Anne said nothing to it at all."

"I wish I had been a bee on the wall to hear that," said Catherine.

"But she returned this morning, all tears, pounding upon doors and calling for the Lady Anne to find out where they have put her child's father."

"What does she imagine that anyone has done with him?" She swept her hand around the stone chamber. "Does she think he's hiding here, in the walls?"

Agnes shrugged, reached for a piece of the bread, examined it, and set it down again. "She does not say. It is all screaming and accusations. I can make nothing of it."

"Then perhaps nothing will come of it," said Ann. "Has there been any word of our lawyer?"

"No, not a sound," said Agnes. "Does he not come here to you?"

Catherine shook her head. "He has told us that the charges cannot harm us."

"It seems they have already harmed you," observed Agnes.

"Indeed."

Ann said, "Do you hear any news from the rest of the Davies household?"

"No," said Agnes. The gaoler banged on the door and she rose. "I will see if I can send someone to find out."

Catherine put out her hand. "Send Oliver. Do not place yourself in any jeopardy, do you hear? And the next time you come, bring me the contents of the blue jar in my still room. Empty it into a clout and tie it up and show no one."

Agnes nodded as the door was swung open. She curtsied and backed out.

Ann said nothing.

The gaoler brought meager meals of soup and ale every morning and night, but Catherine and Ann felt their dresses growing loose in the waists. Catherine's hair got dotted with lice, and she sat by the window at midday while Ann picked them out and mashed them against the wall. Then it was Ann, infested to the undergarments, and they stripped to their skins during the night and beat their clothing against the floor, hoping to dislodge the vermin.

"I will die of the itch," said Catherine, lying under the scratchy blanket she was allowed. "I would give my little finger for a handful of lavender stalks in full bloom."

"Be careful what you say," said Ann. She sat up and scrubbed at her scalp. "I will have you trim me bald when we can lay hold upon a pair of scissors and burn every hair on my head."

Outside, the dark wall showed its blank, wide face. After another three days, Agnes and a chambermaid returned with clean undergarments, soap, and blankets, and they went about making up the cell as though they were taking up residence. A basket held fresh bread and cheese, two bottles of wine, and a small linen packet. They had another empty bucket. "We came with three of the wine, but one did not pass the guard's hands. We will keep you as homey as you please, anyway," said Agnes, shaking out the clothing. "And before the sun is high in the spring sky, you will be coming back to us." She stepped to the window and, gazing down, shuddered a little and covered the motion with a brisk rubbing of her own arms. She set the packet on the table. "What else do you require today?"

"Your company, if you will sit," said Catherine. "Tell us what you've heard."

Agnes folded a blanket and they all sat in a tight circle. "Everyone speaks in whispers. The king's daughters have not returned, but that fat one, that Martin Martins, came once. He makes me sweat." Agnes picked at the hem of the blanket. "He came up behind me like a ghost, just as I was fixing a meat pasty. It makes me afraid to put my hand in my own pocket. Our Sebastian was with him. He no longer turns the kitchen spit."

Catherine said, "What does Lady Anne do? Does he treat her thus?"

Agnes said, "I never go up. I stay in the kitchen and keep my nose to the fire. I have got one of the stable boys to help me with the meat."

"Who else comes?" asked Ann.

Agnes shook her head and said, "Your sister returned. I have heard her voice. It is like—like—"

"Like a horn out of tune?" asked Ann.

Agnes laughed bitterly. "Yes. That's it. I have heard her. And that woman of hers came right down into the kitchen, that red-haired Constance, demanding sweets. Have you noted how swollen she is? Like she's swallowed a wheel. A body would say that she is the one with child."

"Anyone from the court beyond that Martins and his fellows? From the king?"

Agnes said, "No. I would've heard that, even down by the hearth. But there is talk that the other maids have been found guilty of theft. A boy who brings wood for the fire told me that he heard it."

Catherine and Ann looked at each other. Catherine said, "What will their sentence be?" though she already knew.

Agnes shook her head again. "No one says. No one even says their names anymore."

Catherine nodded. "What have you heard of Benjamin, Agnes?"

"I have not seen him," said Agnes. "But I have sent a friend of mine to seek him out. Oliver cannot risk it another time."

"A friend?" asked Catherine. "What friend?"

Agnes cocked an eyebrow. "He keeps the harness. He was given leave to visit his mother who lies ill."

"And where is this mother?"

"Ah. A bit north of London."

"How very convenient."

Agnes winked at Catherine, then caught herself and blinked. "He will bring me what information he can find."

"How does my daughter?"

"She asks where her mother is. I keep her at her letters and tell her that you have business. She sleeps with me."

"That is the best I can hope for," said Catherine. "Has there been anything from my son?"

"Nothing."

The door squeaked open, and the gaoler stuck in his head. "Time enough."

Agnes threw her arms around Catherine. Then she backed off, dropping her head. "Forgive me, Madam. I lost myself."

Catherine held the young woman's hands. "No apologies for being a woman, Agnes. I ache to feel the warmth of another person. Kiss Veronica for me."

"I will return with more goods," said Agnes.

When they were alone again, Catherine sat heavily on the warm spot that Agnes had left. "If Margaret means to stay at court, marriage to Benjamin would suit her nicely."

Ann picked at a fingernail with her teeth. "Margaret will find herself next to us in a cell. She will not be given permission." She spat and went to the window. "Benjamin has deserted us all. I find my trust in God's two-legged creatures waning." Ann sat beside Catherine again and threw the clout from the basket. "I will starve inside these walls." She broke a small loaf in half and bit into it. "Sweet wounds of Christ, this tastes good."

Catherine took the second piece. "No mold?" She sniffed and smelt smoky woodfire and oil. The flesh of the loaf was flecked with bran, but she had never put anything better into her mouth. "Wine," she said, and Ann pulled a bottle free.

The maids had packed two clean cups, and the wine was thick and peppery. The women drank and ate in silence, and Ann licked her fingers when they had finished. The rat pups nosed from the hole, and Ann threw them a crust. "We must save the other for tomorrow," said Catherine. "Agnes may not be allowed to return."

Ann upended the bottle against her lips then, with a sigh, laid it back into the basket.Catherine put her head against the wall and closed her eyes. "Maybe Benjamin sailed to

Calais to find better prices. Maybe Robbie has not been told of all this."

"Maybe," said Ann.

"My father wouldn't let Margaret publish marriage banns against Benjamin's will. He would know of it. Wouldn't he?" Heat bloomed in Catherine's chest, and she opened her eyes. The ribs of the vaulted ceiling of the little alcove in which they sat seemed to her the swollen veins of some hunched animal, ready to spring. She wanted to scratch the surface with her nails, to tear the flesh of the beast. "I am not in my right mind. The wine has gone to my head." Her throat burned, and she thought she might weep. "The hammers have stopped." She lay back against the wall. "What will we do?"

Ann shoved the basket aside with her foot and walked to the window. She laid her head against the dirty glass. "We will sit here and make ourselves merry until we are freed."

"Or until we are taken to trial."

"A trial will free us one way or the other," said Ann.

Chapter Twenty-Nine

Catherine lay watching the stars prick the night sky, while Ann slept beside her. An owl fluttered onto the windowsill and held its reign for a few moments, then dropped away from sight. Catherine laid her hand on her breast and let her heart make itself known for a few seconds. "My soul is burning a hole in me," she said to the darkness, but no one answered. Ann laboured onto her side and resumed sleeping.

The sun was licking at the edges of the panes when Catherine finally rose. Her skin itched, and she poured herself a cup of wine. She wanted ale, but there was none, and her throat felt coated with sand.

Ann opened her eyes and said, "Are you drinking away our store?" Catherine held out the cup, and Ann got up, stretching. "We might as well drink it and hope for more."

"I am losing my hope," said Catherine. "I believe it flew off in the dark."

"You must not. You have always had hope," said Ann.

"I have always been able to feel it, alive at the core of my soul. Here." Catherine laid her hand over her middle. "I used to feel my soul in me like a live thing. I could almost determine the size and shape of it. I cannot find it these days. I feel hollow. Can the soul shrivel and die? Like a flower?

Have its day, bloom and wither? Can it burn itself to an ember and go out?"

"I think my soul is more like a lump of dirt than a flower," said Ann. "It just gets harder and harder." She stared into the empty cup. "We live in a harsh time."

"Like a sun over a desert. Like a vicious sun making a desert beneath it. I feel like a narrow river, dried up in the summer."

Ann poured another cup and handed it over. "Your imagination has got the better of you this morning. You need this more than I do."

As Catherine took the drink, she heard voices commence outside their window. Women chattering. Someone crying out. "What is that?" she said.

Ann wiped at the dirty pane with her sleeve and flattened her cheek against the glass to see down the lane as far as she could. "There's a crowd. A small crowd. A dozen, no more."

"Who are they?" asked Catherine, pushing her aside.

"Don't look. You don't want to," said Ann, but Catherine was already at the window with the stool. A couple of men were leading Marjory and Temperance by the arms. A few women were gathered around them, talking and shouting, and the two girls stumbled along, their heads down. Catherine stepped up to see better. Their coifs were filthy grey, and Temperance's was halfway off of her hair. A priest stepped between them and spoke into Temperance's ear.

"They cannot," said Catherine.

The women who surrounded the girls backed away as they came toward the window, except for one who flung herself down, in front of the girls. "Is that one of the mothers?" asked Catherine.

Ann shook her head for reply.

A few men had joined the progress, mostly following silently with their caps in their hands. Marjory was led past and when Catherine cried out, she lifted her head at the sound, then tripped, falling onto her hands and knees. The priest stooped to assist her. She gazed up at him for a long moment, then gave him her hand and rose. Temperance followed Marjory's path, held at either elbow by a couple of the younger men.

A thin ray of sun shone down briefly, like mercy, but no one looked at the sky. Temperance screamed, and the priest went to her side. He whispered into her ear, but she curled into a ball at his feet, and he was forced to get down to her level and jerk her back up to standing. Marjory watched, and when Temperance was hauled, twitching, to her feet, she adjusted her hood and walked on, straight as a pin, her hands folded before her. The priest opened his book. The men brought up the rear, and then they were all gone and the lane was silent again. A soft breeze blew through the bright morning. Someone fell against their wall, and they jumped back.

"They have brought them this way to let us see it. Good God," whispered Ann.

"Does a good God allow girls to be hanged for pinching a ribbon or a coin?" Catherine wiped her eyes and felt the smear of her own greasy sweat against her hand. "Does a God who is good look on this so-called justice and do nothing?"

The crowd wound its way on by. They turned away from the window. The rat mother squatted in the corner. She was eating her pups. Ann said, "You bitch," and flapped a dirty rag until the animal scurried into her hole.

The day rose and more voices came and went outside their window. Then evening fell, the sun's last light burning at the corner of their panes, but Catherine and Ann remained unmoving in the darkening depths of their cell. They had not eaten their food or drunk their ale, which was brought in silence and now sat growing cold and stagnant in the cheap dishes the gaoler provided. A reflected ray of red lit them up, and Ann said, "I will pour." She gathered her skirts around her and pushed herself to her feet, groaning. "I am stiff as—" she began but stopped herself.

"Go on. Say it," said Catherine. "Stiff as a corpse." She rubbed her shins, then her upper arms.

Ann chanced a look out. "Perhaps they were sent back to Richmond Palace."

Catherine took the cup from Ann's hand and tried to drink, but grief clogged her throat and she began to cry. "They were just girls." She gulped the ale. It was weak and bitter. "Temperance didn't lie when she said the things were left around. We have made our island a trap for children. We lure them in with pretty things and then the men of law kill them. The church fathers kill them, priests and Protestants alike. The king kills them in the name of God." Tears came in earnest then, and she set her cup on the floor and let herself cry. Her joints and muscles were rigid with sitting on the cold stone, and she cried as much at the pain in her body. But she was tired, and the effort of sorrow wore her out. She lay flat out on the floor and closed her eyes. "'When that April with his showers sweet, the drought of March hath pierced to the root,'" she said. "How does it go? 'then longeth folk to go on pilgrimages.' Hmm. Yes. 'the holy blissful martyr for to seek, that hath them holpen when that they were sick.'"

"What is that you say?"

"It is the poet. Chaucer. He speaks of freedom and the many faces that our God shows us. The ways we go about to seek what we must find. Mother taught it to me, when I was a small girl. William loved the poets, too, before he became a father. And then he was concerned with little beyond genealogies. Begetting and begotten. And then he was no longer my William. My children. What will become of them?"

"Stand up," said Ann. "Come, walk with me."

Catherine looked up at Ann's outstretched hand. It was thin, and the blue veins rivered her knuckles. She grasped the fingers and let herself be drawn up to stand beside her friend.

Ann said, "This may be all they will do."

"Is it not enough?" asked Catherine. The weeping threatened the backs of her eyes again, but she swallowed and retrieved her cup from the floor. "To murder girls for wanting a few shiny things?" She pulled the linen packet from her pocket and shook out the juniper, but Ann snatched away her cup.

"Walk. Remember. Your children." Ann curled her hand under Catherine's elbow and began to circle the cell.

Catherine walked, and the movement loosened her muscles. They went around once, then twice, and the third time she stopped at the window and looked out, but the night had fallen and there was nothing certain to be seen outside the circumference of their small world.

Chapter Thirty

The door rattled and squeaked, and the gaoler squinted in upon them. The sun was beginning to stretch its grey morning fingers across the room. "You got a suitor," he said, and withdrew.

Catherine expected the lawyer, Jason LaBranche, and arranged her clothing, but in walked Benjamin Davies. "Catherine," he said, "forgive me."

She thought he was a specter. Then an imposter. She let him gather her to him. He was real enough, and he was himself, but then she pushed against the embrace. His arms stiffened, trying to hold her, but she shook herself loose. She said, "I am very glad to see you. At last. Where have you been? We have waited and waited."

His eyes held a question, but he looked beyond her to Ann. "We must get you out of this place."

"How did you know we were here?" Ann said. Catherine could hear her shoving the blankets aside and getting to her feet.

"A boy from Richmond Palace. A companion of your woman, Agnes. He came to the house the day I returned. We rode up the lane almost as one. I have not even stopped to order my servants."

"You have not been to Richmond, then?"

"No. Has the lawyer been to see you?"

"Nor to see Margaret?"

Benjamin said, "Your Margaret?"

Ann said, "She claims that she is your Margaret."

"What? What is happening?" asked Benjamin. He shook his head. "Has the world gone mad?"

"Sit, Benjamin," said Catherine. "We have much to tell you."

The gaoler stuck his head in the door, and Benjamin shouted, "Get out, man, and leave us be or I will get you gone myself." The man scuttled backward like a frightened beetle and pulled the door shut. Benjamin sat.

Catherine placed her hands flat on the table to keep her fingers from trembling. She opened her mouth, but her throat narrowed, and she breathed deeply. Once. Twice. She was very tired. "You have been gone a lifetime. They have killed the young maids. For theft." Benjamin was shaking his head and Catherine said, "We have seen them taken. They were brought past our eyes. For the benefit of our consciences, I have no doubt." He put his face into his hands, then went to the door and stopped. Catherine looked at Ann. She moved her head sideways a little, a gesture of indecision.

"They have not murdered those children," Benjamin said. He was pushing at the latch. "Tell me they have not."

"We did not see the deed itself," said Catherine, "but the priest was with them. Why else but to take them to hanging? Like a couple of scared rabbits caught with lettuces between their teeth, screaming all the while. It was most horrible. They have not returned."

"Why would they bother to hang them?" The latch would not give way, and Benjamin banged it with his fist. Still it would not move. The gaoler showed an eye, and Benjamin said, "Go off, man!" The eye retreated. "Where has your lawyer been in all of this? I knew his father of old. He was a good man." He ran his finger behind the hook. "I have paid him well to protect you. He was to have his ear to the ground for you."

Catherine said, "Good fathers have had weak sons. We have seen him once and no more."

"Have you been questioned?"

"Not since we were brought here," said Ann.

"I will kill him," said Benjamin. "I will strangle him with my bare hands." He went to the window and tried to open it.

"I think the lock is broken."

Benjamin called for the gaoler, then he lifted Catherine by her wrists. "Look how thin you are grown. And how pale. You need food and sunlight. You need air."

"Margaret," Catherine said. The name came up with a sickness beneath it, and Catherine swallowed some wine to keep herself from vomiting. "She says you are married." She noticed the ragged edges of her nails. "She says that she carries your child."

"The whole of England has gone lunatic. She lies," said Benjamin. "She will not maintain this to my face."

Ann said, "Her tongue does not know the flavor of shame."

"Then we will make her taste it," said Benjamin. "What is the formal charge against you?"

"Common theft," said Catherine. The heat sparked in her cheeks again. "The same charge as was laid at the feet of those two girls now dead. The king's men found the purse of money you gave me, and they say it is just the amount they have found missing from Lady Anne's accounts. And they found the list of names that you left for me. They claim that I aimed to flee the country with the money. And there is a ring missing. They claim that I have it, though I have never laid eyes upon it."

"What about LaBranche? Has he done anything at all?" Benjamin punched the table. "I have paid him from my own pocket."

"Perhaps you should have bought him some brains while you were making your investment," said Ann bitterly.

"He will hear from me. You may depend upon that," said Benjamin. He stood and called again for the gaoler. Then he turned. "Ann, Reg sends you his regards."

"I would give a great deal to lay eyes upon his face one more time," blurted Ann. She pushed the cups and bottle around.

"What is this?" Benjamin lifted the leaves from the little packet that Agnes had brought and crumbled onto the linen. "Catherine?"

"The maid brought it with some other goods."

"I will return before the sun has made his circuit again. You stay here," said Benjamin.

Catherine laughed but the sound lay heavy on her tongue. "What else can we do?"

Chapter Thirty-One

The next morning dawned warmer, and Ann did not scrape a line on the wall for the passing day. There were twenty now, and she had reached the corner. "What difference can it make how long we are here? I cannot recall when I began to mark the time."

"He will come back," said Catherine. The gaoler opened the door, and she jumped to her feet. "What do you want of us?"

He showed an iron bar. "The man says your window's not workin'. I'm gointa fix it." He stepped across and laid the bar precisely behind the latch and pried it free. "You see?"

"We are very fortunate," said Ann.

The gaoler coughed in his throat and walked out, but before he could shut the door behind him, he said, "You have visitors."

Catherine started forward, but it was not Benjamin. Nor was it their lawyer LaBranche. Martin David Martins waddled into the room, followed by Ellers Chandler. Martins was wearing the hip weapon, and he struck his wide-footed pose with his right hand on the gleaming wheel-lock. Chandler placed his hands upon his own hips and trained his narrow eyes on the women.

"Ladies. How do you? I am come to greet you and see to your well-being," said Martins. Chandler grinned like a trained dog.

"Where is your third?" asked Ann. "That flaming Barts? I thought the three of you were like the legs of a stool, unable each to stand without the others."

As though conjured, Ciaran Barts came smoldering through the door.

"I have turned prophetess," said Ann. She turned her back and walked to the open window. "And Sebastian? I suppose you have turned him loose on the Richmond girls again."

"What do you want?" asked Catherine. She wondered whether Benjamin had challenged the men. Perhaps LaBranche had finally done his duty.

"I am here to converse, Christian soul to Christian soul," said Martins.

Ann spat, and Barts shoved her against the wall. Martins guided Catherine to the opposite corner, where her head almost grazed the stones. "Now, Lady Catherine," he said. "You want to be free of this cold and dark place."

"This prison, you should say. This cell where your false accusations have landed us. We will be free, but not by your hand."

Martins' hand slid up Catherine's left side and stopped just under the pit of her arm. He squeezed gently and when she pulled away, he eased her back, close to him. "A man might find a way to see such accusations reversed. Things that have gone missing might be recovered. Papers that seem suspicious might be found to be innocent as the dawn." He stood very near to her now, near enough that his breath warmed her neck. She could feel the hardness of his weapon against her hip. "I might be as good as a loving father to you. Or a brother. A woman needs a keeper."

"What do you suggest?" she said, loudly enough for the gaoler to hear, if he were outside the door. "Will you have me bribe you, sir?"

Martins stepped back. The gaoler came into the room and said, "What goes on here?"

"Nothing," said Martins. "I have given the lady a chance to tell me where she has hidden the goods of the King's Beloved Sister and she refuses, like the liar and thief that she is. I will help her no more. She's a whore, as well, and cannot keep her thoughts from men." He cast a look up and down Catherine and jerked his head toward the door. Barts and Chandler scurried after him. The gaoler gave the two women each a long look and left, locking up behind him as he went.

Ann listened for a few minutes. "Why did he come now?"

"I don't know," said Catherine. She sat at the table and put her face in her hands. "He knows that Benjamin has been here. But I don't know what it means. You heard him bewhore me. Why now? Why? Benjamin. Where is Benjamin?"

"Is that always the bargain?" asked Ann, sitting across from her. "They promise, they take, and then they leave us to ourselves again. It is not a world for women." She drank a deep swallow of wine. "They might as well be done with it. I have nothing left in me to help me endure this."

They sat the whole day, waiting, waiting, but heard nothing except whisperings and boots going by their door. The sun slanted toward evening, and the gaoler put his face against the opening in the door. "You wanting out? Bit o' the sun on your face before it disappears?"

Ann said, "Would you?"

"Yea, I would. Got to be one at a time, though." He jangled the keys. "Got to leave my other man here with the lone woman."

Catherine said, "You go. I will shake out our things. Tell me if it's too bright for your eyes."

"You should be first." Ann touched Catherine's forehead. "Benjamin is right. You need to be outside."

"No. You. I'm sleepy just now." Catherine yawned broadly and went to the corner, where she laid her head down in the cold alcove, using a folded blanket for a pillow. "Go on."

Catherine heard the door open and the swish of Ann's skirt as she went. As soon as the hallway was quiet, she opened her eyes. A dark figure sat at the table, his legs crossed. He was fox-faced and when Catherine sat up, he moved to the window. "Join me, Lady. The air is fresh." Catherine got warily to her feet but stayed where she was. The man was tall and narrow as a strip of gristle. He put his face close to the glass. "There they go," he said, and Catherine stepped over to see. No one. Nothing but a grey cat that streaked by. Catherine backed away, around the edge of the chamber. She took up the blanket and folded it. The man stared out the window and said, "You have much to keep you busy, Lady. You might rest your hands for a time."

There were still some scraps of food, and Catherine sat on the floor to sort through the newest basket. She pulled the paper twist that stoppered the wine with her teeth. "Will you offer me a drink, then?" the man said, and Catherine held the bottle out. He drank it to the dregs. Behind him the sun glimmered on the opposite wall, and Catherine watched its gold reflection on a window beyond hers. Heard the trill of a wren. It was likely searching for a mate to share its nest, tucked up in the wide eaves.

"Do not," she said. "I beg you."

"Ladies shouldn't beg. It shames 'em. Right good that there's no one about but me ta hear it." He set the bottle aside and it clinked gently. He smiled. His teeth were speckled. He reached for her. Catherine slid backward until her shoulder touched the wall. She said again, "Do not," but still he came toward her, weighing her to the floor.

The sun shot a ray into the far window. Catherine struggled to see that spot of radiance, but the man was upon her. He lifted her skirts as she said, "No, no," and pushed against him, but he covered her face with the heavy cloth and then covered her with his body. The light went out. His hand traveled over her breasts and up her legs. Over her belly. Stopped there. "You are a whore in fact," he said, "as well as a thief. In the company of the King's Sister and carrying a bastard?"

"I confess it. I've got a child in me."

The hand withdrew, and she heard the man get to his feet. A boot landed against her ribs. Then another. Catherine cried out and turned away, rolling into a ball. "The others will know of this, and I will be paid handsomely for it."

When she opened her eyes again, Catherine lay alone. The chamber was darker now, the sun tumbled far into the west, and she had to feel for her hose. Her hand touched the empty bottle and sent it flying. It smashed in the corner, and Catherine fixed her dress quickly before she pulled a full bottle from their basket to set on the table. Ann would be gladdened to see that they still had something to drink. Catherine sat and laid her head back upon the folded blanket, curled her feet under her skirt, and turned her face to the wall.

She was in a dream of shouting, surrounded by women shaking kitchen tools and rosaries and screaming something in an unfamiliar tongue when she startled awake. "Ann?" Catherine blinked in the dim room. She heard the door creak open. "It is cold. Don't take off your cloak."

"Indeed it is frosty," said the gaoler. The door closed and was locked again.

Ann Smith dropped to her knees and felt along the stones until her fingers found the basket. The shattered bottle. "How came this broken?" she asked.

Catherine sucked the sore skin on the back of her hand. "I did it," she said. "It is my fault."

"Is there another?" Ann asked.

"On the table," said Catherine. "You must have gone a mile."

Ann found the second cup, wiped it out, and poured. She drank deeply, poured another. She said nothing.

"Tell me what has happened," said Catherine.

Ann drank. The light was blue and low, and Catherine could barely make out her friend's bare head, bowed over the wine. Ann said, "There is no honor in the law. There is no honor in the whole world."

"What has he done to you?" Catherine asked into the dark, but she already knew the answer.

Chapter Thirty-Two

Catherine gently placed her arm over Ann's shoulders. "Has he torn you?"

A great sob wrenched Ann downward, and the cup hit the floor. "I have never been a sight for men. What hell do we live in?" She put her head on her knees and covered her head with her apron. "These men are wolves. I was not even given a glimpse of the sun." Ann seemed about to lose herself in tears, but she wiped her face hard with a scrap of linen and poured herself another cup of wine. "The bastard whoreson yellow-livered coward."

"Shh," said Catherine. "Quiet, now."

"I give not a half a damn if I am heard," shouted Ann. "That vermin has laid his filthy hands upon me when I had no help. He forced me when I was desperate and alone. What man behaves so toward a woman given into his care?" A man's wet hacking sounded for a second in the hall, and Ann turned her head. "Is that you, you villain? Ask a woman to come with you, innocent as a babe, then snare her? Is that what a man does?"

Catherine said, "He has taken you when you had no defense against him. You were distracted. Helpless. They will not blame us."

"Us? What do you mean?" Ann cackled weirdly, as though her throat might crack. "And what has passed here, in my absence?" She lifted a spear of the broken bottle and held it to the dying light. Then she stared at Catherine. "Have they left you alone?" She threw the shard and it tinked against the stone wall. "They have forced you, as well. They have got us separate to use us." She heaved herself to her feet and went to the door. "We will take it to law. Do you hear?"

"He left me be," Catherine said, "but he could feel the child. And I acknowledged it. He is the law, Ann, don't you know? We are at the mercy of the law. He will stand before any judge in the land and testify that I am a slut and then he will say that I tempted him or that he saw me take something from his bench and put it into my pocket. Such a man will say anything to preserve himself. All he wants is the praise of his keepers and the pleasure of his body's desire. Such a man is no man at all. He is a cipher of the law of England. And the law is written in sand." A blast of black cold seemed to overtake her, and she shook until Ann put her face down and wept, until they lay down together and fell into murmuring, trembling sleep.

The night spread its darkness into the chamber, and Catherine eased her aching hand over the cold floor, covering them both with the blanket. Ann swiped at a nightmare, and Catherine rolled her to her side. The stars blinked down through their dirty window, and Catherine lay, watching a frill of candlelight twist in the hallway where the gaoler lurked, until fatigue overtook her and she dropped again into a fitful slumber.

A pale spill of morning woke her. Catherine had her arm over Ann's waist, and her hand was numb. She flexed and made a fist, and tiny constellations of pain lit up through her skin. She sat up and rubbed her eyes. Ann rolled to her back and breathed steadily. The strip of old scar on her throat was a thin, ghastly smile in the early light. Catherine touched her friend's shoulder, and Ann's eyes opened. "Where are we?"

"Still in the gaol," said Catherine.

Ann laid her arm over her face and groaned. "Benjamin," she said.

"What?" Catherine bent closer.

"Benjamin. He will not come. The gaoler told me. He said, 'Your lady's suitor will go before the judge and he will be hanged for a thief himself.' He meant to break me with the news." Ann flung her arm away and sat up. "I believe he has done it."

"You are not broken," said Catherine. She got up and checked the door. No one was in the hall, as far as she could see. "You will be strong." She went next to the window and looked as far either way as possible. "I see no sign of anyone."

"So we are left alone to rot."

Catherine sat again beside Ann. "No despair. Do you hear me? You will hold your head up. It is the only course to take."

"High enough for them to fix a noose over it?"

Footsteps came crunching down the hall, and Catherine laid her hand on Ann's arm to silence her. The little panel in the door slid open, and gaoler's dirty face appeared at the bars. "You awake?" he growled.

"You can see with your own eyes," said Catherine.

"Go on, then," the man said. The key rasped in the lock and the door opened. But it was not the gaoler who entered this time. It was Benjamin.

"Get you back, away from here," he said, and the gaoler skulked off. In two steps, he was beside the women. "They would not give me leave yesterday. I waited outside the court until they drove me off." The women did not move and he went on. "What is the matter? Are you ill? Have they given you aught to eat?"

"We have food," said Catherine. "We suffer from a sickness of the soul, brought on by those beasts out there." She pointed to the open doorway. "Martins was here. And then—"

"Enough," said Ann. She rolled to her knees and pushed herself up. "I will be well in time." She gave Catherine a direct stare. "Enough."

Benjamin was looking at the door. "You will come with me."

"Now? Where are we to be taken?" asked Catherine.

"Away. I have gotten the order to release you. You will come away to the old Davies House for now. The judge has appointed me your guardian." Benjamin showed a paper from his pocket. "John Dudley sent his request to the court to free you. It arrived at dawn. It made an impression." He shrugged. "I paid the fees. This judge was disposed to hold you, but he would not act against Dudley."

"So we are to be your prisoners instead?" asked Ann. She was backing away from the man and when she hit the wall she sagged against it.

"No. What? No. You are my guests." He studied Ann, as though he thought she had lost her reason. Then he turned to Catherine. "I have your daughter. She is with my Diana, and they are on their way to my country house."

Catherine could not stop herself from throwing her arms around him. "Thank God in heaven. Is she well?"

Benjamin closed her in. His face was on her shoulder. "As well as she can be without her mother."

Catherine pulled free. "Robbie? What do you hear of Robbie? What has this done to my son?"

"He is still at the right hand of the prince, the last I heard. I will send a couple of men to be sure of it." He glanced at Ann, but she was staring out the window, chewing on a nail. "I have horses outside." Catherine bent to gather the bottles and cups into the basket, and he added, "Leave those things. They're tainted with this place."

"It is a place of death," said Ann. She hadn't turned. "It kills body and soul in equal measure."

Catherine said, "Then let's be shed of it together."

Ann nodded, and, picking up her shawl, took Catherine's arm and walked out without looking at Benjamin.

The clouds had torn themselves to bits and the sun peered wearily through, white and futile. In the lane, Ann hesitated, as though letting her body accustom itself to new air, and then let Benjamin lead them on. Catherine glanced up, but she could not determine which had been their window. She saw no sign of the gaoler, or any other man.

Three horses stood riderless down by the river, and two of Benjamin's men were holding the reins. The women seized upon the smaller geldings and turned away from the sight of the dark lanes of Southwark. Benjamin threw himself up on his stallion Caesar, pointed toward the bridge, and they were off.

Ann was shifting in her saddle by the time they passed the northern city gate but she wouldn't complain. They rode on, and Ann's eyes remained fixed on the twitching tail of the horse in front of her. Catherine trotted up beside her, and reached for her arm, but Ann shook her head fiercely and kept her eyes where they were. No one suggested stopping for food or drink, even when the midday light shone over them.

It was barely dark by the time they were on the road that led up to Davies House. Here, it had rained, and the mud ruts from cart wheels caused the horses' hooves to slip, but neither Catherine nor Ann cried out. Their mounts plodded on, and when the decayed crenellations of the house showed through the trees, Caesar nickered and stepped up his pace. The others flicked their ears forward and spoke back in snorts and soft whinnies, and Ann leaned forward to stroke her gelding's russet neck. She huddled over the animal's lathered neck until they turned the last corner.

The stable lads were already running up to take the horses, and the front door was opened by Benjamin's boy, Little Jack Huff. Behind him, Catherine recognized Reginald Goodall. Reg stepped down toward Benjamin, but when he caught sight of the women he paused. A couple of maids ran out behind him, and as Catherine and Ann slid to the ground, the girls curtsied and took up the edges of their filthy cloaks.

"Where is my daughter?" asked Catherine, running into the big front room. A maidservant with a warming pan in her hand scurried upstairs, and before Catherine could remove her outer garments, Diana Davies was leading Veronica down. Agnes was with them.

"Mother!" the child cried, and Catherine knelt on the bottom step to catch her daughter. The girl smelt of grass and clean child's sweat, and Catherine's eyes leaked tears, though she tried to blink them away.

Diana sat on the step beside them. "It is good to lay eyes upon you, Lady Catherine."

"And you," said Catherine, swiping at her face and reaching for the young woman's arm. "Agnes, what do you do here?"

"I was asked to go, when Diana came, and she took me. Richmond felt empty as Christ's grave anyway. No one talks now."

Catherine twisted to look up at Ann Smith. "Ann, our Veronica is well and sound. Come, she aches to see her Auntie Ann."

Ann sat on the other side of the steps, and Veronica slid onto her lap. She laid her head against Ann's chest and sighed. "Auntie Ann, what have you brought me?" The girl felt along Ann's ribs and hips. "Have you hidden a sweetie for me?"

Ann's mouth smiled. "I have brought you a lucky stone," she said, digging into her pocket. What she brought out was a chunk of gravel. "This stone has great force in it, and you must hold it tightly in your hand, like this." Ann made a fist. "When you feel that the world has grown too bold for you, you hold this and it will make you hard as granite, impossible to break." She dropped the rock into Veronica's hand.

Veronica lifted it to a nearby candle. Her blue eyes were fixed on the dull surface. "I cannot see its power," she said.

"The power is deep within," said Ann. "And only deep need will bring it forth. Use it wisely."

"I must put it in my jewel case," said Veronica. She pecked Ann on the cheek and hopped up. "May I be excused?"

"Go on," said Catherine. The child ran, Diana scampering after, and Catherine looked at Ann. "What was that?"

Ann gazed up the stairs. "My fingers found it on the ground as he was upon me. I squeezed it so hard that it took my fear away." Ann opened her right hand, revealing the bloody scab stigmatizing her palm. She shrugged. "It was all I had."

Catherine put her arms around her friend, and they sat in silence until the men clambered through the door.

Reg carried Benjamin's cloak, and two dogs from the stables followed them in. One, a rangy hound with ears that flapped around its jaws, shuffled up and stuck its wet nose under Ann's chin. Catherine jumped to her feet, but Ann laughed through her tears, and roughed up the animal's sloppy jowls. The dog crooned and fell onto its side, raising a forepaw to expose its belly for scratching. Ann obliged until Reg whistled.

The dog withdrew, and Reg helped Ann to her feet. "I won't have you grovel on the floor to a badly-behaved animal," he said.

"You don't know how happy I am to feel his dirty old fur." Ann regarded her hands. The fingertips were blackened. "Don't touch me, Reg. I'm not clean."

"Clean enough for the likes of me," he said. "Come on to the hall. Let's have a bite of dinner." He offered his elbow, and she backed away.

"No. I mean what I say. I'm dirty." She looked around. "I must wash." She ran up the stairs before they'd been assigned rooms.

Benjamin watched her go. "What has happened, Catherine?"

Catherine said, "A prison is an unkind place. That's all."

Reginald took a step up, then down again. "What'd they do to her? I've got to know."

"You'll have to ask her, then. In time."

Reg exchanged a long look with Benjamin. "Doesn't matter. Not to me. She's the same woman in my eyes."

Catherine stepped between the men and forced Reg to shift his gaze to her. "You had better be sure of that, Reg. Think. Be sure. Be sure forever or be nothing to her at all. Do you hear me?"

His eyes softened. Then he turned away. "Your dinner'll be cold, Lady. Let me get the maids to serve you." And he walked off.

Benjamin stood close behind her, and Catherine could feel the heat of him. "I've sent two men on the run to bring news of Robbie," he said.

She nodded, closed her eyes, and inhaled. Leather and horse. Old wet wool. It smelt like home.

"Catherine," he said.

She knew his arms were out, and she shook her head. "Come, let's eat the food they've prepared." She opened her eyes and walked into the dining hall. Benjamin followed without a word more.

CHAPTER THIRTY-THREE

Ann did not come down to eat, and Catherine sat at the table with the men until Reg finished his evening meal and, rising, ordered the kitchen girls to take away the unused dishes. He nodded to Benjamin and followed the maids out, pulling the doors closed behind him. Catherine let Benjamin fill her cup.

"Did they ravish her?" he asked.

Catherine drank. "He promised to take her out to feel the sun."

Benjamin poured for himself but did not lift the cup. Instead, he pushed the meat around on the pewter plate with a slice of bread.

Catherine said, "You want to know what they have done to me."

"Tell me if you want to."

"I remained inside. A man was sent to guard me. He touched me. He felt it. I affirmed my condition to keep him off. He could undo me with this knowledge."

Benjamin breathed out through his mouth. "Some men are worse than beasts. I have not forgotten Adam Hastings or that day at the convent."

Resentment tugged at Catherine's chest and her jaw clenched. "You were not there. How could you remember it at all?"

The man drank. "William. Your husband told me what you told him."

Her heart froze against her dead husband for a moment. "He should not have told it. He was broken by it and never loved my son. He could never quite clean his notions of the boy from the stain of his mother." Anger bloomed up in her then. "And he did believe me stained. As though it was my sin. I will not see the same happen to Ann."

"And you?"

"I am in danger of exposure. I will be called both thief and whore."

"I call you neither. And not all men are alike," said Benjamin. "We must get you away from here before anyone comes." He broke the bread and dropped it. "And I don't believe it was the event itself that turned William. It was taking the place of his brother. He wasn't bred for it. And Margaret. His sister poisoned his mind more than his body."

Catherine considered this. "He did not have to be in her company. He might have saved himself an infection and moved to cleaner air."

"I don't mean to speak ill." Benjamin lifted a shoulder. "But blood will run together."

"So it is said." Catherine looked up. "And you. Have you spoken to her?"

"Margaret? Why should I speak to her?"

"She is claiming you for a husband. Saying she is with child. Or have you forgotten?"

"No, I haven't forgotten. But I have nothing to say to it. I am not guilty of it. I wonder if she has gone mad."

"Mad as a vixen," said Catherine. "She will try to convince Lady Anne to force you to acknowledge her."

"Let her try. I will not do it." He had emptied the bottle into his cup. "You might show her a drop of pity."

"Wherefore?"

He shrugged again. "She lies. She plots. But think of it. Parceled off to the convent to keep the family fortune for her brothers. And you, the favorite of your house. You were. I have heard you say it yourself. You have put her down, and she's the last legitimate Overton daughter. She has nothing. No house. No husband. No children. Nor like to have either. She has done everything according to king and church and her father all of her life and is empty-handed as a reward. It must look mightily unjust from her eyes."

"You will defend her to my face?" Catherine burned. "She has also tried to poison my family."

"I know." Benjamin called for another bottle. "Go on to bed, now," he said to the small servant who brought it, and Catherine was alone with him again. They sat, listening to the house settle into the soft night. The rafters above cracked gently. He said, "I am trying to be fair. And honest. I was not the one who freed you."

"No? It looked like you, coming through the door."

"I carried the order, and I spoke for you. I threw them a few coins, as I said, but that was nothing. It was John Dudley. He is the one who turned the key for you."

Catherine stroked her forehead. "That man. That politician. Why would he?"

Benjamin lifted one shoulder yet again. "I can't say. He sent letters to Dover, as well. The man snaps his fingers and suddenly I discover myself undetained. And find I can take you home."

"So you were not lingering there for the wool? Or to avoid me?"

Benjamin shook his head. "Is that what you thought? I was not imprisoned exactly. But a dozen men with swords and a determination to keep a man inside an inn can work their wills quite easily."

"But why?" Catherine asked. "Who wishes us such ill?"

"The judge said I had been mistaken for another man. I was told to go and I went. I saw no prudence in mincing the matter. If I were a guessing man, I would put in the name of that Martins. He seems to have had you much on his mind. But now he seems to have disappeared."

Catherine laid her head back. A cat yowled from a distance, and Benjamin rose to pull the shutters closed, then sat again without speaking until Catherine said, "We will settle this business of the marriage and the child. In public. With you and Margaret in the same room."

Chapter Thirty-Four

For a week, Catherine allowed herself to rest and wait for news from Margaret. She petted her daughter. She listened to Diana Davies prattle. She quietly visited Benjamin's small still room. But by the eighth morning, she could wait no longer and came down, a fur thrown over her shoulders, as the sun rose. Benjamin was already up, directing the servants.

Catherine said, "We should be on the road."

"I have ordered men to search her out. We will wait until we know where she is. What? Do you think you will ride the streets of London, shouting for her?"

Ann appeared at the top of the stairs. Catherine said, "Where would she be?"

"If Agnes has not heard, then I certainly haven't. She is not at Richmond."

Catherine went out to cool her head, just as four men came in, storming up the dust. Benjamin came out behind her. Catherine said, "Who is that?"

"They're mine. The ones I sent to Ashridge about Robbie." The party swung to the ground, pulling off their hats and bowing. Benjamin said, "What news?"

The leader approached and bowed. "Lady Overton?"

"I am she," said Catherine.

"Your son, Lady. We come with sad tidings. Your son has fallen from his horse."

The air went cloudy-white. "Is he alive?" Benjamin's arms were around her, easing her to the ground, and Veronica was running out, crying "Mother, Mother," and Catherine stumbled backward until her foot hit stone and she sat.

"He has a leg wound," said the man. "Sir, do you mark me? Can you make the lady hear? The boy sends word that he wants his mother to come to Ashridge. The prince wishes it, as well. He has ordered it."

The fog around Catherine dissolved into black and yellow spots, dancing like tiny demons before her eyes. She was lifted then, and her daughter was at her side, tugging her skirt.

"Mother?"

"We must journey west, Vere. Your brother calls for us and we will not say him nay. "What think you of seeing a prince's court?"

"Does he wear a golden crown?"

"We will have to find that out for ourselves, won't we?" asked Catherine. "Shall we follow the sun?"

"Yes, Mother," said the child.

Benjamin was already running back inside, ordering food and servants to ride with them. Catherine called for Ann to pack their bags.

"I will stay," Ann said. She pulled open the chest with the finer things. "You will ride the faster without me."

"But we will see the prince!" said Veronica.

"I have no wish to see the prince, kitten," said Ann. She tucked in two heavy cloaks. She murmured to Catherine, "Will you tell him about your condition?"

"I think not. Not now. He's just a little boy. He's hurt."

"Take care, then. Of the boy and yourself. Give him my love."

Catherine put her arms around her friend. "Walk in the fresh air. Eat. Heal yourself."

Ann held Catherine out before her and looked her up and down. "Physician, I might say the same to you. You are nothing but bones. You're not hearty enough for an odyssey."

"And yet I am called to go," said Catherine. "The springtime will mend me."

"I pray that all will be well."

Reg appeared at the door to say that the horses were ready. Benjamin was already testing the belly-bands when Diana came out with a maid, lugging food.

Benjamin turned Caesar in circles, then leapt onto him. Catherine patted her pony and let him smell her. Ann handed Veronica onto the little mare that Benjamin had ordered up for her. She gave two bags to the manservants on the big geldings.

"Are you certain that you are woman enough to ride by yourself?" Catherine asked Veronica.

The child took up her reins. "Overtons ride before they walk," she said, and Catherine's heart twinged at the child's words. "My brother says so."

The way west lay open, and Catherine urged her palfrey forward, praying into the broad blue sky before her that her son would be alive, waiting for her, when they arrived.

Chapter Thirty-Five

Three days of riding under the sun. Three days of dirty inns and narrow beds, without enough linen to serve them. On the second night, Benjamin knocked softly on the door where Catherine lay, but she did not answer, though she lay alone. In the dark, she seemed to see the shadow of Margaret skulking in the corner. Then the eyes of a man. Then the dark bulk of the king himself.

By day, Catherine's haunches ached, and Veronica complained until her mother let her share the palfrey, leading the little mare behind them. The fields were already greening, and Catherine pointed out the ground-dwelling birds in the grasses to her daughter as they rode by. Benjamin kept his distance at the front until late in the evening of the third day. The setting sun splayed its massive fingers across the sky before them, and Catherine held her hand in front of her face. Veronica was dozing, leaning back, and when Benjamin whooped, the child sat up straight.

Catherine allowed herself to look, and here came the man, riding and waving until he circled the palfrey and trotted up beside her, saying "We'll be there before nightfall. I can see it."

"What?" said Veronica, twisting to look up at Catherine. "What does he see?"

"Ashridge," said Catherine. "Where your brother lies."

"Robbie!" the child cried, and she struggled against her mother's arm. "Let me ride with you, Master Benjamin. You are the faster."

"Your mother rides right here beside me," said Benjamin. He touched Veronica's nose. "And you should be commanding the reins of your steed."

The girl nodded and laid her fingers on top of her mother's hand. Catherine said, "What will you say to your brother when you see him? He is laid low with an injury and you must not excite him, do you hear?"

"I will sit by his side and serve him his supper," said Veronica. She reached into her coat and showed the poppet. "I will let him hold Cleopatra." Catherine smiled over the child's head, but her heart squirmed in her chest.

The ladies of the household dawdled at the windows as they rode up, whispering to one another. Only the royal nurse came outside and stood, her arms crossed over her breast, until Catherine dismounted and lifted Veronica to the ground. "Lady Bryan," Catherine said, curtseying. "You see me returned once more into your company, whole and sound with my daughter. How do you this many a day?"

Lady Bryan softened about the shoulders somewhat, and she finally smiled. "Lady Overton. You are thin as a snake. Do they keep you from your own kitchen?"

"No. It has been a hard road. Tell me, how fares my son?"

Lady Bryan pointed to the bags as some Ashridge maids skittered past, dipping to the ground briefly, and the girls lifted the small items from the animals and returned to the house. "He recovers handsomely. He has taken himself to the bed just now. You must eat, and I will see that he is wakened to greet you."

"Have you had any news of my coming?"

"We have had much news of you," said Lady Bryan evenly. She stepped backward and examined Catherine. "Is there anything you would like to tell me more?"

"No, Lady Bryan," said Catherine.

"I see you have brought the man," Lady Bryan said.

"Benjamin would not have us come alone."

"No. I suppose he would not. Come, you will dine." She wrapped her fingers around Catherine's right elbow and tugged. "We will restore your health, at least."

"Would that my good name might be as easily restored."

"Reputation," said Lady Bryan under her breath. "Easily marred. And hard to recover, for a woman. At least you have your head upon your shoulders. And you will be perfect from now to doomsday. We have all laid bets upon that."

Catherine coughed. "And how does the change of life come along? Do your pains still plague you? Have you some relief since last we met?"

At this, Lady Bryan touched her breast and her voice went liquid. "I am cursed with it, night and day. My mouth carries the taste of old coins. And the heats grip me like a demon." She took hold of Catherine's hand. "I am glad to see you well. Come inside. The boy will want to clap eyes on you."

Catherine followed, leading her daughter, while Benjamin and Reg took the horses toward the stables. Inside, the hive of waiting ladies broke apart, some waving briefly, others leaning their heads together before buzzing off. Two women approached to lay their hands on Catherine's arms and say "blessed to see you here, Lady Overton" before they disappeared to hidden rooms. Catherine and Veronica were left alone in the great hall with Lady Bryan, and when, from a distance, the Prince of Wales, surrounded by a flock of young boys, called out, his thin voice echoed through the open space. "Hallo!" he cried out again, as though they were dairy maids returning from Christmas with their families.

Catherine dropped to her knees, and Veronica copied her mother. "Your Grace."

The boy was a winter stick. Catherine watched his skinny shanks come to a stop before her. The fine hose wrinkled around his ankles. He said, "Stand up, stand up and let me see your face." Catherine rose to her feet and pulled Veronica up beside her. "Mother of Robert Overton. It is pleasing to see you come when your son is in need." He regarded Veronica and bent to study her face, hands planted on the flat planes of his hips. "Are you a good girl? Do you mind your elders?"

"Yes, Your Grace," murmured Veronica, glancing up at her mother.

"And do you obey your brother?"

Veronica shifted her weight from one leg to the other. "Yes, Your Grace."

The prince nodded, his eyes narrowing slightly. "Girls should learn to obey," he said. "Brothers are meant to guide their sisters. And sometimes sons must guide the mothers." He nodded to them both, then turned and signaled to two serving men to follow. The boys swooped into formation around him. The women stood unmoving until he had disappeared with his train around the corner.

"And where is the lady-maid?" asked Lady Bryan. "Your Ann?"

"She did not feel well after our ordeal," said Catherine. "She is too weary to ride far just now and stays at Benjamin Davies' house to recover. She would not be a burden to you."

"There is no burden in this house," said Lady Bryan, swatting the air. "There are rooms for all. The king sees to it. As long as she is clean."

"And what do you hear of Kat Champernowne? I mean, Kat Ashley?"

"Still an Ashley, still governess to the Lady Elizabeth. Content, I believe, though it is a task I would go out of my way to evade."

"I've seen her lately," said Catherine. "Elizabeth. She seems, well, high-spirited."

"Overwrought and hysterical, you might say," murmured Lady Bryan, "if you were allowed to say anything at all of the prince's sister. She is too much the mother."

Catherine went after Lady Bryan into the great dining hall, where silver dishes of food were being laid out. She heard the men's voices, but they went on by. "Eat," said Lady Bryan. "There is always food. I will return."

The table offered meats and bread and a large dish of steaming carrots, dotted with green leeks. Jugs of red wine and ale, surrounded by clean cups and goblets. A little maid came to Veronica's side and said, "May I serve you, Madam?"

Veronica squealed and clapped her hands. "I am a Madam, Mother!" She flounced onto a chair, set Cleopatra on the table beside her, and nodded at the maid.

Catherine sat next to her daughter and filled her own dish. "Do not overstuff," she said, but the bread was so soft and sweet that she could barely contain herself. Benjamin came in with Reginald, and they took their places across from Catherine.

"By my soul, the food is good," said Catherine.

Benjamin opened his mouth, but Lady Bryan was in the doorway before he could speak. "Your son asks for you."

Catherine was on her feet. "Lead on."

Robbie's chamber was on the second floor, and he lay alone in a vast bed. A man sat beside him with a volume of the gospels in his hand, and he rose at Catherine's appearance and moved silently, head bowed, through the door at the back of the room. Catherine stopped at the sight of her son, pale and small in the middle of the wide mattress, but Veronica ran past and had almost leapt up beside him when Catherine grabbed her. "No, he's injured."

Robbie smiled at his sister, and Catherine laid her hand on his brow. "My dear son," she said. "I praise God to see you healing."

The boy struggled among the heavy bedclothes to sit up. "Hallo, Lady Mother. And you, my sister. Kiss me." Catherine lifted the girl and she pecked her brother's cheek.

Catherine moved to the foot of the bed. "May I look, Robbie?"

The boy nodded, and Catherine uncovered his leg. His right foot was wrapped in pristine linen. It looked normal enough. It was not swollen. "What dressing have they put upon it?" she asked, and Lady Bryan said, "The physician says it is not broken."

Catherine unknotted the cloth and rolled it back until the ankle was exposed. A small island of bruise, already yellowed at its borders. She put her thumb against his arch. "You can wriggle your toes?" she asked, and he showed her. She stroked the bones and found them straight and strong. "A poultice of thyme would settle the blood. I see no need for the wrap."

"Will I ride again, do you think, Mother?" Robbie sat up, watching her work.

"I expect you will," she said, "but only if you vow to be more careful in the future."

"Set my sister here beside me," he said, and Catherine helped the girl onto the bed, where she patted his hair.

"How does the boy?" Benjamin Davies stood in the doorway. Reg was behind him, and Benjamin stood aside and let the serving man enter.

"Master Robert," said Reginald.

"You were my father's man," said Robbie. He stared beyond Reg to Benjamin Davies. "And what do you do here?" His gaze slid to Catherine. "Why is he here?"

Catherine's breast sparked. "Master Davies was your father's faithful friend, and he has done Reg a kindness by taking him on. You know this, Robbie."

Robbie scrutinized Reg, then Benjamin. He said to Catherine, "Do tell us what has happened in London. They say some of the girls in your care confessed thefts and treasons. That they spoke ill of the king and wished for his death. Their mothers should have been whipped for letting them go to the devil."

"Never. They never said such things," said Catherine. "They were silly children who were tempted. They should have had their knuckles rapped and been set to milking the worst-tempered of the cows. That's all. To kill young girls for having the judgment of young girls—"

Lady Bryan cut in. "Young girls often decide badly."

"You have taught me," Veronica said, "Will they kill me, Mother? For being a young girl?"

Catherine's throat filled with embers, and she said, "You are a good girl, Veronica."

Benjamin said, "It is the fault of these new, rising men, and the constables and lawyers. They must have the courts filled and so they listen to slanders against gentlemen whose greatest crime is to wear their sleeves out of fashion and old farmers who cannot remember the Pater Noster in English. And helpless girls."

Catherine stole a look at Lady Bryan, but her attention was fixed on the window. Robbie, however, had gone scarlet. "You question the reforms? Our laws?"

"I do not," Benjamin said. He walked over to the bed and gazed down on the angry boy. "I question the punishment of English citizens on only the word of men who are paid to find someone to accuse. Or think they will be paid. Some men in this land are so corrupt that they would condemn their own mothers to death because their dugs dried up. The court relented toward your own mother only because they had orders that forced them to do it. They accused her on libels and would have convicted her on a lie. They might have put her head in a noose. You might be grateful to see your mother alive."

Robbie ignored Benjamin and looked full at Catherine. "I have forgot myself, Mother. You and your companions are most welcome." His mouth lifted into a shadow of a smile. But his blue eyes remained cold.

Chapter Thirty-Six

The night was alive with voices, and Catherine lay in the big bed she was assigned, listening to whisperings in the hall. Twice, someone ran past her room, but the footsteps faded before she could get up. Veronica slept beside her, unaware of the noises. Catherine laid her hand on her belly. She wanted Ann. By the time the dawn yawned across the east, grey and foggy, she was up, dressing herself. She roused her daughter and sought out her son.

But Robbie was not in his chamber, and Catherine hurried on down to the dining hall, where she found Benjamin surrounded by the ladies of the house. When Catherine walked in, he elbowed his way across to her. "I am as welcome here as the sweat. I should ride back to London."

"You seem to have gathered quite a little court," said Catherine.

"They want to know about you," he said. "Let me go. Your son would be glad of it."

Lady Bryan came in and sat at the head of the table. "Ah, Master Davies. You mustn't mind young Robert. These boys change with the wind." The servants brought in more food. "Come. Eat." She beckoned to Catherine, and Benjamin took a chair at the foot of the table.

"It is not as easy as that," Benjamin said. He was forced to raise his voice to be heard the length of the room.

Lady Bryan approached to speak more softly. "I see how it is. When the recent storm has blown by, the black mood of the king will pass with it, and all will be well."

"Yes, all has been so well under the king," said Benjamin.

"What do you say?" asked Lady Bryan.

"Nothing," said Benjamin. "I say I would have Lady Catherine well."

"Put it out of your mind," said Lady Bryan. "She is free now. No one will speak any more against her."

Catherine snagged a fistful of bread and bit it. "Where is Robbie?"

"Up and about," Lady Bryan said.

"The injury does not seem severe," said Catherine.

"Perhaps not. But the boy insisted that he would see his mother. You are his best physician."

"Do not call me physician. It's not permitted."

"What will I call you, then?"

"Mother will do for me."

"Then mother you will be."

Catherine hacked up a bit of unchewed crust and did not look at Benjamin. Robbie was wheeled in on a chair, pushed by a young serving man. Beside him walked a golden boy. Yellow hair, a burnished gold silk jacket, and bright brown hose. He smiled around at the women like a tiny courtier. Robbie Overton said, "Mother, this is my riding companion."

The radiant child bent into a theatrical bow, and Veronica slid from her chair to stand before him. "I am Robbie's sister," she said. "And who might you be?"

"He is Guildford Dudley, Sister," said Robbie. "Perhaps if you grow up to be beautiful, he will marry you."

"You are Jane Dudley's boy," said Catherine. "Your mother and I have served the Lady Anne of Cleves together."

The little boy smiled up at Catherine like a mischievous angel. "I know of you, Lady Catherine. My father saved your neck when you were called bad."

Catherine knelt. "That he did, and I will always be in his debt." The boy smiled again. He was as perfect as a human could be, and Catherine's heart suddenly blazed for Jane. No wonder she was so child-proud. "Your mother is a fine woman."

"My mother obeys my father," said the child, "but my father learns what orders to give from my mother. My mother says that you know things. She says that you have some magic in your touch."

"My ankle does not pain me this morning," said Robbie, wheeling between them. "Your poultice works its charm."

Catherine turned to her son. "God puts the healing properties into the plants. The hands of mortals can only bring them to their proper use." She sent the serving man away and pushed the chair up to the table.

Benjamin was sitting across from them, but the boy did not greet him. Instead, he said, "Where is our Reg, Mother?"

Benjamin said, "He is rubbing down the horses."

"Do you mean to steal my mother away so soon?" The boy set his eyes upon the man. Guildford Dudley jumped onto a seat next to Robbie and helped himself to food. Veronica tugged on Catherine's skirt.

Catherine said, "Benjamin has accompanied me here. He sees to the Yorkshire property for us."

"That land will be mine one day," said Robbie. "And the house."

"It will, Son, God willing," said Catherine. Her hand was steady on Veronica's head.

They finished the meal in silence, and Catherine, pleading fatigue and taking Veronica by the hand, excused herself to her rooms.

Veronica sat on the bed, swinging her legs. "Will I marry Guildford Dudley, Mother?" she asked.

Catherine laughed. "That is just boys' talk. You will marry whomever you choose."

"And where will I live? If my brother has our house?"

Catherine studied her daughter's face. So serious for a little girl. She looked almost like Elizabeth Tudor. "You will live in your own home."

"And where will that be?"

Catherine pulled her daughter onto her lap and held her. "God will show you, Vere. Keep your eyes open and see what is before them. Let no one tell you what you observe. Do you hear me?"

"Yes, Mother." Veronica struggled free, and Catherine let her go.

The door opened, and Robbie's extended foot entered, followed by Robbie himself in the chair, and the serving man pushing him again. "My ankle will be pleased by another of your poultices."

Catherine said, "Come in and entertain your sister while I go and make it for you."

Robbie nodded at that. "Get on, Vere, and my man will give you a ride in the hall."

Veronica scrambled onto her brother's lap, and the man pulled them out, pivoted the chair and trotted down the hall. Veronica squealed and buried her face into her brother's chest, and he put his thin hand on the back of her little coif. Catherine watched until they got to the far window. She turned away so that they would not see her tears.

She took the servants' stairs down to the still room, and was bent over a bowl when Benjamin's hand touched her collar. She said, "Robbie could walk today. He could run. He has scarcely a scratch."

"You have not even seen whose hand is on you."

Catherine did not move. "I know your fingers well enough."

"Your boy would run indeed if it would run me off," said Benjamin.

"He is a little boy yet, and he is jealous of his mother." She did not look at him. "You should see how he loves his sister."

Benjamin put his arms around her waist and nuzzled the back of her neck. "We could be gone from England before the summer is fully here. But I will steer clear of your son in the meantime."

She twisted to look into his eyes. "If you think it best. He is only a little boy."

He kissed her on the nose before he answered. "I think it safest," he said. "He flies very near the sun."

Chapter Thirty-Seven

Robbie Overton decided to walk again on the seventh day. Catherine had wakened every night, drunk on the scents of the room, feeling her body change. She could not allow Robbie onto her lap, even if he still felt the desire to ask. The last morning she opened her heavy eyes to the sound of children's voices trilling in the hall outside her chamber door. Veronica sat up and, throwing off the covers, said, "That's my brother," and ran out the door. Catherine followed, tying a robe around herself and straightening her nightcap, just in time to see a tiny troop charging around the far corner, Veronica trailing after them in her night dress.

"Daughter!" Catherine called. "Do not chase those boys!"

Veronica stopped and almost popped her thumb into her mouth but wiped her lips instead and hung her head. Catherine knelt and her daughter ran into her arms. "They do not want me."

"They do not know what they want. They are just boys. Come, let us spy upon them." She lifted Veronica and, propping her over the knot of the new baby, carried her to the stairs, where they had a view of the broad gallery below. The prince appeared, a twiggy colt of an heir, and the boys gathered about him like a stable of restless young horses.

Prince Edward beckoned with one hand, and Guildford Dudley trotted to his side. Catherine heard "How is our Robert this morning?" and her son stepped forward and bowed. He ran after the others when Edward turned on his gold slipper and dashed away.

Lady Bryan joined them. "He shows his father's royalty in every movement, does he not?"

Catherine swallowed. "He is his father's son."

"Thank God for him. Your boy looks well, Catherine."

"Well enough to chase after his prince," Catherine said. "It is time for us to travel back."

"We will miss you. You could bide here. The king wishes for his son to have the best care. I would like to have you by my side. Send the men away and stay."

"It is not for me to lay hands upon the prince," said Catherine. For a moment, she thought on it. The beds, like soft fields. The rich food, cooked by others' hands. But she could find that at home. She said, "My son, as you say, is healed."

"Ah," said Lady Bryan. "Still, you might stay. Unless there is some pressing reason that you cannot." She patted Catherine's shoulder and walked down the stairs, holding the hem of her skirt away from the pointed toes of her shoes.

"Will you remain here?" asked Benjamin, who had come up behind them. "Would you?"

Veronica said, "I will go. I have my own mare. I have no need of a prince. He is just a boy."

Benjamin guffawed, and Catherine clapped her hand over the girl's mouth.

Downstairs, as they sat for their morning meal, Robbie came skidding into the dining gallery and slid into a seat beside her. "You cannot leave, Mother. I am barely upon my feet."

"You are flying through the air," said Catherine, "as fast as gossip. Your prince will be glad to have you back in his company. And I must see to your home."

The boy regarded the fish that lay upon the plate. "My home. Yes, Mother. You must go, it seems. And I must stay with the prince." Robbie shoved a wad of bread into his mouth, and at a call from beyond the room, was gone. His eyes did not fall on Benjamin, and Catherine saw no more of her son all the day.

Chapter Thirty-Eight

The Ashridge servants had them packed by the next morning, and Catherine waited in the front courtyard for Caesar to be bridled. Veronica's little mare pawed impatiently at the gravel, and just as Benjamin came around the corner of the palace, leading his stallion, the troop of boys appeared at the front door. "The prince waits for you, Mother," said Robbie. He cast a frosty glance at Benjamin but kept his narrow body turned toward Catherine.

She followed him inside, leading Veronica by the hand, toward the receiving room, where the ladies who kept the royal boy parted fluidly to let them through. Robbie Overton stood before them. "Sister, come and tell me good-bye." He held out his arms and Veronica skipped to her brother. "Does our mother allow you to play all the day?"

"What?" said the child. She held up the doll but the boy ignored it.

Lady Bryan announced, "The prince will bid you farewell, if you think it best that you go." She looked at Catherine.

Robbie Overton marched away, with his sister capering after him. Benjamin said, "Courage," and held out his arm for Catherine. She refused it. They crossed the great front hall into the room where the skinny prince saw petitioners and penitents. Edward Tudor occupied a carved chair that was too large for him, and his feet struggled to find the nap of the carpet. His arms sat awkwardly along the wide sweeps of polished wood, and when he nodded, he seemed to be getting his balance on the bow of a great ship.

Robbie Overton bowed and moved to one side, folding his arms behind his back like a miniature courtier. Someone had provided him with a slim dagger which he wore on his right hip in a black leather sheath. One of his toes gently tapped the floor.

Benjamin and Catherine knelt. Veronica walked away from her brother and joined them.

The prince struggled to the floor and stepped forward. Robbie Overton stood beside him. From behind the chair stepped Guildford Dudley. The pale, royal hand came out and rested on the air above Catherine. "I give you my blessing and this warning. A mother's example is a gem in the crown of her son's good name. Or it is a stone in his shoe. The sin of a mother stains her children. Be virtuous, Lady Overton. And obedient."

The benediction ended and Benjamin relaxed. He coughed lightly. The air moved, and Catherine thought someone whispered "whore," but when she dared a glance up, she saw only the shining Guildford Dudley, whirling his bright little cape as he withdrew. Her son and her prince stood over the adults, unmoving, like a pair of righteous cherubs, stiff and formal, their expressions distant as the stars and cold as the gaze of indifferent gods.

Prince Edward waited until they had risen and then extended his hand over them again. "Go safely, Catherine

Overton," he squeaked. "Your Robert will be at our right hand."

Catherine backed away from the diminutive blessing. Robbie embraced his sister and whispered into her ear. The prince gave her a thin gold ring set with a tiny garnet, and Veronica gasped and held it up for her mother to see.

"Your Grace is most generous," Catherine said, hearing an echo in her head from years past.

Lady Bryan stepped forward and embraced Catherine. "Our prince is already kingly," she whispered. "And your daughter is a beautiful girl. Take care, Catherine. England has eyes everywhere."

Catherine made her arms envelop the other woman for a moment. Then she led Veronica away.

Robbie did not touch his mother until they were outdoors, and when he hugged her, his arms were tight, his body stiff. "Ride with honesty, Mother," he said. "It is a rare enough companion for a woman."

She did not look back as they headed away. But as they turned onto the wide lane, her eyes slid off to the side. The distant building seemed painted onto the thick air. The day was already hazy with new heat.

Catherine bounced along, greeting strangers on the road with a nod, watching her palfrey's ears twist forward and back. They passed three men at a crossroad, cloaked in old blankets. One of them wore a leather patch, and Catherine felt the one eye following her as they rode by. A fly lodged in her palfrey's left ear, and she reached out to catch it. Mashed it and flicked it away. Rode on. The day grew warm, and she tossed off her cloak. Bored, she slid her fingers along the velvet ear again, and the animal yanked his head to the side. "My ride is annoyed with me."

"It seems so," said Benjamin, "but he will have to endure his misery. As do we all."

"My son will prosper with the prince."

"He seems to grow well enough under that sun."

"He is not directly in Edward's inner circle of boys," Catherine said, "so he will get less of that heat. Perhaps some obscurity would be safer for him."

"He seems safe where he is. He looks close enough, to be sure."

"The Dudley boy is certainly a forward duckling, isn't he? He is a friend to Robbie. It may be good for them both."

"Yes."

Catherine flicked the reins against her palfrey's neck, and he flinched. "Tell me he does well there, Benjamin. Tell me that Robbie will grow up to be a good son. A good man."

"Oh, Catherine. You ask me to foretell what no one knows. Goodness gets a foothold in a boy's soul or it does not. And it can be dislodged any time by a kick of Fortune's toe. He is your son and you love him."

She sighed. "He loves the rule of law."

"Will Fortune kick me?" asked Veronica.

"Pitchers have ears," said Catherine. "You must seize your Opportunity by the forelock, Daughter, and drag her so that Fortune's boots cannot get at you."

"Look!" said Veronica. She held up her right hand. The ring sparkled in the light, and she giggled. "I am the prince's favorite! Fortune wouldn't dare to kick at me!"

"Quiet, Vere," said Benjamin. He looked back. "Do not show the ring."

"What is it?" said Catherine.

"We passed three men, back at the last crossroad. I didn't like their looks."

"Were they ugly?" asked Veronica. She'd tucked her hand into her skirt.

Benjamin laughed. "Ugly as Satan. So ugly they had covered their faces." He looked again. "I think they have let us go by."

Catherine's guts were icy. "How long do we ride today?" she asked.

"To the end of the light," said Benjamin.

Catherine cocked her head and considered it. "It is such a long ride."

Benjamin said, "Do you not trust me even to steer you right on a road?"

Catherine looked at him, but he stared ahead. Margaret's tale had almost become a fairy story in her mind, with the man so close and her sister-in-law so far away, but memory settled in like an evil angel, spurring her indignation. It ached along her sides. They rode along for a few seconds in silence, and she decided. "I will go as far as you take us this night."

He nodded and spurred Caesar up to Reg. They conferred, heads together. Veronica continued to admire the winking of the little stone in her ring, now hidden on her lap. Catherine settled back into her saddle and let the palfrey follow the waves of dust his master raised down the long road.

Chapter Thirty-Nine

They walked into a village at dusk and Benjamin stopped at the first crossing to peer down the lane, left, then right. He spoke to Reg, pointed forward, and led them to the next junction. Again he looked one way, then the other. He shook his head and walked on. Reg then halloed and pointed ahead, and Benjamin waved for the party to follow him forward.

They turned into the courtyard of an inn with a sign of a red dragon, and Benjamin threw his reins to a scrubby boy who had wandered up, scratching his head, from the stable. Catherine and Veronica rode up behind the men, and Catherine jumped to the ground and helped her daughter down. "Where are we?" she asked.

"The Red Dragon Inn, Madam," said Reginald. He took the back door. He was too tall, and Catherine watched as he ducked and went into what had to be the kitchen.

"I can see a sign," said Catherine. The courtyard was cramped with piles of firewood and broken barrels. The building itself appeared to list southward, and the frames of its low-browed windows matched the short door into which Reg had disappeared.

"You will be happy enough for the night," said Benjamin. "Wait here for me." He threw the boy a coin and walked the palfrey and Veronica's mare to the stable. When he returned, he was grinning. "All is quiet. We'll be safe here."

Catherine followed him around to the front, and let him hold the door for her and Veronica. She had to step down to enter. The rest of the men had gone in the back way, and the three of them stood in the gloomy public room. She waited until her eyes could bring shapes into being. The innkeeper called came forward and bowed. "Lady Overton. Honored to have you here. Supper is laid. I hear your road has been hard. I am glad you found your way to us." The table was covered with roast duck and platters of carrots and leeks. Loaves of white bread and jugs of ale. Catherine took the edge of a bench and a manservant filled her cup. She sloshed the ale around until the colors of the candles, swimming in its golden surface, loosened her mind and she could swallow.

The innkeeper sat at the foot of the table and helped himself to meat. Catherine looked to Benjamin, but he was stuffing his mouth and said nothing.

"What did you say these men looked like?" the innkeeper said.

"Three," said Benjamin through his chewing. "Wrapped up in dark clothes. Blankets over the top. I couldn't see their faces. One had only a single eye. He wore a patch."

The innkeeper shook his head. "Not talk much of thieveries on the roads hereabouts." He pushed the platter of meat up the table. "Never heard anything of them. No one-eyed men around here."

Catherine said, "You two are acquainted. The Red Dragon. You are a Welshman."

Benjamin smiled into his cup. "You think we all know each other?"

Catherine's face flamed and she chewed her lip. "I'm a fool. Forgive me."

"As it turns out, we do, Catherine." He pointed at the innkeeper with his knife. "This is David Jones. Wouldn't stay in my brother's service."

"Wouldn't say a word against your brother, sir," said the innkeeper.

"No, you wouldn't," Benjamin said.

"And so, those men this morning?" asked Catherine.

David Jones shook his head a second time. "These parts are quiet, Madam. If there were men hunting down travelers, we would know of it."

"That's good to hear," said Benjamin. "We will sleep the more soundly." But his eyes still held worry.

In the morning, Catherine slipped out of the bed, wrapped herself, and walked down to the warm kitchen. The early sunlight struggled against the small windows of the Red Dragon, and by the time she could make out a low line of scrubby apple trees in the yard, Benjamin had come down, stretching. A chambermaid crept in behind him, and he said, "Girl, pour us some ale."

The maid searched around until one of older servants heard the racket and, still in her nightclothes, lifted two goblets from a corner cupboard and set them before Catherine and Benjamin. "The ale's in the cellar, sir." She flounced a little curtsey, cut the younger girl a look of contempt, and disappeared.

"Go see that my boots have been polished," said Benjamin, and the smaller maid brightened. She went out just as her older fellow was returning, and they let a wide swath of air blow between them as they passed in the doorway.

The bigger maid poured for them both, and, leaving the jug on the table, picked up an egg basket and left them alone. "She's a good worker," said Catherine.

"They're all fine in their ways," said Benjamin. "They're just children. Not too much danger for them out here in the country. No jewels much, or fine things lying about."

"A pleasant situation for them," said Catherine. She melted a little toward the man.

"I wish you had stayed in the country. People say the King's Sister keeps a loose household. I should have taken you out of it."

"It was the king's choice, Benjamin. A lady's palace should be a harbor, not a snare." Resentment tugged at her thoughts. "But her position did not loosen the noose on Margery and Temperance."

"Christ's bones," said Benjamin. "The law is a tyrant."

"And the king makes the law."

"The king exists with the parliament," countered Benjamin.

"And he is the husband and father of it," said Catherine. "And its pope."

"It is not a peaceful family. May God forgive us all, because we surely do not forgive each other."

"God has been mighty quiet these last years."

"Then we will make the best of the quiet and call it peace."

"I have heard of some kinds of peace that make quiet seem a grave."

The smaller girl returned with the glistening boots. Benjamin slid them on and stood. "Catherine, don't be angry with me. We have done no great sin, have we?"

"Sin, yes. A great one? I can't judge that anymore." He'd moved nearer to her, and she touched his side. A muscle moved under her hand, and her heart leapt. "The woman gets the fault laid at her door when the man rides away with a clear conscience. We are all sinners, are we not?"

He laid his hand gently on her shoulder and guided her toward him. "And we are all redeemed already, are we not?"

He smelt good, fresh and green, and Catherine let her head fall against his familiar chest. His body moved against hers, and she trembled. "I must hear the admission from Margaret's own mouth. I would rather be alone than pecked at by rumour."

He set her away from him. The innkeeper came into the room, and Benjamin gripped his host's hand, just as Reg entered from the front to say that the horses were saddled.

"We must go," said Catherine.

Benjamin said, "You heard our lady, Jones. I am gone."

CHAPTER FORTY

The horses were assembled in the front courtyard, and Reg was checking their hooves. They were on the wide road before the sun had lifted its crown over the eastern treetops. Reg stayed behind, and the other four servants rode before them. Veronica complained until Catherine let her come onto the palfrey. She gave the mare to Reg, and then she lagged, trying to picture Benjamin with Margaret. She still had a maid's shape, and those fine hands. The Overton women all had fine hands. Hers were rough, and the nails were brittle.

Benjamin pivoted his horse and stopped. "Where are you? Has that palfrey turned to stone? We will be at the house before you leave the grounds of the inn."

"I don't want to muss my clothes," called Catherine. But she heeled the flanks of her ride. The palfrey swiveled its head and bit her toe.

Benjamin said, "Come, let me in on the women's secret."

"The country has a large king and a young prince," said Catherine. "That has been all of my musing."

"You are a great prophet, Lady Catherine. We would have no news at all if it were not for you."

Catherine fussed with Veronica's coif and ignored him until he pulled his stallion's head around again.

They rode almost without speaking until they were in the open country. The cold breath of spring still clouded the fields, heavy with bright dew. Then they entered a wooded stretch, and Catherine relaxed in the friendly shade and drew her fur wrap up to her chin. Veronica was dreaming, slack-mouthed, in the crook of her arm. She twitched, her mind working on some private child's matter. Catherine remembered something her mother had said to her, in those days when she was turning into a woman: "All men are different. All husbands are the same."

Catherine was working her brain on a retort. An answer to a dead woman. She stuck her heels into the palfrey's flanks and Veronica jumped.

They rode on, the men urging them, faster, now, through the villages and farms, woods and open wilderness. A few walkers stepped aside as they clopped up behind, and a few people came outdoors to watch, but no one raised more than a distracted hand in greeting. Benjamin turned in his saddle and watched any man on a horse until he was out of sight. The sun ruled the day, pushing fat clouds along as it made its progress across the sky. Then it tumbled, and their shadows grew longer, canting off to one side, as the air grew cold again. Veronica's stomach complained loudly, and Reg produced an apple from somewhere among the folds of his clothing. She chewed at its flesh as they rode along.

Catherine barely knew she was on her feet again when they turned in at the lane to Davies House and slid to the ground. The saddle had cramped her muscles, and, taking Benjamin's hand, she stumbled with little Jack Huff past the hulking front door. The great hearth in the dining gallery raged heat, and she fell onto a stool gratefully, holding her palms to the flames. Benjamin ordered food and drink, and Ann came running in.

"How does the boy?" she asked.

Catherine drank the ale that was set at her elbow. "He does very well. He had nothing but a bruise, no more than this." She held up her thumb.

Benjamin said, "Catherine was asked to stay."

Ann raised her eyebrows. "They must hear nothing, out there."

"Oh, they hear," said Benjamin. "We were subjected to more admonitions than a priest would deliver. If we had been ordered to be any better, I would have thought they meant to send us to the angels forthwith."

"What does Robbie know?"

"Only of the prison. And of the maids. It was enough. Lady Bryan had her eyes much on Benjamin."

"She has seen him in your company before," said Ann.

"And she has not forgotten it, either." Catherine drank. The ale was good, but she said, "It tastes like dirt. Like mortality." The liquid came back into her mouth, bitter and bilious, and she forced it down again. "At least it is not bouncing." She looked around the dim room. "My tongue is ruined for taste tonight."

Benjamin set down his own cup and wiped his mouth with the back of his hand. "Bring wine."

"I am almost slain," said Catherine, rubbing her haunch. "The only thing I want is a bed." But she up-ended the cup and emptied it.

Ann said, "Don't you want the story of your sister-in-law?"

Catherine was suddenly overcome with the cold and moved to the fire. She sat on a stool near the hearth, watching the wisps of her breath disappear into the darkness. The flames cast a wedge of gold light over the floor, and Catherine pulled herself inside it. Benjamin turned his chair to face her, and Ann came to sit at her feet. Agnes came in with a maid, and Ann said, "Veronica, there's your friend Agnes. You go up with her."

Catherine said, "Go up, Daughter." When their footsteps had gone into silence, she said, "Tell us."

"Yes," Ann said softly. She put her hands to the fire. "The word from Overton House is that Margaret left there in a rage. And from London, that she has settled herself into Benjamin's town home, maid and all."

"So we will travel to London." Benjamin stood, sending his chair skidding backward. "She will have to open our door to us."

Ann idled her hand over her skirt. It was fine, embroidered at the hem. She had kept it covered with the shawl, but now she cast the outer garment aside. "I expect she will claim you for herself, Benjamin. She seems to have taken your house for her sanctuary."

"I am no priest and my home is no chapel."

Ann said, "Here is one of your men in the shadows. James! Come in and tell them what you told me."

A servant edged into the room and slid forward until the flickering light caught him. Benjamin dragged him into the circle. "What do you say? Does she mean to stay?"

The man James twisted a short lock of dark, oily hair and spoke to his boots. "She had a letter delivered to her, as though she was the lady of the house. When she opened it, she fell on the floor like a woman almost killed and said she was your wife and that you wouldn't be wed to no other. We didn't rightly know what to do, her with her fine clothes and all."

Catherine said, "So she is mistress of your property, Benjamin."

Ann looked at Catherine. "And a bed in his house."

"She is no such thing," said Benjamin. "This is a farce she plays to get attention for herself. She is afraid and looking for a place to hide. She should have stayed in Yorkshire."

"We will see," said Catherine. "I must get myself to the bed." She staggered up, and Ann caught her arm. Catherine vaguely hoped that her clothing was free of lice.

When they were closed in upstairs, Catherine said "My God, it is good to see you." She pulled Ann into her arms. The familiar warmth. The clean water smell of her hair. "You're a little fatter," she said.

"Diana has been stuffing me like a plowman." Ann pushed Catherine away to look into her face. "How is Robbie? Tell me truth now."

"He's well. The injury was nothing. He wanted me to come so that he could scold me, and when he saw that Benjamin was with me, he wanted me to go. He is hard. I have never seen a child with such a skin of anger on him."

"The world has made him so. But you're his mother, and he must love you."

"He loves his sister," said Catherine.

"All men love their sisters when they're little."

Catherine set her hand on her belly. "He will not love this one." She looked up to see Veronica by the door to the maid's room, thumb in her mouth. "Daughter, come here." She removed the thumb. "You will mar your ring."

Veronica's eyes widened. "Auntie Ann! Look at what the prince has given me!"

Ann admired the small stone. "You already shine like a great lady, Vere, and it is plain for all to see."

The little girl twirled, and Ann swatted her on the rear. "Now off to bed with you, so that you will not grow bags under your lady-eyes."

"You must tuck me in, Mother."

"You have been in too many strange beds lately," said Catherine, and she swooped the child up and carried her to the narrow bed in the tiny adjoining room. Agnes was already snuggled in, and Catherine laid Veronica beside her, kissed her head, and pulled the door closed. Ann was bent over the basin and she looked up with a dripping face. The rafters barely gave her room to stand straight, and Catherine touched one of the beams. "It is a short building," said Ann. "It is a good thing that it's not lower, or our feet would punch through the floor."

The laughter burst from Catherine, so hard that she doubled over with it to stop the sound. "Ah, Christ in the East, Ann, it is good to hear your voice."

Ann sat on a stool, dried off, and stared at the closed window.

"You can see nothing there but the reflection of the candle," said Catherine. "Come over here and drink with me."

"The world is nothing but reflections and shadows," said Ann. She took the cup Catherine offered. "I search for my face and see a darkness in the shape of a woman."

"We are all shadows in the night. Look again in the morning and you will see a different view."

"Perhaps. But we may appear only as pale specters, under the eye of the sun."

"We are free. Let us celebrate it." She clinked her cup against Ann's and they drank.

Ann gazed at her reflection in the window. "Will you keep this child with you? And you unmarried? Robbie will be against you, for certain."

"He will." Catherine examined the dark drink. "One evening's carelessness and the world is made perilous for a woman. It is unjust."

"My flowers have come and gone, so I am safe. What do you think? Can you still want any man after all of this?"

Catherine lifted a shoulder. "I will not have Margaret's leavings and I will not be with a lying husband. Robbie, poor boy. Veronica can keep William's picture in her locket, but Robbie turns himself the wrong way out to keep himself shining in the prince's eyes. Mark me, someone has told him that he's a bastard, though he will not say it. I wonder if someone has said that his mother is a whore. His talk. You would not believe your ears. He has taken some book on women's faults to heart."

"Go back and fetch him. He can be in his home, whatever he is called."

"He is planted too deep in the royal household, and he needs to stay. But it breaks my heart for Veronica. Will she have to be disinherited because she's a girl? My mother would not have done it. Folks called her hard, and they said she had the temper of a devil. Perhaps she did, but the strait ways of the world made her as she was. She was never so mean-spirited as she was when the king moved against us."

"No one of us bore that well," observed Ann. "It turned us against each other, at the end. It shames me to think what Furies we became."

"But she had some love in her, though it was not out for plain view. My mother would have left me all she had to give, if it had been left in her power to do it."

"And as it turns out, you have it all anyway." Ann mused, pulling her lower lip. "Then do as she would have done. Give Veronica the convent buildings. Have your father will his house to her. The boy can have the big house and the little village. The girl will have the smaller house and big village. How would that be?"

Catherine refilled their cups. "You have a genius for management, Ann Smith. Now can you tell me what to do about Margaret?"

Ann looked almost like herself again. "Now there's a temper that we cannot lay at the king's door. Toss her from the high window. Her head is soft enough to land upon without injury. Or if Benjamin does not prove true, let him catch her for himself."

"Benjamin says I should show her some compassion." Catherine pulled off her sodden shoes. "He has catalogued her misfortunes for me. In truth, they're not few."

"And he aims to win your heart with this sort of talk?"

"Beshrew me, he's a fair man, if I think on it with a level mind." She threw one of the shoes at the wall. "I believe Reg would like to ride by your side."

Ann sucked inward. "He might think he does. But I saw as well as you did what happened to William. He loved you.

He was good, at first, and fair as you claim Benjamin is. And even he couldn't bear to think that another man had touched you."

"It was his station. Being the heir was forced down his throat, and it ate him from within."

"Station. It is all their talk." Ann said, "I once heard of a house cat who swallowed a great mouse. So eager she was to have this mouse that she swallowed the beast without biting it first. And the mouse resented its captivity and began to chew its way out. The cat could not disgorge the mouse for its large size and died of her prize. The mouse, finding itself at liberty, went on to devour many a sack of flour."

Catherine mused on the tale. "Am I this mouse?"

"This was a mouse of monstrous proportions. A mouse of estate, you might say. A mouse of station. And woe to the cat —or the man—who swallows the lure of high estate in this land."

"William fought it as well as he could. Reg is different."

"Not great, you mean?" Ann stood and began to loosen her dress. "Too low-born to care who's rutted his woman?"

"No! You know that's not what I meant. He knows where he is in the world and he knows himself. If he'd been born a lord he'd be a lord. William was born a younger son and he didn't know how to be anything else. The same is true of Benjamin. But he doesn't care a fig about his brother's position. He prefers some sheep for himself."

Ann pulled off the heavy dress and sniffed her armpits. "I still stink. I need a better wash. I cannot even move my elbows in this room."

"You smell like yourself," said Catherine, but she stepped to the door and called the chambermaid to bring warm water.

Ann spoke in a whisper. "I'm sorry. I'm not myself these days. You say right. Reg is good just as he is."

While they waited, Catherine tried to untie the laces at the back of her own dress, but she couldn't reach them. Ann did the task nimbly, and Catherine was down to her own shift by the time the girl brought the heated ewer, set it on the table, and scooted out. Catherine said, "Give me your hand," and she gently wiped Ann's scarred palm. "Are you injured? Inside, I mean?"

"No."

Catherine scrubbed her own neck, then under her arms. She lifted her feet one at a time, and after running a clout around her toes, rinsed the clout, washed between her legs, and hung it over the edge of the basin. She stood, hands raised, before the dying fire until she was dry, then covered the embers and sat. "Tell me the truth."

"I don't bleed much, but at my age I wouldn't expect to. It hurts me some to ride." She nudged Catherine. "He wasn't big enough to tear anything." Her shoulders fell. "But my soul."

"Oh, Ann," said Catherine. She held her friend in her arms, but Ann did not cry. "Men do not know what it is to be a woman. They break us open and then blame us for being broken."

Ann said, "They sing praises to women's beauty, and then chastise us for looking into mirrors. They demand freedom of conscience for themselves in order to leave us, and in the same breath demand perfection of us. They think they can use and discard us and that we will miraculously restore ourselves to maidenhood and find another."

"Perhaps all will be well when we know the truth about Margaret."

"Perhaps the king will decide that England is too tight a fit for him and he will sail off to the New World and never be seen again," said Ann, pulling away.

Catherine tried to smile, but she couldn't hold it. "He will squat here until he dies." She shuddered.

"Do you see signs of mortality on him?"

"He's not at Ashridge, but Lady Bryan says that the leg will not heal. An open skin lets infections in. A world of corruption swirls around us, beating to get inside. He is melancholy as a bear and roars at his men. I say he will never live to see his son married." She let her hair fall down and untangled it with her fingers.

Ann said, "And so we will have a boy king. God help the kingdom that is steered by a child."

"I think God has cut us loose from the port of heaven already. Jane Dudley's son is among the prince's train. The inner circle. They are like a herd of hot colts, nipping for position."

"Colts step into holes sometimes. They break their legs," said Ann.

They crawled under the linens, and Ann reached over and pinched the last taper to death. Soon, she was breathing in her steady nighttime rhythm. The night held no moon and the darkness wheeled over them all. Catherine lay in the blackness, listening to her friend. She wondered what window what Margaret lay looking from, conjuring her own demons against Catherine's return.

315

CHAPTER FORTY-ONE

The next morning, the room stank from the ewers of dirty water and Catherine's muddy clothes, strewn over the planks of the floor. Catherine sat up, holding her nose. Ann was beside her, flat on her stomach with her arm hanging over the edge of the bed. Agnes was talking in the next room, and when Catherine stepped from the bed, as quietly as she could, Ann said, "Are we going already?" She hadn't moved, but her eyes were open.

"The light is up," said Catherine. She peeked into the hall. "No one else is stirring yet, though." The hall was as familiar to her eyes, it seemed, as the ones in Overton House.

Ann rolled out and stretched. "You are as punctual as a rooster, Catherine. And every bit as welcome at dawn."

Catherine opened the window. The cold had moved back in. Fast-moving clouds usurped the early sun, and she threw some kindling onto the hearth and took the wash water down to the kitchen herself. The cook was rolling out pastry, and heaps of cold meat and onions waited in a bowl next to it. The ovens gave off a hellish heat, and Catherine went on out, tossing the water into a shallow ditch.

She was barely dressed. She shivered. She should go back inside. Wake the others and be ready to ride. But she

316

hesitated. The cold invaded her breast, and her teeth chattered. She wanted to know the truth. Of course she did. And then what? To know Benjamin for a lecher and reject him? And then what to do with the child?

A maid came rushing across from the little dairy shed, hauling a bucket of milk, and she almost walked flat into Catherine. "Madam!" she startled out. "You are nearly blue with the cold. Have they locked you out?"

"No, girl," said Catherine, taking the other side of the bale. "I was just going inside."

The girl smiled, happy to have her load lightened, and Catherine said, "Have you any yarrow in your stores?"

"I will see," said the girl. They set the bucket beside the cook.

"Do you know how to make a tea of it?"

"I do."

"Make me a strong batch, if you have it, and bring it up to my chamber."

Catherine made her way up the stairs and met Benjamin standing at the big central hearth. He said, "Can you bear to ride again so soon?"

"I have ordered a tea sent up for Ann." Benjamin tried to draw her to him, but she said, "I must wait for the tea."

"You ordered it sent up."

"Ah. Yes. So I did." Catherine backed a step. "Ann must be well enough to ride." Her shivering began again, deep in her belly and reaching to her shoulders.

Benjamin said, "Do you shudder at the thought of my touch now?"

"No," she assured him. "At the cold." But the fire was blazing.

"Go drink that tea."

She let Benjamin kiss her on the fingers, then she said, "I will fetch Ann," and ran off before he could see her face.

Catherine gulped deep breaths all the way back up the creaking steps, and she found Ann glaring at the cup and pot on the table before her. Agnes and Veronica were walking her poppet across the bed.

"We must heal," she said, but Ann pushed away the brew.

"I need real ale," said Ann.

"It's good for you," said Catherine.

"It stinks." She picked it up, tasted it with her tongue, and set it down again. "By the crucified Christ, that stuff will be the death of me. What is it? Hay?"

"It knits a woman's insides together," insisted Catherine, thumbing the cup back. "I will put honey in it if you want." She poured for herself and drank it down.

"You can dissolve diamonds in it." Ann pushed the cup away again. "Give me some good strong ale. That will cure me."

Agnes pulled Veronica onto her lap and fixed her coif.

Catherine said, "You must drink this. It's better than ale."

"That brew tastes like horse piss."

Veronica sniffed the tea and asked, "What tastes like horse piss?"

"Nothing," said Catherine, taking up the cup. "Your Auntie Ann is feeling much better."

Veronica put her hand on Ann's knee. "How do you know what horse piss tastes like?"

Ann laughed her whole laugh at the child. "I am going in search of ale. A woman's drink, not an animal's." She got up from the chest she'd been sitting on and flipped Veronica's bag onto her shoulder. "This one weighs nothing. Vere, have you got all of your skirts in here?"

The child put out her lip. "I haven't got but a few. You and Mother have piles of them."

Agnes placed her hand on the girl's head. "I brought changes for you and your mother, tadpole, in my chest. And when you are my height, pretty gowns will fall from the trees for you."

"What? From the trees?"

"She is teasing," said Catherine. "We will have new ones made for you. Here, put this in with your things so that it doesn't get any dirtier than it is." She unwound the green band from her waist that she had worn for the prince and folded it so that the flowers, picked out in golden thread, were turned inward. "We will take enough to keep us. In case we do not return here."

Benjamin knocked, and, when they called for him to enter, stepped inside and saw the women's things piled together. He hefted one side of Ann's chest. "You can't take all of this. Come, let's get on the road. Catherine itches to play our lady knight, who will ride up to the castle and lay siege."

Catherine's cheeks scorched. "Don't mock me."

"Do you see me laughing? I will stay by your side like your best gallant. And then you will be forced to take pity on my plight and offer me your hand."

"Benjamin." Catherine reached for his fingers, then dropped them. Ann pushed Veronica out the door and Agnes followed, pulling the door shut.

He said, "And you will let me languish in my misery until then?"

"You are not miserable," said Catherine.

He took her hand and she let him pull her toward him. "I am miserable. I know you better than any man has. You have pushed and pulled me for years now and I am stretched to your will."

"So you say and so I am sure you believe. But a woman wooed and a woman wed are two different creatures in a man's eyes. I would rather shake hands and be friends than distrust you."

"Friends?" He put his arms around her and she let her head fall back. "Would you say we are friends?" He brushed her lips with his, and his beard tickled. She pinched her mouth tight to keep from sneezing. "What, do I taste so bad as all that?"

She stroked the bristles on his upper lip. "It's that." Then she did sneeze. He let her go and she fished in her pocket for her handkerchief. She blew her nose and said, "You do not need me."

"What I need is this," he said. This time he took her face in his hands and kissed her full on the mouth.

Catherine let herself lean on him, let her hands cling to his jacket. He was warm. Or the heat came from inside, her ribs searing her heart. She gasped, pushing him back. "I am burning up."

"You see?" he said. "You were frozen, and now you are on fire. For me. Do you want me upon my knees?" He started to go down, and she tugged the shoulder seams of his jacket.

"Someone will come in and see you."

"Let them see," he said. "Ouch." He rubbed his left shin. "You see what you bring a man to? I grow too old for courtesy and will have to resort to simple begging."

"Now that I would like to see," said Catherine. She reached for his hair, but the door opened and Ann came back in. Catherine jerked her hand back.

Ann said, "The men are mounted. The men outdoors, I mean." She bit back a smirk.

Benjamin bowed formally and scooted from the room.

Ann plucked up the other bag. "You have made a great deal of progress in the loading."

"We have been discussing business. The fleeces."

"Fleecing. What else would you talk to a man about?" A couple of manservants had followed her in. "She has decided to leave them after all." They bowed and went out again. "Are you going to tell me or let me wonder?"

"There is nothing to tell. He's a man. There is an accusation. I must know the truth of him. And after that I don't know where I will go."

"Accusations. We know of them, too. You could find yourself yoked to something worse, for all that."

"Or not yoked at all. Not to anything but my own sins."

"Oxen wear yokes," said Veronica, dawdling in the doorway. "They smell bad."

"You see? Out of the mouths of babes—" said Catherine.

"I'm not a baby," pouted Veronica.

"No, Vere, you're not." Catherine pinched her nose. "But you're wiser than your years, and your mother doesn't like bad smells."

Chapter Forty-Two

The sun had retreated to a high place in the pale sky as they mounted and rode toward London. The grasses flattened in the wind, and sheep turned their shorn backs to its whipping. Catherine slouched into the fur lining of her travelling cloak and watched for early cyclamen and violet. Twice they passed by small woodlands with flowers, but the men were slumped onto their saddles, and Catherine let them go by.

Agnes, riding one of the pack animals, had a Davies maid and two of their manservants as companions, and they chattered along, as though they were all out for a pleasure ride. Veronica was nestled in front of Ann, who had her eyes on Reg's back, and Catherine let her palfrey slow to a walk. Ann sidled back to ride beside her. "I expected to see you in the lead."

"I'm afraid," said Catherine. "I want to go home." The child was already dozing and Catherine said, "How can she sleep so soundly?"

Ann touched Veronica's head. "She's not seen enough of the world yet." They rode on a while. "I bleed," she said.

"What, again? So soon?" Catherine pulled on her reins. "We should not have started."

"No, no. May be a tiny bit of a tear. I should have drunk your tea." She made a fist and squeezed. "We can turn north. We can take Agnes and a couple of the men. We can do it now."

Catherine chewed her lip. "And I will be a coward if I do. And then I will never know."

"That's true."

"How is your hand?"

"Healing. Stiff. I will be able to forecast storms."

"I have begun this. I must not stop until I have landed upon a shore. I hope it is a friendly one."

They passed through a field, bright with new corn, and Catherine's eyes wandered over the hedgerows and wild verges, searching for medicines. She spied out a stand of columbines in bloom and pulled her palfrey to a stop. Reg turned when Ann called out, and they all waited while Catherine waded through the weeds and plucked a bunch of the purple blossoms. She handed a few to Ann, then to Reg, and finally to Benjamin. She kept the last and held them up to the sun. "Do you see? If you look from the base, you will see the five doves."

Ann leaned from her saddle and squinted. "I see flower petals."

"They are the doves of peace. The messengers of God." Catherine rubbed the blossoms vigorously between her hands. "You do the same. It is the lion's flower and this will give you courage. Now the lion lies down with the dove and we will win our battles with evil."

Ann said, "This is not your customary sort of physic, Catherine. This sounds like the superstition of old."

"Maybe it is," Catherine said. "But I will have all the strength I can muster."

Ann crushed the blossoms between her palms. The men did the same, exchanging an amused glance, and Veronica demanded one.

Agnes huddled into herself and said, "I'm too cold for rituals, Madam."

Catherine pulled her cloak off and tossed it to the maid, who wrapped it around her shoulders, pulled up the hood, and closed her eyes. "Keep it," Catherine said. She watched her daughter mash her bit of plant between her pale hands, then regained her saddle. They rode on.

The sun had lost its throne at the top of the sky when Catherine spied the high roofs of London. They stopped outside the city gates. The men went off to the trees and the women to copses by the streams to relieve themselves. Catherine kept watch while Ann washed her clouts and shook them out. No one looked her way when she hung them from her saddle.

The Davies courtyard was crowded with Davies servants, but Catherine's thought, as they rode in, was all on William, how proud he had been to bring her here the first time. She'd been carrying Veronica in her arms, and William had shown them off to Benjamin. And now, here was Benjamin, looking to her for some sign that she would walk in at his side.

The servants came running, and Benjamin turned to them instead. "Where is she?"

"In her chamber, sir," said one of the men.

"Her chamber? She has no chamber here." Benjamin marched them back through the front door. "Get some drink for these women," he said, and Catherine led the others into the dining gallery. The room was dark and unscrubbed, the table greasy. "This place looks like a shambles," Benjamin shouted. "Where are my chambermaids?" A couple of girls brought in cold meat and ale, and he took one by the arm. "Have you spent your days sitting and watching the dust grow?"

"The woman—" the girl said, dipping her head. "We stay out of her way."

"Go on," he said. "Hide yourself. You can do the cleaning later." He traced a letter in the grease on the table. "It's not fit for you to sit here, Catherine. Go upstairs and take the chamber on the left. Freshen yourselves before the whole house gets into a frenzy."

Catherine went, with the others in tow. The clouts at the basin all felt rough and smelt of mildew, and the bedclothes were stiff as winding-sheets. "Open the shutters," she said to Agnes as she poked at the dead kindling. "If we cannot have water, at least we might drink some air."

A maid came in with a torch to set the fire, and the beams creaked like old bones as they moved around the room. Someone slammed a door. Ann shook out her cloak, and the floorboards clicked beneath them. The new flames nipped at the logs in the hearth. A voice sounded somewhere, raised in anguish. Or anger. Then nothing. The low clouds slowly sealed the sky. Someone knocked, and Ann withdrew to the next room. Catherine called and the door opened.

Benjamin walked in and took Catherine by the elbows. "She has been found."

Catherine's ankles and feet shocked with cold. She could almost feel his breath on her throat and the fine hairs on her neck prickled. She could not move. "Agnes. Take Veronica."

"Will you not go down?" asked Benjamin.

She could not stir. Benjamin sat on the hearth, and the fire was behind him, a halo of flame. His long, curly hair stood out and Catherine was put in mind of a burning bush. She laughed, and he said, "You find me amusing?"

"No," she said. "My fancy carries me away."

"We are no strangers, Catherine, nor giddy children. We have known each other too long. You have asked me to bring you here and so I have. And now you stand there. I don't know what to do to win your faith."

"My faith?" Her knees shook. Her feet would not go forward. "You would ask me that when we're tossed from one belief to another. It's a wonder that the isle of England doesn't sink under the weight of our errors in faith."

Benjamin looked away. "I meant your faith in me and you know it right well."

Benjamin spat into the hearth and Catherine sat on the bench. He put his hand on her thigh. She did not move it away. "Say to me outright that Margaret is lying. That you are not promised and that you have not been abed with her."

Benjamin smiled. "Jealousy? I can see that you are green-eyed, but are you possessed of the devil that goes with it?"

"You answer me with questions."

He put his arm around her waist and pulled her onto his lap. He pressed his lips against her neck, then nuzzled her jaw. "Will you not allow me to prove myself in public, as you asked?"

Catherine's arms went liquid, and her legs ached. She sat astraddle him and let him kiss her mouth. His lips were hot and soft, and she held him to her. She was afraid.

He stood, hauling her to her feet. "Downstairs. Come on, Catherine."

"I won't be made a fool before the entire house."

"I would never make a fool of you. And what of me? My reputation is not so stellar that I want the whole world gaping at me. I want this settled as much as you do. She is in my house, Catherine."

She raised her left palm, then lowered it and held up the right. "Swear it to me."

Benjamin took the left one between his own and kissed it. "It is an insult to God to swear. Christ tells us to speak truth plainly," he said.

She withdrew her fingers. She would have to hear it. "We will go down, Benjamin."

But Margaret Overton was not in the great entry hall. Nor was she dining. Catherine searched the back courtyard while Benjamin questioned the maids. Catherine had entered the small stable when it began. But it wasn't a call. It was a cry. A wail. Then a shriek.

Chapter Forty-Three

Margaret Overton lay in the front hall, twitching and moaning, when Catherine came running back in. Benjamin and Constance knelt on either side of her, holding her arms down. Her head twisted back and forth, and Constance was trying to force a wooden spoon between the afflicted woman's teeth.

Benjamin said, "Catherine, will you help us?"

Catherine pushed her way past Constance and pressed her hand down on Margaret's forehead to stop the thrashing and said, "Margaret. It's Catherine. Do you hear my voice?" The woman began to thump against the floor, first her whole body, then her legs.

"She's got a demon in her," offered one of the kitchen maids from a corner. "We found her under the stairs, down on her knees like a goat."

Catherine tried to pry open one of Margaret's eyelids, but her head tossed from side to side. "Give me the spoon." Constance let loose and Catherine wedged it into her mouth.

One of the maids had begun to pray to S. Valentin, and Constance said, "Skull shavings. Is there a tomb?"

Benjamin said, "What?"

Constance said, "Scrapings of a man's skull. It is the best treatment for falling sickness."

Catherine studied Margaret. The color in her cheeks was red as raw meat. The color of life. The color of exertion. "Hold her more gently," she said. "Let her work out the fit."

Benjamin said, "A skull?"

Catherine resituated the spoon. Margaret opened her eyes and Catherine saw recognition there. This was no falling sickness. "You're upsetting the whole household," she said.

Margaret closed her eyes again and flopped. Catherine held her head down and said, "Skulls are an old remedy for falling sickness. The German physicians have proved it ineffective."

"Will you let her die then?" asked Constance.

"She is not on her deathbed," said Catherine. She sat back, curling her legs under her. Margaret flailed more slowly. "They say that Julius Caesar suffered the falling sickness. And Petrarch. It is often said to be a sign that God has entered the body."

"Does God enter the body of a woman?" asked the maid. She'd stopped her praying and crept closer.

"If God is God, He may enter the body of whoever pleases Him," said Catherine. "Do we not speak of Christ as our husband?" She pressed harder on Margaret's forehead.

The maid leaned over Catherine to look at Margaret. "Then what is the cure?"

"Some recommend tisane of mugwort or foxglove," said Catherine. "It has never been clear to me how it is to be administered without choking the victim, but we might try. Valerian is said to be efficacious." She looked over her shoulder at the young maid. "Go and check the stores. Do you know what the letter 'V' looks like?" The maid shook her head, and Catherine made the sign with two fingers. The girl nodded and ran off down the back stairs. Catherine bent her head close to Margaret's ear. "You do not suffer from the epilepsy." She said to the others, "Leave us."

Ann and Reginald were coming downstairs together. "How does Margaret?" Ann called as they approached. "We have almost been bowled over by the maids."

Benjamin herded everyone away, and Catherine said again, "Margaret." She put her hand on the heaving chest and waited until Margaret opened her eyes. Then she drew the spoon from her mouth.

"Where am I?" said Margaret Overton.

"You have suffered a fit," said Constance, and Catherine said, "Get away, Constance. Go." She smoothed Margaret's dress. "They say the falling sickness has come upon you." She let her hand move on past the bodice to the skirt. A child was blooming there, to be sure. Margaret's belly felt much like her own.

The wind blowing through the front door brought in the spicy scent of the city, urine and old meat and horse sweat, and Margaret pulled back her coif to let her hair free. She breathed in, closing her eyes, and laid one hand over her breast. "So you are arrived. I am never to be free of you. It's no wonder I am ill."

"You were not in danger, except from yourself," said Catherine. She pushed herself to her feet and stood back to let her sister-in-law gather herself and rise. Margaret's back was to the door and to Catherine she seemed a dark blotch on the bright canvas of the day. "You have revived splendidly." She called Benjamin, who appeared from the dining gallery with the others. Catherine took a breath, blew it out. Said, "And now that we are all assembled and recovered, shall we settle this matter of a marriage and a child?"

Margaret's features flattened, and Constance trotted to her side. Ann and Reginald moved to Catherine's right. The young maid crept up to the edge of the staircase to watch.

Benjamin regarded both groups. "You line up like armies on the field," he said, "when you should be a family. There must be truth among us all."

"How should we be a family when there is neither love nor trust among us?" asked Margaret. "My father and my brothers made those properties what they are." She thrust Constance forward. "This is my brother's child, and she is no more bastard than that one is." She pointed at Catherine. "Your mother was a whore. You know what you are. And your son along with you. My brother knew it, as well. Will I stand before my father in heaven and tell him that I have let his land and tenants go out of the family and into the hands of this woman and the children of her sin? That you have all and I have nothing? That I did nothing to regain my position?"

Margaret's face showed lines of strain, and the rims of her eyes flamed as though she might weep. Constance stared at the floor, her hands folded neatly in front of her. She could have been Margaret's daughter. She could have been Veronica's sister.

Catherine's thoughts flew back to a Christmas when she was a child, still the foundling of Mount Grace Priory. The Overtons had not yet placed their daughters in the convent, and the name only meant the great family who had bought the old properties, the ones that had once belonged to the prioress's family. Catherine had been sitting, at that very prioress's feet, absorbing tales of holidays of old. The snow had come deep that year, and the nuns had gathered by the fire under the reading room. The hearth was green with fir boughs, and someone had hung mistletoe over the one window. Far past sunset, the old nuns sat with Mother Christina, once Christina Havens, drinking wine and warming their feet. At midnight, they exchanged gifts— embroidered linens, candied fruits, soaps scented with daisy or lavender. For the first time, Mother Christina let Catherine stay awake, and after the stroke of twelve she pressed into the girl's hand a parchment roll. When Catherine flattened it across the stone pavers before the fire, she saw a drawing of a building, surrounded by fields studded with sheep. When Catherine asked what it was, the prioress said, "Havens House." Mother Christina leaned down and tapped the sheet. "This was my father's home before the Overtons took it. Everything was Havens back then. But he died." She sat back and drank. The firelight etched the bones under her skin, and she said, "Keep that, Catherine. And remember that it is Havens House. It will always be Havens House, and the village below it is Havenston."

The prioress had been her mother. And it was her sin that had brought Catherine into the world to be the heir to that house. Something turned deep inside her, and Catherine said, "But I am an Overton, too." She could almost see it, the fields outside sloped down toward the village. The old center rooms, thick as a castle's keep, embroidered with the new wing and ornate door the Overton men had added. And beyond it, the village, still called Havenston. The past would always haunt the present, like the face of a risen, but bloody, Christ. "The house was my family's before it was yours. It was my husband's. It will be my children's."

"You may fashion a legitimate ancestry out of your pride," said Margaret, "but I was born a true daughter of my father from my mother's married bed." She pulled herself up straight, but Catherine remained an inch taller. The two women were within striking distance, and Catherine felt her fists clench. Her fingertips thumped. She clamped her teeth against her lower lip and began to count in her head.

Benjamin stepped between them. "I want no scratching between sisters," he said, "but Margaret, you must deny this story of our marriage now."

"You deny it?" asked Margaret.

Benjamin's expression softened in disbelief, as though his sternness had been made of wax. "You will not maintain this to my face, will you? Before witnesses?"

"Here is my witness," Margaret said, yanking Constance forward again.

Benjamin shook his head. "No true witness will say we are married."

"I will say this," said Constance. "You came to Overton House on pretense of seeing to the wools and the works in Mount Grace. You made love to my mistress. You spoke loving words and on those words you won her bed. It is a marriage before God if not before a priest. It is a consummated marriage. And you have got a child upon her body. And we will have Overton House and Catherine will go back to Richmond to work in the kitchens, where she belongs. And no one will know her and no one will care. And her bastards will have no names at all."

"The girl has grown quite a tongue," said Benjamin, "but I will not have my mouth bridled on her word. And if you've got a child in you, then God help it because it's got a liar for its mother, and that sin will land upon its innocent head."

"It is your child," Margaret insisted.

"And how do you reckon anything of mine has gotten inside of you?" Benjamin said.

Margaret blanched. "You. You drank of an evening. Every evening. Perhaps you do not remember."

"There is not enough wine in all of France to fortify me for such a deed. Or to make me forget it." He beckoned to Reginald. "I am done here." The man bowed and they headed for the stairs.

"Wherefore would you go?" asked Margaret. "You belong here. With me." She pulled at his arm and he jerked away. "You no longer want me?"

"I never wanted you," said Benjamin. "You are as brazen as a stable yard goose. I wonder that the lightning does not bolt from the blue and strike you."

"Benjamin," Margaret said. "Will you leave me desperate and alone?"

"I will leave you as I found you. I have spoken kindly to you. And this is how you serve me?" And he walked upstairs, Reginald following. Ann looked at Catherine, and she said, "Go on with them."

"I will not stay where I am scorned." Margaret huffed out.

Catherine went after her, hooking her arm in the courtyard. "Wait."

Margaret turned, but she did not free herself. The two women stood, linked, and Catherine saw beneath her sister-in-law's face the girl she had been when she entered the convent, a spoilt, angry daughter flanked by a prideful brother and father. Her mother had ordered in the clothing and small luxuries for the private room while Margaret had watched, blank-faced, with her twin huddled behind her. That twin was dead. The parents and brother also dead. And the absent brother, Catherine's William, also gone now to God. Margaret's skin was threaded with care lines, and in them Catherine saw a map of their lives—their paths leading relentlessly back to those days of their nunnery, when Margaret had been the wealthier, but Catherine had been the more favored.

But Margaret spoke truth when she said that Catherine had been the bastard, the child of her mother's and her father's secret sin. The pity came up in her like fever, and, even as the memory of Margaret's crimes spilled over her, she could not drench it.

"Whose child is that?" Catherine said. "Sister, tell me the truth. Were we not once friends, back in the days of our girlhood?"

Margaret let her fingers twist into Catherine's sleeve. "You have all the glory of my fall. You have overthrown me, and I have nowhere to go. Nowhere to be. No husband and no position. And no brothers no more." Her speech broke, and she let her arm fall. "I have hated the very ground you stepped upon, even though it is Overton soil. You're the mare who rides over my heart in the nights. And now you trample me by daylight, as well. I have shamed myself beyond repair. You will hear it all anon, flying in on the wing of rumour, but

I have no wish to speak my dishonor to the open air. Let me go in peace."

Peace. "Go, Sister." Catherine released her, and Margaret sent Constance for their horses. Margaret walked to the road, and over her head, Catherine saw some ravens, scrolling their black marks across the clear sky. "I wonder what they seek," she said to no one.

Ann came out at the sound of the animals being brought around. Margaret and Constance, with their men, gathered themselves and left. No one spoke. No one wished anyone fair weather or fast hooves. "Look," said Catherine. "The birds want something."

Ann shaded her eyes. "Food and shelter. They have each other and they settle their disputes with a few cross words."

"An unkindness," said Catherine.

"Oh, they have no real feelings," said Ann.

"No, I mean that is what we call them. 'An unkindness of ravens.' I have heard them called 'a constable' after the king's ravens in the Tower." She listened as the riders clopped away. "We are the same," she said to the space her sister had occupied.

Ann said, "You and those birds?"

Catherine said, "'And since that I so kindly am served, I fain would know what she hath deserved.'"

"What is that?" asked Ann.

"The poet. Thomas Wyatt. He wrote of being shamed by a woman."

"Benjamin has not been shamed," said Ann. "At least not by Margaret."

"It is not only the men whose shame matters." The birds settled into the trees and began scolding one another. "An unkindness indeed. Come, Ann. We must finish this journey of ours. We ride to Mount Grace. If this child is to live, its mother must find her way home."

Chapter Forty-Four

They were back at the country Davies House, at least part of the way to Yorkshire, the next day. Catherine and Ann had only to bring down their bags and chests to be ready, and they spent the hours helping the maids prepare meat and bread and apples. Benjamin finally came to the kitchen, searching out Catherine.

"You will come upstairs and dine with me. Let these girls do the work."

"Come on, Catherine," said Ann. Her face was pimpled with sweat. "We've been working like Trojans for hours."

At the table, Benjamin was triumphant. "Your sister is conquered. Martins has vanished. You are free. And I am here by the grace of a sonnet."

"How is that?" asked Catherine. She flopped some meat onto her plate but did not eat it.

He settled and folded his hands in his lap. "Did I not tell you the story? When they took me before the judge down in Dover, he required me to prove that I was the man I said I was. I offered to describe the translation I have done of the Psalms. To say the last sonnet I penned. But he stopped me after only a few lines. I think I proved myself well enough."

"You have translated the Psalms?"

Benjamin's face twisted into a wounded expression. "You think me incapable of rendering them?"

"You have written a sonnet?"

Punching his chest with the side of his fist, Benjamin pushed his chair backward. "What? Now you think I cannot rhyme? Make a conceit?"

"I think of you as making money more than love poems."

"Ah, then. I will have to show you my many depths." He tried out a grin with one side of his mouth, and Catherine felt her cheeks warm. But then he turned sober. "The judge had no interest in seeing them, I will tell you that." He ripped a chunk of bread from the loaf and mopped up the sauce around the leg bone on his plate.

"I thought it was Dudley who got you set free."

"Well, perhaps he played his part." Benjamin flushed.

Catherine said, "Recite me a verse or two."

"What? Oh, I'm tired," Benjamin said. "The road wearies a man's memory. How is this? 'When a man rides by a fine lady, all his wits will turn into gravy.'"

Catherine said, "That is the worst rhyme ever to assault my ears. And the verse halts like a goose with a bitten foot."

"You heard me plead for mercy. And yet you have wrung a line of poetry from me."

"It sounds wrung, in truth," said Catherine. "It's no wonder you were driven from Dover."

"You will have to keep me, then, until I can perform better. You may test me or my word, at your leisure, when I have had some sleep. I will make you a verse on any matter you choose."

Catherine trained a look on him. "And you will seek your liberty by this test?"

"I may instead be sentenced to put my head in a yoke, my Lady Judge."

"Enough of this," said Ann. "I am weary with our work." She took up Veronica's hand. "Will you go to bed and keep me company? I'd rather listen to you giggle at your dreams than endure this man's wit."

Veronica yawned. "Yes, Auntie."

"Agnes?"

"My haunches would be glad of a mattress."

They waved their goodnights and retired. Reg watched Ann walk away from his place at the bottom of the table, and Catherine said, "Come here, Reg. I want to see your face. Move into the light."

Reginald looked into his cup, then lifted it and came up. He sat across from Catherine, where Ann had been. "Here I am, Madam. It's a countenance you've beheld many a time."

"And never one that showed a lie," said Catherine. "You will ride home with us?"

"If I am asked."

"You are. But it's a long road and we will be much in each other's company. We know that men's minds change over time."

"Women's, too, if I might speak openly," said Reg.

She nodded. "Right enough. But Ann Smith is not fickle. She's the most steadfast being I have ever known, man or woman. She is more than a sister to me. And what injures her wounds me."

Reg peered into the cup again. Then he looked into Catherine's eyes. "You're wanting me to leave the lady to herself?"

"I want her to suffer no more harm."

Benjamin laid his hand on Catherine's arm. "Who can promise that another will come to no harm?"

Catherine pushed back the bench and stood. "Any one of us can work for good."

Benjamin said, "But the work of our hands is not always matched by what our hearts wreak on us. And the world."

Catherine looked down at Benjamin, but his eyes were shaded by his long lashes and the tumble of dark hair. Then at Reginald, who waited without moving. She said, "I must sleep.

Forgive me. I don't know what I say. I will not see Ann harmed. Not a hair. Nor played false." She plucked a bottle of wine from the table, and Benjamin handed her two cups.

Ann and Agnes were already asleep, and Catherine lay beside her friend but her eyes would not close. The logs whistled softly as the fire whisked through them, and to Catherine it sounded like a melancholy song. Then one cracked and fell. She rolled over, put her arm into Ann's, and slept.

Before the second day was showing its face on the eastern horizon, Benjamin and Reg had horses out for the men to load. The noise in the hall woke the women, and they were dressed before the servants came to drag the chests down.

Catherine found Benjamin at the table. He said, "And now you will ride by my side and smile upon me?"

"I will be moving forever," Catherine said, "like the sailors of the old stories."

"Every sailor wishes for home," said Ann, "and hopes for a smiling welcome when he arrives."

They finished eating without speaking further and threw themselves into the saddles once more. The clouds scudded along above them, tracing a pale crown around the low, bloody sun, and Catherine closed her eyes and let the light twist into colors behind her lids.

"How will Margaret travel, without more than the clothes on her back?" asked Catherine.

Ann yawned. "She has money in her purse and two men to ride by her side. I wonder that your mind still works on her." Catherine shifted in her saddle, unwilling to speak, and Ann said, "You are growing. Do you feel life yet?"

"No. But I feel the weight in my hipbones. I hope Eleanor has gotten the corn into the ground." The cold day blew around them, and Agnes pulled Catherine's fur cloak up to her chin. The wind gathered and shook the trees, and Catherine almost wished she hadn't given it away. She settled back into a thick woolen blanket, dreaming of warm fires and a jug of red wine. It was going to be a long ride.

And it was. Benjamin kept looking behind for signs of followers, but no one appeared, and soon they all faced forward and rode hard. Hours of spitting, cold rain, and sudden bright glaring sun. Joints of hard mutton and stiff bread eaten in the saddle and washed down with weak ale. When the sun dropped into the west, they all stumbled into an inn, barely seeing the fish stew laid before them. A thin mattress. A short night. Catherine and Ann washed in the icy water of their basin and dragged themselves onto their saddles again the next morning, before the sun had opened its great cold eye.

Another day, then another, then another, and Catherine ached so much across her belly that she wondered if the child had lain sideways in resentment. They rode past woods and broad fields, into villages and out again. The men stayed ahead, whistling and exchanging tales that made them laugh. Sometimes they sang a snatch of old melody. But Catherine and Ann rode in silence, while Veronica tried out the men's songs or recited parts of the psalms. More days and more nights. The season moved backward as they pushed northward, and soon the tender blossoms had become buds, then the buds bare tendrils of green trying out the air. The sheep here were not yet shorn, and the cows showed their ribs as they ruminated over moldy winter hay. Havenston had to be close by this time. It had to be. Catherine could not help herself from looking backward. The road lay empty behind them.

Another day wheeled by. They passed through yet another wooded stretch. The branches here showed the first nipples of bud, and a few brave crocuses opened their mouths to the sky, but the view was mostly grey studded with brown trunks of leafless trees. The sun yawned on the western horizon. "What mother would ride into such a dull season for the child she has never met?" asked Catherine.

"Only every mother alive," answered Ann.

The words bit at Catherine's mind, and she twisted her hood to loosen her hair.

Ann, unaware, spoke on. "Women will meet an army to let any ugly, dim-witted baby come into the world without the stain of sin upon its head."

"And why should any child be marked by sin for being born?" said Catherine. "It is monstrous. Why should a few words, spoken between a man and a woman, change the nature of a child? It is not even a child yet. We are all born with the original stain upon our souls. Does it not make us equals in the eyes of God?" She shoved her right hand into her pocket and her finger found the pennyroyal that she had taken from the still room of Benjamin's country house before they had gone to Ashridge. It was brittle, and it brought her son's face into her mind

Ann said something in reply, but a shout drowned her words. The men had stopped ahead. They faced another party of men. Many men. They brought their horses to a stand across the road. The strangers wore cloths wrapped around their faces. "Stop," said one. He drew a sword from his side and pointed it at Benjamin. Two men sat on either side of the leader, swords also drawn. Catherine turned. A dozen men blocked the road behind them.

Benjamin motioned Catherine and Ann up behind him. Reg brought his horse over to stand next to Benjamin's. Ann pulled her palfrey beside Catherine's. Veronica had opened her eyes at the noise, and Ann bent to murmur into her ear.

"What is it?" Catherine called. "What do you want of us?"

Benjamin and Reg approached them, and the Davies servants circled Ann and Catherine. "I will have your cases and bags," said the stranger. He brandished the sword, and Benjamin reached for it, but he pulled the weapon back and trained it on Benjamin's face. "Drop your goods."

Ann yanked her reins and dug her heels into the animal's sides, forcing it backward. She held Veronica tight against her.

"Ann!" shouted Catherine. "Wait!"

"Let her go, Lady Catherine," said the thief. He turned the weapon in her direction.

"How do you know me?"

"The palaces whisper your name, Lady Catherine. They say you have wealth that you keep hidden. Many secrets that you keep inside you." He shouted over her. "Take it all."

Catherine gazed at the long road that unwound beyond the dark figures and their companions, while the chests were unloaded. The heaviest ones, brought by the Davies servants for Benjamin, clunked to the ground. Horses' hooves thudded in the dust behind her, and the other men grunted and chuckled. A clasp clacked open. "Good stuffs here, man," said someone.

"Have done and be gone," said Benjamin.

"I know you for one Benjamin Davies, a Welshman," the leader said. "The Welsh are a race of cheats and liars. They eat cheese and fart."

Benjamin's face flooded with blood. "The king himself is a Welshman. You speak slander and treason." His hand was on the hilt of his dagger, and four of the bandits drew on him. Catherine sat very still.

The thief's eyes glittered. "I slander no one. And I would keep my hand where it lies, if I were a man in your position." He backed his sorrel three steps. His partners did the same. He raised his left hand and crooked a gloved finger. Catherine turned in her saddle to see their horses disappearing in a blur of dust.

Catherine kicked her palfrey and faced forward, expecting the others to have gone, as well, but now more strange men surged from the woods on either side. Their swords were out. Two of the Davies manservants behind them went down without a sound, and Catherine grabbed Ann's reins and kicked her own ride. Veronica shrieked, and Benjamin charged Caesar forward. Reg was already fighting, his weapon out, but Catherine could hardly see him for the dirty gloom and the dull flash of blades. Benjamin was stopped between two horsemen, and Catherine's palfrey shied away from another man, who had come up on her side, and smacked flat into Ann's mare. Catherine fell, rolling to avoid hooves, and then Ann was on the ground beside her, flattening herself over Veronica. Agnes screamed from somewhere, and Catherine felt a hand grabbing the cloth of her bodice and pulling her to her feet. She jabbed backward with her elbow, and when she felt the grip loosen, she shouted, "Run, Ann. Agnes! Run."

Ann was with her, clutching the child, as they fled into the trees. It was darker here, and Catherine ran northward, as well as she could tell from the light. A fallen limb tripped her, and she fell, but Ann's fingers were on her arm, lifting her, and they kept going until the sounds of steel on steel, of cries and groans, were far behind them. Catherine buckled into the loam beside a great oak, and Ann collapsed beside her. Veronica groped for her mother.

"Come here, child," whispered Catherine, gathering her daughter to her chest. Ann was heaving for breath. "Are you stabbed?"

Ann felt her bodice and arms for tears in the fabric. "Bruised from the fall." She cocked her head. "If our clothes had been lighter, we would all be run through." Her palm bled, and she tore a piece from her shift to pack it.

Catherine's skin buzzed all over, and her guts fluttered and tossed. "Agnes. Did she run? Where is she?"

"I don't know," Ann murmured. She lay back on the mossy roots. "My brains are drowning. Can you hear anything?"

"No." Veronica was shaking, and Catherine rubbed the small limbs, hard. "You're safe now, girl," she whispered. But she listened for footfalls, a voice, anything creeping through the silent woods. Her left wrist and thumb throbbed, and she pulled back her sleeve. "I'm damaged here." She had an old scar from a dog bite, and it sang with pain.

Ann took her hand. "Is it broken?"

Catherine waggled her fingers. "I must have landed upon it. But not broken." She tore a strip from her own shift. "Can you wrap it?"

Ann made the bandage, and they moved on until they found a cover of firs. An owl dropped onto a low branch over their heads and watched a while, then lifted its broad wings and hoisted itself into the darkness. Catherine startled at a snapped twig, but it was only a badger that waddled by without taking note of the shivering women. They lay huddled together, listening, while the stars picked their way across the night sky.

Chapter Forty-Five

Catherine must have fallen asleep, because the east was growing silver before she had said all of the prayers she knew. Her eyes were gummy, and her cheek was numb from lying against the damp ground. She shook Ann.

"I'm awake," Ann said. Veronica was sleeping between them on a mat of softened needles.

"Let me take her," said Catherine, but Ann shook her head and lifted the child. They crouched and made their way to the next wide tree, stumbling from stiffness and fear. Catherine studied the sky. "This way," she said.

"Are we going north or back to the road?"

"North. You think the road is better?"

"I think alive is better," said Ann. "Did you see aught of Agnes?"

"Maybe she ran another way," said Catherine. "Did you recognize any of them?"

"They were masked," said Ann.

"They were waiting for us," said Catherine. Veronica was alert, staring. She'd put her thumb in her mouth, and Catherine let it stay. "We cannot be far from the village."

They walked, then trudged, then stumbled forward, searching through the trunks and branches for anything familiar. The day waxed and waned. Finally, a spiral of smoke mingled with the mists of the evening fog, and Catherine followed its thin twist in her mind's eye all the way to its source at some woman's hearth. She said, "That comes from a chimney," and Ann lifted her eyes from her boots. "We're almost home."

"Where is home, Mother?" asked Veronica, squirming.

"There." Catherine pointed. "Can you see the fire? That's our village, named for your family."

"Overton," said the child. "The village is Overton?"

"Havens. It's Havenston. You remember it."

The girl pushed herself up in her mother's arms. "How are we Havens? We are Overtons."

"You'll understand one day," said Ann.

They crouched in a thicket near the high road, watching for stragglers from their party. For the armed men. Catherine's stomach grumbled loudly, but she pressed her hand to it and waited. The bulge of new child pressed her onward, but she waited until the sky was dark to take a chance and broke out, staggering up the high road. She almost did not know where she was. The hedges were trimmed, and the verges of the road had been mowed all along the way. But the sturdy house of Peter Grubb, the constable, was unmistakable, and his old mare nickered from the stable as they passed. He and his wife were probably already asleep, but Catherine turned up the little lane anyway and pounded on the door. "Peter Grubb!" she called. "Open for us!"

The eye-hole slid open. "Who's there?" said a woman's voice.

"It is Catherine Overton, Mistress Grubb. And Ann Smith and my little daughter Veronica."

The door opened and the woman, dressed only in her nightdress and cap, stepped out and caught Catherine as she fell.

"Christ's wounds, what has happened? Ann Smith, what has befallen you?"

"Murderers and thieves," said Ann, dropping into the front hall. She laid her head on the dusty woven rug.

Catherine slumped onto a chair. "Thank God," she said. She could have kissed the stones of the floor, but she was too tired to bend.

"Who's here?" Peter Grubb himself appeared in a ratty jacket, tossed over his night shirt. The white froth of his hair caught the fresh moonlight. "Light me a taper, Wife."

"It's Catherine Overton." She dragged herself up so that he could see her. "We have been set upon."

Peter Grubb hurried to the front door, and Catherine heard him bolt it. "Have you brought killers into the village with you?"

Mistress Grubb flicked him a look. "They are half-dead. Get them a drink, for the love of God, Husband." She laid a little hot spit on the last word.

"I'm figuring a man can be allowed to protect his own house," muttered Grubb, but he shuffled off in the direction of the kitchen just the same.

Catherine's heart was still lodged up under her collarbone and she forced her breath downward. "We had a party with us. We were almost within smelling distance of the village and men came upon us from the woods."

Peter Grubb returned, bearing a tray with drinks. "Come out of the hall. Drink and settle your minds."

In the front room, Mistress Grubb poured for them all, latched the shutters, then squatted and took Veronica's chin in her fingers. "Has anyone hurt this child?"

"I am whole," said Veronica. "My Auntie Ann put herself between me and those awful men." She stood straight to show herself, but her legs shook.

Mistress Grubb smiled and released her. "You come with me, girl, and you can have whatever suits your fancy." She took Veronica by the hand and disappeared into the back.

Peter Grubb settled himself into his chair. "Now tell me, Catherine Overton. What do you do in Yorkshire?"

"I live here," said Catherine. "It is my home."

"You have been away a long time."

Catherine's skin rippled all over with fury. She could feel Ann behind her, watching, and she counted ten before she spoke. "I am returned to settle my affairs."

"Your affairs." Grubb drank, then set the cup aside and steepled his fingers. "There has been gossip of your affairs. I did not expect to see your face."

"Did you not hear us? We have been set upon. We have no one and nothing except what you see before you."

"Well," said Grubb. "The world is a dangerous place. I figure you need rest."

"I expect they do," said Mistress Grubb. She still had Veronica by one hand. "This child is well-nigh dead for terror, and these ladies have kept their lives with the courage of lions. Now, Husband, I am going to make up a clean bed for them, and you will hold your tongue and let them sleep."

Catherine thought that tears would spill from her, but she clenched her teeth and said, "I know not how to thank you."

"I figure there's no thanks needed," said Peter Grubb. "I figure that a woman's got a right to her home as much as a man. Can you not find them a bed, Wife? They look dead on their feet."

Mistress Grubb bit her lip. "I am upon the task, Husband."

The women replaced each other's bandages with fresh linen and crawled into the one unused bed. Catherine's eyes were swollen and gritty, but she could not hold them open, and they lay in a row, the child between them, until the morning cut a bright swath through the shutters and Mistress Grubb was knocking on the door and slipping into their room.

"There's bodies found on the London Road."

"How many?" said Catherine.

"Five, they say. Four men, one woman."

"Where are they?" asked Ann.

"Taken to Overton House for the laying out. My man is called on to go."

"Then we are gone with him," said Catherine.

Two geldings had been rounded up, and the Grubbs' stable boy was holding them when they came outside. Ann hopped onto one and set Veronica in front of her. Catherine let the boy help her and they were already moving as he let go of the reins.

It was only a few minutes' ride, and they found the front courtyard of Overton House alive with horses and men. Catherine's steward, Eleanor Adwolfe, presided, big-bellied, out front, with her husband Joseph.

Catherine hung back, letting her horse chomp at the old weeds drooping along the side of the lane. "That's one of Grubb's watchmen from the village."

Ann pointed. "But look there. I see Reg." She kicked her horse and was off. "Come on!" she yelled over her shoulder.

They were almost within spitting distance of the house when Eleanor raised her eyes. "Is it you?" she called. "Madam?" She ran to Ann's side and held onto her leg, but her eyes were on Catherine.

"Still casting a shadow," said Catherine, sliding to the ground.

"They've brought four men and poor Agnes, oh, Madam, and they've been saying that you were killed and dragged off by the murderers."

"Agnes?" Ann jumped down and pulled Veronica close. "Where is she?"

"Downstairs somewhere. Some of the watchmen are there, and those others that rode up. I don't know who they are and they all say they want in."

"What others?" Catherine pulled her hood closer to her face.

"I don't know them," said Eleanor. She searched the yard. "I don't see them now. And Master Benjamin's run mad."

Catherine let the hood fall back again. "He's here?"

"He brought the bodies," said Eleanor, but Catherine was running toward the house.

She lost Ann, who veered off to follow Reg, but no one stopped her as she found her way down the back steps. The kitchen table held two Davies men, stretched shoulder to shoulder. The men of the watch sat on the benches on either side of the dead forms. Catherine said, "Where is the woman?"

They didn't look at her, but she recognized Samuel Cobb from the village. He slung a thumb over his shoulder without noticing her face and said, "In t'other room."

Catherine retreated down the narrow hall, peeked into the laundry and saw no one, and tiptoed on down to her still room. She pushed the heavy door open and there she was, on the old convent table. Agnes still wore Catherine's old cloak, but the furred hood was dark and damp on one side with her blood. The woman herself was pale and stiff, and Catherine pulled a stool beside her and sat to pray. She put her head down and closed her eyes. She'd said only "Mother Mary" when she heard footsteps and jerked upright again. "Who's there?"

Benjamin came in and Catherine stumbled to her feet and into his arms. He said, "I thought you were taken."

"And I feared you were dead." Tears scorched the backs of her eyes but they would not fall and she was blinded. Someone tapped on the door and she felt her body being set a decent distance from the man.

"It's only me, Madam." Eleanor came in, her belly swaying before her, and shut the door. She took the other stool and Catherine sat, blinking her vision clear.

"I will leave you to the work," said Benjamin, and left.

"When does the baby come?" Catherine put her hand on Eleanor's apron. It was seven months gone, at least.

"In June, I judge. I felt life more than four weeks ago. Look how low I swing. I think it is a girl at last. Three boys are enough for Joseph."

"Where are your sons?"

"In the stable. Joseph sent them to hide when the men came into the lane. And they'd better stay there, or they'll get the back of his hand."

Catherine put her hand on Agnes's unmoving breast. "This breaks my heart in twain." She stood and peeled away the filthy clothing. "Have the watchmen seen this?"

"They have been occupied with the men. Two of Benjamin's. The other two are men that nobody knows. They say that three or four escaped with marks on them."

Catherine folded the cloak and laid it aside. "This was mine."

"I know," said Eleanor. "I thought it was you when they brought her in."

Eleanor pulled off the dead woman's soiled shoes while Catherine rolled down her hose. The younger woman said, "I will get water," and disappeared. She returned quickly with a full basin. Catherine handed her a clout and she lifted one of Agnes's feet. "This girl never hurt a soul."

Catherine's air snagged in her throat. No one disturbed them as they cleaned and covered the body. Catherine rinsed her hands. She was sweating, and she pushed her hood back and ran her wet palm over her own face. "I wish I could cleanse my mind as easily."

"You lack food and sleep," said Eleanor. "The body must have nourishment and rest. I have learnt that of you, Madam. Stay quiet here." She closed the door as she went, and Catherine was left alone to pray for her lost maid, to say her apologies to God, and to listen to the strange voices murmuring through the walls of Overton House.

Eleanor returned with bread and cheese and wine, and she laid it on the mixing table. Catherine's stomach suddenly coiled and rumbled, and she sat gratefully to the food. The bread was warm, like biting into a summer cloud, and, when she took up her cup, Catherine let the wine sit on her tongue for a few seconds before she swallowed. Perhaps it would soften the accusing voice in her head.

Ann came in and latched the door behind her. "I have locked Veronica in a chamber with Reg."

"The constable is old, and there is no judge in the village," said Eleanor. "The law has no teeth, if you will pardon my saying so."

Catherine said, "For some of us, it has the bite of a mad dog."

"Who is in there?" A man pounded on the door, and the three women jumped. "Have you the dead woman?"

"She is here," called Eleanor. "We are cleaning the body."

"Who is 'we'? Speak up!" Thudding again, rattling the latch.

Catherine flung open the door while Eleanor covered Agnes. Samuel Cobb stood in the hall. "Is it you breaking down my doors around my ears?"

"Lady. I thought you was absent." He retreated a step. "There's so many folks comin' and goin' on the roads these past hours." He watched his toe move on the pavers. "A man doesn't know where they get to. And with these dead—"

"The constable knows I've arrived, Samuel." She pointed back, into the still room. "Do not remove the body. We have just washed her."

"I won't touch her, Madam." He shuffled over to the table, where he stood, hands folded, and stared down at Agnes.

Catherine led Ann and Eleanor through the kitchen, past the abandoned dead men. She opened the door and saw, out in the garden where her most delicate herbs had been, beds of rose spikes. Ann gasped and Catherine cried out, "What is this?"

Eleanor said, "Your sister ordered it the day she arrived. She had the bushes with her, on wagons. She said it is the fashion to have roses. I would not give her the kitchen girls for the planting, but she ordered the men to do the deed. I have spared what I could, Madam."

"Well," said Catherine. The rose was her most favored flower. "They will smell sweet when they bloom." The remaining vegetable patch was tidy and weeded. "Thank God you have kept something. It looks like a small paradise."

Eleanor said, "That's the sun, gilding the dirt. In the rain it looks dark and greasy."

"May be," said Catherine. The thorny twigs stood naked as skeletons, but Catherine could imagine pink and red blossoms, blowing in the wind. "I will not pull them up. We will have a new space plowed up for the herbs." Two dairymaids came from the cow barn, swinging buckets of milk as though their progress through the world went on undisturbed by death. A striped cat trotted along with them, and Reg was walking behind, holding Veronica by the hand. When the girls stopped in front of Catherine, Veronica captured the cat and sat with it, yowling, on her lap.

"Puss won't be kept in chains, little Veronica" said one of the maids. "She'll claw if you don't give her some liberty."

Veronica let go and the animal scrambled away. It shook its head and allowed the child to pet it behind the ears before it sauntered off to stand under the bucket between the maids.

"Your daughter will not be kept indoors, Madam," said Reg.

Catherine shook her head. "I am without words. It is Eden come again, at least on this side of the house."

Eleanor said, "Very like, Madam. But today it seems to have sprouted a serpent."

<h1 style="text-align:center">Chapter Forty-Six</h1>

Peter Grubb had already gone back and was walking the high road of Havenston when Catherine rode down with Ann and Joseph. "No one here has seen any men who don't live in the parish," called the constable, "but I will bring in every mother's son for interrogations."

"Benjamin is speaking to the watch." Catherine dropped heavily to the ground beside him. "We are become a nation of courts and solicitors."

"Of gaols and gallows," added Ann. She led her pony a turn to calm his spirits and hopped off.

The sun's glare followed them, and Catherine felt it like a reproachful eye on her. She lowered her head and her hand found the short post of a front gate. "This is Gladys MacIntosh's cottage," she said, just as the woman herself stood from weeding her rhubarb bed. She was planted like a squat pillar in their line of sight.

"Lady Overton. It is you, clear as a summer day."

"How do you, Mistress MacIntosh? And how does our village?"

"See for yourself." She raised her gnarled hand. "Women are busy with the wool. The village makes its way. The constable has been warning us of thieves and murderers, but by my troth you will not find them here."

The shrubs and hedges prevented Catherine from seeing all of the dwelling, but the branches had been rough-hewn back from the road, and the gravel was swept and clean. She could see at least two new sets of shutters. A whirr of wheels sounded like a distant hive of bees. "You prosper, then."

Mistress MacIntosh waddled forward and leaned upon her gate. "Master Davies brings the payments at the quarter-year. Gives it direct to the wives. Makes the husbands complain some, and there's one or two that take it downright evil, but it's a sight better than 'twas. You see."

"I will walk," said Catherine, "without the law, begging your pardon, Master Grubb." She wrapped her reins around the gatepost and, followed by Ann and Joseph, forced herself onward. Roofs were patched and doors hung straight. Small flocks of buff and white chickens and ducks. A few geese, hissing their discontent. Half a dozen fat pigs in boarded sties and a nanny goat tied beside one neat garden. The inn yard was laid with new stones and the front door stood open. Catherine didn't stop until she came near the spot in the road further up. She believed that it would still be defiled with blood, that she could not mistake it, but she found herself searching up and down for any sign of the place where William had died.

"I have lost him," she finally said. "He is gone entirely."

Joseph stood off, unwilling to come close to her thoughts, but Ann scuffed her sole over the stones. "The world has grown a new skin."

Catherine nodded. She watched a young woman run from a back door, chasing a short-legged dog. It was the house she'd bought after William died, for former nuns. At her last count it had housed six women and three orphan girls. Someone inside rang out a laugh. She said, "And now how will we know ourselves?"

Ann grunted. "We will learn to live in our new selves, whatever they are." She squinted into a yard. "The entire village is made new. This is your doing, Catherine. The child of your genius."

"Not mine alone. It was William and Benjamin too."

"Don't give it over to them. It was your conception to have the women in the village do the spinning and weaving. Yours alone. And to pay them a wage. That house." She pointed at the nuns' house. "That's yours. Your city of ladies."

Joseph coughed and said, "Not meaning to be a long ear, but I heard what you were saying. My faith goes with Ann's. Even Master Davies says so." He grinned. "Have you felt Eleanor's belly? She says it's a woman child this time. A summer child. I would like to have a little daughter to sit on my knee."

Catherine nodded. "Please God it will be, and one as lively and good as her mother." A door opened nearby and she patted Joseph on the arm and went toward the woman who appeared. "Hallo, Goodwife Cartwright. How do you and your small ones?"

The woman curtsied and backed into the little house, where the dirt floor was packed and smooth, and the spinning wheel was set between the hearth and the small window. A bushel of yarn lay wound into skeins in the corner and Catherine dipped her hand into the fluff.

"Better, Madam, than ever we have before. The children wind the yarn and Master Davies brings the money. I do the spinning. My Maggie is learning at my hand and we will be turning out twice the lot this time two years on, God willing."

Catherine checked the joints and surfaces of the wheel. They were well-oiled and smooth. The girl showed herself and demonstrated her skill. Catherine gave her a coin and Maggie Cartwright dropped to her knee and closed her hand over the money.

"It is a wonder," Catherine said.

"A wonder and a sign," said Mistress Cartwright. "Turn of the wheel, Lady, if you'll pardon the expression. We're up now, sure, you'll say. I hope there's not a fall coming."

"Why would it fall?" asked Catherine.

The woman coughed.

"Say it freely."

"Word's gone about—" Mistress Cartwright dropped her face into her hands and rubbed hers cheeks hard. "You were in prison and would never return. There. It is said. Some say that you were taken for a common thief." She raised her eyes. "Not that I have anything to say against you. Your man comes regular enough and takes the wools and delivers the monies. So there it is. But your sister followed him out of this village like a hawk after a hare and now my husband says there's banns been read over at Mount Grace for you and him, or for her and him, you that can't be married, neither one of you. The talk is that the king's gone stark mad and cuts the head off any woman who looks sideways at him." She took a breath and let it out with a huff. "Now I have said it and it can't be taken back."

They stood in silence for a few seconds. Catherine stared out the open front door. A striped cat trotted from behind a hedge, stopped to sniff at the leaves, then backed against the lower branches, tail raised. He shot a spray of his scent, hindquarters shivering, and went on his way. A woman yelled somewhere in the distance. Another door slammed a few houses down. The wheel sang.

"And what have you heard of a child?" Catherine said finally.

"Well. There's some say the Overton children ought to be seen now and then. And then there's some say they need to be at the court, learning to be fine." She lifted her shoulders.

"I meant Margaret Overton. A child of her own."

"She goes about with that red-haired maid, you know. They say the girl is a child of the dead Robert Overton's blood and ought to be recognized. That she's already the niece to Madam Margaret anyway and might as well be called a daughter. They say legitimacy is a fine point of the law nowadays and not to be regarded." Mistress Cartwright seemed to measure the progress of the morning by studying the lay of the sun's rays across her front garden.

"You speak wisdom. I thank you." Catherine ducked out and found Ann and Joseph, already mounted, in the high road. Peter Grubb was nowhere to be seen. She pulled herself into her saddle, clicked her teeth, and flopped the reins. The pony jolted forward at a trot and Ann rode up close to her.

Catherine said, "Did you hear what she said of the king?"

Ann said, "I would have had to stop my ears with her wool not to hear."

"And I have worked to steer her back into his bed. I have prayed for it."

"Lady Anne, you mean."

"Yes. And she has been always kind to me. I have lied, straight to her face, and have smiled like a cat in the cream when she spoke of being queen."

Ann plucked a speck of dust from her skirt. "You thought it best."

"I thought it best for me. And would I not have put a witch's potion in her cup to make her beautiful to him if I had had the skill? I have played her like a piece on one of her game boards. To smooth my own path."

Ann kept her eyes straight ahead. "And you failed. So there is no sin done. But to yourself."

"If a failed wish is no sin, then Margaret has committed fewer sins than we have laid at her charge. Did you hear what she said about banns being read?"

"I did."

"I wonder what Benjamin will say to that."

"We can know before the sun has dropped another hour. You still have to decide what's to be done about this child, and if you make this marriage, you will answer for it to the king."

"Let's hurry. If the banns are for Benjamin and Margaret, I know what I must do." She spurred the gelding.

But Ann reached over and held onto Catherine's arm. "You will shake something loose at this pace, and then you'll have to be married in your sickbed."

"You seem sure that those banns are for me. Who would have ordered them?" Catherine reined in her ride and put back her head to let the sun strike her face. "The Lady Anne will have no marriage at all."

"May she find happiness in remaining the King's Sister."

Catherine was riding with her eyes closed, letting the sky etch its unreadable script into the blackness behind her lids. Ann said only "Who is that?" and Catherine dropped her head to look. A rider was coming at them, churning a foam of dust behind.

Ann said, "Joseph? Who is it?"

He shook his head. "He comes at quite a pace."

They lost the rider around a corner, then he reappeared, coming at them at full speed. It was Reg. He had to turn his gelding three times to bring it to a halt. The horse took its stand with its forelegs extended, blowing through its nostrils.

"What is it?" asked Catherine.

"Master Benjamin says we must get you to your father's house. He suspects that more men will come here, and we must be gone. He is already saddled to ride to Mount Grace. He has your daughter. You must come and meet him on the road."

Chapter Forty-Seven

Catherine and Ann kicked their horses into motion. At the crossroads beyond the House, they saw Benjamin, with Veronica propped in front of him, ahead on the road to Mount Grace, and they all gave their animals their heads. The hedges and ditches rushed by as though they fled down a green river. They came into a long open stretch, and the sun hit Catherine's face. She could see bright color—red and yellow—pounding at the edges of her eyes, and as the gelding's hooves bumped along like the beat of her heart, she matched her breathing to his. Her belly ached, and she held it with her free hand.

"Have a care," called Ann. Her voice seemed to come through Catherine's skin. "Don't fall." She slowed, and Catherine pulled in her reins.

Catherine tried to say yes, but she hadn't the breath for it. Ann called, "She cannot keep this pace," and Benjamin turned Caesar and waited. Ann said, "We needn't knock her about to save her life."

Catherine's horse blew through his nostrils, unhappy at the sudden change, and Caesar chomped at his bit. Catherine could see the impatience on Benjamin's face, but he murmured to their mounts and settled them into a walk. The little party passed tenant houses and broad fields of sheep. They banged over the old wooden bridge that spanned the little river and by the time the sun was casting a gold gloaming light, they were passing the first cottages to the west of the village of Mount Grace. Then Benjamin leaned forward in his saddle, and Caesar pricked his ears to run, but Catherine's mount had begun to wheeze from the journey, and she said, "This one is as tired as I am. I must be getting fat. I will break him."

Benjamin's Caesar still strained forward, and he said, "Ho now, boy. Steady." The panting of her own horse echoed through Catherine, as though she could hear his animal blood speaking. She wondered if the animals caught the moods of their riders.

They started up the last hill, and Benjamin said, "We're here. No one can catch us now." Catherine knew this hill as well as she knew the shapes of her own feet. The hedges were clipped more closely than in her childhood, and three new cottages had been built for the workers, but the soft roll of the land, away into the gorse, was unchanged. As a child, Catherine had thought it had flowed away to God, who had laid down the swells and dips around Mount Grace at the beginning of time.

Catherine clicked her tongue to stop her horse at a trough at the side of the road. Ann slid off, and Catherine followed, rubbing the lathered neck while the gelding drank extravagantly, snorting into the water and swishing its muzzle about. "We can walk from here," said Catherine, and they led the horses the last mile. They were sweating more than the animals by the time they trudged into the village. Catherine could still not stop herself from lingering at the path to their old convent as they walked by, though it had been a drapery for years now. The broken stained-glass windows of the church had been replaced with plain leaded panes, and the doors stood open. The buildings cast a long shadow over the road. A man walked out of the convent and peered at Catherine. It was one of their young weavers, the son of an Overton farmer, and when he recognized her, he bowed and called, "Lady Catherine!"

She stopped. "Do you know if Father John is at his home?"

"That old man. Yes, he's here. Sitting at the public house if he's not sitting in his own front room."

Catherine smiled. "He keeps regular hours?"

"Regular as the sun in the heavens," the young man said. "Regular as the king at his table."

"Take care how you speak of the king," said Catherine. He bowed again and they walked on. Beyond her father's home were the village square and the large house of the Justice, Kit Sillon. Same as ever, the unmoving center of a changing world. Ann took the reins and they headed through the gate toward the stables. John Bridle's man was leaning against a post, picking his teeth with a twig.

"Lady Catherine Overton," he said, throwing down the stick and reaching for the reins. "You have purchased a fine new ride."

"He's ridden a hard way and needs water. They all have."

"Yes, Madam," he said, "and rub-downs as well."

Catherine's father was coming around the hedge toward her. John Bridle had widened in the last few years, and his girth made walking a complicated event involving both forward and side-to-side motion. Catherine embraced him, and he said, "I thought I was dreaming, to see you atop that demon. And that is Ann Smith, as I live and breathe."

"It is," said Ann.

"And here is my granddaughter," he said, reaching for Veronica. "I may have a sweetie for you in my kitchen, little lady. Come and kiss your old grandfather."

Veronica hesitated, then went to him. "I like strawberries very much."

"Strawberries you shall have, then," said John Bridle. He nuzzled the child's hair and looked up, over her head, to Benjamin. "And here is the man."

"You see three of those before you," said Benjamin.

"I only see one for my daughter."

Catherine said, "You have put up these banns?"

"In a few places," said John Bridle. "Here and there. Perhaps one or two got stuck beneath a bench." He grinned at Benjamin. "Just following the gentleman's orders."

So they were not for Margaret. "Father, how do you?" Catherine asked. She pushed herself back to arm's length to observe him. His face was netted with threads of blood, but his vision looked bright, and he held her hands with a young man's strength.

"I do as well as any creature under God's eye," he said. "He keeps me in bread and good ale, and the village thrives with the new works. I have babies to christen and I'm grown fat enough to keep the widows off me." He patted his protruding gut. "It keeps me safe from temptation."

"Gluttony is also a sin, old man," said Kit Sillon, behind him. The Justice's beard had whitened and he stooped as he clung to the oak post, staring at Catherine from under a set of startlingly opulent eyebrows.

John Bridle put his head back and laughed at the setting sun. "God has made me a wide man, as He has made you a narrow one, Sillon. It will not kill either you or your soul to be a bit broader in all ways. And it is no sin to thank God and enjoy His gifts."

The left side of Sillon's mouth crept upward. "That is why I bring my moral questions to your door, Father John. And now, here's your daughter, come to ask your favor. What do you think she'll want this time?" A puddle collected in the right corner of his mouth as he spoke, and Sillon brushed the spit off with the back of his left hand and slung it into the road. The good eye found Catherine, then shifted to Benjamin. "You wonder, don't you? What I suffer?" He laughed and let the drool run freely over his lip. "Age. That's not a thing even a woman with learning can halt. Think you can heal that?" He lifted his right arm. The fingers were brittle as old branches, and the hand trembled in the air. "Nothing for that but the grave and some hope of resurrection in a younger form."

Catherine said, "The body will run headlong toward the tomb despite our efforts." She took Sillon's ruined hand and straightened his fingers. The nails had yellowed, but someone was keeping them trimmed and clean. "Your wife does this?"

"My wife died almost a twelve-month hence. I have a man who does for me."

Catherine nodded. "The most any one of us can do is slow our race back to dust."

"You will be wanting the agreement to this marriage of yours?"

"If you have it finished," said Benjamin.

"Finished and dry and paid for by this new father of yours." He aimed a finger at Benjamin. "You will not have title to the Overton properties or the Havens properties though you may claim profits from the sales of the wools gained thereon." The finger wavered toward Catherine. "You will not sell the Overton lands or buildings away from your son without written permission of a court."

"You have put your name to it?" asked Benjamin.

"Signed and sealed. And if the king hangs me for it, my miseries will be at their end."

"And the Havens lands?" asked Catherine.

"What Havens lands? Havens is Overton now." Sillon flung a hand at John Bridle. "You'll also have whatever this old reprobate leaves you, and you can do whatever you want with that. I will be gone to the worms by then anyway. Race to the dust, as you say."

Father John bowed his head and they all let a solemn few moments pass, until Sillon said, "Why do we waste our time loitering in the road like a pack of idiots? I suppose you two want a church, like any other young couple. Bridle, you're the one's been whispering the banns. Will you perform for them and risk your neck?"

Catherine chewed her lip. "I am a widow with no man over me. I have been a Havens and now I am an Overton. I will marry if I choose."

"So it is the same tune as ever," said Sillon. "You women will have your heads. Or the king will have them."

Catherine bristled. "Wherefore are you so sour, Master Sillon? I've not seen you in many a day."

"And many a fine day it was, when I saw neither a Havens nor an Overton on my doorstep. But here you are, like the plague following the sweat. I must tell you, Lady Catherine, seeing you does not put me into a dancing mood."

Catherine turned to gaze down the open road. "I have not traveled here for a frolic," she said. Sillon, behind her, gave no answer. Low storm clouds had rolled themselves out like a sheet of pewter over the sky. The old convent walls were dull grey in the low light, and Catherine could smell the tang of new woolens and water. She wondered if the river behind the buildings ran high from the spring rains. "Our old rooms are stuffed with goods for sale," she said to no one. "God has likely shut his ears against us all. I hope the king follows His lead."

"What's that? What's that you say?" demanded Sillon. "Turn your face and speak to me directly, girl. You're not so high and mighty these days that you needn't look a man in the eyes."

Catherine turned. "I beg your pardon, sir. I was just thinking of what we have done to the village. And to the buildings where we once prayed. All of us women, together."

"I will bring the agreement on the morrow. It's too late for a wedding tonight." Sillon worked his way stiffly back down the front walk. The right foot scraped along, and Catherine could now see that his entire right side drooped, as though the flesh were dissolving. He muttered as he walked. "The scriptures say a man can pray anywhere he is, so I will leave you and your father to it. Sweet Christ on the water." He wiped his mouth and slung the matter away. "Will I never see the end of this family?"

"Not yet," called Father John after him. He smiled sadly. "And are you ready for marriage then? With no more of your family present?"

Catherine regarded her father's worn face. He had never married at all, and yet here she was, as well as a woman might be. She looked at Benjamin. "Ann and Veronica will be my family," she finally said. "And Joseph and Reg."

The sky glowered darkly above them, and Veronica had fallen asleep on her grandfather's shoulder. John Bridle said softly, "How does my grandson, Daughter?"

"Still among the pages at the prince's court. He is against this marriage, Father."

John Bridle nodded. "Will you marry this man with that curse on you?" He pointed at Benjamin and they all followed the arc of his finger. But before Catherine could answer, he said, "Margaret Overton claims you are already married to her. Yes, the word has reached me here. She says she carries your child. She says it was done at the House. That you made a promise and consummated the union."

Benjamin said, "I deny it."

Catherine said, "It is nothing, Father."

The old man lifted an eyebrow. "The consummation?"

"Father," said Catherine, and she tried to smile. "The world's ways have infected you."

"It's a disease I've learned to live with," he said. "And you say nay to this story?"

The sun ripped a scarlet seam in the western clouds. Catherine hooded her eyes with her hand. "Benjamin tried to be a friend to her. Men act without foreseeing the consequences."

"As do women," said her father.

Catherine's face stung. "And women bear false witness to maneuver themselves and their families into better positions. Their battles are often held on the field of gossip."

"As are men's," said her father.

Catherine nodded again. "You have me cornered there, Father. Except that when men gossip, they call it the current news."

"You win the match," said her father. He turned once again to Benjamin. "Will you marry my daughter with a free conscience?"

"I will."

Catherine watched the sun tear its way into full view. "Will you perform a marriage with a free conscience? We are sinners, you know."

John Bridle said, "Can we do anything in this world without sin?"

"No," said Catherine. "We sin, every one of us."

"Without sin, we would have no need of Christ. And so our sin brings us around at the last."

"If we confess to it." Catherine wiped her brow with a clout.

"Have you aught to confess?"

"I am one with the other sinners of the world. No more or less."

"Well said, Daughter."

Catherine said, "Have you got those sheep up to a second shearing in a season?"

John Bridle clapped her on the back and Veronica woke with a start. "That's my daughter. We might try feeding the ewes white bread and good ale this year. Can you imagine the fleeces springing from them then?"

"I have always said that cruelty to God's beasts shows a shallow heart," said Catherine.

"Will we stand here discussing the weather, as well?" asked Ann. "I thought I was riding from some demon come to carry us off to prison, and now it begins to look as though we will spend the night philosophizing and then start the haying directly."

"Have you heard it all, Father?" asked Catherine. "Of our time in the prison? Of this Martins, this king's man? He travels with a flame of a man named Barts and his shadow Chandler. They know what we do, and they will report ill of me if he sees a payment in it."

John Bridle stroked his beard. "I hear the news now and then from London. But we are not in London. It is a long way away. We sometimes must make our own law. So, Daughter. Will you marry him?"

Catherine laid one hand across her middle. The other went into her pocket, where the pennyroyal lay. It crumbled between her fingers. "I will do it."

Her father regarded the sky. "I'm one with Sillon. No marriages in the dark. Day for nuptials, night for making heirs. Come on to my kitchen, Granddaughter," he said, swinging Veronica. He bowed to Benjamin. "We will meet you and your men at the church at dawn."

Chapter Forty-Eight

Ann took Veronica to bed, leaving Catherine alone with John Bridle. They sat in the kitchen with a jug and a loaf between them. The priest slapped the knife against the bread board until Catherine set her hand on his wrist. "You will make me mad with that noise. What's on your mind?"

"Your sister-in-law." John Bridle stared into Catherine's eyes. "And you. Are you well? Too well?"

"Can a person be too well?"

"A woman can be doubly well. As well as two people. A well of wellness."

Catherine smiled and poured herself a cup of wine. "You may say it, Father."

"You grow fat in the waist. Your eyes are blue beneath. You look like your mother when she was—. Well, it doesn't bear expression."

"When she was carrying a child? Can we not speak of my mother without shame? Even now, with her so many years underground?" She shoved back the stool and stood. "It falls on the woman always, does it not? The sin is the mother's, and she must purge it from the child." She sat again. "Yes. You know my face as you knew my mother's, shining with guilt."

John Bridle rose to place his palm against Catherine's cheek. "You shine, Daughter, but I will not call it sin. Your mother's sin brought you into this world and I would not have it undone to save my soul. And if she sinned, I sinned as greatly as she did." He retook his seat and hacked at the loaf. "I sometimes read on the Greek authors and wonder if they did not see further into our souls than we do. What if God returns us to this world to live through our own purgatories in new bodies? What if we purge out our sins by being born again? And who could be born, or born again, without our mothers wanting men?"

"Father, you have turned pagan. And I thought we had rejected the purgatory as a superstition of the Roman church."

"Perhaps we have. We must say that we have. But we burn, do we not? For love. For children. For wealth. Perhaps we return in new bodies to burn the Hell out of us before we fly to heaven to stay. And I hope one day to meet your mother there, sin or no sin. And any sin you have contracted through her has been purified by your mind. And now, to bed, so that you are not a dull bride." He left the butchered loaf where it lay, pushed himself to his feet and, handing her the cup, shooed Catherine from the room. "If you are certain. There may be shame yet to come."

"I am sure of almost nothing these days. But I trust Benjamin's word. And I will do what can be done for this child."

Upstairs, she undressed herself in the firelight, flinging her clothes over a bench without ceremony, and sat on the floor like a maid and stared into the flames as though they would send her a sign of what the next morning would bring.

The morning beyond that. The rain swished against the window, but the wind said nothing she could understand.

Catherine woke in the grey dawn with her head on the floor. The fire, uncovered all night, had died into ash, and her hair was tangled. She had been dreaming of ravens, dozens of them. They had come in through the window and perched on the chairs and bedposts, the hearth and the chests. One had landed before Catherine and stood, bobbing its black head at her. It had turned first one gold eye on her, then the other. Its great beak clopped three times, then it said "Margaret." At that they all began to beat their wings, screeching "Margaret Margaret Margaret" and Catherine had opened her eyes to the silent room. Then a wren resumed its morning song on the windowsill, singing a melody that sounded like "secretive secretive secretive."

Catherine pushed herself to her feet and rubbed her stiff shins. Her back hurt, and she'd let the cup roll away, dribbling wine as it went. She couldn't rub the stain from the stones, and the maid would know she had spilled her drink. Let her see. It was no crime to drink wine in her father's house.

Her father's house. Catherine went to the door and called for a chambermaid to bring her fresh water, and while she waited she shook out her clothing. Footsteps hurried up and down the hall, and soon Ann's familiar thump hit the door.

"Are you awake?" Ann came in with Veronica, who hopped onto the bed and squirreled under the covers with her poppet. Ann ran her hand over the top cover. "You haven't slept here."

"I fell asleep on the floor. I was here. Alone. I think my body was crying out for rest."

One side of Ann's mouth smiled. "No matter to me where you lie or who is lying with you."

"Why do you sleep on the dirty floor, Mother?" asked Veronica. She popped up and ran to the window, throwing it open. The wren fled, and Veronica waved her Cleopatra at it as it went. "Go, bird!"

Catherine laid her hand on her daughter's hair. "I lost the time and was awake before I knew I was asleep. God gave me no time to find my pillow."

Ann rubbed her arms against the early breeze. "It's your wedding day."

The girl came in with the water, and Catherine stripped to bathe. The water was warm enough to soften her tight muscles, and Catherine held the wet clout on the back of her neck. She bent her head one way, then the other. "I have the headache this morning. It runs clear down my back. I am becoming Jane Dudley. I wonder if we have any willow bark." She clutched her head in both hands and stretched downward. The pain slid away and she finished washing, pulled on the skirt and bodice. Ann tied her up in the back and helped her on with the sleeves. Twisting her hair into a simple knot, Catherine fixed her coif and called it good.

John Bridle's kitchen was spotless, and his three girls, all Bridgettine novices from Syon House once, were fresh and clean, their hair tied back and their aprons white. One of them was squatting on a stool, picking pin feathers from a chicken and a second was kneading bread on the corner table. A pile of cabbages lay in a basket on the floor beside a bucket of eggs, and the third maid was pulling the dead leaves from them. When they saw Catherine, the girls curtsied before returning to their tasks. "Will you eat?" asked the oldest. She indicated the big plank table that was pushed up to the window. It looked out over the back, toward the stables.

"Your kitchen is pristine as a palace," said Ann, and the girl's face flamed with pleasure as she spread a slice of bread with strawberry jam and pushed it on a plate toward Veronica.

"Here you are, small mistress. Eat that all up."

Catherine took a seat with the widest view. The side garden was still winter-dull, with layers of straw over last year's rows. The gravel looked raked and washed. She stood and stepped out into the blue morning. The scent of the earth made her smile, and she squatted to turn the young, translucent leaves of the lettuces in the raised salad bed, then picked one and held it up to the sun. It looked almost gold, she thought, like a shard of stained glass. She tucked the straw up around the necks of the tender plants and moved on.

"Do you mean to marry today or not?" John Bridle said. Catherine startled, and he took her arm. "Your man will be waiting for you."

"Sillon tells truth about the law. We do not make it."

Father John put his arm through Catherine's. "But I do make the marriages in Mount Grace. Come then. You don't want to go with dirt under your fingernails."

They walked through to find Ann fixing Veronica's coif. "Will we go to find you a father, child?" asked Catherine.

"Where do we find the fathers?" the girl replied, and the priest lifted her.

"We find them at the church door," he said, and led them out.

The village was closed up against the cold, and Benjamin emerged from the inn with Reg and Joseph. John Bridle set Veronica down in the old stone porch of the church and waited until Benjamin stood next to Catherine and took up the fingers of her right hand.

The priest said, "Will you love each other as the scriptures require, and forebear the quarrels and the daily betrayals that mark the lives of husbands and wives? Will you care for each other when your hair grows grey and your eyes are too gummed for lust? Will you live together in peace and depart contentedly when you must be in different places? And not harp at one another with the foul notes of jealousy or gamble each other's money away?"

"This sounds like no vow I have ever taken," remarked Benjamin. He was looking at Catherine.

She smiled. "My father is no ordinary priest."

"And we are no ordinary folk, are we?"

"No, Husband."

Ann pushed them closer together. "Will you or won't you? The questions still hang in the air unanswered and my toes are numb with cold."

"I will," said Benjamin.

"I will, said Catherine.

"And so it is accomplished," said the priest. "I will record it in the parish record and it is done, come what will." Benjamin bent to put his lips gently on Catherine's, and the priest said, "Time enough for that. I have not et this morning, and I will blow away with the first wind if I don't get some bread in me." He added, "You're man and wife, by the grace of God, and I urge you to have some grace in your lives. Come, Ann Smith, lead me and my granddaughter to my table." He stepped onto the path and waved. Kit Sillon came labouring toward them. "Go to my house, man," the priest called. "There's a cup for you."

"You are my father now?" asked Veronica, wedging herself between the couple and staring up at Benjamin. "We could have found you any old where."

John Bridle's front door stood open, and they all retired to the kitchen, where the chambermaid served ale and bread and cheese with stewed apples and fresh cream. But Catherine had no appetite, and she went to the back window and watched the garden slowly waking. She pushed the pane open, and leaned out. She could hear the distant drone of spinning wheels. A lark sang a note from the top of a tall fir, and dozen bright birds burst from the boughs and hurtled themselves across the sky.

"Mount Grace lies in layers," she said. "This one lies over top of the village of my memories. Those last days, when the king's men destroyed us. There was blood in the pavers, thick as dark honey. I would wager it can still be seen, if you move the bales of wool. I recall sitting in this room as a girl, and you teaching me my letters. I sat at that very table and you would guide my right hand with your own." She glanced over her shoulder at her father. "It was to prevent my using the left hand, wasn't it? Mother Christina would beat me if I picked up even a stone with my left." She turned. The priest and the judge sat at the table, watching her. Benjamin leaned in the doorway. Ann and the maids had disappeared.

"I was meant to go to court. You know that, Father. Then I ruined my chance. Then I decided I was better off to stay. Then I wanted to go, and go I did. And now I both want to go and to stay. I am here and not here every minute of my life."

She leaned back on the window and laughed. "I am both woman and child all of the time. How can you bear my company?"

Benjamin silently withdrew, and Catherine heard his steps on the narrow staircase.

"How can I bear to be without it?" her father said.

"William loved me. And we know how that story ended."

"William is in his tomb. Don't shackle yourself to a ghost. You didn't cause his death, nor did you cause his grief during life."

Catherine sat across from the two old men and clasped her hands. "I know that. Nor did I make myself the child of a priest and a prioress, but these events live in our blood, do they not?"

"How thin is your blood, that it can only hold a few years' events?"

She rubbed her forehead, as though the motion might put her thoughts into place. The morning birds argued outside the window, and she put her hands over her ears and closed her eyes.

"You cannot disappear that way," her father said.

"Like water in summer." Catherine opened her eyes. "The river behind the convent used to fill a pool near the large willows. It was a shallow place, and old Sister Veronica used to take me there in the warm weather to cool my feet. But when the weather was hot, the water would dissolve away and leave nothing but old roots and nests of dead leaves. I would cry." Catherine laughed at herself. "And then she would walk me out under the sky and promise me that God would send the water down again when He had made use of it. I used to stare up at the sun, wondering what God's feet looked like." She tried to laugh again, but her throat closed against it. "Father, I have wronged my sister-in-law. And the king's sister."

The front door opened and closed, but they did not move. Father John said, "That Margaret is a blight and a plague, God forgive me for saying it. If she is with child, it had to be got by an angel of God. No man but a saint could do it."

"You are my father, and you take my part. But, mark me, I have been a player in whatever evil she has done."

Ann came into the kitchen. "The village is out."

"They expect some celebration," said the judge.

The priest called for his girl. "Open the door so that we may call our neighbors in. Sillon, wipe that devil's glare from your face or you will frighten the children. Put on your bridal smile, Daughter, and wipe your mind clean. Go greet your well-wishers."

Someone called a hallo, and the old judge scooted out of the kitchen with Ann. Catherine and John Bridle waited until they heard Simon, the old innkeeper, call out "Where is this groom?" then gathered some plates of food from the pantry and walked into view.

"Boy!" called Sillon, and a child squeezed through the people gathered in John Bridle's front garden and stepped inside. "Bring me that chestnut mare. Put the Spanish saddle on her."

The kitchen was full of women now, and the men massed in the sitting room. Sillon squinted through the front shutter. Benjamin came down and stood with Catherine by the hearth. She put on her modesty, ducking her head as the men wished her husband well in getting a son, but she was watching the embers extinguish themselves under their ashes.

"And are you asleep, Catherine Havens?"

She looked up into the freckled face of her old friend Elizabeth Aden. She was holding out a crock and Catherine could smell the honey.

"Look at you," said Elizabeth, pressing the jar into her hand. She stepped aside to reveal a young girl, with bright brown hair escaping her coif. "Say hallo to the woman who brought you into the world," Elizabeth said, and the girl curtsied.

"She's a beauty," said Catherine, but the sight of her brought tears to the backs of her eyes and she put her face onto her old friend's shoulder to hide them. "You recall that summer," she whispered.

"Indeed I do." Elizabeth pushed Catherine to arms' length. "And here you are, yet again. And my bees are as fat as the sheep of the fields. Where is Ann Smith?"

"Here! Elizabeth! Have you still got the bees?" Ann was hailing her from the stairs, and Elizabeth kissed Catherine on the cheek and waved. "Be well, Catherine."

Catherine watched them embrace, Elizabeth lifting Ann's chin to examine the old cicatrice across her throat. Benjamin took Catherine's hand, but when she met his eyes, he said nothing.

The food was gone within the hour and the morning wound into afternoon, then evening. More ale was brought and dancing commenced in the yard when three men took up pipes and began to play. Catherine had almost fallen asleep on her feet when the priest said, "Will these young folks not be allowed to go to their bed?"

"I'm not so young," Benjamin called, and the men hooted.

"Young enough," someone yelled.

"Out, now," said the priest, shoving at the nearest man. It took him and Joseph and Ann and Reg together to empty the house and grounds, Catherine handing out soft pairs of leather gloves her father had provided. Finally she sat and pulled off her shoe to rub her sole.

"Upstairs," said the priest.

"Not yet." Sillon was at the door. "I thought that rabble would never clear themselves out. Come on with me before you take yourselves up." He glared and went out.

Catherine slipped the shoe back on and followed Benjamin outside. Sillon stood there, holding the halter of a young, golden mare. On her back was a burnished leather saddle, stamped with blossoms and leaves and studded with brass. He handed Catherine a paper. "Here's your agreement. And here is your wedding gift. Do not overfeed her. She has the appetite of a queen's ride and will founder too easily." He held out the leather strap and frowned.

Catherine wound the halter around her hand and pulled the mare forward. The animal pushed her silky muzzle into Catherine's hand and snuffed. She smelt sweet and green. "She is fit for a queen. I have no words to thank you."

"Ah, women have too many words anyway," said the old judge. The bushes of his eyebrows rose and fell. "Treat her well, Catherine Havens Overton Davies. You will sit her as she should be sat." He moved forward and crooked his arm enough to pat Catherine on the shoulder. "Well, then, you be a good girl." He rubbed at his eyes and shuffled off, muttering to himself.

The stable boy took the horse, and Reg retreated to the kitchen with Ann. Catherine heard them playing with Veronica. Joseph said his good-night and said he would sleep at the inn. John Bridle said, "I will have another glass before I retire." He shook Benjamin's hand and embraced his daughter. Then he was gone.

"And that leaves only two," said Benjamin. "Wife, you must guide me to my bedchamber."

"And so I will," said Catherine. She took him by the hand and led him up the stairs.

They'd been in proper beds before, but in her father's house, Catherine put out the light before she allowed Benjamin to untie her coif, then her sleeves, then her skirt. He knelt to slip it down and he laid it aside on the floor. Then he ran his arms up her legs until he had her by the hips. He lifted her and laid her on the bed. She watched him in in the dusky light as he undressed and crept in beside her.

"May I touch you without fear?" he asked.

Catherine laughed quietly. "What have you ever feared?"

He raised himself on one elbow. "Men of law. The plague. Hurting you." He bent over her and kissed her mouth.

"Do not lie to me," she said.

"Never. I vow it. I will only lie on you." He rubbed his face down her breasts and her body warmed to him. His arm came around her waist, setting her higher on the sheets. "Here I am."

"And I," whispered Catherine. "I am here for you. And I will love you." Her muscles went hot and she pulled him over her.

CHAPTER FORTY-NINE

The moon was up, shining a vindicating light upon the house. Catherine slid from the bed and searched the shadows in her father's garden. She had made the decision herself, and now she would be victorious and happy. Should be happy. But the king would have to be told. And her son. And Lady Anne. A storm festered in the far west, but for now the sky was bright. The high road was a silver ribbon, and a lone badger waddled up the grassy verge. An owl swooped across its path, and Catherine crossed herself. She turned, but Benjamin was sleeping on his stomach, one arm out where she had lain. She had better join him again, she thought, and slid back into her spot, barely moving her husband as she adjusted herself for rest.

The eastern sky was blushing with the dawn when Catherine opened her eyes again. Ann was calling from downstairs and soon there was pounding on the door.

"Come in," said Benjamin. He covered Catherine with the blanket and scratched his jaw.

Ann peeked around the door. "I suppose you will break your fasts in your bed like a duke and duchess."

"I eat wherever I choose," said Benjamin. "Bring me some pickled oranges, Sister, and the hind foot of an elephant, stewed in almonds."

"I will pickle you, man, for sure," Ann said, "and what's more I will bring you your man's hind foot, kicking your breeches onto you. There is bread on the table downstairs, if you can rouse yourselves." The door closed and Veronica's voice shrilled, laughing. Ann was probably carrying her over one shoulder.

"So begins married life," said Benjamin. He tossed off the covers, smacked Catherine with a kiss, and jumped up. "Get dressed, Wife, and let's go claim our thrones. No man will dare come between us now. Nor woman neither. And if they try, we will go away on a boat, together. "

They had eaten and were on their horses within the hour. The sun had been overtaken by clouds, and Joseph pulled off his coat and threw it over Catherine's shoulders as she climbed onto her new mare. Veronica wormed her way into Ann's cloak. Reg checked her reins, and Ann touched him briefly on the shoulder, but he simply nodded and took his own saddle. John Bridle shook Benjamin's hand and kissed his daughter. Kit Sillon did not show.

"A rough coat sometimes covers a good dog," said the priest, and Catherine smiled despite herself.

"Thank him again for the mare," she said, and John Bridle nodded. They turned onto the high road toward Overton House.

They were all day riding, Catherine and Benjamin side by side, and Veronica chattering to Ann behind them. The wind blew in rain, and they bent into it, but it only lasted an hour, and the late sun dried them. They stopped once to eat their cold meat and bread, but the road unwound before their eyes, and no one wanted to stop.

Catherine's eyes were drooping as they turned the corner and saw the grey tops of Overton House. "We're home," Catherine said.

"Home," said Benjamin. "It's finished." He spurred Caesar and the others whooped behind and gave chase.

Catherine kept her mare to a comfortable walk, and, as she approached her house, grew sober, seeing the chambermaids on the doorstep looking mournful. "Agnes," she said, and Benjamin wheeled around to meet her.

He leaned over to squeeze her hand. "We'll respect the time."

The stable boys came running as they dismounted, and the chambermaids dropped to their knees. Catherine said, "Up, girls."

The eldest looked but did not rise. "There are men here. A fat man and his companions." Eleanor came outside. She wore a frown.

The loyal Overton kites spiraled, low, over the House, and one by one they set their feet down on the air to slow themselves for landing. They disappeared into the gorse in the far field, and Benjamin said, "Just as I feared. Where are these men?"

Eleanor took the reins from Catherine, and Ann threw hers to Joseph.

"They were searching the house," said Eleanor. "They're armed. I don't know where they've gone, but they've not gone far, I'll wager my soul."

"Ann, take Veronica to the back." Catherine slid heavily to the ground and shouted at the broad stone front, "Who is in my home?" No answer. "Go," she said to Ann. "Lock yourself in the laundry." She called again, "Where are you? Show yourselves."

Not a sound. Benjamin said he would check the stable, and Catherine walked inside and up her own stairs to her old rooms. The air here was fragrant with lavender and rosemary, frost and fire. But the bed curtains were filmy with the dirt of disuse, and when Catherine shook a corner, a cloud burst from the fabric. One of the chambermaids had lit the hearth, but the winter scent hadn't fully burned off. The bed was turned back, and Catherine let her hand wander over the musty linen, over the side where her first husband had slept. His favorite glass still stood on his side table, and the bed curtain was still torn where he had caught his heel one evening in a moment of passion. She put her nose to the pillow and inhaled. She fancied that she could still smell his hair from deep in the goose down, that woodsy savor of a man who liked the outdoors. Did the feathers recall the shape of William, who had lain here how many hundreds of times? The canopy above reminded her of the days when they'd been happy to be in bed together.

The house was too quiet, and when a branch slipped and exploded in sparks, Catherine jumped. She almost tripped over one of her old chests in the gloom, opened and half-emptied. "Who is here?" she shouted again, but again no one answered. When she opened her door, Benjamin grabbed her and covered her mouth with his hand.

"They're coming back in," he said, backing her in and shutting the door behind him. He cocked his head toward the door, then set her on the edge of the bed. "Listen, these men have a warrant that looks royal."

Catherine's throat had iced through. He let her loose and she rolled over the bed and ran to the window. The sun was tangled in the far trees. An Overton dog ran out of the stable, barking and whirling, and one of the horses nickered from inside. Men's voices congregated somewhere below. Another dog, a strange one with long legs and a spiky coat, rushed out, growling. It leapt onto the Overton hound and the two dogs rolled in the dust. A group of men strolled from the stable, and one of them whacked the Overton dog with a stick and the thing fled, yipping. The stranger, whining, held his ground against the newcomers. Catherine felt the dirt ground into her plain green skirt and brushed at herself. She could feel the slick smudges of sweat that surely marked the underarms and back. She was afraid, and it made her filthy.

Joseph appeared from the stable and stood before the group with his hand readied on his hips. And there they were. Martin David Martins and Ciaran Barts and Ellers Chandler. Their servants lingered behind, staring up at the face of Overton House. Martins stood at the front of the pack, posing for a moment as though he knew he was being watched. Even in the gathering darkness, he was resplendent in red jacket and soft tan breeches. He wore pale silk hose and his codpiece featured gold embroidery and two small green tassels. The shining weapon was fixed to his side, just where his body began its alarming spread toward the ground. Barts was dressed in brown, more sober than his companion, with soft breeches and solid riding boots. Chandler was in black, like a hangman. He carried a whip and was trying to brandish it in competition with Martins' shining wheel-lock.

Benjamin said, "They have been through the house once. They claim to have found what they sought."

Ann came out of back door, and Catherine could hear her voice. "What do you do here? You are out of your element."

Martins' face tightened. "Woman, have you come to claim your trouble? You must forgive me, but I've misplaced your name. I don't keep the names of all the servants in my books." He wobbled forward. Barts stepped up behind him. Chandler, as always, followed, looking with his thin arms and skinny legs in the dark clothing like a spider stepping across its web. Joseph looked from Ann to the men and finally deferred to the woman.

Catherine recoiled from the window and bumped against Benjamin, who put out a hand to steady her, but she could still hear them, Martin insisting "Your lady is a thief and a whore."

"Get you gone," said Ann. "Set yourselves back into your saddles and turn your faces toward London."

"You are now mistress here?" said Martins. "I give my congratulations for your raising. But I have business. I come in the name of the king to arrest your lady for rank whoredom, against the king's dignity. He takes pity upon his sisters who maintain their faith. Your lady should have submitted her will to his."

"He cannot," whispered Catherine. Her chest began to sing with pain, and she could not get her breath. The sun slipped downward, blazing out a flare to blind her. "Benjamin, he cannot." Joseph seemed to be speaking, but Catherine couldn't hear through the whistling in her ears. The men were arguing. The sun dropped another notch in the sky.

"I will meet them," said Catherine.

"Not without me," said Benjamin.

Catherine tiptoed to the corner, and flattening herself against the wall, peered down. The front hall was empty, the door standing open. The air twirled with dust, slowly working circles through the shafts of candle light. A small grey cat stood on the threshold, sniffing the interior as though trying to decide whether to enter. Catherine stepped out, then down. The risers felt hard underfoot, and the click of her soles seemed to echo. But no one showed. She reached the entrance hall, where the cat looked up and meowed once. Then it fled in a streak.

No one was visible in the long gallery to the left, and Catherine moved over the carpets as quietly as she could toward the back stairs. She bent and listened. Voices somewhere below."Someone has arrived," said Benjamin from the entry hall.

Ann came panting in. "Another man—" she said flailing her arm at the door.

"I heard," said Catherine.

But it was only one, squinting into the dim hall. "Lady Overton," said John LaBranche. "Madam. I'm here to save you. Master Benjamin. You are here." He walked in and curled his soft fingers around her arm.

Catherine went bloody-minded. "You. You! Save me, you say? Save me? You might have done that weeks ago, and what did you do? Not a thing! How much of Benjamin's money did you spend to sit at your writing desk and do nothing?" Her voice spilled out of her, shrill as a caught rabbit, and she put her hand on her breast.

"I followed Martins and Barts and Chandler all the way along, but you were not here," LaBranche said. His spectacles were almost opaque with dust. He still wore the same worn boots and cheap jacket. "I have stayed at the Havenston inn. A very pleasant place. I have come for you."

"You've come to sniff out a fee," said Benjamin. "I do hope you have enjoyed the sights along the way."

"You may hire another lawyer if it pleases you," insisted LaBranche, "but I maintain that I am here to serve you."

"Your service kept me in prison." Catherine opened her mouth to go on, but Benjamin touched her shoulder. Martins and his men were behind the lawyer.

"We have found you out at last," said Martins. "And you, LaBranche, I thought we had lost you back in Nottingham. Excellent navigation, man, to make it so far on your own. I hadn't thought you had it in you. What a man will do for a handful of coins." Barts sniggered, and Martins stepped around the lawyer to take Catherine by the elbow. Barts took her by the other arm. "You must come with us. LaBranche, if you mean to defend this woman, you may begin at any time. It will be good finally to see you practice your profession. You are a man of law, am I correct? That's the rumour in London town though I have never seen the confirmation."

"Let her go," said Benjamin.

LaBranche glanced over at Catherine, but he didn't move to disengage her. Benjamin took Martins by the shoulder. They were all crowded together, and Catherine felt the men's breath like a choking fog about her head. "Get away from me," she whispered, and tried to push Martin and Barts aside. But they wouldn't go. The pair pressed in, gripping her elbows so tightly she could feel their nails through her wool sleeves. Benjamin drew his dagger, but they were too close for him to take a safe aim.

"You have no authority," said Catherine. "I have served in the household of the King's Beloved Sister, and I will go with no one who does not come in her name."

Martins coughed out a laugh. "The name of a woman is nobody," he said, trying to shake Benjamin off. "The name of a woman signifies the master to whom she belongs and nothing more. The name of a woman is a hole into which a man must drop his meaning and his seed. A woman makes nothing happen." He finally let himself stand, fastened between Catherine and Benjamin. "I might have helped you if you had wanted me. Had wanted me to."

"You have your spies in Dover, too. And at Ashridge. Don't you? Where is this warrant you claim to have from the king?" asked Benjamin. He backed a step, the dagger now fully out. "Let me see it."

"I have the warrant upon me," said Martins. "You have already seen such a thing. Many times, I think. The woman is a common whore. And a thief. I will maintain it."

Catherine said, "I will not go."

"You think to make a cipher of me, do you?" asked Martins. "No woman dirties my name and walks away." He slid up close to her, and she could see the evil shine in his eyes, smell the sweaty clothes. He whispered, and spit gathered on his lip as he spoke. "A woman had better stick her head in the dirt than put me down. I am known in the court. No woman says no to me." He unbuttoned his jacket and Catherine dropped her tired head.

He wore a silk belt. A green belt, woven with gold thread. "That is mine," she choked out. "That was in—"

"In the closet of the King's Sister?" said Martins. "You imagine that you own anything you see, Lady. It will not go well with you to show such avarice. Luxury is a woman's sin."

"It was in the case," she said to Benjamin. "The case that was taken from us along the road." She looked back at Martins. "And where do you hide your eye patch?"

Benjamin said, "You're certain that's yours?"

Catherine said, "I am sure as the grave."

Benjamin's face paled, then flamed. "You son of a dog," he said, pushing Catherine aside. "I will kill you where you stand."

"She is no innocent, and we will take her," said Chandler.

Martins laid his hand on the wheel-lock as Benjamin swung back the dagger. Barts scrabbled at Benjamin's arm, and they grappled, but Barts could not hold on and Benjamin slammed him to the floor. Martins straightened, the weapon aimed at Benjamin. "I have found the missing ring, and now we will go, this woman and I. It will be the two of us, like love birds, side by side. We know she likes a man." He took her sleeve again with his left hand. Barts scrambled to his feet.

"Take your paws from the lady," said Benjamin. "She is my wife. She is free by order of the court, and you will take her nowhere. Put down that damned thing."

"Your wife?" said LaBranche. "She can't be. It is against the king's law."

Martins said, "Get back, Davies, or we will take you along with her. A court order to a woman is like meat to a puppy. It's offered to get it to behave." He guffawed. "Don't act the fool. You've taken a whore. It is no secret." He paused, cleared his throat, spat on the floor. "A woman cannot be an heir to great lands nor order the king's men to stay or go. The land will be entailed to the Overton boy who serves the prince. He is a great favorite, I hear. It is sad for us all that his mother is so fallen. But then she is a woman, and sin is to be expected." Martins turned again to Catherine and bowed as though he were her manservant. "I will see to it that your son's interest in his properties is guarded well. I may have him appointed as my ward until he reaches his maturity. It will be of great profit to us both."

"You will not." Catherine smacked him, catching him unawares with her left hand, and sent him lurching against the wall. Two paces brought her to him again, and she hit him once more, this time with her left fist. He went to one knee, and blood spurted from his nose.

"You hyena!" he yelled, covering his face with his unencumbered hand. He pushed himself up the wall, the bulk of his wide haunches flattened against the plaster. "You are the harpy they say you are! You have all seen it!"

Barts and Chandler grabbed her and dragged her off the man, and Benjamin went for Barts. Chandler and Catherine struggled, but she couldn't get herself loose. He tore her left sleeve off, and tossing it behind him down, took her by the bodice and began shaking her. LaBranche was shrieking in short, high squeaks, and Catherine held onto Chandler's hand, trying to keep him from stripping her before the whole company. Martins, reeling forward, staggered to get at her from the other side. The weapon wobbled. Benjamin stood to meet him, but Ann had followed Martins and was pulling at his shoulder. Martins reeled backward, and the wheel-lock's surface flashed, brassy in the slant sun. Benjamin was trying to get Chandler's hand free from Catherine, and now Reg was in the room, beside Ann, and Catherine was shouting, "That thing, that weapon," but no one heard her.

They scuffled, and Catherine stumbled, pulled, dragged herself backward, still caught by Chandler and stuck between him and Benjamin, trying to land blows on each other. Catherine shoved Chandler with all of her strength, but he would not let go. Over his shoulder, she could see a golden wink in a narrow shaft of light as Martins raised the wheel-lock, braced it over his left forearm, and aimed at Benjamin. Reg grabbed at Martins' arm. Catherine wrenched herself as hard as she could, but the men would not be moved. The shot went off, flooding the entire room in smoke.

Chapter Fifty

It was all arms and legs and shouting. Someone and then someone else had fallen on top of Catherine, and she cried out, "You're breaking me! I cannot breathe!" The pressure of bodies was lifted from her, and she waved the smoke from her vision. "Benjamin? Where are you?"

"Here," he said, sitting beside her. His dagger lay on the floor. He was feeling his doublet.

The sulphurous clouds twirled and twisted away, and Martins appeared, frozen a few steps from them, the wheellock dangling from his right hand. He was staring, open-mouthed, at Benjamin. LaBranche stood beside him, and as the air cleared, he covered his mouth and wheezed out something like a cry.

Catherine dragged herself to her knees. Ann was beside her, saying "Are you hurt? Where, where are you hurt?"

But Catherine was not shot. Chandler lay where he had fallen, and the blood had already stained the floor by his side. On the front of his shirt bloomed a black flower, fringed with red. Benjamin crawled over to the man, but his eyes were open, fixed on nothing in the world.

"You have murdered your own man," said Benjamin. He pushed himself to his feet and regarded Martins, who still held the weapon. "And you have murdered one of Catherine's women, who lies downstairs. You will answer for it."

Martins lifted the wheel-lock and looked at it, as though he had only just then realized that it was in his hand. "You," he said. He seemed to be talking to the weapon, but then he raised his eyes to Benjamin. "It was you. You were preventing us from discharging our duty. Barts. You saw. And you, LaBranche. You saw." He pointed with the wheel-lock at the lawyer, who was clinging to the doorframe, and LaBranche threw himself face down.

"Let me have that," said Benjamin. "You have done enough harm for one day."

"You will have to take it from me," said Martins. He waved the weapon wildly, first at Benjamin, then Catherine, even at LaBranche, who screamed again and ducked his head.

Benjamin was on him in two steps, wrenching the firearm from Martins' hand. The fat man tottered, then flopped down where he was. It was like watching a rotten bladder of wine collapse on stone. Ann lifted Catherine and held her, drawing her skirts away from the blood.

"We must ride," announced Barts. "At once. Martins, up with you. I will fetch the horses." He knelt and pulled at one of Chandler's arms, then let it drop without ceremony. "This man is dead."

Barts addressed himself to Catherine. "As the lady of the house, you will arrange for the burial of this man who has died in your custody. I will inform his family what accident of fortune has befallen him. Martins, get up from there! We ride. Now."

Catherine said, "Now I am the lady of the house? When you kill your own and leave them lying in their blood? What say you to this, Master LaBranche? Are there not laws against murder in this country anymore?"

LaBranche touched his fingertips together and pursed his mouth. His upper lip glistened with sweat. "The law contains many statutes that pertain to the act of causing death. First —"

"Jesus on the water, will you shut your mouth?" said Benjamin. He took hold of Martins' arm and shook him.

Martins jiggled like a rat in a hound's jaws. "It was a mishap," he squealed. Then he indicated Ann. "That woman. That damned woman. She pulled my arm and interfered with my aim. She is to blame." Benjamin flung him away.

Ann let loose of Catherine. "You will not lay your murder at my feet. LaBranche, if you can pull your fingers apart, you might get a constable and have this man arrested." The lawyer did not move, and she kicked him in the shin. "Go, man. On your horse. That animal with the four hooves that you left in the courtyard."

LaBranche stumbled outdoors and away, and Martins scuttled around the other men. He squatted at Chandler's side and ran his hands into the man's breeches pockets.

"What are you doing?" asked Benjamin. He tried to haul Martins to his feet, but the man was so bottom-heavy that he rolled away.

"He was my companion. I will have something to take to his mother." He crawled back toward Chandler, and Benjamin shoved him with his toe.

"Get back. You will not take anything from here." Benjamin pushed at Martins again, then again. "Hand over that warrant."

Martins sat and stared at Benjamin's knees, then he gathered himself to his feet. It was like watching a small mountain rise from the base of a hill. He glared around. Benjamin would not be moved. Barts said, "Come on, man, give up the field," and Martins sat on the stairs. Benjamin prodded him, and the fat man produced the warrant, dropping it on the pavers. "This is not signed," said Benjamin. Martins didn't move again until they heard horses out front, and LaBranche pranced in, followed by Peter Grubb.

The constable walked to the body, then knelt, stroking his chin. "I figure a man that shoots his friend is bound to be punished twice." He struggled to his feet. "Who's the villain here?" They all pointed at Martins, and Grubb shouted, "Come on." A pair of his watchmen brought manacles and bundled Martins and Barts out. Grubb turned back in their dusty wake. "You will prepare the body?"

Catherine nodded, and the constable was gone. "There is not enough of England to hide their heads from the eye of God." She turned back to Chandler and, lifting the jacket edges, ran her fingers into the pockets that lined the garments. The large ones contained handkerchiefs and gloves, a small bag of coins. A dried nosegay. A short love message from someone named Alise. Catherine worked her fingers up near the collar. There, on the left, above the heart, was a tiny pocket with a flap and a button. She twisted it open and reached inside.

"Here it is," she said. She held up the ring. It was a deeply colored ruby, set in gold fretwork and surrounded with pearls. Catherine let a spear of light sparkle through it, then rolled it into her palm and held it out to Benjamin. "All of this over a man's wounded pride. And a stone." It lay, a sanguine spot in the middle of her hand. "This belongs to the King's Sister. I have seen it on her very finger. Mine is only a garnet."

"And now this poor fellow will pay for it under a stone," said Benjamin, toeing Chandler's arm.

Catherine lifted the ring toward her husband. "I must take it back where it belongs." She stared down at the dead man's face. A silent circle of servants had appeared at the head of the stairs above, and Benjamin nodded at them to carry Chandler away. "Where do you want him?"

"In the main kitchen," said Catherine. "Then in the chapel."

Benjamin offered a hand and pulled Catherine up beside him. "We must show ourselves now."

The tall oaks outside moved in a sudden wind, and the sun's rays shimmered through the windows like coins falling. Catherine said, "I will get the girls to clean up this floor."

Veronica's voice came piping from downstairs. "What is all the noise? Where is my mother?"

Ann said, "The child mustn't see this," and went.

Catherine watched the open shutter bump gently against the window frame. Far beyond them, a dog barked. A kite wheeled past, one dark initial against the sky.

Benjamin said, "The king may be merciful when we bow and show your great belly."

"He is so very well known for mercy," said Catherine. The wind set the curtains fluttering, and Catherine put her hand on the silk. It felt greasy and old. "How much water would wash this clean again? Maybe we should leave the shutters open and let the storms do what they will." She turned. "I will send for my father to say the words for this man. We will put him in the Havenston churchyard."

Someone moved at the top of the stairs, and they all looked up. Sebastian came stomping down and presented himself. "I stand before you, Lady, as your prisoner. It was I who set them onto you and now I am abandoned in the enemy camp."

"Sweet Mother of God," said Catherine.

Benjamin said, "What have you got to say for yourself?"

"I have nothing to say," said Sebastian. He drew a narrow knife from his boot. "I will be required to stand trial." He placed a hand on his throat. "They don't allow no neck-verse to servants, even if I can read as well as the next man. But I will not go. If they require me to go, I will not. I will swing from that window first." Sebastian's face was chalky and his eyes were liquid. "I will stick a hole into my heart before they will lay their hands on me." The blade shone with a dull wickedness when he held it up. "It is long enough to reach my soul."

Benjamin swiped the knife from his hand in one motion. "Now I have saved your soul from damnation and you will ride to your fate and sing your song to whoever cares to listen. You're a weasel." He cuffed the man on the jaw. "Reg! Bring me a rope."

CHAPTER FIFTY-ONE

The road south gave them time to accustom themselves to married life, sleeping together on lousy mattresses and moldy pillows and riding side by side by day. The Davies House was already alive with news of Master Davies and his new Lady, and they spent one night in each other's arms on the best bed in the house. They made love in silence, Benjamin careful not to lay his full weight upon Catherine's belly until she pulled him to her.

But Benjamin was not summoned to court. No word arrived from Ashridge. A letter came from John Dudley, saying that Benjamin was directed to Calais, where a load of his wool was said to have been abandoned, unclaimed by any merchant. Catherine had been ordered to Richmond Palace.

They parted in London, Benjamin promising a straight return. Reg and Ann went with Catherine. Only Jane Dudley came out as they rode up, Catherine in the lead and Ann behind her, holding Veronica. As they were deciding their words, Jane said, "At last you come. We have heard the story. The king has heard of it. And the prince."

Catherine curtsied low. "Rumour has wings but few wits, though if you have heard of my marriage, you have heard true."

Jane stood back to let them enter. "Yours and your sister's as well. The king does not say a word about you."

"My sister?"

"Come inside." She sent Ann downstairs and the men around back. "Leave the girl here." When they were alone, she appraised Catherine. "You are with child."

"I am."

"She is waiting for you." Jane went toward the receiving room, where Anne of Cleves perched on her big chair.

Catherine fell to the floor in front of the Lady of Cleves. "I have offended you most grievously, My Lady." She withdrew the ring from her pocket. "But I come having rescued your jewel, to restore it to you."

"Bring it to me," said Lady Anne. Catherine began to rise, but Lady Anne stopped her with an upraised palm. "Little Veronica, give it to me." The child plucked the gem from her mother's hand and delivered it. She sat at the feet of Anne of Cleves.

"Which is the more prized of these jewels?" said Lady Anne. "A ring or a daughter?"

Catherine chanced a look up. "My children are always my chiefest gems."

"Get up, Catherine," said the King's Sister. She put the ring on her finger and shoved herself out of the seat. "Jane, we will go to the game room." She took Veronica by the hand and they went, Catherine in a daze at the rear. They settled around the familiar table, and Jane began to deal out cards. No one picked them up. Veronica folded her hands and sat still.

"Your sister Margaret has behaved very bad," said Lady Anne. "Our messenger say that she has married a manservant. Someone from the Overton House."

"Who?" asked Catherine.

Lady Anne said, "You do not know your own servants?"

"Margaret has gathered servants of her own," said Catherine.

"She have cursed herself. This cannot be undone."

"It is I who have behaved cursedly, Lady Anne. But I have made a redemption in marriage. Benjamin is a gentleman."

"A redemption?" said Jane Dudley. She gave Catherine a withering look. "Your man had better make his fortune in the wool trade. And you had better set yourself to the work below with a vengeance and work your salvation with your hands."

"I am allowed to stay?"

"It is required." Lady Anne lifted a card and set it back where it had been. "You are to be in a purgatory. We will see how long it lasts."

"And how hot it will be," said Jane.

Catherine's eyes leaked tears, and she could not stop them. Veronica crawled over onto her lap, and Jane patted her hand. "You have been preserved by your sister's greater ruin. It is a most grievous fall."

"Beshrew me if I don't pity her. The world spins too fast for me. I don't know what to say."

"Your son is very silent," said Jane. "And you are not to send any letter into the prince's house."

Catherine said, "He will come back to me in time. He must."

"Go now," said the King's Beloved Sister. "I play alone." She smeared the cards into a pile, and Catherine went.

But Jane was with her, and before Catherine descended, she said, "The tide has turned and you will not be much in the king's thoughts here."

"Are Lady Anne and the king friends again?"

"The king has friends enough. He has lately turned his attentions to another widow. One not as irregular as you have been. She is noble and good. The prince has warmed to her."

"And Lady Anne's hopes are at an end?"

"She never had a hope. Not a true one. Keep your head low, Catherine, and pray for your soul. No one has forgotten your past, and all of the king's sisters are to be impeccable. Too many of them have fallen. You have done so under a lucky star. You have much to do to win back your character."

"I will undertake it," Catherine said. "And what is the lady called, the king's new favorite?"

Jane laughed, but she was not smiling. "You will appreciate the irony of it. She is a widow of good reputation, and her name is Catherine. Catherine Parr." Then she walked away.

Catherine took up her daughter's hand to begin the next journey. The unborn child shifted within her, and, with great care, she set her foot down, upon the first of the slick, uneven steps.

THE END

About the Author

Sarah Kennedy

Sarah Kennedy is the author of the novels *Self-Portrait, with Ghost* and *The Altarpiece, City of Ladies*, and *The King's Sisters*, Books One, Two, and Three of The Cross and the Crown series, set in Tudor England. She has also published seven books of poems. A professor of English at Mary Baldwin University in Staunton, Virginia, Sarah Kennedy holds a PhD in Renaissance Literature and an MFA in Creative Writing. She has received grants from both the National Endowment for the Arts, the National Endowment for the Humanities, and the Virginia Commission for the Arts. Please visit Sarah at her website: http://sarahkennedybooks.com.

If You Enjoyed This Book
Visit

PENMORE PRESS

www.penmorepress.com

All Penmore Press books are available directly through our website.

THE ALTERPIECE

BY

SARAH KENNEDY

It is 1535, and in the tumultuous years of King Henry VIII's break from Rome, the religious houses of England are being seized by force. Twenty-year-old Catherine Havens is a foundling and the adopted daughter of the prioress of the Priory of Mount Grace in a small Yorkshire village. Catherine, like her adoptive mother, has a gift for healing, and she is widely sought and admired for her knowledge. However, the king's divorce dashes Catherine's hopes for a place at court, and she reluctantly takes the veil. When the priory's costly altarpiece goes missing, Catherine and her friend Ann Smith find themselves under increased suspicion. King Henry VIII's soldiers have not had their fill of destruction, and when they return to Mount Grace to destroy the priory, Catherine must choose between the sacred calling of her past and the man who may represent her country's future.

PENMORE PRESS
www.penmorepress.com

CITY OF LADIES

BY

SARAH KENNEDY

It's midwinter in 1539, and Catherine Havens Overton has just given birth to her second child, a daughter. The convent in which she was raised is now part of the Overton lands, and Catherine's husband William owns the properties that once belonged to her mother's family. With a son, Robert, and her new daughter, Veronica, Catherine's life as the mistress of a great household should be complete.Henry VIII's England has not been kind to many of the evicted members of religious houses, and Catherine has gathered about her a group of former nuns in hopes of providing them a chance to serve in the village of Havenston, her City of Ladies. Catherine's own past haunts her. Her husband suspects that Catherine's son is not his child, and his ambitions lie with service at court. Then the women of Overton House begin to disappear, and though one of them is found brutally murdered nearby, William forces Catherine to go to Hatfield House, where the young Elizabeth Tudor lives, to improve the family's standing—and to ensure, for her own safety, that she is as far away from connections to her old convent as possible.Reluctantly, Catherine obeys, only to find herself serving not only the Protestant Elizabeth but also the shamed Catholic Mary Tudor. As the murders in Yorkshire mount up and her loyalty to the Tudor sisters grows more complicated, Catherine must uncover the secret of the killer and keep her dream of a City of Ladies alive.

PENMORE PRESS
www.penmorepress.com

 Carrie Welton

by

Charles Monagan

Eighteen-year-old Carrie Welton is restless, unhappy, and ill-suited to the conventions of nineteenth-century New England. Using her charm and a cunning scheme, she escapes the shadow of a cruel father and wanders into a thrilling series of high-wire adventures. Her travels take her all over the country, putting her in the path of Bohemian painters, poets, singers, social crusaders, opium eaters, violent gang members, and a group of female mountain climbers.

But Carrie's demons return to haunt her, bringing her to the edge of sanity and leading to a fateful expedition onto Longs Peak in Colorado. That's not the end, though. Carrie, being Carrie, sends an astonishing letter back from the grave and thus engineers her final escape—forever into your heart.

PENMORE PRESS
www.penmorepress.com